DAVID DONACHIE was born in Edinburgh in 1944. He has always had an abiding interest in military history, including ancient Rome, the Middle Ages, the British navy of the eighteenth and nineteenth centuries, and the clandestine services during the Second World War. He has more than fifty published novels to his credit with over a million copies sold. David lives in Deal, the historic English seaport on the border of the English Channel and the North Sea.

By David Donachie

THE JOHN PEARCE ADVENTURES
By the Mast Divided • A Shot Rolling Ship
An Awkward Commission • A Flag of Truce
The Admirals' Game • An Ill Wind
Blown Off Course • Enemies at Every Turn
A Sea of Troubles • A Divided Command
The Devil to Pay • The Perils of Command
A Treacherous Coast • On a Particular Service
A Close Run Thing • HMS *Hazard*
A Troubled Course • Droits of the Crown

THE CONTRABAND SHORE SERIES
The Contraband Shore • A Lawless Place • Blood Will Out

THE NELSON AND EMMA SERIES
On a Making Tide • Tested by Fate • Breaking the Line

THE PRIVATEERSMEN SERIES
The Devil's Own Luck • The Dying Trade • A Hanging Matter
An Element of Chance • The Scent of Betrayal • A Game of Bones

HISTORICAL THRILLERS
Every Second Counts

Originally written as Jack Ludlow
THE LAST ROMAN SERIES
Vengeance • Honour • Triumph

THE REPUBLIC SERIES
The Pillars of Rome • The Sword of Revenge • The Gods of War

THE CONQUEST SERIES
Mercenaries • Warriors • Conquest

THE ROADS TO WAR SERIES
The Burning Sky • A Broken Land • A Bitter Field

THE CRUSADES SERIES
Son of Blood • Soldier of Crusade • Prince of Legend

* * *

Hawkwood

A Crusades Novel

SOLDIER
OF
CRUSADE

David Donachie

McBooks
Press

Essex, Connecticut

McBooks Press

An imprint of Globe Pequot, the trade division of
The Rowman & Littlefield Publishing Group, Inc.
4501 Forbes Blvd., Ste. 200
Lanham, MD 20706
www.rowman.com

Distributed by NATIONAL BOOK NETWORK

Copyright © 2012 by David Donachie writing as Jack Ludlow
First published in Great Britain by Allison & Busby in 2012
First McBooks Press edition 2024

British Library Cataloguing in Publication Information available

Library of Congress Cataloging-in-Publication Data available

978-1-4930-7621-5 (pbk. : alk. paper)

∞™ The paper used in this publication meets the minimum requirements of American
National Standard for Information Sciences—Permanence of Paper for Printed Library
Materials, ANSI/NISO Z39.48-1992.

To Richard & Marguerite
friends through thick, thin and all the
bits in between

PROLOGUE

The defenders of Durazzo knew the Apulians were coming and, if they had eased the passage of the first forces that had landed on the Adriatic shore under the French nobleman, the Count of Vermandois, they were less inclined to welcome the next to arrive for the very sound reason that they entirely mistrusted their motives. The knights and nobles accompanying Vermandois had been seen as honest Crusaders, needing to traverse the lands of Romania with no prior aim other than to aid Byzantium in throwing back the infidel Seljuk Turks from the very borders of Constantinople, the ultimate aim to then move on and free Jerusalem and the Holy Places of Palestine from the grip of Islam.

The armies of Southern Italy were different; led by a member of the family of de Hauteville, whose collective military prowess had kicked Byzantium out of Italy, the mounted Norman lances they commanded counted as the most formidable warriors in Christendom. Many of the foot soldiers were Lombards who, if they marched for pay and plunder, would be fully trained to do battle and loathed the old Eastern Roman Empire for the hundreds of years of what they saw as the suppression of their right to rule themselves. Such a combination had breached the eastern boundary of Romania twice in the last fifteen years as invaders not friends and, even worse, they had enjoyed a high degree of success in both battle and conquest.

The walls on which the watchers of Byzantium now stood, as well as many other castles and towns, added to great swathes of the lands of ancient Illyria, had been taken from them, only wrested back after much blood and even more treasure had been expended. The Apulians, always inferior in numbers, had been commanded by men of genius and if the now dead father, Robert, Duke of Apulia, had been seen as the devil incarnate throughout Romania then he was not in present times to be outshone in black-heartedness as well as ability by the present leader, his natural, first-born son, Bohemund of Taranto.

'I am told he is such a giant, this Bohemund, that he can pick up and consume a man whole, Father.'

'Children's tales,' John Comnenus replied to his too impressionable son. 'To demand the likes of you cease chattering and go to sleep, but it is true he is reputed to be a meaty fellow. Your great uncle the Emperor had a sight of him outside these very walls before you were born, and if you can mark one man for his size in the heat and confusion of a great battle, that tells you of his stature. It is said that he even made look human the giants of the Imperial Guard.'

'What is it that they feed these Normans that they are so tall as a race?'

'They are raised on a diet of arrogance and greed.'

8

'Odd that,' replied the ten-year-old Comnenus, his tone deadly serious, 'I heard it was apples.'

The laughter that produced echoed off the formidable walls of the port city but the humour was not long-lasting; it was known the fleet bearing Bohemund and his army had departed Otranto and Brindisi three days previously, so given the distance and even sailing easy to allay seasickness, it should be in sight by now. Unlike the approach of Vermandois, the foppish brother of the King of France, who had come close to losing his life by drowning in stormy seas, the Adriatic was flat calm and those who knew how to read the weather, master mariners who had sailed these waters all their lives, pronounced that with the nature of the sky added to the direction of the wind such conditions would likely hold for days.

John Comnenus, *topoterites* of Durazzo, had been given a task to perform and it was one to be applied only to the host from Southern Italy, more specifically to Bohemund. Prior to landing he must swear an oath to the Emperor Alexius that would bind him to the aims of the papal crusade and, if possible, imperial service; in short, the Count of Taranto must make assurances that he had come to aid Byzantium and not under the guise of assistance to attempt that which had failed before: outright conquest.

The Norman leaders of Southern Italy had eyes on the imperial purple, hankering after it as an adornment for their own shoulders. As a race they were avaricious for land and plunder, no better than the Viking forbearers who had settled along the banks of the River Seine and so harried the Frankish king that he had been obliged to cede to them the whole peninsula from which they now took their name. That had not stilled their appetite; formidable warriors, they had become a permanent menace instead of an occasional one and had increased so much in numbers that they threatened not only France but also neighbouring Anjou and ultimately their own suzerain, the Duke of Normandy.

Those who first came south to Italy were the rebellious, the landless and the discontented, amongst who were the first two de Hautevilles, subsequently to be joined by five more brothers. Employed as mercenaries to fight for Lombard independence they had, in less than fifty years, cast aside their erstwhile paymasters, then wrested the centuries-held provinces of Langobardia and Calabria from imperial control, before invading and conquering Saracen Sicily. Despite the odd reverse, they had bested Byzantium in battle after battle to become, first, counts of Apulia, and then, after papal recognition – that body too had suffered more than one military defeat at the hands of the Normans – had become acknowledged in their ducal titles.

Never likely to be sated they had turned their gaze east, seeing the remains of the old Roman Empire as weak and ripe for a fall. If they had tried and failed, that had not dented their desire – what better way to introduce the force necessary to accomplish total conquest than under the guise of this religious endeavour called a crusade? So the man who commanded at Durazzo was not about to let such a puissant general as Bohemund ashore without that pledge of loyalty.

To aid his cause John had the ability to deny them a landing at the western end of the Via Egnatia, the road to Constantinople, added to the lure of a trouble-free passage with plentiful supplies provided en route that would obviate the need to forage or, more importantly, oblige the Norman leader to raid his own chests of gold to pay for the things necessary to keep his army fed. Given such advantages he was sure he could impose the imperial will on Count Bohemund as well as his senior captains. The man who spoilt this comfortable illusion of security came while the *topoterites* was eating in his own chamber.

10

CHAPTER ONE

'One of the piquet boats approaches, Your Honour, and she is flying an alarm pennant.'

Comnenus was confused and it showed both on his face and in his reply to the messenger from the battlements. 'If we are not overburdened with friends, I cannot think who would be an enemy so threatening as to cause a piquet boat to hoist an alarm pennant?'

'The Norman devils?'

That answer had about it the air of, 'Who in the name of the Lord else, you fool?'

Comnenus carried the burden of having his place by family connection rather than experience and that showed in an occasional lack of due respect from those whom he commanded.

'They are supposed to be coming in peace, fellow – and even if they are not, how would ill intent show while they are still afloat? I fear our sailor has overplayed what he might have seen. Still, we

11

cannot ignore what it says. Send to the captain of the garrison to man the walls.'

'It was he who sent me to you, Your Honour, and he has already ordered that done.'

The thought for the titular commander could not be avoided: such a precaution had been carried out without the courtesy of informing him, just as the message regarding the approaching piquet boat had first gone to his second in command. Was it that which induced a knot in his gut or the notion that there may well be an approaching threat? Durazzo was a prize after which many lusted and one any man who held it for the empire feared to lose.

Enemies outside of Apulians he could easily conjure up: the Venetians or the Genoese with their great fleets, Saracens from North Africa or any of those in alliance with Bohemund. For the nephew of the Emperor, Durazzo was an even heavier burden, so an impatient John Comnenus was at the quayside when the fast-sailing sandalion, having unseated its mast and laid it along the thwarts, slid through under the water gate portcullis, the man in the prow shouting his message.

'The demons have landed at Avona.'

'Have landed?'

'The whole Apulian host is ashore, My Lord, and the first companies are already marching inland.'

'Headed to where?'

'I did not hang around to find out – some of their galleys came to seek me out and I ran.'

Aware that all eyes were upon him Comnenus was quick to respond. 'Then that we must find out first.'

Horses were quickly saddled and a party of lances gathered to

12

escort the *topoterites* as he rode out to locate what might be an army more intent on conquest and one which would find scant force to contest its passage. On a coast dotted with smaller ports, deep bays and open beaches there were many places to land but Bohemund had chosen well, for too many of those led nowhere but into a barren hinterland of impassable mountains. Comnenus did not know the topography as well as many of those he led; he was soon made aware that Avona provided a route, albeit a hard one, through the high coastal hills to a point where the Apulians could join the road to Constantinople at a point well inland.

As he rode he was cursing himself, even if he lacked sufficient force, for not providing the numerous places with the kind of protection that would have at least alerted him prior to them getting ashore, a landing he could have then rendered more of a risk, while being acutely aware that such an opinion probably existed among his subordinates. Now he was working to catch up with events, not, as he wanted to be, in control of them.

Forced to push their horses beyond what was wise it was a weary and dusty party of riders that overlooked the newly set up encampment, a mass of smoking campfires, tents, horses and fighting men that filled the well-watered plain and soon made any attempt to count their numbers futile. John Comnenus felt less than stately as he made his way, with only two attendants, one an interpreter, through the Apulian lines to approach the great pavilion above which flew the banner of the Count of Taranto.

Blood-red, it was crossed with the blue and white chequer of his de Hauteville family and there was no doubt, even if he had never clapped eyes on the man, who was waiting at the entrance to greet him; he had not, since he arrived to command at Durazzo, been left

13

short of descriptions but, even so, the dimensions of the man shocked him and Bohemund was not alone in that.

Not himself small, Comnenus was aware of being in the presence of not one giant but two, though there was a small margin of difference between Bohemund and the very much younger fellow at his side, he being the shorter by three finger widths. If they overawed in size while he was astride his weary horse, that was made more manifest when Comnenus dismounted to find he had to tilt his head well back to engage the eye of either. Both were bareheaded, the youthful fellow's skin a deep bronze from exposure to the sun, his hair blond above a handsome face.

The to easy-to-recognise Bohemund was fair too, but with the reddened countenance of his northern race. They were a match in style and dress, both in chain mail hauberks, wearing over that the white surplice dominated by a single red cross that Pope Urban had designated as the device to be worn by the men he had called to Crusade, this to underline that they were Christian warriors who, if they came from different locations, were dedicated to the same holy cause.

'Does the *topoterites* of Durazzo address the Count of Taranto?' the interpreter asked, in the Frankish tongue.

Bohemund looked at the speaker before lazily letting his eyes turn back to Comnenus, it being an act designed to underline his authority as well as his indifference. 'You may speak in Greek if you wish, I was born and grew up among those who used to be your subjects.' He turned to introduce his younger associate as the eyes of the *topoterites* flicked in that direction. 'As was my nephew, Tancred, Lord of Lecce and Monteroni.'

That caused the Greek leader's eyes to linger on the younger fellow,

14

for he had heard of Tancred, son of the late Marquis of Monteroni, known as 'the Good', a Lombard loyal to the Norman cause who had married Bohemund's sister, Emma. The tale told of Tancred spoke of a similar fidelity to his uncle, as well as a fighting ability and sharp mind that underlined his maternal bloodline.

'Then you will know that when you land unannounced on the shores of Romania that I see it as a hostile act.'

Bohemund let a smile play about his lips. 'Hostile or unfriendly?'

'Is there a difference?'

'There is, *topoterites*, for if I were hostile you would be still inside yours walls of Durazzo and I would be encamped without them.'

'To no purpose but death and starvation.'

It was Tancred who replied, his tone a lot less civil. 'My uncle has been inside those walls before, *topoterites*, and has slept many nights in the chamber you now occupy. Do not doubt he has the means to do so again.'

Comnenus looked around him at the men gathered to listen to what should be a private exchange, foot soldiers, not lances, and by their colouring Lombards, all of whom would speak Greek. 'Am I to conduct a negotiation in public?'

'What negotiation?' Bohemund enquired.

'Regarding the conventions you must obey if you are to cross Western Romania to meet up with your confrères in the capital.'

'I have an army and a route, why do I need conventions?'

'The Emperor commands it, just as he commands that you take an oath of allegiance to him before you can march.'

Bohemund made great play of looking around, and his men close by, knowing he was preparing a jest, began to chuckle. 'I see no emperor, so where have you hidden him?'

'You cannot expect such an eminent person to come to you.'

'No, *topoterites*, I cannot and neither can he ask of me that I swear to anything when he is not present.'

'Then I must forbid your passage.'

'With what?' Tancred snapped.

Comnenus felt safe enough to reply with open disdain. 'I hold the key to the supplies you need to progress and they will not be released to you if I do not permit it to be so. It is a long way to Constantinople and you might find all that awaits you in the mountains is hunger.'

'Supplies?' Bohemund said, his hand going to the point of his chin. 'I will tell you this, we come on the call of Pope Urban to aid your Emperor to push back the Turks, a request he sent to the synod held last year at Piacenca.'

'The cross you wear on your breast speaks of another purpose.'

Bohemund responded with a distinct growl and short points accompanied by a fist slapping into a huge hand. 'The infidels stand between us and Palestine. The Pope has tasked us to aid the empire on the way to Jerusalem. If we respond to that it is only justice that in such an act Alexius Comnenus, your uncle, I know, should feed us. The supplies are there, so we will take what we need and I promise you we will take no more.'

'And if I contest that?'

'Then prepare to spill blood.'

There was silence then, for there was an unspoken truth known to all: Comnenus did not have the power to impede this Apulian host and Bohemund was as aware of the fact as he. Even to try to sting them he would have to denude Durazzo of any protection, which, given it must remain defended, would be a deep dereliction of his duty to his uncle. He had the option of making the progress of Bohemund and his host a

16

difficult one, or as easy as such an inherently fraught enterprise could be.

'Which would be a waste, *topoterites*,' Bohemund added, 'given we have come to coat the earth with the blood of your uncle's enemies, not that of his own men and certainly not that of his family.'

'I am minded to provide an escort.'

'Something,' Tancred replied, 'given to those in need of succour, like pilgrims. We are not pilgrims.'

'We move out on the morrow, *topoterites*,' Bohemund pronounced, 'our aim to join the Via Egnatia at Vedona, and be assured I know the terrain well. I will give no trouble to those who do not trouble me. Now, allow me to offer you some refreshment in my tent.'

After, Comnenus thought, you have humiliated me in front of your Greek-speaking army.

'I must decline,' he said, 'for I have the command of Durazzo and that I must protect.'

'No doubt you will send to Alexius to tell of our arrival.'

'I shall.'

Bohemund could not keep the wry tone out of his voice. 'News to delight him, I'm sure.'

The despatch John Comnenus sent off to his uncle that night was full of foreboding about the intentions of the Apulians and while he was careful in his recommendations – he did not ask for troops with which to contest their passage for the very sound reason they did not exist – he did ask for gold with which to bribe Bohemund's half-brother and primary enemy, the reigning Duke of Apulia, Roger de Hauteville, known as *Borsa*.

Rendered a bastard by the papal annulment of his father's first marriage on the grounds of consanguinity, Bohemund saw himself

17

as the rightful heir to his father's domains; *Borsa*, first son of the second wedding to Sichelgaita of Salerno, had claimed his rights as the legitimate successor and his formidable mother had secured that for him. The two sons of Robert had contested that right over many years and Bohemund had wrested much of the Apulian domains from his half-sibling, who was, militarily, no match for him in the field or in the loyalty he could command from his subjects. Thus he would be easily tempted to stir up trouble.

If *Borsa* could be bribed to take up arms, that might force Bohemund to look to save his Italian possessions; in short it might oblige him to hurry home with his army, a repeat of the well-funded upheavals that had saved the empire in the past. This he did on the grounds that such an army and such a presence on the soil of Romania, regardless of the stated cause, was too dangerous for imperial security.

He also felt obliged to send ahead messengers to deny the Apulians easy access to supplies and, for all the weakness of the forces he commanded and the responsibilities thereof, Comnenus despatched in his wake a strongly armed party to ensure that they continued to progress east and did not succumb to the temptation to set down in any one place. That it was no more than a gesture Comnenus knew, but he thought it one worth making.

The despatch from Durazzo reached a ruler who had enough troubles without worrying about Bohemund of Taranto, though his arrival, as well as the method of it, underlined a difficulty that would be the devil to deal with. In calling for help from the Christian powers of the West, Emperor Alexius Comnenus had already got a great deal more than he had bargained for and the primary part of that was standing before him now, a charismatic preacher called Peter the Hermit.

On his own Peter was not a problem; he was a holy man with the simple tastes of his title, ascetic enough to fast regularly, humble in his person, a man happy to live wholly by the tenets of his Lord Jesus Christ and who even looked – tall and thin, with his great beard and the way he leant on his full-length crook – like an Old Testament prophet.

The problem was the nature of the multitude he had inspired with his sermons, for, if there was a body of knights amongst those he had led to the East, the mass was an unruly mob containing, amongst the pious majority, some of the dregs of Europe. This host had come to the capital of Byzantium in their onward search for absolution for the entirety of their sins, this to be granted to them when Jerusalem was once more a Christian city.

From what Alexius Comnenus knew – he would admit his knowledge was incomplete and would remain so until a papal legate arrived – Pope Urban had talked only of the remission of past sins for those who took part in his Crusade. Peter, in his enthusiasm for the cause, had elevated that promise to a guarantee of entry to paradise for any who took up the challenge, which, if it had enthused many thousands of the genuinely devout, had also gathered to him those with a great deal to gain from such a pledge, a mass of ne'er-do-wells with crimes against their name from which they needed pardon if they were not to burn for eternity in the pits of Hell.

'My people are good simple folk, Your Eminence, easily led astray.'

They are not all that, Alexius thought, though he was too much the diplomat to say so. There are murders, rapists, thieves of every sort included in your rabble and they are beyond control even by a saintly fellow such as yourself. That was not a criticism of Peter, who saw only good where other men saw a less palatable truth, and

19

the evidence of his error had reached imperial ears long before his followers saw the walls of the city.

Peter's so-called 'People's Crusade' had left a swathe of destruction all across the lands of middle Europe – the Jews in their path had suffered most, with much slaughter of those who refused to convert added to the burning of synagogues. It had even led to armed conflict once they were inside the boundaries of the empire as they ravaged the countryside through which they passed. On coming to Constantinople they had posed a threat to the city itself and even more to the public peace, added to which Alexius had been required to feed them while they committed arson as a cover for their manifest transgressions.

He was still doing so but now at a pleasing distance; recognising that matters would not improve he had them shipped across to the town of Civetot, on the southern shores of the Gulf of Nicomedia where their depredations were out of his sight as well as those of the inhabitants of his capital. Yet it was far from being without concern given their continued dismal behaviour; he felt a responsibility, if not for their well-being at least for their survival, and the reports he had told him that their conduct had not changed – they were doing to northern Bithynia what they had been stopped from doing within the walls of Constantinople.

Having made his statement in support of the masses he had led here, Peter was obliged to wait for a spoken response – that was the way it should be: no man, however saintly, had the right to hurry a Roman emperor in his musings.

'It concerns me,' Alexius said finally, 'that your people do not confine themselves to the area around Civetot that I have granted to them and in which they may reside till the crusading armies arrive. They raid out from the lands around the port and risk, in their foraging and, dare I say it, plundering, to upset the Turks of Nicaea, who will not sit idly by and let the lands they control be ravaged.'

'*Your* lands, Eminence, Christian lands.'

Tempted to underline the nature of possession, Alexius demurred; Peter held a simple view that all lands were the property of his Christian God, while the Emperor knew that the sword of Islam held greater sway.

'While the supplies you send us are adequate,' Peter continued, 'and you are to be thanked for your Christian charity in providing such, there are those who have come to expect, given they are set upon God's work, that they deserve more.'

'What is it you require, Peter?' Alexius asked suppressing a sigh. Tempted to tell Peter to go to the devil he knew that bribery was so much easier than condemnation.

'More grain, a better supply of meats and also wine.' Peter was about to go on, when the noisy arrival of a high Byzantine official obliged him stop; the fellow, a much trusted aide and close imperial advisor called Manuel Boutoumites was obviously intent on speaking to the Emperor without delay, which he did when signalled to speak.

'Majesty, news has come from Xerigordos. A party of knights has attacked the town and taken the fortress there. It is reported they intend to use it as a base to raid deeper into the Sultanate of Rüm.'

If Peter the Hermit was astonished at the language such news produced and from a man said to be as pious as Alexius, it was a measure of the shock and anger the Emperor felt, even if this had been something he feared. Xerigordos was well beyond the range of any previous raid, and worse, it was a Turkish fortress, if not a very important one. Such an act was both premature and dangerous: the last thing Alexius wanted was to stir up trouble on his borders when he was too weak to easily contain it and the military aid he expected from Europe was yet to arrive. He did not count the knights who had come with the People's Crusade to be that, a fact Alexius made plain to the Hermit once he had established the size of the force engaged, a mere five hundred men in all, the majority foot soldiers.

'The Turks will not let that stand.'

Peter was taken aback and it was plain on his face. 'Can you not support them, Eminence?'

'No I cannot, so it falls to you, good man, or a messenger sent by you, to tell them to withdraw at once.'

CHAPTER TWO

It had all started so well for the men who took the Castle of Xerigordos, as it had for the whole People's Crusade. The fertile northern plains of Bithynia seemed entirely clear of any defence and Kilij Arslan, the Turk who had taken to himself the title of the Sultan of Rüm, remained within the formidable walls of Nicaea and seemed passive regarding the arrival of these thousands of pilgrims as well as indifferent to their activities.

Having settled around Civetot it was only days before marauding parties set out from the coastal town to bring mayhem and destruction to the surrounding countryside, in much the same manner as they had done on the way to Constantinople. Much of that pillaging, in terms of distance, was constrained by the lack of suitable transport for the mostly foot-bound and untrained host, but that did not apply to parties led by well-armed and mounted knights, most notably those raiding under the banner of Reinald the Alemanni.

Ranging further afield they had enjoyed complete freedom to despoil any settlements they found while paying scant attention to the religious or vassalage ties of their victims; it mattered not whether they were Christian Greeks or Turks and infidels. They represented booty for men who had come to the East seeking to gain profit from the Crusade as well as forgiveness. Finally the old and badly repaired fortress of Xerigordos, as well as the town that had grown around it, fell to Reinald and so easily that he, as well as the force he led, saw it as divine approval. The desire to partake of the fruits of that capture led to their downfall.

Three days of feasting, some pleasant slaughter of the menfolk and violation of the women, ended when a force of Kilij Arslan's Turks appeared that outnumbered them three to one, the men Reinald led forced to take refuge in the run-down castle. There was no time to gather supplies of any kind, not that the town could provide much after it had been pillaged, but the real difficulty came when the Crusaders found that there was no water supply within the walls, a crippling handicap in a part of the world where, even in early October, the temperatures could be scorching.

Such a debilitating predicament was not aided by the need to constantly man the walls and, over several days, fight off well-coordinated attacks, which meant hails of deadly arrows from the numerous archers to which the defenders, with only lances and swords, had no way of replying. Reinald's casualties, for that reason alone, had been bad from the first day of siege and had worsened since, till the number of shallow graves multiplied. Men became too weary to bother to bury their dead, and bodies, thrown over the parapet, were now rotting at the outer base of the castle walls.

Then there was the choking smoke, behind which Turks advanced to the very walls to set ladders against the parapet and engage in close combat – to a man already suffering from thirst, that on the lungs had a doubly nauseating effect, yet despite such tactics they repulsed assault after assault by deeds that would have been valorous in a better cause. But the need for liquids was the greatest drawback; after eight days, when the blood of their now dead horses was no longer available to ease their thirst, when they were reduced to dropping their leather girdles into the sewers then sucking them for a modicum of relief, or using what little urine their bodies produced to try to assuage their rasping throats, it was time to talk.

'Do you think they know how badly we are placed?'

Reinald croaked this to one of his knights, a Lombard called Argyrus who, having served with the Normans, knew the Frankish tongue, as he watched his enemies prepare another assault. Really the question was: can you think of anything by which we can negotiate that I might have missed?

'It was their castle, Reinald, they must know. That was why the garrison was too small to hold out against us, why we found it so easy to capture in the first place.'

'There is no sign that anyone is coming to our relief.'

'Do they even know we are under siege?'

Reinald conjured up enough saliva to sound as he had done a week before, arrogant and angry. 'They must know, Argyrus, but they do not care.'

'What will you offer?'

'Only our swords, it's all we have. Prepare a truce flag.'

The man in command of the Turks, a general called Elchanes, came within hailing distance, but he was not so trusting of Christians that he would come close enough to be struck down by a lance – not that the defenders had many of those kind of weapons left; too many had been cast at the men seeking to overcome the walls – with what followed being long-winded and confusing.

Elchanes had a Greek interpreter who could communicate with the likes of the Lombard Argyrus; he, in turn, had to translate for Reinald, though in truth there was little to discuss. To stay inside the walls was to die; to leave their protection was to rely on the word of the Turkish commander who seemed willing to accept them into military service as long as they came as a body.

Yet if Reinald was the leader of his small force it was far from homogenous – his men came from many different lands and nor was he so respected that he could issue orders and demand they be obeyed. They had a say in their fate and that led to a great deal of argument, with many reluctant to take up arms against their co-religionists, the very people with whom they had traversed many hundreds of leagues in order to seek salvation, set against those who were prepared to set that aside for a chance to live, on the very good grounds that their all-seeing God would observe they had no choice and thus forgive them their sin. A few even claimed that having come on Crusade, they enjoyed prior absolution.

'And let me see a way to escape, brothers, and, with God's aid, I will take it.'

That cry from a lone voice swayed the meeting and gave Reinald the right to offer them into the service of Kilij Arslan, a message Reinald sent from the walls just before he ordered the gates to be opened and for all of his men to stay gathered in the castle courtyard where they had debated their fate. The Turkish archers, who fought on both foot and mounted, trotted in on their small, fleet ponies heading right and left, an arrow nestled in each bow and eyes on the gathering that

26

meant the slightest untoward move would result in a swift release.

Once they had fully encircled the Crusaders their general entered, surrounded by men with drawn swords, and Reinald, dragging Argyrus with him, walked forwards to execute a low bow. A hand signal from the Turk brought forward a man bearing a skin of water from which, much to the chagrin of their watching followers, the two men greedily drank. There was no sympathy in the act; Elchanes wanted them to be able to speak clearly.

'He wants to know why we have come to this place, Reinald,' Argyrus said, when the first words were spoken.

Reinald was looking at Elchanes, without his metal and leather helmet now, so his dark eyes, being unshaded, were visible. There was not much of an expression in either those or on his round and dark-skinned face, with skin heavily marked by pox. The lips were close to being as black as those eyes, thin and unsmiling.

'He must know that already.'

'I suggest,' Argyrus replied, 'that it would be wise to humour him.'

'Tell him that we came to save our souls from eternal damnation.'

That was twice translated and the reply came back. 'Such a wish is a simple matter, all you have to do is acknowledge the Prophet.'

'We are Christians.'

That needed no translation and by saying it Reinald got a clear reaction, a look of real hate crossing that cratered Turkish face. The shout that came from Elchanes had every bow up and pointing, each archer picking a target, and Argyrus was obliged to tell Reinald that the order had come to lay down their weapons on the ground.

'Weapons with which we have offered to serve the Sultan.'

Those words had no effect; the reply came back to do as they were commanded or die. While most complied, a goodly number declined only to suffer immediately as each took at least one arrow in the upper body and many of them several, which hastened those who had hesitated. The Turkish general then yelled a command accompanied by a huge sweep of the arm for the Christians to move out through the gate that rendered translation superfluous.

Bereft now of swords, daggers and shields, Reinald led his men out of the gate to where the main body of the Turkish force, weapons at the ready, was stretched out facing the curtain wall, against which the captured Christians were obliged to line up, the archers from within the fortress taking station on the parapet above their heads. Elchanes rode though the gate and yelled out another order, which had Argyrus, once it was given to him in Greek, crossing himself as he spoke.

'We have a choice, Reinald, to convert to Islam or to die where we stand.'

'He accepted our terms.'

'Look at his eyes, Reinald. If he ever did, he does not do so now.'

What followed was horrible to observe. One at a time men were dragged forward and asked to forswear the religion into which they had been born. Those who accepted were spared, had their hands tied and were led away, those who refused immediately had their throats cut to the neck bone with a dying prayer on their lips, their bodies dragged away to be thrown onto a rising mound of dead flesh. Reinald and Argyrus, when their turn came, took the same course as the majority and forswore.

'Ask what is to become of us, Argyrus, now that we have converted to Islam?'

The reply came back, once translated, with an accompanying laugh, to tell the survivors that the Sultanate of Rüm always had need of slaves.

* * *

Word reached Civetot within two days, and if the fact that men had died was enough to enrage the multitude, the forced conversions to Islam were even more maddening to the more vocal priests and the deeply religious amongst the host, preachers every bit as inspiring as Peter the Hermit. A council was immediately called with the general opinion, much pushed by the divines, being that such an infamy could not be allowed to pass. The whole of the People's Crusade in their thousands should shoulder their weapons and move out to attack the city of Nicaea, many loudly acclaiming that they had stayed passive long enough.

A few voices demurred, but they were wiser than the mob or the priests, for they tended to be the men who knew about warfare, mounted knights, amongst whom the most vocal and respected was the Frenchman, Walter Sansavoir. He pointed out that the city they were proposing to assault had repelled several attempts by the armies of Byzantium to overcome its formidable walls. Those who disagreed with him, and some of them shared his fighting experience, argued that by moving they would oblige those very same Byzantine forces to come to their aid and the combination must overwhelm the defences.

In the end it was the prospect of plunder that swung the vote towards action, indeed the very nature of many of the people that made up the People's Crusade. Stark indeed was the truth when set against what had gone before, which was in too many cases no more than rank religious hypocrisy designed to mask naked greed, this from adventurers who had thought of nothing since setting out from their European hovels and manor houses other than the fabled riches of the East. The more honest pilgrims were souls with no fear of death; had not Peter the Hermit promised that if they perished on this venture their entry to heaven was assured? So overwhelming was the sentiment to march that those who disagreed could not stand against it.

The host that set out next day was indeed formidable if seen from a distance and spread across the landscape: three hundred plus mounted knights trained in the art of war, at least the same number who at some time in their lives had borne arms in battle as *milities*, able to use pikes for defence and axes as well as sharp daggers in close combat. The remainder, and they were several thousand in number, were stave- and pitchfork-carrying peasants so fired by their faith to be sure that when they came to the walls of Nicaea, they would, like those of Jericho, tumble to the sound of their combined prayers.

In such a ragged army there was scant discipline and if Walter Sansavoir had agreed to take the lead, he did not have anything like overarching control; what he had was dispute if he even attempted to issue an order, so that midway through the second day, as much due to heat as disorderliness, the host utterly lacked any kind of cohesion and that was exposed when before them they could observe, on an open plain with no protection from a flank assault, a large force of disciplined Turks advancing to meet them and one of which they had gained no prior warning.

'We should have tried to withdraw,' reported a Lombard knight called Sigibuld, his torn, cross-bearing surplice still covered in his own blood, mixed with those with whom he had fought, the whole overlain with dirt of a battlefield and a long and dangerous flight. 'Many suggested it but Walter Sansavoir asked how it could be done with a rabble over which we had little control when advancing.'

'The enterprise was foolish,' Alexius replied, his voice weary. 'You should never have gone beyond Civetot.'

'We did not expect to meet Kilij Arslan in open battle,' Sigibuld protested.

'The Sultan led them in person?'

'They cried out his name when they attacked.'

'What a price to pay for a lesson known to every soldier,' said Manuel Boutoumites, titled *Curopalates* and thus high enough in rank as a trusted advisor to speak unbidden in the presence of his Emperor. 'Never underestimate your enemy.'

Alexius nodded and a lifted finger was a signal for Sigibuld to continue, which he did in a voice devoid of emotion.

'We tried to form up as best we could. Walter had we knights take up position to the front, mixed with the men who knew how to use weapons so that we could present a defence, the aim to let the Turks know that any attack would cost them dear. The rest we sought to keep to the rear but they would not listen, so convinced were they, egged on by the priests, that God would surely smite their enemies before they even came within longbow shot. I think they expected bolts of lightning to come from the sky.'

'The Bible tells us it has been so,' intoned Peter the Hermit, which got him a look from a more secular emperor. 'The Old Testament tells of many times when God has interceded to protect his flock. Think of the parting of the Red Sea . . .'

That had the courtiers in attendance shifting uncomfortably, for if they were good sons of the Church they were also men who knew that miracles were caused more by imagination than divine intervention. There were soldiers of the empire amongst them too, like Boutoumites, and they had to work hard not to scoff at the old man's words. Alexius gave Peter a look that, if it was gentle, demanded his silence, then indicated that Sigibuld should continue with his tale.

'The priests had them kneel and entreat before the Turks launched their assault, as if the power of prayer alone would stop them from

31

attacking. They were still at their devotions when the first arrows landed amongst them, and packed as they were the bolts did great slaughter. It was as if the shock broke their spirit, for they set up a great wailing and gnashing, many claiming that God had deserted them. They began to rush about both in front and behind we fighting men and lost what little unity they had possessed.'

'Easy meat for the Turkish archers?'

Sigibuld dropped his head when Alexius said that, his voice seeming now to come from the depths of his belly.

'We could not move to break up their formations without we trampled our own people, this while the mounted archers got to our rear, dashing forward to fire an arrow then withdrawing before we could inflict any damage upon them. Kilij Arslan then sent his swordsmen into the melee of pilgrims. Many who died were on their knees begging for forgiveness, the rest began to scatter, running in all directions, which left we fighting men to face a full assault from a force greater than our own with the need to do battle on both flanks as well as to our front.'

'How many survived?' Alexius asked, cutting across Sigibuld.

He did not want to hear what this Lombard was about to tell him, of the butchery which followed and how it was achieved; he had fought the Turks too many times himself, had seen their mounted archers ride forward and, while still moving, launch a flood of arrows at a defensive line cowering under shields. In his mind's eye he could see how that would, on an open battlefield, pin the defenders so that their enemy could get round their flanks and begin to crush them between twin pincers in a way that meant resistance would be flattened.

'If there is indeed place in heaven,' Sigibuld continued, avoiding the direct question, 'for those who perish on this venture, then surely the likes of Walter will gain entry and glory when they do. Many knights fought on even when their bodies were pierced by the Turkish bolts and took many of the infidel with them before they finally fell.'

'And you, Sigibuld, how did you get clear?'

That made the Lombard pull himself up to his full height; there was in the question the accusation of him being less of a man than those he had named. 'We were still mounted and when those we had chosen to lead were slain it was obvious that no other choice presented itself but flight. The Turkish horses were blown from their previous exertions and sluggish in pursuit, but more in our favour was the way their compatriots fell upon the bodies of the dead to strip and mutilate them.'

'How many got away?'

'Around seventy knights.'

'And the pikemen?'

'They, being on foot, were less fortunate. Some did survive by throwing away their weapons and hanging on to our stirrup leathers.'

'And where are they now?'

'Defending Civetot, Highness, which is why I have come on here and in haste, stopping not even to remove the blood and filth from my person. The town and the remaining pilgrims are at risk if the Turks keep advancing, for there is nothing of a fighting nature to prevent it. I have come to ask that you either provide men to defend the town or send ships to withdraw the people left behind, the women and children as well as those too old or infirm to fight.'

They could smell Civetot long before any of the boats sent to bring off the remaining pilgrims ever sailed into the Gulf of Nicomedia, the great bight, on the southern arm of which the wretched town sat. Never a place of beauty it was ravaged now, the churches burnt shells and the homes of those who had lived here torn down into dust. Rotting carcasses of flesh leave a high odour in a warm climate, yet it was testament to the amount of slaughter that it could be discerned so far from the shore that there could be no doubt what the sailors would find when they set foot on the beach.

Kilij Arslan had indeed come on from the massacre described by Sigibuld, to attack a settlement bereft of any means of resistance. There were survivors, but few, the kind who had rushed into the sea and managed to stay afloat as the butchery was accomplished on land. There were also those the Turks had thought dead, buried so deep in a pile of bodies that the fact of their still breathing was undetectable, a few dozens from the many thousands to tell the tale of what had occurred, about a host who had no interest in conversion to Islam but only in killing what they saw as a plague.

There had been others who avoided the massacre: young women and boys who could be sold into carnal servitude, the few fit men who had not marched off with the army able to work as slaves aboard galleys or in quarries. For the rest they were killed; women not of tender years were of no use and neither were small children, infants and newly born babies. The old were despatched as a matter of course and the Turks had gathered those they had slain into a great mound of suppurating flesh that had left the ground around it, where their tuns of blood had leached out from the ferociously administered wounds, as soggy as a bog.

Peter the Hermit had come as well and many wondered at his silent thoughts as he surveyed the death of both his hopes and his Crusade. Was his faith still intact? Did he think, like the victims over whose bodies he prayed must have thought, that their dreams were delusions? Or did he believe these souls to be martyred and already in paradise? No one asked Peter and he was not speaking.

'Go back to Constantinople,' said the man Alexius had put in command of the ships, 'and tell the Emperor that the People's Crusade is no more.'

CHAPTER THREE

The Apulian army was unaware of what had happened ahead of them and would have shown indifference if they had been told – what else could be expected of a force of peasants? Many were experienced mercenary soldiers who had previously marched along the ancient Via Egnatia, as were the mailed and mounted Norman knights who moved east with them, not least their leader. Just over ten years previously the then Duke of Apulia, Robert de Hauteville, had been obliged to curtail a second bite at conquest, required to go home to suppress an insurrection of his ever-discontented barons, whose natural bellicosity had been watered by Byzantine gold.

Bohemund had been entrusted to continue his father's invasion, and given that he had suffered an ultimate reverse, not all of his memories of this land were ones to be covered in a golden glow. The memory dimmed even more as he recalled that the deeper he had pushed into Macedonia and Thessaly the greater became the difficulties for the forces he had led, as much from the terrain as from enemy action to slow his progress, as well as the determination of the Emperor Alexius Comnenus to bring him to battle on a field of his choosing.

If there had been many successes, in the end he had been beaten by a combination of factors: campaign weariness after endless forced marches, a dearth of plunder and a lack of reinforcements added to that staple weapon of the enemy he faced – wealth with which to bribe his father's Apulian subjects as well as Bohemund's captains in the field. Both led men who fought for no higher cause than their own personal gain, a right his followers had exercised when he had been forced to absent himself from the campaign at the same time as an emissary, a fellow Norman in the imperial service, appeared from the Emperor Alexius laden with treasure, an act which broke the cohesion of a tired army and led to an ignominious retreat.

Unlike on his previous incursion Bohemund had no desire to push his men in the kind of swift march required to seek and wrong-foot an opponent, he being in no hurry to get to Constantinople. Other large bodies of Christian knights were on the way from Northern Europe and Germany, one of which, from the Duchy of Lower Lorraine, should already be near the capital having taken the route through Hungary. They would join those who had embarked from the ports of Bari and Brindisi under Hugh of Vermandois.

Bohemund, busy gathering his own forces in the port cities which he controlled, had met to talk with and entertain Vermandois, as well as to seek some measure of his opinions on the forthcoming campaign, only to find himself conversing with a vainglorious fool who had never independently led men in a real battle. This boded ill for the future since, given his royal connection to the King of France, Vermandois saw himself as the leader by right of the whole enterprise. That was not an opinion Bohemund accepted and he had enough respect for Alexius Comnenus, even if he had never met him, to believe he too would smoke that Vermandois was a dolt.

It was most certainly not one likely to be shared by the other powerful warlords who would follow in the wake of Vermandois, especially the contingents from Toulouse and Provence, reputed to be commanded by the men who had first responded to a personal plea from Pope Urban. Likewise, those from Normandy, Flanders and England would have men in their ranks who would not readily take commands from another, for they included amongst their number the second son of William the Conqueror. It was good fortune that Count Hugh's brother, the King, clearly a man of some sagacity, had sent with Hugh his constable, Walo of Chaumont, who was both a good soldier and, being a high official of the French Court, a practised diplomat.

So, several bodies were reported to be ahead of the Apulians and would thus be earliest to the Byzantine capital, there to meet with Alexius and to have set the terms by which the Western armies would help to reconquer imperial lands, news of which would come to Bohemund before he reached Constantinople. Prior knowledge of what would be asked for would allow the Apulian leader to play a better hand, for, if Palestine was the ultimate aim, that presaged a long, arduous campaign over hundreds of leagues and difficult terrain, fraught with as many difficulties as opportunities.

Unlike some of the other leaders who would answer Pope Urban's call to Crusade Bohemund was too experienced a warrior and general to be blinded by the mysticism of the enterprise. If the aim was sacred the task was military and that required those who undertook it to be pragmatic. Added to that he was a near neighbour and recent enemy who knew Byzantium too well to just accord them the kind of Christian brotherhood likely to be spoken of in other bands of warriors, most tellingly its troubled history and endemic lack of stability.

No one who aspired to or wore the imperial diadem could ever feel safe and that had been too often proved over centuries in a court full of intrigue, where either violence or poison lay behind every marble column. He had grown up with tales of both in execution; the deposed ruler if he was not killed was at least rendered harmless by having his eyes put out.

Alexius Comnenus, now in his fifteenth year of rule, had lasted longer than most. He might have come to power through a kinder deposition, but he had acceded to the throne in a palace coup that saw his predecessor, himself a usurper, despatched with eyes intact to live out his days in a monastery. It was just as likely that there were plots being hatched to remove the present incumbent of the imperial throne regardless of his abilities, which were manifestly high. That was the nature of the polity and had been since the time of Constantine, founder of the city that bore his name.

Whoever ruled Byzantium was required to be well versed in the devious arts of intrigue as well as deception and Alexius would be no exception. Bohemund surmised he would seek to use the forces granted to him by Western religious fervour to further the aims of the Eastern Empire. That he would do so was not to be despised; no ruler who wished to secure his throne could afford to behave in any other fashion. Yet it was as well to be aware that such priorities would colour every act of Byzantine support; Bohemund was prepared to sup with his one-time enemy Alexius, but he would do so with a long spoon.

The first task once all the contingents converged would be to push back the Seljuk Turks. They had been advancing west over many decades, as much an enemy to their Mohammedan co-religionists as the Greeks, Jews and Armenians over whom they now ruled. They had steadily eaten into the Eastern Empire, making their most telling gains after the disastrous Battle of Manzikert a quarter of a century previously. There the flower of the Byzantine army had gone down to a disastrous and total defeat that included the capture of the then emperor, Romanos Diogenes.

That reverse proved so comprehensive that Constantinople had never recovered the initiative, indeed it had struggled to hold on to what it still possessed on the southern side of the Bosphorus and had asked, many times and to no avail, for help from their Christian brethren of the West. These pleas for aid were sent to Roman pontiffs who had enough trouble on their own doorstep, often from the Normans, more regularly from the King of the Germans, to even think of what was happening in the East.

Added to that there was a definite schism that was far from being healed around certain disagreements about priestly celibacy, the proper way to conduct the Mass and the use of unleavened bread to denote the body of Christ. More tellingly divisive was a refusal from the Patriarch of Constantinople to acknowledge the Vicar of Rome as head of the entirety of the Christian Church, both Orthodox and Latin, these matters now fifty years in dispute.

Left to its own devices, Byzantium had struggled. The Turks had expanded their gains against a weakened empire to become a threat to the imperial capital itself, in possession of the heavily fortified city of Nicaea, within three days' marching distance of Constantinople, having established what they called the Sultanate of Rüm, an Arabic corruption of Rome, which went some way to establish their aims. One day they aspired to take all of the Eastern Roman Empire; what kept them in check now was not Byzantine resistance but their own ability to fall out amongst themselves.

Pope Urban, in receipt of lurid tales of how maltreated were pilgrims to Jerusalem, mocked, robbed and even forced to convert, called for a crusade to free the Holy Places of Palestine. This could only be accomplished in alliance with Byzantium, for they held the narrow water crossing from Europe to Asia, added to which no military force could invade or move south without their aid and support, both in terms of supply and cooperation.

Thus the two aims had coincided and set in motion these great armies. That the Emperor would want to control the enterprise was certain; what he would be willing to grant in terms of plunder and territorial possessions if successful was as yet unknown, for if it was faith that brought many to answer the crusading call, personal advancement added to both territorial gain would not be far behind.

These were the thoughts, made up of memory, experience and speculation, that filled the mind of Bohemund, the subject of conversations only with his nephew Tancred, the one person to whom he would occasionally show his innermost feelings. Yet there could be no conclusion; too much – personalities, the outcome of future battles – was open to speculation. That was not a situation that made the leader of the army anxious, it being that with which he had lived since he had first been old enough to reason and to fight.

Even if the Apulians had wanted to move swiftly a rapid advance was barely possible; the old Roman road, acceptable as a trade route for merchants and their goods-laden donkeys scarcely served for an army of thousands. It stood as an emblem of the polity that was supposed to keep it in good repair; everything was on the perish and that meant progress was naturally constrained. In places, like the high mountain passes, it had been part washed away by winter mudslides and was barely negotiable; even on level ground there were gaps where the polygon stones that were supposed to provide the pavé had been stolen to be put to other uses by locals well able to ignore the central imperial authority, leaving the road in places a quagmire after even a modicum of rainfall.

That lack of firm rule posed the next hindrance to the daily movements as the hill tribes, never wholly subdued by Byzantium, sought to alleviate the poverty of their miserable existence by a continual set of raids on the Apulian baggage train, but more persistently on the supplies provided by Byzantine storerooms and farms to which Bohemund had helped himself, despite protests, both those carried in carts and that on the hoof: grain, pulses and peas for the men, oats for the horses, and cattle to be slaughtered and provide occasional meat. Worse were the depredations on the herd of spare horses without which no mounted force could go into battle.

The raids were sharp affairs, short in duration, happening in daylight as well as in darkness, the sole object to swiftly steal what could be carried off in the time between launching an assault and the speed with which the nearest mounted party could react to chase the intruders off. That brought forth another difficulty – pursuit was dangerous to a small party of lances; to follow the tribesmen into their own mountain terrain left the Normans at great peril from ambush, while to mount a greater incursion just saw the raiders melt away to higher ground.

On the rare occasions when the tribesmen had been cornered

they had proved they could fight; these people saw themselves as the descendants of the armies of Alexander the Great and it was from this high country that had come the men who, under his leadership, had conquered half the known world.

Many of the Apulian host, if asked, would not shrink to compare Bohemund to that military titan and it had nothing to do with his remarkable height and build; he was the son of Robert de Hauteville, acknowledged to be the greatest soldier of his time and known to the world, for his cunning and cleverness, as the *Guiscard*. The family from which Robert sprang, a string of brothers, having come from the depths of the Contentin in north-west Normandy, had risen from owning nothing but their weapons and their horses to become mighty warriors and the ruling line of Southern Italy and Sicily.

Bohemund's half-brother now held a trio of ducal titles while his uncle, another Roger, was the Great Count of Sicily and master of that island, even if, in title, he was supposed to be a vassal of his namesake nephew. Originally fighting in tandem with the *Guiscard*, Count Roger had, with papal blessing and encouragement, completed the conquest of the island, defeating both the Saracens and Islam in what had come to be termed a "Crusade", similar to that taking place in Spain against the Moors. More pleasing to the papacy was the way he had dealt with the Orthodox form of religion, to which the mass of the Greek population adhered.

They looked to Constantinople for spiritual guidance and Roger was working to replace that with worship in the Latin rite, rededicating churches, encouraging priests and monks from the north as well as setting up abbeys and monasteries into which they could move to spread the Creed as set out by Rome, so if anyone stood high in papal favour and personal power, it was he.

Added to that, the Great Count held the line between his two nephews, *Borsa* and Bohemund; the latter would have taken everything without his uncle's intervention. That was another plus for the papacy, who found pious and malleable *Borsa* easier to deal with than the combative Count of Taranto.

All three had risen on the efforts of the men of their family that preceded them, first and foremost the eldest de Hauteville who had outmanoeuvred the slippery Lombards, a race that sought to use them only as military mercenaries, going on to outwit those fellow Normans who saw him as a subject not an equal. William had begun to carve out in south-east Italy what would become the Duchy of Apulia, aided by brothers Drogo, Humphrey, Godfrey, sometimes Mauger, then Robert and Roger.

Collectively they had wrested South Italy from Byzantium and stymied the King of the Germans, the so-called Western Emperor. The de Hautevilles had overawed and humbled a succession of popes and many times they had fought such enemies, Byzantium included, individually; more seriously they had been obliged to face them in varying combinations where luck and enemy dissension had played as much a part in victory as Norman fighting skill.

To the men Bohemund led it was as if all this ability had been distilled into one man. None could doubt his Norman heritage and not just because of his height and colouring. In single combat he had no peer and as a commander of men he cemented their allegiance by example and his selfless acts of individual bravery. If amongst his captains there were many who would dispute with him, for the Normans were by nature a fractious race, to the rank and file Bohemund of Taranto was the greatest of his tribe. On this day, with the light fading, he was preparing to embellish that reputation by undertaking a task many would have delegated to others.

'Let me face an army in battle before much more of this.'

These words were uttered as he stripped off his top clothing to leave himself in dark-brown smock and breeches, an act that in these high mountains made the heat from the nearby fire welcome. Not that he could get too close, for he did not want to be seen, not that anyone trying to observe such a large encampment would have found such a thing easy. They were spread along the western shores of Lake Ohrid, where the old Roman road skirted the edge of a stretch of water so long the other end was invisible in daylight.

'This is no task for you, Bohemund.'

Looking at his nephew Bohemund just grinned as he slipped a long dagger into a sheath in his belt. 'I cannot bear to be so pricked by these people, Tancred, and do nothing.'

'What you should do and I tire of saying it, is order others to undertake what you propose to do yourself. You risk the whole enterprise when you risk yourself.'

'I have not swung my sword in anger since we left Amalfi, so it is time to see if it still performs as it should.'

'Take it out on a tree trunk.'

'I'd rather cut a human trunk in two and from neck joint to crutch.'

If that came with a smile, both men knew it to be possible. Tancred's uncle carried an accumulation of muscle that over near forty years, since he could first wield a wooden sword as a mewling child, had become directed to the act of killing by either axe, mace or sword most of his Lombard levies would struggle to even swing. Added to that, Bohemund never ceased to hone his skills and neither did his confrères; even on the march a little time was set aside for the practice

45

of the art of combat, the daily ritual of swordplay, lance work and mounted control that made the Normans the most formidable of warriors.

'Your father would not do this.'

'He might have done so, Tancred, when he was younger and less concerned with affairs of state, for he was ever mischievous.'

'He was cunning and wise. This is neither.'

Others who had also stripped off their outer clothing, twenty lances in all, were making for a part of the shore where no fires burned and where the fishing boats Bohemund had ordered to be commandeered from the local lake dwellers, who had come to sell their catch, were assembled. Beyond that lay unlit black water, for the skies had clouded over for the first time in days to obscure both moon and stars, though there was a modicum of light that allowed to be made out the outline of the surrounding mountains.

'My father was ever keen to surprise his enemies and in that I am no different.'

'I think you flatter these hill tribesmen when you term them enemies. They are a rabble not a host.'

'They are like an itch I cannot scratch and I mean to end what they are about, for the losses we are sustaining are not to be borne, especially with horses.'

'Alexius Comnenus will provide replacements from the imperial stud when we get to Constantinople.'

'Trained destriers?'

'Horseflesh as good as.'

'No, Tancred, even an emperor cannot do that. They do not breed in Byzantium the kind of mounts on which we rely. Horses to ride, yes, pack animals in abundance, I am sure, but those that can face an unbroken line of enemy lances with horns blowing, shields clashing and not flinch?'

'Then let us hope you succeed, for if you do not we could lose more tonight than we have had stolen on the march so far.'

They were the bait, mounts the tribes knew were the most valuable to the Normans, now at pasture in an area where they looked to be a target for theft, animals just as valued by the raiders but for different reasons. A horse able to carry a fully mailed and equipped Norman knight into battle, men of some stature who were also heavy in their equipment, were the very kind of creatures to cope easily with the routes between high hills and deep valleys of the Macedonian uplands. Destriers were bred and trained to be fearless and they were not high in the shoulder either, another benefit to clansmen who tended to be short in the leg.

In so persistently questioning what Bohemund proposed to do, Tancred knew he was close to exceeding his standing and openly acknowledged it now; he might be second in command but there was a serious age difference of seventeen years. He had served by Bohemund's side for a long time, first as a squire and then as he grew to manhood, as his right-hand shield. Even so, care had to be exercised when questioning the actions of any commander and he feared what he was saying was close to insubordinate.

That got him a huge hand on his shoulder and a squeeze. 'Never fear to question me, you of all people, Tancred, for your bloodline more than permits you the right. Your mother is as much of the *Guiscard*'s blood as I and, I think, had Emma been of our sex she would have made a formidable soldier.'

Tancred grinned, the firelight picking up white teeth in a weather-darkened face that took the sun like his Lombard father; if he had loved and esteemed the man known as the Good Marquis of Monteroni he was doubly proud of being the grandson of Robert, Duke of Apulia.

'You may live to regret saying that.'

'You'll know when I do, for I'll fetch you a buffet round the ears as I was obliged to do when you were younger. Now make sure once we are departed that those tribesfolk do not surprise us by employing boats too. Guard the shore and guard it well and make sure the men near the grazing fields know what to do when they hear my shout.'

Bohemund grabbed his sword and strode down to where his men, equally armed, were gathered, stooping at the water's edge to scoop up some mud, which he rubbed vigorously into his skin. Seeing this, the men he was leading did likewise and with a minimal amount of residual light they manned the boats and cast off, rowing in a wide and Stygian arc to a pre-chosen landing spot, arrived at by using those faintly silhouetted mountain tops. As ever, at the prospect of action, blood seemed to course faster than normal through Bohemund's veins, and using a route he had studied so hard it was imprinted in his mind, marked by the shapes of bushes and trees, he led his men to where he thought he could spring his trap.

First the party had each to find an individual spot in which they could comfortably stay, somewhere whereby their stillness would allow any wildlife to become accustomed to and begin to ignore their presence, with either a bush or a tree to protect their backs and sat so each would be alone with their own thoughts, for there could be no talking and being elevated in terms of rank made no difference – Bohemund was as privy to such meanderings as any man alive, in his case a stream of memories of battles, sieges, raids carried out on

48

fast-riding horses, not destriers, of friendships made and promises broken in a world where allegiances shifted with the wind. What it did not do was interfere with the acuity of his hearing.

Even the most skilled intruder moving over a night-time landscape will make a noise – the snap of a branch, even a twig, the rustling of dead leaves and in some cases, though not this one, a quiet curse to acknowledge the pain of kneeling on a stone or cracking an elbow against something unseen. These hill tribesmen were children of the country in which they lived, who had started out playing as a game what they were now undertaking with serious intent. Had the wind not been coming off the lake and over the horse lines they would have picked up the strong scent of their adversaries, a blend of human odours added to a mixture of ingrained horse sweat and leather.

Bohemund had his sword raised before his face, the cold steel of the blade touching his nose, in his other hand a small stone he had gathered, now as warm as his flesh, aware that there were intruders crawling by, probably within touching distance though not in sight. It is easy for imagination to provide clues to what is not there but having soldiered since he was barely breeched he had enough experience to discern the difference between the real and the illusory. Now it was time for his nose to twitch at the rank smell of an unwashed body tinged with a smoky tang that spoke of a man who spent too much time near a wood fire in a place where there was the lack of a decent chimney.

To move so slowly in the dark required great discipline and Bohemund was seeing in his mind's eye what the tribesman he could smell was doing. First a sweep must be made of the ground in front, a slow arc of movement to identify potential obstacles or objects to be circumvented or, if it were a high growing weed or rushes, flattened. The next advance would be no more than the distance that arm could reach and then the exercise would need to be repeated. Touch a tree by its bark and the crawler would have to decide to go right or left, seeking, from the memory of a long day's observation of this very terrain, the best alternative; make no noise on the way to your quarry, knowing you can make as much as you like in reverse.

Whoever had been close to Bohemund was past him now, his nostrils full of the mixed odours of disturbed plant life as well as the munching destriers and he had to calculate how long to wait. Like his knights the intruders would be spread out in a long line; concentration in numbers was too dangerous, for the exposure of one meant the rest would be required to either withdraw quietly or flee noisily. In the end it was the lack of sound that decided him, the certainty that a decent gap had been opened up between those silently waiting and the crawling raiders.

Cautiously he stood, making no sound until he was fully upright. The single loud ping of the stone on his sword blade enough to alert his men and if it would bring to a halt those they were intent on foiling he hoped it would make them pause for only a second, to wait for a repeat. Lacking such a thing should induce them to carry on for Bohemund wanted them close to the horse lines and their eyes as strained as their thoughts before he took any action.

He was blessed with a voice that matched his size and weight, so when he shouted it carried far enough to seem to bounce off the walls of the surrounding mountains. In an instant the ground in front, some fifty paces distant, seemed to explode as the oil with which the ground had been soaked burst into flame. There was no darkness now and the intruders who stood up in shock were silhouetted against the blazing brushwood that had been laid as soon as the light faded. Behind those flames stood a line of mailed Norman knights, the swords reflecting now bright red to orange from the conflagration.

Those who had got to their feet had no option but to try to flee and thus they provided easy kills for the line of men they could now see standing between them and safety. But the real problem lay with those not prone to panic, for as Bohemund closed the distance between himself and that line of fire, he knew that in the undergrowth were hidden men with sharp knives and little hope. Again his voice boomed out, telling his men to employ their blades like scythes to root out those in hiding, who had only one hope: that they could wound then move so swiftly when discovered as to get past those seeking to cut them down.

With senses heightened to the level needed to stay alive in battle, Bohemund picked up the flash of a knife blade as it swept towards his lower leg, the aim to so maim him that he would be unable to easily control his weapons and certainly with his ankle tendons sliced be unable to run in pursuit. Swiftly moving his leg out of the way he swung at what was no more than an outline on the ground, aware as soon as his sword struck flesh that he had done so, not just for the cry that came up to his ears but for the way the contact between steel and bone jarred his forearm.

All around him his men were doing the same, either flushing out their quarry and cutting them down as they sought to flee or skewering them as they lay still on the ground. There was no mercy given and none received, for two of his men took knives in the vital parts of their guts from men desperate to escape. As the flames died down the men on the Lake Ohrid side of the fires pushed their way through to add to the depth of slaughter until it seemed there was no one left to kill. Yet Bohemund doubted that to be the case; it was dark, one or two of the tribesmen would manage to escape. So be it, they would pass back that raiding the lines of the Norman host was a game too deadly to play.

'Tomorrow at first light we will gather up the bodies, to be hung from trees at every league on our line of march. Let the tribes up ahead have a warning of what they face should they seek to steal from us.'

'And I say John Comnenus too,' Tancred later insisted, for he was strongly of the opinion that the *topoterites* or even his uncle the Emperor had encouraged such raids.

'Perhaps,' Bohemund acknowledged. 'But content yourself that you will never know the true answer to that.'

'Perhaps we will find out when we get to Constantinople.'

Bohemund shrugged. 'By then this will be history and of no account.'

'It will tell us how we are viewed.'

'That we know already.'

CHAPTER FOUR

The Apulians knew they were being trailed by part of the garrison of Durazzo and if their presence was an irritant it could be no more than that. Previously invisible, the pursuit had only come into view because of the time it took to make a difficult crossing of the River Vardar, so swollen that even at the point at which it could be forded it was flowing fast. For mounted men that presented little difficulty, for those on foot the rigging of manropes strung between driven-in stakes acted as an aid. But getting the carts and livestock across would take time, so Bohemund led his main body away so as not to churn up and make impassable the eastern riverbank, though he left a small rearguard on the western side lest the men sent by John Comnenus be tempted by the sight of so much easy plunder.

If the aim was to hurry them on their way, in that they failed utterly, as much from the acts of their own commander as any other factor. Thanks to John Comnenus and the time given to act upon his instructions, supplies had ceased to be plentiful and that meant no haste was possible; the army was required to forage and buy, which slowed progress, none of which much troubled the man in command. He moved at his own pace and went out of his way to be pleasant and courteous to those Byzantine officials and traders with whom he was obliged to do business, which aided him in building up a picture of the present state of the imperial domains.

The empire was stronger than the times in which he had campaigned previously; if Alexius had been a brand-new emperor in the days when the Apulians had first encountered him in battle he had not only survived invasion but had also taken a firmer grip on the imperial possessions than his recent predecessors, most notably in terms of tax collection, reputed to be ferocious. This revenue, for centuries, had served as the bedrock of imperial power, the Eastern Roman Empire being fabulously wealthy if properly administered.

It lay at the hub of the trade route between East and West and with the customs duties that brought in, Byzantium could gather so much gold and treasure to its coffers and had accumulated so much over the eight hundred years of its existence, that even after a great defeat like Manzikert, a degree of safety could be bought by the hiring of mercenaries, usually from the very enemies the empire had been fighting.

That was the kind of force Alexius now mustered. Led by Greek generals his army consisted of few natives, more of mercenary Pechenegs and Bulgars, even a contingent of Turkish archers, while at the peak stood the Varangians, the personal guardians of the Emperor. At one time made up exclusively of formidable axemen from Kiev Rus, it was now more likely to contain fighters from the old Viking heartlands of Norway and Denmark, as well as embittered

Anglo-Saxon warriors who had departed a Norman England where they had little chance to prosper.

'Not an army I would choose to lead.'

This opinion was advanced by Robert of Salerno, another relative of the de Hauteville family through too many connections to easily enumerate and one of Bohemund's senior conroy leaders. In the mix of marriages between Normans and the leading Lombard princely families over sixty years, there existed a web of cousinage in various degrees that it would need a learned monk to untangle. This Robert was black-haired and saturnine of complexion, though he did have dancing eyes.

'It was one that put up a good fight at Durazzo,' Bohemund replied. 'And remember, under Alexius I was bested by that same combination more than once.'

'Only in defence, Uncle,' Tancred insisted, 'they never attacked and drove you from the field.'

Bohemund acknowledged that with a nod, for, if memory made him uncomfortable, the conversation had started with that very proposition while waiting for the baggage train to cross the Vardar, the prospects of offensive aid from the Byzantine armies should they and the Crusaders ever get to grips with the Turks, the shared opinion being that, the Varangian Guard apart, little reliance should be placed on them.

'And that has its own dangers, for there is no love lost between we Normans and the Anglo-Saxons as was proved at Durazzo, where we first encountered them.'

Robert and Tancred had heard the tale of the battle outside the walls many times before, yet Bohemund was obliged to tell the story again, of how the *Guiscard* had met and defeated Alexius Comnenus for the first time and shortly after he had assumed the purple. The men of the then Varangian Guard, many of whom served the usurper Harold of England at Senlac Field, had come into Byzantine service after the Norman Conquest.

Tall, blond and wielding huge axes, they had advanced and thrown the Apulian battle lines into disarray. It was the *Guiscard*'s second wife, Robert of Salerno's Aunt Sichelgaita, who had rallied the broken force and saved the day. If Bohemund had hated her with a passion – she being mother to *Borsa* and had ensured his elevation to the duchy – he was obliged to acknowledge her ability. The Varangians died to a man rather than withdraw.

'Which, I hope,' Bohemund concluded, 'neither of you will ever be foolish enough to do.'

'They were brave,' Robert replied, those eyes alight.

'They were stupid,' came the snapped response, as some kind of commotion broke out to the rear, Bohemund standing to see what was afoot. 'Never be afraid to retreat and live to fight another day.'

The shouts came from a fast-riding messenger and, indistinct at first, they soon assumed more clarity, not least because many of the Apulian knights were grabbing their weapons and heading to remount their horses. It took a mighty shout from their leader to stop them and still they remained until the message was relayed to him, that the Durazzo soldiers were attacking his baggage and there were insufficient men left behind to drive them off.

'Robert, take two conroys back and force them to withdraw, but no more than that.'

'They are stealing our possessions.'

There was no doubt the conclusion that induced: such men were required to die.

'They are a pinprick, no more, and I do not want to arrive at the court of the Emperor with the blood of a massacre on my hands. I require him to think we are come in peace.'

'But—'

The interruption was harsh; Robert of Salerno had too much Lombard blood for Bohemund to indulge him in the same way as he did his nephew. 'Do not dispute with me, do as I say and quickly.'

'Do we come merely in peace?'

Tancred posed this enquiry as Robert of Salerno, shouting out commands, rushed to mount his horse, a question answered after a lengthy pause to the sound of thudding and departing hooves, a subject never satisfactorily established since the day they set out to join the Crusade, abandoning the siege of rebellious Amalfi in the process, much to the chagrin of its titular suzerain, Roger *Borsa*. It followed from a very public dispute about the policy being pursued by the increasingly unpredictable *Borsa*, an argument in which he had insulted Bohemund and even managed to alienate the more equable Roger of Sicily.

In essence it came down to which of the *Guiscard*'s sons the Normans would follow, which only a fool like *Borsa* would put to the test, especially with news of the papal crusade circulating throughout the whole of Italy and knights like Tancred extolling what might be gained by participation. Even the Great Count, though unwilling to take part himself, had seen the possibilities – to no avail; Bohemund would not be moved and without him there was little chance of raising the forces necessary.

If *Borsa* had provided the proverbial straw that broke his half-brother's back, the younger man was still curious about the precise nature of Bohemund's motives in taking up the Crusade; what were his immediate aims and more importantly what did he envisage in the longer term? He might be a good son of the Church but he was not and never had been the kind of religious zealot like *Borsa*, who wore hair shirts and allowed his thinking to be swayed by the intercession of priests.

Nor was it a mystery that he chafed at being a vassal to such a weakling. He had taken to the field immediately upon his father's death in an attempt to gain his inheritance and if it had not been for Roger of Sicily, Bohemund would have been successful. That formidable power stood between him and success, always on hand to aid his weaker nephew if the stronger one looked like achieving his aim, while never so backing *Borsa* as to utterly cement his power. The balance, of course, gave Roger more security in Sicily than the prospect that either one should triumph.

If it needed Western aid to free Byzantine territory from the Turks it would require that same aid to hold it and prevent its recapture. The only way Alexius Comnenus could achieve security and keep that military presence in place would be to grant control of possessions to the leading Crusaders, but did they want that? It was impossible to know if those making their way east were intent on the capture of Jerusalem and personal salvation or were seeking to gain a slice of that fabled eastern wealth for themselves.

'I have no mind to do for Byzantium that which it cannot do on its own merely for gratitude.'

'Remission of sins once we free the Holy Places?'

That got Tancred a long look before any reply came; his nephew knew him too well to think that his primary reason for coming east. Bohemund, if he made obeisance to God, as all men must, did so with reservations brought on by too many remembrances of the times when divine intervention had been seriously lacking when it came to his life and good fortune. He had never seen a fiery cross in the sky as he went into battle, nor heard a heavenly shout of encouragement from on high as armies clashed, and if God was a doubtful champion his servants on earth were less to be admired. Had not a reigning pope, for his own cynical ends and several talents of gold, helped his father annul the marriage to Bohemund's mother, thus rendering him and his sister as bastards?

'There is a hard road between here and Jerusalem.'

'But are we here as friends or, as John Comnenus feared, as enemies? You are being given free passage over territories you fought for previously but he and his uncle obviously suspect your aim to be the same as it was a decade past.'

'He would be a fool not to consider the possibility that I have come for Constantinople but he will also reason that alone it is nought but a dream. It would take the combined might of every Crusader to even think of taking the city and even then it would need trickery too. I have not seen the defences but I have heard enough of them to know they are formidable.'

'Could such a combination be assembled?'

'That depends on Alexius and the trust he can create. What is being asked of us is a great endeavour. I have no desire to march several hundred leagues to the south without I know that my lines of communication are secure and cannot but believe that others will think the same.'

'There is no advantage to Alexius in not providing full support.'

'True, and I think he will do so as long as it suits his purpose. But what if that changes, and even worse, what if he were to be replaced?'

'He is a strong emperor, the best for a century.'

59

'Strong emperors have fallen before, to a deadly potion or the secret knife, but all these things you have raised are in the future and unknown even to God.'

A stirring of recumbent warriors and an outbreak of cheering killed off any further discussion and had Bohemund and Tancred looking to observe the return of Robert of Salerno, the most obvious sight and easy to see at a distance the severed head dripping blood at the top of his lance. Bohemund's anger rose in line with the increased roars from his knights, who saw only the fruits of a successful encounter and nothing of what it might lead to. By the time Robert was ready to dismount the cries of praise were raining down on him from all sides so that the man in command, even if he had wanted to publicly berate him for disobedience, knew how badly it would play with the men he led. A wise leader knew when to hold his tongue, so he had little choice but to confine his disapproval to a glare, while speaking softly to Tancred.

'Tell him, in private, that if he ever disobeys me again, and so openly, it will be his head that adorns my lance tip.' In a louder voice, which he had to work to keep under control, Bohemund asked Robert, 'How many did you kill?'

'Half at least, the rest fled, but they killed many beforehand. They were mainly archers who saw our drovers as an easy target and had no stomach to face the lance.'

'And the crossing is secure?' Tancred enquired.

'All our baggage and livestock will be on this side before the sun begins to dip, cousin.'

The system of imperial messengers, fast riders and a ready supply of change horses, so important to the expansion of the old Roman

Empire, generally failed to function properly when the wearer of the diadem was weak or ruled for a short time. Alexius had restored it to something akin to its legendary efficiency and he required the service to function more now than he had ever needed it in the past. Thus he knew what had happened at the Vardar ford within a week, the news followed within days by a messenger from Bohemund explaining it as a mistake by an overzealous subordinate.

Of more interest to Bohemund was the news, when his messenger returned, that one of the main crusading groups several thousand strong, led by the Lotharingian Godfrey de Bouillon, had arrived and what had transpired when the Duke of Lower Lorraine met to talk with Alexius. He sent for his nephew and together they set out to walk the encampment heads close in conversation.

'I suspect Alexius is demanding from him the same pledge his nephew wanted from us, but neither de Bouillon or his leading captains are prepared to freely give it.'

'And the nature of the oath?'

'Acknowledge Alexius as suzerain, hand back to him any possessions taken back from the Turks and rely on his generosity when it comes to the rewards for success.'

'A wise ruler rewards his own people, not strangers.'

'A thought that will have occurred to Duke Godfrey.'

Bohemund had several traits he shared with his late father, one a gleam that came into his eye when some ploy or stratagem had just occurred to him. With the *Guiscard* it had often turned out to be some telling notion of how to break down a stubborn defence by subterfuge rather than force but it was not always so. Even as a young squire Tancred had observed his grandsire in his dealings with his fellow Normans as well as subject Lombards and Greeks. That curious twinkle was an indication that he could see into their souls and find the right words – or would it be bribes? – to hold them to him.

'I sense you have a plan.'

Bohemund smiled. 'Not a plan.'

'Yet it must involve this Godfrey de Bouillon.'

'Bouillon has already declined to accept that which Alexius demands, but for what reason and how strong are his objections? If he is a good leader he will know what we know, that to advance into Asia Minor puts us at the mercy of Alexius, and that increases the deeper we travel.'

'So he may consider it prudent to secure that before setting a foot on the other side of the Bosphorus?'

'Are you with my thinking or ahead of it?'

'You will write to him with observations that might lead him to the conclusion you seek.'

That got a smile from Bohemund, this time a sly one. 'And how do you think he will respond?' The response was a shrug of ignorance from the younger man. 'He will not, if he has any sense. De Bouillon does not know me and Alexius will seek to ensure that any message coming from me or any of the other leaders are his to read.'

That was the way of the Byzantine court: a secret was only that in terms of its value and any emperor would pay high for access to anything received by Duke Godfrey. Yet if Bohemund was serious all he would do, even if he was careful, was alert the Emperor to a potential threat.

'It is one of which he is already aware, Tancred,' Bohemund replied, when his nephew voiced those concerns. 'Alexius sees me as a hazard, witnessed by his instructions to his nephew not to let us land without a pledge of loyalty.'

'And you see value in increasing the knowledge of that threat?'

'I will have to deal with him when we get to the city and it may be that I cannot avoid making the promises he requires, but an emperor with concerns is one more to my liking than a man free of worry. I am seeking to remind him that any such undertaking as a pledge of loyalty runs both ways.'

'So it is a ploy to get him to keep his word?'

'It is a means of reminding him what risk he takes if he breaks it.'

'You cannot be certain he will get to know the contents of what you write.'

'I suspect that de Bouillon cannot emit a quiet fart that Alexius will not know about within the hour. This might take longer but I have no doubt the contents will be gossiped about by someone.'

'And if you're wrong?'

'Then no harm will be done and de Bouillon will know what I would hint to him if we were talking together face-to-face.'

The letter, when it reached Godfrey de Bouillon, came as a surprise merely by the name and seal of the sender – why would a stranger write to him and have it delivered by a messenger who refused to give his own name? He had heard of the Count of Taranto, of course, who had not, for his deeds were the stuff of travellers' tales. Nonsense mostly, Bouillon thought; no one was as gigantic as the fellow was reputed to be and no one could have carried out the actions in battle ascribed to him. Bohemund was of the same mystical cut as his father. Tales of the activities of the *Guiscard* had travelled the length and breadth of Europe and the way he was spoken of was just as foolish as the gossip told of his bastard son.

The letter was, in any case, strange, talking of security of supply being paramount before the Crusaders ever crossed into Asia Minor, that to do so without concrete assurances would be folly of the highest order. Read one way it was just that, a set of concerns, but it seemed when perused more than once it had another meaning, only a hint, but there, that the best way to secure the necessary line of communication was to have firm control of it.

'Is it truly from Bohemund?' asked his brother, Baldwin, with whom he had discussed the contents at length and to no real avail; it was still ambiguous. 'They are famed for their trickery in these parts and it may be this has been forged to test you.'

'The messenger was a Norman, or at least he spoke with their nonsensical twang.'

Baldwin had to look away then to hide his expression; he saw his elder brother as a bit slow and too pious for his own good, albeit he was a doughty fighter and a talented commander in the field. But he was also the barrier to security and opportunity for an impoverished younger son who stood to succeed to his title; Godfrey was childless and given his attachment to chastity likely to remain so. He had sold off great swathes of territory to the Church to fund his Crusade, eager to gain absolution for sins no one but him thought he had committed, and he had thus severely depleted what could be inherited. If nothing could be found on this venture Baldwin would be left with his small demesne and a straitened purse to add to the slight comfort of sibling goodwill.

'There are Normans in Byzantine service, brother.'

'I do not like this much,' Godfrey responded, waving the letter.

'Then best not reply; let Bohemund stew if it is from him and wonder at your thoughts.'

'I have no wish to make an enemy of him by seeming arrogant.'

That, to Baldwin, was typical of his elder brother: he always saw his own faults before those of others. 'Better him a foe than Alexius.'

Godfrey dithered, but Baldwin pressed home that as the best course of action and eventually persuaded his brother to give the letter to him for safekeeping. He also made sure, for a fee and in a very short time, that the contents were copied and made known to the imperial palace. Let the Emperor decide if each phrase written had a double meaning.

CHAPTER FIVE

Alexius Comnenus was in receipt of other clarifications regarding the activities of the Apulians over the following months, which stretched well into the new year of Our Lord 1097. Being himself an experienced general he was well aware of how hard it was to control thousands of fighting men, so he took at face value Bohemund's apologies for the transgressions of his soldiers: a small fortress sacked against his wishes, those selling supplies beaten when the buyers thought they were overcharging, in one case a whole town set upon for a refusal to sell them cattle; such lapses were to be expected.

More alarming were reports of what was happening with the body that had followed as soon as improving weather allowed them to cross the Adriatic, this led by the Duke of Normandy, Stephen of Blois and Robert of Flanders. The marauding tribes that had troubled the Apulians were bad enough, but the locals en route were sick of feeding passing armies, added to which the supply of the things necessary for their well-being, requested by the imperial governors, had dried up. This obliged them to forage for supplies and since there was a fine line between that and outright sequestration there had been uprisings to which the local Byzantine commanders had felt obliged to give military support to those over whom they ruled on behalf of the Emperor.

Yet more Crusaders were now making their way down the Dalmatian coast under the fabulously wealthy Provençal magnate Raymond of Toulouse and including in its ranks the papal legate, Adémar de Monteil, bishop of Puy, and they were suffering, if anything, more in the way of local obstacles, not least from the barbarous Pechenegs who as a tribe – mercenaries apart – had ever been a thorn in the side of Byzantium. The Crusaders were finding they had to fight their way across Romania and special envoys had been despatched to facilitate their progress.

'Who could ever have imagined they would come in such numbers?'

The person in receipt of this enquiry from the Emperor, one made many times previously, as they traversed the corridors of the Blachernae Palace, was the trusted Manuel Boutoumites. Added together – those on the way combined with those already camped around Constantinople – the figures were staggering: Alexius had reports that the armies totalled near fifteen thousand mounted men and twice that on foot.

The *Curopalates* responded with a wry look and a tone of deep irony to make a point that lay at the heart of imperial concerns: to what purpose was such a force assembled? 'Are they truly devout to give up so much, or are they spurred on by greed?'

'I do not doubt,' Alexius replied, 'that some are, just as I have no doubt that there are genuine pilgrims amongst them.'

'Not Bohemund.'

The Emperor smiled, though it was not a name to often bring such a response. 'No.'

'Turn him away, Highness, tell him he is not welcome and send him and his men back to Apulia.'

'I cannot, Manuel, for to do so would create a rift with the other leaders. If I say I have no faith in one of their number, then I risk implying I have no trust in any.'

'I would advise it as sound policy to create division amongst them. Advise Godfrey de Bouillon that Bohemund told you of his attempt at communication to diminish him in your eyes.'

'While I think it best to fashion a shared purpose. The key to holding them in check is this papal legate, Bishop Adémar. I must make common cause with him so he can remind these Crusaders of why they came here and to where they must proceed.'

'And if he cannot control them?'

Alexius did not need any elaboration on that point; such a body of armed men camped around the city would present a threat too great to manage. All he had in his favour, apart from the walls of the city, was that supposed piety – the need to move on to Palestine, added to the other salient fact: that to act in unison they would need a leader and from what he had so far been able to discern that was not a position any one of the great nobles, much as he supposed they would hanker after it, was likely to gift to another.

'Then I must,' Alexius replied. 'By a physical separation if no other way presents itself.'

He spoke these words as they entered the audience chamber, a room large enough to make his voice echo off its high-arched ceiling. Numerous assembled courtiers were waiting, while the tall àxe-bearing Varangians stood guard, one to each of the numerous malachite pillars, with yet more taking station by the dais on which sat the imperial throne, their eyes seeming dead in the fashion of men engaged in such a duty, gaze fixed forward.

At the heart of Byzantium was a deep sense of the value of ceremony to establish the near divine position of the emperor, honed over centuries and which harked back to Imperial Rome. Thus when Duke Godfrey de Bouillon and his entourage of senior adherents entered the huge chamber it was to the sound of blaring trumpets. There he found Alexius Comnenus seated on his throne, dressed in a purple cloak threaded with precious embroidery and on his head the jewel-encrusted diadem, stones flashing in the sunlight streaming in through the openings in the walls, that same radiance picking up the masses of gold, both in objects and decoration, with which the audience chamber was blessed. In his hand he had the imperial insignia of axes and fasces fashioned in solid gold.

If the eyes of the imperial guards flicked, then it was to the weapons these men wore; few were ever allowed into the imperial presence bearing arms and commonly no man was allowed to approach the Emperor with anything that could be used for sudden assassination. This was an exception, a ceremony by which these Western knights would bind themselves by solemn oath to the Byzantine cause. They would use their swords as a substitute for the holy cross, while to drive home the depth of that pledge Alexius had caused the reliquary bones of several apostles to be brought to the Blachernae Palace from the Basilica of St Sophia, which each Crusader would be required to kiss.

The perfumed eunuch who had coached these men in the necessary protocol, whom he thought to be rank-smelling barbarians, had stressed that they were not to come too close to the imperial presence, while Alexius, in his majesty, kept his eyes fixed at a spot above their heads as they approached the line of dark marble tiles they had been told was the limit of their advance. There they were announced one by one, the Duke first, the rest in order of precedence, one obvious omission the name of Baldwin of Boulogne, though the youngest brother, Eustace, was present. On completion they were required to go down on one knee and only then did they come under the imperial gaze, this while that same courtier read out the oath they had agreed to take, first in Greek, then in the tongue of the Franks.

If it was somewhat less than Alexius had desired – Godfrey de Bouillon, Duke of Lower Lorraine, had insisted he was vassal to no man and was not about to become one even to a Roman Emperor – it met the needs, as the ruler saw it, of Byzantium. They promised on the threat of eternal damnation to pay due attention to his advice, to respect his office and those who bore his commands, to return to his control any possessions taken back from the infidel which had once been imperial property and to reserve to him the fair distribution of any treasure captured in their progress.

The apostolic relics were then brought forward to be kissed, each man making a personal and whispered vow to act as an agent of the one true God, the effect on Godfrey to bring tears to his eyes. First the thigh bone of St Peter, crucified upside down in Rome, then a forearm bone of St Bartholomew, skinned alive then beheaded, a finger of St Simon the Zealot, sawn in half while alive, and finally the skull of St James, stoned and clubbed to death in his ninth decade. The message was plain to all: these are men who have martyred themselves for their faith, can you do any less?

'Duke Godfrey, we bid you stand,' Alexius said, adding to the wish with an upward lift of his hand, his voice changing to include the entire assembly. 'We see before us a noble servant of Christ, a man who has already given much to the sacred cause and will go on to give more.'

Another gesture brought forth two men carrying between them a small casket, which was set down before Godfrey.

'In order that you should know that you have our favour, and as some recompense for the sacrifices you have already made, not least in loss of land to fund your endeavour, I wish you to accept from our hand this small token of our imperial regard.'

A sharp command brought up the lid of the box, to reveal that it was full to near bursting with gold coins. If the Lotharingian knights strained to see, there was scant curiosity from the assembled courtiers; to them such as was being gifted was but a token, enough to impress a barbarian, scarce a quantity of treasure to raise a Greek eyebrow.

This was the second such ceremony in a few days; there had been another for Count Hugh of Vermandois accompanied by Walo Lord of Chaumont. The brother of the King of France stood so low in the mind of the Emperor that he had been given no more than a single gold ring, personally placed on his finger by Alexius and followed by a kiss on the cheek, and when they had fallen to talking about campaigning it was to the experienced Constable Walo that Alexius addressed more of his thoughts.

Alexius called forward Manuel Boutoumites, his favourite soldier and closest advisor, to tell Godfrey de Bouillon what he already knew, for Vermandois had been given the same instruction at his swearing.

'His Highness wishes that you break your present camp outside the city walls and, along with the body of men led by the Count of Vermandois, cross to the southern side of the Bosphorus. There we have prepared lines for you to move into and in which His Imperial Highness desires you remain until the rest of your confrères arrive, keeping the peace until it is time for a united advance.'

That had been a stumbling block in negotiations, for there was not a man present who had failed to mark the fate of the People's Crusade. The combined forces of de Bouillon and Vermandois were not sufficient to stand against the leader of the Sultanate of Rüm should he seek to likewise dislodge them. Protocol demanded that Boutoumites make in public the assurances that had previously been made in private.

'Be assured that the infidel Kilij Arslan is elsewhere, far to the east doing battle with his fellow Turks, the Danishmends. They are mortal enemies, thank the Lord.'

Which meant that only their separation, mutual hatred and rivalry kept Byzantium safe, but again the fate of the People's Crusade hung in the air; that easy victory had convinced the Sultan he had naught to fear from an army of Western knights, leaving him free to pursue other territorial aims.

'Should he break off his attacks and move back west we would know as soon as he marched and we have the means to forewarn you and withdraw you back to the outskirts of the city.'

'This is my wish,' Alexius added, slapping the axes and fasces into his palm.

Diplomacy, of which he was a master, precluded him from explaining his real reason: he wanted as much of a separation as could be achieved between these men and those yet to arrive. As for the need to recross the Bosphorus, should they seek to effect a combination, that they could not do without his aid and assistance for only Byzantium had the means to transport them.

Separation would severely diminish the numbers that could pose a threat to the city itself, while at the same time imposing restrictions on any chance of them intriguing together against his position. The strictures on good behaviour would only be proved by their actions but only a fool would make the same mistake as Peter the Hermit's rabble and provoke the Turks.

For all that, one observation would have stood out: while Godfrey might be unsure if it was a wise move to make a binding promise, his brother Baldwin was certain it was not, no doubt the reason he had absented himself and declined to join in the taking of the oath. In essence, for Alexius, this was a test of both Godfrey's intentions and his control over all of his vassals, especially Baldwin, for it was no mystery to Alexius that he relied on his younger brother for advice.

If Godfrey declined to hold to his word, or could not control his own men, then the oath just taken was meaningless. If he did and could then that would ease the fears of Alexius for the future, given he discounted Vermandois as militarily useless, even if the men he led were of good quality and had Walo of Chaumont to temper their titular leader's follies. He would know that at least one of the more worthy Western leaders would oblige him by obedience and that had to set an example for the others to follow.

For the Duke of Lower Lorraine the reason to comply and cross the Bosphorus had little to do with the wishes of Alexius Comnenus, more to do with the temptations to which his men were exposed by proximity to the city and the effect upon both their martial spirits and their souls. If his soldiers were barred from easy entry to Constantinople – only six were allowed inside the walls at any one time to gawp and pray, which he endlessly encouraged them to do – that did nothing to stop the devilish enticements coming out to his encampment.

Loose women, traders of shoddy goods, sellers of cures and questionable relics, even Orthodox divines seeking to detach them from the Roman Creed. Better they were in a camp far from such inducements and one in which they could recover, with the help of his priests and his captains, the true purpose of this endeavour.

'Good,' the Emperor concluded, adding a gesture to indicate they were dismissed. 'I will have our imperial gift brought to you before you depart.'

Alexius was satisfied; Bohemund would find it much harder to engage Godfrey de Bouillon in any conspiracy against the city as long as the Bosphorus separated their forces, while the Apulians were not strong enough, alone, to pose a threat if he took reasonable precautions against some clever trick. They would arrive soon and that would create another test of his diplomatic skills; could he shift them too away from the city before the other contingents appeared?

Such considerations were thrown into confusion when word came that Bohemund had called a halt and was preparing to spend Easter at Hebdomon, several days march west of the city, raising the fear that he might be waiting for the Duke of Normandy and Raymond of Toulouse, who must approach along the same Via Egnatia, creating a dangerous combination. A message to say he would come on himself did nothing to allay these anxieties, for to many at the imperial court the Count of Taranto was the spawn of Satan.

'No,' Alexius responded, when he heard that said. 'He is of the seed of his father. If the *Guiscard* was famed for anything it was never to do that which was expected of him.'

The forces of de Bouillon and Vermandois were gone by the time Bohemund arrived at the head of his *familia* knights, a body of twenty lances who acted to protect his person in battle. Tancred, once one of their number, had been left behind with the army, which would only come on to Constantinople once the terms by which they would ally themselves to Byzantium had been agreed.

The first thing to notice was the lack of any forces camped outside the city, the next the outer walls themselves, fifteen or more cubits in height and reputed to be half that thick, with dozens of towers so spaced and protruding as to allow archers to pin down anyone trying to assault them. Bohemund, having heard them described many times, had suspected exaggeration, but not even with that information could he be prepared for the actual sight.

More than seven Roman *mille passum* in length, they ran from the southern arm of the so-called Golden Horn to circle round the northern edge, there to join the sea wall which enclosed the entire city. A great chain barred access to the Bosphorus, which would have to be overcome before that flank could be threatened. To overcome what he could see was not enough, for behind that obstacle stood three more sets of fortifications all kept in decent repair, the last, the Servian Wall, protecting the very core of ancient Constantinople: the Great Palace, the Hippodrome and the greatest church in all Christendom, the mighty Basilica of Santa Sophia.

Men had been on duty to warn of Bohemund's approach and a strong party, led by Manuel Boutoumites, set out from one of the city gates to intercept him. The identity of the new arrival, given his physical features, could not be in doubt, yet, just as legend did not do justice to the walls of the city, what Boutoumites had heard did not do justice to the Count of Taranto and this in a city not short on freakish giants. It was hard not to be astounded, even more difficult to not let it show.

Boutoumites called out his title once they had come within talking distance, following that with his own name and title of *Curopalates*, which got him a nod but little else.

'Should I be flattered?' Bohemund asked finally, which got a quizzical response. 'I have been told of you, Boutoumites, and I know how high you stand in his counsel. You are spoken of to me as his right hand by those who write to me of such matters.'

The Byzantine replied unsmilingly, far from pleased that the Apulian general was so knowledgeable about the intricacies of the imperial court, even more so that he made no secret of it.

'It has been my duty to greet every noble Crusader on their approach to the city, so no, to feel flattered would not be appropriate.'

Bohemund produced a wry smile. 'Truly, Alexius asks much of those he holds dear, to be no more than a doorkeeper.'

'He has the right to ask what he wishes of any one—'

The interruption was swift. 'A notion to be put to the test, would you not say?'

'I was about to add, of his subjects.'

'Which I am not.'

'When can we expect your army?'

'They will come on from Heboomon when I call them. I thought it best to discuss the future with Alexius beforehand.'

'You make it sound as if the future is in doubt.'

'You tell me, counsellor and right-hand man, is it so?'

'If I knew the answer to such a question it would not be my place to provide it.'

'So is it time to find out and lead me to where I will be accommodated?'

'If you look behind me, Count Bohemund, you will see a line of carts approaching. They bear tents sufficient to house you and your escort.' The calm expression, which Bohemund had worn since the first greeting, changed to one of obvious irritation, which delighted Boutoumites, much as he tried to disguise it. 'It has been imperial policy not to allow those coming to our aid to reside within the city walls, for fear that, through misunderstandings, they might incite trouble with our citizens.'

The look around the landscape was slow and deliberate for it begged the question that, if there no armies encamped there, where were they?

'Duke Godfrey de Bouillon and the Count of Vermandois have led their forces across to the north shore of the Gulf of Nicomedia, but you will know this, surely, given you seem to know so much about what we say and do.'

'And your army, Boutoumites, where are they?'

'Inside the walls, where their duty requires them.' He might have just as well said to keep you and your kind out, but diplomacy left that unspoken. 'His Highness the Emperor desires to speak with you, but he has many other matters to occupy him. Once they have been attended to I will come for you and take you to him. In the meantime you will find that those approaching carts have upon them fodder for your mounts, food and wine for you, as well as cooks and servants to both prepare and serve it. His Highness wishes you and your knights to feel welcome.'

'And how long must I wait upon "His Highness"?'

The Byzantine General could not fail to note the way Bohemund emphasised that honorific, which was close to an insult, and the change in his facial expression left Bohemund in no doubt he wished to say 'as long as he damn well pleases'. When his did speak his voice was tight.

'It will be no more than my master deems to be necessary. Until then you and your men may enter the city in numbers of no more than six at a time and without weapons, to pray if you so desire as well as to marvel at the sights the imperial capital can offer. I will send a messenger out in the morning to enquire if there is anything you need.'

'Like the courtesy of being treated as an equal?'

Boutoumites enjoyed responding to that. 'No one is equal to a Roman Emperor!'

It was three days before the summons came, time in which Bohemund examined the outer walls of the city in some detail, an act which did not go unobserved by those defending them, and such was his reputation it made them nervous, so much so that he acquired a distant escort of mounted lances. He also visited within the city and marvelled at the Hippodrome, while trying to imagine it in use, packed with a hundred thousand screaming and gambling Greeks, with teams of four-horse chariots racing round seeking to either overtake or tip into the dust their opponents.

Constantinople was full of magnificent churches, abbeys and monasteries, seemingly one on every corner, but none compared to the Great Church of Santa Sophia, where he went to pray beneath the great vaulted dome, a wonder of construction that seemed to defy physical reason. If he had been escorted when outside the walls he was near to hounded within, followed by a crowd of the curious, some even so taken with his person as to wish to touch him, as if doing so would ward off the danger he was known to represent or establish if he was, as they had been told, the offspring of the Devil.

This carried on as he inspected the three sets of inner walls, less formidable but still objects it would be hard to overcome, while a ride around the sea wall convinced him that the city could not be taken without the besieger had a large fleet to impede supply and the means to get beyond that great Bosphorus chain. Those of higher ranks than this horde of peasants who watched him on his progress – and he suspected one was Boutoumites – thought the city impregnable, but there was no such thing as far as the Count of Taranto was concerned.

Back outside the gates he looked at the outer walls again, knowing Constantinople would be a hard object to overcome, possibly the hardest he had ever seen, yet he could not help but wonder what his father would have made of such defences. He had been told Bari and Palermo could not be taken, yet he had captured both and if the *Guiscard* had never seen the fortifications of Constantinople he had dreamt of them often. These thoughts got him back to his camp, where he found Tancred waiting for him, keen to report that his army was well situated and anxious to know what was happening.

'Nothing yet.'

'What is Alexius playing at?'

'Being an emperor, nephew, making sure that I know who has power and who does not.'

'How long will that take?'

'Not much longer, for if I am not summoned he knows that I may well ride away, to tell all of our confrères of the insult he had heaped upon me. But let us set that aside and eat together, for I have walked many a league this day and my stomach rumbles.'

'Is the city as magnificent as they say?'

'More, Tancred, it is staggering to think how many people live within its walls and the sights are wonders. Rest here tonight and perhaps, if Alexius still plays the despot, we may go tomorrow and you shall see for yourself.'

'Riders approaching, My Lord.'

Leaving the table and Tancred, Bohemund went to the entrance to his sumptuous and spacious tent and observed the sun was setting behind the single fellow approaching, sending long shadows across the flat plain on which the city stood, while picking out the spires and domes that sat atop its hills. It also burnished the armour of an unescorted Manuel Boutoumites, which could only have one meaning. Having been relaxing over wine and conversation with his nephew, Bohemund had one of his men keep the Greek occupied until he was clad in his Crusader surplice, while his horse was saddled and brought to the entrance, Tancred being told to keep out of sight, an instruction which mystified him.

When the Count of Taranto emerged it was to find the *Curopalates* surprised at his presumption. Bohemund could have said that him coming on his own, and not sending the usual messenger, only left him to draw one conclusion: he was being summoned. But that would have provided no amusement.

'I have been expecting you, Boutoumites. As you see I was dressed and waiting. Now let us not do that to your Emperor. It is desired, is it not, that we meet at the Blachernae Palace?'

The last was a guess, if not a wild one, but the implication was again obvious: I have spies within your court and I know everything I need to before you deign to inform me.

CHAPTER SIX

The outer wall of Constantinople was so extensive it seemed to take the entire contents of a glass of sand to ride to the point of entry, which meant darkest night had come by the time Manuel Boutoumites and his charge arrived outside the Blachernae Gate, a pair of great doors studded with iron bolts and some silver-topped to denote the imperial device. This was flanked by two massive crenellated towers, the whole area illuminated by the same array of lit torches that lined the city parapet all the way to the southern stretch of water known as the Propontis.

Unlike the many previous gates they had passed, closed for the night, these were wide open, yet it was testament to the nervousness of the garrison that a strong body of archers stood guard, so fearful were they of the reputation of the man coming to visit their ruler. Looking backwards at that line of flickering and diminishing points, which, due to the arc of the walls, disappeared halfway, brought home to Bohemund, more than daylight had done, just how immense was the Byzantine capital and what kind of force would be required to invest it.

To overcome the outer defences was only the first part of the battle, as his observations on his tour of the inner city had underlined. Even with a whole crusading army and adding a powerful fleet, which they did not have, it would be more like the fabled siege of Troy than anything he had experienced previously in his years of fighting, a decade in duration and likely requiring some kind of ruse to bring about success.

Such conclusions had played upon his thinking over the time of waiting and they were still present now as they approached the entrance to the Blachernae Palace, a residence that had become the favoured accommodation for Alexius Comnenus. He rarely entered the Great Palace at the heart of the city, Bohemund suspected because too many of his predecessors had been murdered there. The second reason for the shift to the Blachernae was comfort: it occupied a hill to the very north of the city in an area well away from the crowded stink of the old urban heart and the elevation gave the occupant good views in all directions, it also being high enough to benefit from any available and cooling breeze.

There was a third compelling purpose to such a place of residence: Constantinople was a city much given to riot, at times when food was short and prices rose to levels the lowest could not afford, at others when some event set the population at loggerheads with whoever wore the imperial crown – excessive taxation, some perceived insult to the Orthodox religion, to which the populace was much attached – or just a long-lasting heatwave in an overcrowded city. Being at the north-eastern tip of the city a threatened emperor could make a quick and easy escape till things settled down.

Again it was only torchlit illumination that gave a clue to the massive dimensions and gilded magnificence of what was now the administrative centre of the empire. Diminished that polity might be, but the palace reeked of a wealth almost impossible to quantify, while within the walls were the men, and they were numbered in the several hundreds, who carried out the business of government, most of them eunuchs.

Thinking on such a body, Bohemund could not but help reflect on their reputation for intrigue, jealousies and in-fighting; to him such leanings seemed to seep from the shadows thrown onto the walls by torchlight. Every time an emperor fell, there was always some powerful eunuch at the centre of the conspiracy to topple him.

The Varangian Guard lined the corridors through which he and Boutoumites passed, each with breastplate, helmet and axe; they were trusted to be armed in the imperial presence yet it was also true, and had been since the days of Ancient Rome, that any Praetorian Guard were the first to be seduced, which made them as much a threat as a safeguard. If these men sought to appear indifferent, every eye flicked a little in Bohemund's direction, for passing them was not just a fellow warrior and one who well overbore them in height, but also a near legendary one; if some looks carried a glare of hate it would be from an Anglo-Saxon.

Finally they entered the same large chamber, which unbeknown to Bohemund had so recently witnessed the deference of Godfrey de Bouillon and his captains. There were no courtiers present now, just the guards and, sat on his dais, the Emperor Alexius dressed not in purple, but in what looked like workaday garments, a smock edged with embroidery of an almost archaic Greek design, albeit made of very fine linen. When he got up to greet Bohemund, the thought arose in the mind of his visitor that it might be because only by standing on his elevated platform could he look him in the eye.

A short period of silence ensued as two men who had only ever seen each other on a battlefield and at a distance carried out a mutual examination. Alexius was of medium height and had the chest and shoulders of a fighting man while his legs, where they were visible, showed strong and muscular support for that upper body. His skin was olive-coloured yet pale and spoke of an indoor life, made to look more luminous by the many oil lamps, the nose prominent and slightly hooked, the lips full and sensuous, while the gaze from his dark-brown eyes was steady and unblinking. The voice, when he spoke, was deep and composed, strong enough to create an echo in what was a near empty and high-ceilinged chamber.

'Count Bohemund.'

That got a slight dip of the Norman head. 'Face-to-face, Alexius.'

'Highness!' whispered an irritated Manuel Boutoumites. 'Show respect.'

That got a low chuckle. 'I have shown enough respect by the time of waiting, then coming when summoned.'

'A proud Norman, then,' Alexius said, with a ghost of a smile. 'Not much given to bending the knee?'

'I do so when I am seated.'

That brought a full smile to the lips of the Emperor and a sharp intake of breath from Manuel Boutoumites, for it was a clear demand for a chair; few were the people allowed to sit in the imperial presence outside the immediate family, and even they required permission. It was plain from the ensuing pause that Alexius knew he was being challenged, that Bohemund was demanding to be treated as an equal not a subject. It was also obvious he was thinking through the ramifications of either agreeing or a refusal.

'Let's you and I retire,' he said finally, looking around the large chamber, 'to somewhere more informal.'

'To where we can speak in private.'

'You may wish to say things others will not take kindly to hear.'

'Highness?' Manuel Boutoumites asked, who realised that he was not to be included.

'Please wait here, *Curopalates*, to escort Count Bohemund back to his camp.' The hesitation of his advisor was palpable and the reason obvious. 'Do not fear for my person, the Count is unarmed, and if he seeks to use those great hams of his to break my neck, one of my guards will chop them off.'

There was a moment, when Alexius descended from his dais to ground level, when he registered his comparative height and it was not one that spoke of ease. Accustomed to respect for his title this was a not a man to be easily overawed; imperial splendour – and the Blachernae Palace, even near empty, had that in abundance – would not impress this particular Norman, with his steady gaze and a body stillness that spoke of a high degree of self-control. For a second Alexius felt discomfort, before abruptly spinning round to walk away, his mind full of thoughts over which he had mulled many times.

Of all the Frankish knights supposedly coming to the aid of Byzantium – and many of them were a mystery in terms of their personal aspirations – Bohemund was likely to be the most dangerous and the most difficult to control, for he had no respect for an empire which he and his family had fought both for and against. Nor could he easily believe in Bohemund's piety; if faith had brought the likes of Godfrey de Bouillon to his city and might be bringing on those who followed, Alexius could not believe that such a cause had prompted this man to take part.

His ambitions in Southern Italy were far from secret, nor was the frustration he felt at the need to acknowledge his half-brother as both Duke of Apulia and his suzerain, or that this was a compromise forced upon him by his Uncle Roger, who, instead of supporting his right to the lands he had conquered, would have taken the field against him had he refused to settle for what he occupied. Set against that, also to be proved when all were present, he was probably the most accomplished leader in battle, a fact to which Alexius could personally attest.

In the latter stages of his father's invasion of Romania, with the *Guiscard* obliged to take the bulk of his lances back to crush rebellion in Apulia, Bohemund had been massively outnumbered at every turn, and if he had lost a battle or two, many more times he had inflicted defeat upon the armies Alexius had led by the employment of superior tactics, the sheer physical force of his Norman lances or by some act of individual courage that had rallied his men to mount what would appear to be a futile assault.

Added to that prowess was the trouble he could cause, if disgruntled, by stirring up resentments with his fellow Crusaders. In the formulation of imperial policy Alexius had quite fixed aims: to throw back from his borders the Turks who, if left in peace, would threaten the city of Constantinople itself, something he lacked the means to achieve. Three times he had sought to retake Nicaea, each attempt ending in failure; perhaps with these Western knights that could be brought about and the infidels defeated to create a true buffer between them and the capital. If they moved on south, every step taken towards Jerusalem was one that would provide enhanced security for Byzantium.

After passing through endless corridors, Alexius led Bohemund into a private and much smaller chamber, where two servants awaited him, as did food and wine, the latter poured on command. Both he gestured should leave and when they obeyed, though they left the door ajar, he indicated that his guest should occupy a capacious divan, before personally handing him a jewel-encrusted goblet, he sitting down opposite in a curule chair. The goblet Bohemund took, but he did not drink from it until Alexius had done so first, which did not go unnoticed.

'You think I might poison you?'

'More I think that someone might seek to poison you, Alexius, and that I would suffer by inadvertence.'

'Did you not see I am well protected?'

'As well protected as many of those who preceded you, such as Nikephoros.'

Alexius smiled; he suspected Bohemund was trying to needle him by mentioning the previous emperor. 'He was a weak man, I am not.'

'Was it not a mistake to spare his eyes, in fact his life?'

'I did not invite you here to discuss the events of the past, Count Bohemund. I wear the diadem now and it is with me that men must deal. Why have you come here?'

The sudden change was designed to throw Bohemund off guard; it failed because he had been waiting for it. 'I answered the call of Pope Urban.'

'So you are bound for Jerusalem?'

'I have had to point out to many of those who follow me that such a goal is a very long way off and much stands between what the Pope might desire and what can actually be achieved.'

'Are you saying you do not think the Crusade will succeed?'

'You know what I am saying.'

'It concerns me that you may have other things in mind.'

'Like an attack on the city?' Alexius nodded as Bohemund took a deep drink. 'That is ambition long since put aside. I do not have the strength to attempt such a thing.'

'Yet you do not deny that such a possibility excites you?'

'No, any more than that you would like to regain from we Normans the provinces of Langobardia and Calabria. Like me, Alexius, you lack the ability to make that dream become a reality.'

'And what of your fellow Crusaders?'

'Since I do not know them I do not know their minds.'

'So you did not seek to garner support from Godfrey de Bouillon?' Answered with a look of bewilderment Alexius continued. 'You did write to him, did you not?'

'Only to see if his views on what we might face coincided with my own.'

'And the others yet to arrive, have you communicated with them?'

'Why should I when I suspect that their gaze is fixed on the Holy Land, as is mine?'

Bohemund interpreted the following silence as a lack of belief, which was hardly surprising. But if Alexius knew that he could not send the Apulians packing for the effect it would have on other Western knights, so did the man who commanded them.

'It is vital that all of you cooperate with Byzantium.'

'We will not get far, Alexius, if we do not, nor will we get far if we do not cooperate with each other.'

Alexius was quick to discern the meaning of that. 'You see trouble ahead?'

'I hope for the opposite but I would be a fool, and so would you, not to count it as a possibility. A divided command is a dangerous one.'

'Why did you stop your progress at Heboomon, why is your army camped there?'

The change of tack was a deliberate attempt to fend Bohemund off from where he was obviously headed – the answer to a divided command was a unified one and who better to head that, with imperial support, than a Norman whose worth he knew? Aware that Alexius was not going to allow himself to be dragged into a discussion of that, Bohemund answered the question with a pre-prepared and wholly specious answer.

'To ease your concerns, given I had no idea that Vermandois and Bouillon had departed and crossed to Bithynia. I thought that the addition of my Apulians to their forces, sitting outside your walls, might cause you anxiety.'

Alexius allowed himself a ghost of a smile. 'And if I requested that you do likewise?'

'If that is your wish I am happy to meet it, as long as my men and my mounts are fed and watered.'

'You have heard of the oath taken by Vermandois and Bouillon?'
'I have.'

'Then I am bound to enquire if you will make the same pledge.'

Bohemund feigned surprise, but he did it well. 'Is not that the reason you have called me to your palace?'

Alexius was just as good at masking his true feelings, yet to a sharp eye a sudden need to blink was as good as a shout, even if, in revealing he had reacted when he should not have, the Emperor kept his eyes closed; that response had taken him off guard. He took his time to open them once more and fix his visitor with a firm look.

'You have come prepared to swear?'

'I will do so now, if you wish, Alexius, and to you alone.'

The reply was slow and soft. 'No, Count Bohemund, let it be done with due ceremony and in the presence of witnesses. I would have you swear too on the holy relics kissed by the others so that you know you are risking eternal damnation if you betray the pledge you make.'

'Anyone would suspect you did not trust me.'

Alexius was too shrewd to respond to that direct challenge, even if it came with an amused smile. He stood and indicated the door. 'I will send my *Curopalates* to you on the morrow.'

Bohemund was escorted back to his encampment by a squadron of cavalry to find Tancred pacing back and forth, worried that his uncle had walked into some form of trap. If many of the tales of Byzantine intrigue were lurid they were not without some basis in fact; over the centuries people had been regularly killed in cold blood and the methods were the stuff of nightmares. Pick a pear from a tree and it might have been filled with a fatal toxin, accept an imperial gift of, say, a gold casket and there might be a famished and venomous snake waiting for you to lift the lid. It was rumoured that they had even perfected such a thing as a poisoned cloak, for that was a common imperial gift and a mark of respect.

'I daresay Alexius would like to see me dead, but it's not something he can at present afford.'

'What's he like?'

'You can make your own mind up, Tancred; we go to the Blachernae tomorrow to take the same oath as Godfrey of Bouillon and Vermandois.'

Tancred could not hide his surprise. 'You intend to swear?'

'If we are to proceed I have little choice.'

'The risk—'

'What risk – swearing on the relics of saints?' Bohemund snapped. 'That would give me pause; it would give most men pause.'

'If you go to Santa Sophia the divines there will show you many things, including two heads of John the Baptist. I have heard it said that men with such a feature exist, but they do not do so as biblical prophets. One of those heads must be a fake and that throws doubt on any others, so how do I know what I am being asked to swear on is a true relic or some fanciful object dug up by some dreamer or fraud?'

'An oath is an oath, made to God even if the relics are dubious.'

'Which I will keep as long as Alexius keeps his, and think on this, nephew! Alexius Comnenus was once given the military title of *nobilissimus*, the first to be so termed with the highest rank the Emperor could bestow, and that was for his service to his predecessor, to whom I think you will agree, he must have made an oath of loyalty both before he was granted the title and at the ceremony of investiture?'

'Of course,' Tancred replied, for he knew what was coming.

'Where is the one-time Emperor Nikephoros now? In a monastery praying that the man who swore that oath does not suddenly see cause to have him strangled. I will make the pledge that Alexius demands and I will hold to it as long as he does the same. That is the warning I sent him in that letter to Bouillon, which, to ease your curiosity, he had plainly read.'

Bohemund knew his nephew was troubled and he was aware why: the younger man had more fear of divine retribution than he but it was not just that. If his own motives in coming on Crusade were mixed, those of Tancred were less so. He could recall only too clearly the way his nephew had sought to persuade him to take up the Crusade outside the walls of Amalfi, talking of the opportunities for wealth and plunder, never stating the other possibility: that a young warrior with a strong arm and a small inheritance, the fiefs of Lecce and Monteroni, might carve out for himself in the recovered territories possessions of his own to rank with those of his de Hauteville forbearers.

'I cannot swear, Uncle.'

'You do not have to, I will swear for myself and the forces I command.'

'That includes me.'

'It might not always be so, Tancred.' Their eyes locked for a long time, until the young man nodded to say he understood: one day he would strike out on his own behalf and with his uncle's blessing. 'Go back to Heboomon and prepare to lead the army across to the Gulf of Nicomedia, I will deal with the Emperor Alexius.'

Bohemund did not wait for Boutoumites to come to him; he was outside the Blachernae Gate at first light with his *familia* knights, helmeted, in chain mail, wearing his great sword, his snow-white surplice with the bold red cross and loudly demanding entry, which was granted but not to the audience chamber. Knowing that they must wait until all was made ready they did so in the Church of St Mary, on their knees before the shrine to her memory, like knights at vigil over a dead leader. Bohemund was aware as he stayed still in his devotions that a stream of the curious came in to cast eyes on this epitome of the Norman warrior until eventually the messenger came.

The ceremony was the same as that attended by Godfrey de Bouillon and his captains, the same clutch of courtiers, the same guards at the pillars and Alexius on his dais in full regalia. Called upon to come before the Emperor he and his followers, still wearing spurs, made a noisy entry to the airy and spacious chamber to kneel before Alexius, swords acting as crosses, where the same oath was required and given, the relics brought forward to Bohemund to be kissed in turn.

'It pleases me that we are at peace, Count Bohemund.'

'I too, *Imperator*.' Alexius could not help but smile; if Bohemund was not about to address him as 'Highness' he had found a way to show his respect with the ancient Roman title. What followed was not so pleasing. 'And I ask that to seal such a peace you swear, on these same holy relics, that you shall give to our Crusade all the aid that is at your disposal to provide.'

If that set up a buzz amongst the eunuchs, it infuriated Alexius and he made no attempt to hide his anger. 'You doubt that I will do so?'

'No, but it would ease my soul if I knew that you were as committed to me as I am now committed to you.'

The gesture that fetched to the dais the thigh bone of St Peter was a sharp one and, with a glare at Bohemund, Alexius bent to kiss it, but he did so in silence, no words were spoken. Unbidden Bohemund stood and his men followed.

'My army is ready to march, all they require is to be told where to embark. I would beg to be allowed to stay in the city to ensure that the supplies we need with which to campaign are bought and stored, also that ships are available to carry them to where they need to go, which I will be right in assuming is Nicaea.'

'That must be the first objective,' Alexius replied, still seething. 'But I would wish your senior captains to swear the oath too.'

'When I pledge it is on behalf of them all.'

The silence was long, for here again was a problem about which it had to be considered if it was worth making a stand. Eventually Alexius nodded, having decided it was not, stood himself and descended to ground level, where he removed the heavy diadem and handed it to a grovelling eunuch.

'There is something I wish to show you.'

Alexius turned and left the chamber, Bohemund alone following to a door through which the Emperor had disappeared. On entry the Norman was dazzled by the light of hundreds of candles, but it was not their illumination that hurt the eyes so much as the way that reflected off what was stacked in the room, objects of gold and silver in a quantity Bohemund had never seen assembled in one place, bolts of the finest silk dyed in a multitude of colours, trays which on closer examination were covered in precious stones. Try as he might to maintain his composure, it could not be done; Bohemund actually gasped, for all the revenues of his domains, which were substantial, would not add up to this is in a decade.

'You will have heard that I rewarded Hugh of Vermandois and Godfrey of Bouillon for their oath of loyalty to me.' That got a cautious nod, for it had been used to tell both men how they stood in imperial regard, the Frenchman with his derisory ring and de Bouillon with his casket of coins. 'So that you will know how highly I regard your acceding to the same, I wish that you will accept the contents of this small chamber as a reward for the services I know you will render to me in the future.'

'This is all for me?'

'It is,' Alexius replied. 'And may it let you consider what you might gain by keeping to the oath you just took.'

Bohemund nodded, but he was thinking, as well as securing supplies he must find a ship and a trusted captain to take this treasure back to Bari. There was too much to transport over the terrain they were about to cover and its value in his homeland vault would be much greater than it would be in Constantinople.

CHAPTER SEVEN

The camp to which Tancred led the army was as well ordered as the sea crossing that got them to the shores of Asia Minor, ample open barges for horses that made easier the loading and unloading, given they never lost sight of the sky or the Bosphorus shore; not that it was simple, transporting horses over water was a skill that the Normans had learnt in Calabria. They could not have conquered Sicily without it and much of the lesson came from how to sedate the most awkward and skittish animals with potion provided by Basilian monks. Such tricks had been passed by to their fellow Normans at home and the *Guiscard* had always claimed that, without his aid, the man they called the Conqueror would never have got his mounted knights to the battlefield of Senlac.

Assembled on the Galata side it was a full day's march to the camp at which Alexius had decreed the Crusaders should assemble. Aware of their coming the Byzantine officials who controlled the province had already designated an area in which they could pitch their tents and set up horse lines in close proximity to running water, this from specially dug shallow canals, and to get there the Apulians were obliged to pass through what was, in many respects, very like a Roman legionary encampment of ancient times.

A main roadway ran through the centre with an oration platform in front of a series of large pavilions on one side and a parade space opposite, while the tents, cooking and latrine pits of the previous arrivals lay beyond. The sight of their fellow Christians, especially the fabled Norman warriors, engendered much curiosity amongst the men of Lotharingia and Central France, bringing them to stare, and being soldiers the new arrivals were the subject of much diminishing ribaldry, which had the commander and his captains needing to enforce restraint on men who took badly to insults regarding their manhood.

Within an hour Tancred had raised a de Hauteville pennant above one of the central pavilions to join those on the adjoining tents of Godfrey de Bouillon and Hugh of Vermandois. But he did not linger to seek their company; before the flag raising he had set his knights to constructing a manège in which he and his lances could properly exercise, the kind of facility with which they had honed their skills, first in Normandy and then in Italy. If there had been training on the Via Egnatia it could not compare with what they undertook now, which was designed to get them back to the peak of those abilities which struck so much fear into their enemies.

The task was to create a large area of soft ground, sandy if possible, big enough to work their mounts, into which thick poles were driven for sword practice, others to bear sacks and shields to be attacked with lances at saddle height as well as a false shield wall behind which the Apulian foot soldiers would gathered to create as much of a cacophony of noise as they could so that the destriers approaching such a defensive line got accustomed to the din and were able to ignore it. Working in conroys of ten, the standard Norman fighting unit, they practised wheeling and manoeuvring their destriers, these then combining into larger groups so that everyone understood and responded to the same commands.

When not yelling for their mounted confrères, Bohemund's Apulian *milities* were also engaged in training, albeit of a simple repetitive variety: when to move forward or back, to left and to right on which call of the horn, the recognition of certain banners that would presage an attack, a retreat or a warning of incoming flights of arrows, which required them to kneel and cover their heads with their shields. If the other Crusaders trained for battle too, none did so with the application of the men from Italy.

'So when do we get a sight of your giant Bohemund?' asked Godfrey de Bouillon when, a few days later, Tancred finally dined with them. 'Our cousin of France assures me I will be astounded.'

Vermandois, himself tall, but gangly rather than sturdy, was nodding, which did nothing to disturb his carefully barbered golden locks, nor show any hint of intelligence in his pale-blue eyes; having met the Count of Taranto in Bari he had, no doubt, been vocal in his impression. The contrast between the two northern magnates was striking: Godfrey had a barrel chest and seemed near as broad as he was tall due to the shortness of his treetrunk-like legs. Tancred had an amusing vision of him bestowing a kiss of peace on Bohemund's knee instead of his cheek, but even holding such a thought he also had to acknowledge that de Bouillon appeared to be no fool.

'He promises to come when he has ensured that when we advance we are fully supplied with goods already purchased.'

'A task for one of the Emperor's minions,' Vermandois snapped, his eyes flashing for once. 'Not for one of our rank.'

Behind him, his brother's constable raised his eyes as Tancred responded.

'He is spending imperial funds and I think when we are outside the walls of Nicaea, you will be grateful that his efforts are no charge on your purse.'

'An attack on Nicaea is yet to be decided,' Vermandois snorted.

That had Godfrey's eyebrows twitching – Walo adopted a bland expression – for it was a comment from a fool: if it had not been yet discussed, this due to the absence of the leaders of major components of the army, it had to be the primary aim. There was no way to move south and leave such a powerful fortress untouched and sitting on their line of communication to Constantinople. Besides, Alexius would insist upon it being recaptured as part of his bargain with the Crusade, not least so as to protect his own capital.

Tancred could guess what made Vermandois so waspish; if he did not know that his aim of overall command was never going to be fulfilled, he must have sensed it by the way he had been treated in Constantinople. He would have heard of the rewards Godfrey received set against his own meagre ring and both would be smarting if they knew of the largesse showered on Bohemund. Thus the name of whoever did acquire the position was of much import to Vermandois. He suspected, and so probably did Godfrey of Bouillon, that Bohemund had remained in the capital to make his case to Alexius and to also be the first to impress upon the likes of the Duke of Normandy and Raymond of Toulouse his fitness for the role.

How simple it would be if such concerns had any basis in fact; command of the host was going to be a chalice charged with a fair degree of poison, given that Pope Urban had signally failed to anoint anyone with the responsibility. The list of names provided too many candidates and Godfrey, a reigning duke who had been forced to fight hard to maintain his position in his domains, had at least a claim to be one of them. He was also by repute a staunch Christian utterly dedicated to the cause; you did not have to be long in the camp to hear how much he had sacrificed of those lands and titles to get here, especially from men who were loyal to his brother.

If Raymond of Toulouse could advance a right to the command, being the first to pledge his service to Pope Urban, so too could Robert, Duke of Normandy, an assertion that would be backed by his powerful brothers-in-law, Stephen of Blois and the Count of Flanders. The fact that none could match Bohemund in the experience of leading large forces on campaign meant little; he had concluded that without either papal or imperial input the command would remain diffuse. If it were to prosper, the Crusade would become a meeting of minds rather than under the direction of one single intelligence. Any attempt to issue orders by one of the individual leaders would only result in dissension.

Messengers streamed back and forwards from Constantinople on a daily basis, Tancred keeping his uncle informed of what was happening on the shores of the Gulf of Nicomedia, he likewise kept abreast of events in the capital, this while others, such as the contingent from Normandy and Flanders, crossed the Bosphorus to join them. When Raymond and his Provençal army finally arrived to camp outside the capital, the largest contingent so far, no one was left in doubt as to how angry he was at the troubles he had encountered, which sometimes descended into pitched battles, in crossing Macedonia and Thessaly.

He and Alexius had not enjoyed a happy meeting, for proud Raymond had point-blank refused to swear any kind of oath to the Emperor, promising nothing more than that he would do no harm to any present or former possessions of Byzantium. Then he and some of his leading nobles came on to the Gulf of Nicomedia ahead of his army, not willing, given his previous troubles, that they should move until he had seen and approved of the encampment.

In the collection of pavilions the largest had been set aside for a place in which to meet and it was there that Tancred took his place as the acting head of one of the crusading contingents, with Robert of Salerno as a sole supporter. That his youth attracted looks he was aware, just as he was conscious that in standing in for Bohemund his voice would carry nothing like his uncle's weight.

A glance around the room showed him now familiar faces, including the sad countenance of the much diminished Peter the Hermit, as well as those of the fresh arrivals. Raymond of Toulouse was a man who repaid close study, for he had about him an air that impressed Tancred. Of medium height he had a high colour, set off by golden hair and a stern brow made more so by thick eyebrows, this over a much broken nose. It was not just that he looked like a warrior – the leaders all had that air, even in some ways Vermandois, and it certainly resided in the Constable of France. It was more a cast in the eye that marked him out, for it had about it something of the confidence exuded by Bohemund.

The one non-warrior, if you discounted servants there to supply food and wine, was Bishop Adémar of Puy. He had come with Raymond, trailing a reputation for being of clever mind as well as a calm one. The personal representative of Urban he had been tasked with overseeing the papal enterprise, though not in a military sense, something from which he maintained his office and priestly vows debarred him. Tancred guessed that was so much stuff; de Puy knew that these men would no more obey a divine than any other one of their number. Having led the assembly in prayer and asked God that their efforts be blessed he took a seat along with everyone else and opened the gathering, looking straight at Tancred.

'We are saddened that your uncle is not with us.' The voice, if it was soft, was not weak, nor was there any blinking when Tancred returned his questioning stare, looking into a round, smooth face set in a substantial head, in which the eyes seemed large and the nose and mouth seemed unnaturally small. 'However, we are sure that it is only duty that detains him.'

Was that a barbed comment or a priest speaking the truth to assuage the concerns of others? It was impossible to tell, but Adémar did not hold his gaze on Tancred, he let it roam around the room, to rest on each of the powerful magnates in turn, naming them and all of their titles, as if such a thing were necessary. That done, his smooth face took on a look of gloom, albeit without the production of one single wrinkle.

'It is a sadness with which we must live that a man's intentions can always be called into question, even if he is blameless. As I look at this assembly, so puissant and remarkable, I see much justified pride yet I am forced to have you recall that pride is a sin. The endeavour upon which we are about to embark will be both difficult and hazardous. If we have God to sustain us we also have the means through base human motives to put many obstacles in our path.'

That brought forth various ways of denying possession of such a thing as pride; throats cleared, the odd bark and one outright vocal dismissal from Vermandois, which brought from Adémar a slow and engaging smile.

'Be assured that priests are not immune, and an elevation to a bishopric does not much alter things. You here assembled represent the very best of Christendom. You have given up lives of ease and comfort to come here, I know.'

That too got various reactions, for not all had abandoned ease and comfort, though Vermandois was nodding as he picked at a bowl of grapes. Those serving under Godfrey de Bouillon and his brothers, Baldwin and Eustace, came from a patrimony in constant turmoil, while Robert of Normandy, known as *Curthose* for his shortness of leg, had left behind a duchy at constant threat from his brother.

William Rufus, the eldest son of the Conqueror and now King of England was determined to unite the twin parts of the paternal domains, an aim that was only frustrated by too many difficulties at home, yet he caused endless trouble in Normandy. It was maliciously rumoured that *Curthose* had come east for peace and quiet, not more conflict. There was one truth that had emerged through loose talk by his men: he had mortgaged his duchy to William Rufus for the fabulous sum of one hundred thousand crowns, which, if he had not already spent it all made him one of the richest of the assembly.

'Yet,' Adémar carried on, 'if we are all poor sinners there is wisdom here too, enough of that to allow for the putting aside of arrogance so that the common good may be served. I, as you know, am not at home on the field of battle but I have made it my business, since tasked by Pope Urban, to put my mind to a study of the art of war. While I will openly admit to being a novice in such a gathering I do have, I think, sound judgement and, I hope and pray, divine guidance.'

That got another slow study of the room, as though Adémar was seeking to discern where each man stood. Tancred thought it a clever ploy; if the Bishop could not lead by experience of combat he could act as the honest broker between those who were knowledgeable, the next words from his mouth cementing the notion.

'Yet we are bound to be beset by differing views so I propose that what we have here gathered be the norm. Let us call ourselves the Council of Princes and set as our task to act always as honest and open in matters of policy, as well as men who can accept that when a majority favours a course with which they might disagree, that is the one which should be adopted.'

If Bohemund had been present, Tancred was sure all eyes would have turned on him to see if he would accept such an arrangement. As it was they were laid upon Raymond of Toulouse, including those of Adémar, which obliged the Count to react. The answer was not long in coming, showing that he had a clear sight of what was attainable as well as that which needed to be done.

'As of this moment we are not obliged to engage in speculation. Our first goal stands four-square on our path. If we are to have any discussion, it would have to be plans of how we are to take a fortified town that has thrice sent Byzantium packing.'

'Then let us make haste to be outside the walls,' cried Vermandois, with brio.

'Tancred,' Raymond said, ignoring him. 'Your uncle will have spoken to you of this.'

'He has, My Lord.'

There was real discomfort in becoming the centre of this much attention and as he replied he wondered if the tremor he could feel in his voice was obvious. Had he been standing he was sure his knees would have been shaking.

'Then it would serve us,' Adémar asked, 'if you would share his thinking with the council?'

'The observations he made to me concern the old Roman Road, which provides the route we must follow to Nicaea, and he asked that I reconnoitre it. It does exist but is so overgrown in places as to disappear. In the mountains there are the usual problems of mudslides and falling boulders, but at least it is defined. Where it is visible on open ground it is in poor repair and it would thus be easy for our forces to wander off it. The Emperor Alexius stressed when discussing tactics with my uncle that when we march it must be as a compact body, for the Turks are adept at forcing battle on dispersed forces. He cites the fate of the pilgrims led by Peter the Hermit.'

That had the old man's lips moving in silent prayer as the others present used gestures to underline that they were very different from that rabble.

'Then,' Raymond declared, 'that must be our first task. To clear the road and mark it clearly.'

'Which requires,' Adémar interjected, 'that one of you here present accept the duty.'

'We are not mere villeins,' cried Baldwin of Boulogne, his act of speaking getting him a glare from his elder brother; supporters at such gatherings whispered to their leader, they did not take the floor themselves unless invited to do so.

'Let the Byzantines repair their road,' said Vermandois, agreeing with him. 'Is it not to their advantage to have it in good order?'

'Which means,' Tancred insisted, 'sending back to the Emperor a request for the bodies needed to carry out the task.'

Raymond cut in again, his voice strong and commanding. 'There is no time for that. Let each host provide a contingent.'

'Well said, Count Raymond,' cried Adémar, 'for it is only by joint effort that our enterprise will succeed.'

This took no account of the fact that Raymond's army was still on the other side of the Bosphorus, but it was nevertheless agreed, as was the opinion, again advanced to Tancred by Bohemund, that even on a clear road the Crusaders would need to move in groups, given the ability to supply the men along a roadway was constrained, while what pasture existed for the mounts would be destroyed if overgrazed. Things would be much improved if it were given the means and time to recover.

'I myself will toil on repairing the road,' said Godfrey de Bouillon, unaware of the sibling glare that produced behind his back. 'No man can stand idle when the work of the Lord needs to be done.'

'Well said,' was the chorus, but none of the other magnates volunteered to work with him.

It took thousands of men and two weeks to clear and make usable the ancient road that led through the mountains to Nicaea, work which was carried out undisturbed by the garrison of that city, men who could not fail to be aware of the strength of the approaching host or the intended target of their labouring efforts, the common opinion being that they felt so safe behind their walls that the prospect of investiture was one they did not fear.

Tancred, in company with Vermandois and Robert, Count of Flanders, led the first major component south, Walo of Chaumont coming on later with Godfrey de Bouillon and Robert of Normandy, then finally Raymond in company with the forces of the Emperor Alexius. Several thousand men strong, on horse and foot followed by carts, oxen and a number of camp followers, such a body presented a tempting target on a highway now cleared and lined with white crosses, one that led across open country and on through mountainous defiles. A screen of cavalry was strung out to the east as well as ahead to ensure they could not be caught unawares.

With them came Manuel Boutoumites, as the personal envoy of the Emperor and a man who had attended a previous siege of Nicaea, his task, which he was plain seemed a thankless one, to offer the Turks an opportunity for honourable submission. Tancred tried to be affable but it was not readily reciprocated; he suspected the Byzantine soldier saw the Westerners as barbarians and that coloured his manner. It seemed, too, he had limited faith in the notion that they could succeed where his hero Alexius had failed, and he had just cause.

The first sight of Nicaea from the high hills, lying as it did on a fertile and open plain bounded on one side by a huge lake, brought enough pause on its own. The massive walls as well as their extent brought forth some appreciation of the task they faced as a whole army, never mind a partial one. Not quite as forbidding as Constantinople, they were a full three *mille passum* in length, twenty cubits in height, surrounding the city on three sides, interspersed with close to a hundred towers, which rendered any assault on the base deadly and that took no account of the deep double ditches that would have to be crossed to even get close.

Debouching onto the plain, the Crusaders made no attempt to approach the walls or to cut off entry and exit by the roads that led out of the landward gates. That would have been futile anyway; the city sat on the western edge of the mighty Askanian Lake, ten leagues in length, that came right up to its walls and was reached by an indented watergate. On a midsummer day the still blue waters seemed endless as they disappeared into the haze made by the late spring sunshine acting on water still cold from winter.

'Now you can see why we failed,' Boutoumites growled, as he

and the other commanders rode closer to the walls to reconnoitre. 'It must be taken by assault for they cannot be starved out nor deprived of water.'

Tancred, ensuring with the pressure of his knees that his horse stayed out of longbow shot, replied with an insouciance he did not feel. 'You have not seen the walls of Bari. They were just as high and they too were supplied by sea.'

'My forbears built the walls of Bari,' Boutoumites snapped, angry, for the loss of that great Byzantine port had sounded the death knell of imperial hopes in Southern Italy.

'And my grandfather,' Tancred replied, in a deliberately cold tone that matched the other man's ire, 'took it from you when everyone, including those he led to the walls, believed it was impossible.'

Boutoumites produced a sneer. 'You would summon up the ghost of the *Guiscard*?'

'Why would we need to,' Tancred replied gaily, 'when we have Bohemund, his son?'

'Do you not mean his bastard?'

'Advice, *Curopalates*: never use that word in the presence of my uncle, for if you do he will smite you so hard you will need two coffins in which to be buried.'

'I require a truce flag and an escort to the main gate.'

In time-honoured fashion the defenders had to be given a chance to surrender, that was the way of things in Asia Minor as well as Europe. Matters differed somewhat, for, instead of merely delivering an ultimatum from his saddle, Boutoumites required that the gates be opened and that he be allowed to enter. Nor did he emerge as the sun went down, which had Vermandois at first, and subsequently

Flanders and Tancred, wondering if he had decided he was safer with the Turks than with them.

He stayed inside for three whole days and that had them thinking he had been killed and they awaited the sight of his head on the walls, but he emerged looking hale and unmarked, dressed in fine silks which could only be gifts from his hosts, to tell his eager companions about his attempts to broker a surrender of the city with the governor Acip Bey.

'Three days to establish what?' was the unified response.

That got a sneer from Boutoumites, who took pleasure in informing them that such negotiations were not carried out in the barbaric fashion common in Europe; offers had to be advanced, but with great subtlety, never anything like a definite statement – Tancred suspected that meant bribes of money and offices to this Acip Bey to betray Kilij Arslan. These inducements had to be given careful consideration and the full meaning and value explored. Could there be more and what was best for those in receipt; was it wiser to accept or reject? All this carried out in the midst of much ceremony and endless flattery.

'And?' the Count of Flanders demanded.

'They said no.'

CHAPTER EIGHT

Encamped on a well-watered and fertile plain, the force that set up camp outside Nicaea was in no danger of either deprivation or, it seemed, physical attack, though it had to be acknowledged that the inhabitants of the city existed in even more comfort, which no doubt excused their reluctance to attempt an exit and drive the Crusaders away. The air of unreality lasted until Bohemund arrived on the just visible shore with ships full of supplies, curious at first, displeased second and then furious when he fully understood the situation. Not only was the partial force outnumbered and completely exposed, but they had no idea when the rest of the main forces, both Crusaders and Byzantines, would join them.

Tancred had felt the lash of Bohemund's tongue many times in his life, but not since he had been a callow and easily tempted squire. As a boy he had been both handsome and wayward, inclined to go off on what he thought of as escapades and his seniors saw as outrageously risky adventures. Very often there was a wench attached to his disappearances and if his uncle was no prude – he enjoyed the company of women as much as the next knight, albeit he preferred them refined – he became heartily sick of the way Tancred seemed incapable of passing up on an opportunity, regardless of how much he put himself at risk by partaking of it.

Many times his squire had been told that one day he would wake up from laying with a woman in what was enemy territory to find his coxcomb sliced off, that was if the knife was not used to slit his throat. They were dalliances; the situation now was worse and the only concession to the younger man was that his uncle took him to a private place to berate him.

'Where are the Turks?'

'In Nicaea.'

Bohemund was good at concealing his anger if he needed to; he did not now. His frown was deep and the look in his eye incensed and for once, though there was not much between them in actual height, Tancred felt small.

'I do not mean them and you know it!'

Aware he was under a cloud Tancred was determined not to show it; he was, in his own mind, just as much of a de Hauteville as his uncle and with that went the family pride. 'If you mean Kilij Arslan he is well to the east.'

'You know that for certain?'

'The Byzantines have assured us it is so.'

'*Was* so, Tancred!'

'We would have been told if he had moved west.'

'By whom?'

'The rest of the host or the Byzantine army.'

'And where are they?'

'On the way to here, I presume.'

'You presume? Close are they? Days away? A week?'

Failing a response it was superfluous to point out that Tancred did not know, and neither did Vermandois or the Count of Flanders when the same question was put to them. Nor was it necessary to point out that had the Sultan of Rüm appeared with even part of his army – the fast-riding mounted archers, for instance – and aided by the garrison of Nicaea, Bohemund would have arrived to find the bones of the entire force littering the ground, a point he made with some force, if less obvious fury, to Tancred's fellow commanders.

For once the problem of the Crusade was not men hankering after authority but the lack of anyone willing to assume it; seeing each other as at least equals – if anything, Tancred stood slightly lower in the firmament – none of the trio, even the haughty Vermandois, had taken the responsibility for the whole.

'Gather up your men and what supplies you can easily move. We will find a position we can defend and one from which we can hastily depart if the enemy shows. Send the fastest messenger you can back north and find out where the rest of the army is.'

The gravity of their error had struck home to Tancred and it was scant excuse to say he had only acquiesced in what was a common point of view. Determined to re-establish himself in his own estimation as well as that of Bohemund, he spoke up loudly.

'A retreat through mountains puts us at risk, especially those on foot.'

That gave Bohemund obvious pause and after a second he nodded. 'I have ships full of supplies offshore. Those of us mounted can get clear and outrun any pursuit. Designate their captains to lead the *militias* to the shore and we will embark them.'

'What about the supplies?' asked Vermandois. 'You will not have space for both.'

'Those we will tip overboard, Count Hugh, for it must be plain, even to you, that if we are driven away from Nicaea we will not need them.'

It took several beats of his French heart to take cognisance of the implied insult in the remark 'even to you'. He swelled up to protest and to demand an apology, only to deflate when the obvious occurred to him: he could not openly challenge a giant like Bohemund of Taranto to anything that might end up as a test of arms.

'Do as I say and do it now!'

'They were preparing to break camp when I arrived, My Lord, with Godfrey de Bouillon and his attendant priests leading the way. When they depart the camp the forces of Raymond of Toulouse will come on from Constantinople to join him.'

'Preparing?' Bohemund sighed; if the returned messenger was telling him what he had feared it was not what he had hoped.

'I was told that they were waiting for the Emperor, and were only going to move when he did so.'

'And has he?'

'There is a Byzantine force based in a separate camp at Pelekanum and Bishop Adémar is assured they are about to march.'

'Has the Emperor departed Constantinople?'

'They have had no news of such a departure.'

Bohemund spun on his heel and called for Manuel Boutoumites to be fetched to his presence. Waiting for the summons to be obeyed he eyed the state of the defences he had set up on the steep slope that had at its back an entry into the higher northern hills, which included a second circuitous pathway to the shoreline. Large boulders had been dislodged and rolled down to the level ground, where they would break up the cohesion of any formations seeking to advance towards the Crusaders, especially mounted.

Between those the ground had been cleared of stones so that the horsed portion of his force could descend rapidly and safely to engage the disorganised enemy, the Apulian Normans held in reserve for a disciplined final charge to cover a retreat; they were, quite simply, much more effective than the men led by Flanders or Vermandois. On the highest peak within plain sight a piquet had been set to keep a watch to the east for any telltale dust cloud, which would herald the approach of the Sultan.

Boutoumites was slow in responding, making the very obvious point that if the Count of Taranto could order the other leaders about he was not to be told what to do. A good-looking fellow, with full lips and a flaring set of nostrils, Manuel Boutoumites found it easy to display arrogance and he was doing so now, not least in the flaunting of the silks with which the governor of Nicaea had rewarded him. Putting aside the temptation to fetch him a buffet round the ears, Bohemund forced himself to smile.

'I require you to counsel me, *Curopalates*.' That changed the man's expression; no one had used his honorific title since he had left the Byzantine court. 'And I am sure you will do so freely and honestly.'

'I cannot think of a reason why I should lie,' Boutoumites replied, his original arch expression quickly reimposed. If size forced him to look up, his countenance implied he was doing the opposite.

'No, I did not mean that. Forgive me for being so clumsy.'

That got a firm nod; Boutoumites, despite any dealings he had had with this giant, was sure he was dealing with an ill-educated barbarian and one he expected to be maladroit with words; had he been able to see into the mind of the man to whom he was being so condescending he would have shuddered. Bohemund was thinking that all he would get was lies, that he could easily get the answer to the question he was about to pose by tying this swine to a stake and sticking a heated sword point up his arse. Tempting as such an act might be, it would not sit well with Alexius or probably his fellow Crusaders, so he continued in his emollient tone.

'I merely wish to enquire as to what level of force the Emperor will send to Nicaea?'

'He will despatch whatever force he thinks is necessary, Count Bohemund.'

'Not his entire army?'

'He will not denude the city, he dare not.'

'But the numbers will be what?' That got a shake of the head that implied ignorance. 'You were not told?'

'I did not enquire.'

In a career of much fighting, there had also been in Bohemund's life a high degree of negotiation; results were not always achieved by force of arms so he was well versed in the arts required. He had dealt with his fellow Normans, who were devious enough but as nought compared to the wily Greeks of Italy and the slippery Lombards who had once ruled over them. Boutoumites was lying; he did know, but he was never going to say.

Being the son of the *Guiscard* had many more advantages than just those physical, his father's sobriquet derived from the old Norman word for a fox; others less well disposed said it meant a weasel.

Bohemund had not only inherited the parental sword arm, he had also inherited much of his sire's natural guile.

'Such a pity he has no intention of coming to Nicaea himself.'

That made Boutoumites stiffen and when he spoke his voice lacked any degree of sincerity. 'Who said this was so?'

'You just did, or rather you omitted to say he would lead here whatever force has been assembled, and be assured I can smoke his game. If my nephew cannot fathom why you spent three days within the walls of Nicaea, I can.'

It was in the dark and well away from Flanders and Vermandois that Bohemund apprised his nephew of his thinking. Below them, at the foot of the slope, large fires burned between those great boulders, illuminating the ground on both sides to deter any kind of sneak attack.

'Are you saying Alexius will not support us?'

'He will, but it will be nothing but a token force.'

Sensing incomprehension, Bohemund reprised points he had made previously about the primary aim of any Byzantine ruler: the preservation of a much-threatened empire came first, second and last.

'Alexius must take account of the notion that we will fail. He must also consider that now we are fully assembled we might turn on him, so he will not expose himself in person.'

'Which is a foolish idea now we are on the wrong side of the Bosphorus. The supplies in those ships of yours will not last for ever.'

'Now you are showing good sense but let us take the first point. Look at what we are: Christian knights far from home, seemingly held together by faith and with no fighting man in command. It is not hard to see the whole host falling apart, and if it did so where would that leave Alexius? Facing an angry Sultan of Rüm, for we could not have got to the gates of Nicaea without Byzantine aid.'

'So Boutoumites spent three days discussing failure, not success?'

'I suspect he spent three days explaining to the Turkish commander that his master was powerless to stand in our way, while hinting that should we be forced back Kilij Arslan would be compensated with gold for any losses he felt he had suffered. Given such a hint the demands of the Turks would have been outrageous. Boutoumites took all that time to get them to agree to something Alexius would be comfortable with.'

'Which leads me to wonder why we carry on.'

That got Tancred a gentle slap and even in the dark he could sense the wry smile. 'We are on God's business, nephew, not that of Byzantium.'

For all Bohemund's anxieties no threat appeared, either from the east or from the city and as soon as the forward elements of the forces led by Godfrey and Robert of Normandy arrived he rode back to meet up with his fellow leaders and a truncated Council of Princes was held in the open air – Raymond was absent ferrying his Provençal army across the Propontis. This took place on a rocky outcrop hard to surreptitiously approach, the only place in which they could discuss matters without being overheard.

The Bishop of Puy introduced Bohemund to the gathering as if that were necessary and while the Count of Taranto was greeted by a nod from each of these magnates there was little overt cordiality in the act. Adémar had met him before, if briefly, in Constantinople and if their conversation had been amiable it had also been non-committal, so he felt the need to establish what had been arrived at previously.

'It was agreed, Count Bohemund, that we would put aside our conceits and act collectively in our decisions and our actions.'

There was a certain amount of tension in the pause that followed what was obviously a question, and Bohemund took some pleasure in letting that last for several seconds; but in truth there was only one way to reply. Appraised by Tancred of what had happened at the first council, his uncle was well prepared, for he too had formed the impression that Adémar intended to exert some form of control, using his papal appointment and apparent independence as a lever. The leader of the Apulians would have a voice and a strong one in any proposal advanced and as to the capabilities of his peers when it came to battle tactics that would only be established in combat.

'My Lord Bishop, I cannot conceive of any other way to proceed.'

The response came with the blessing of a handmade cross. 'You gladden my soul, my son.'

Looking into that smooth, round face, so capable of dissimulation, Bohemund wondered what the cleric was really thinking, apart from feeling the satisfaction at still being in full control of the council. For example, what had he been told by Pope Urban, for Bohemund had met the Pontiff? Barred from Rome by a German-supported antipope, Urban had called a synod for the South Italian bishops in Bari, which made him a guest of the man who held the great port city.

At various meetings Bohemund had gently but forcefully denied a papal request to surrender and hand back some of the lands he had taken from his half-brother and to cease making raids into the territory *Borsa* presently controlled. The other hint was that they should, as a Christian and a family duty, for the de Hautevilles were papal vassals, join forces to help Urban gain his rightful place in Rome.

The threat of excommunication had hovered over the request to surrender both territory and aggression, only for it to be made obvious that it was not a sanction that bothered the man who might labour under it, any more than it had constrained his sire – the *Guiscard* had been excommunicated three times. When it came to attacking Rome to unseat an antipope and his German backers, Bohemund could see no advantage for himself; *Borsa* might do the bidding of a pope, so in thrall to priests was he, Bohemund would not, which if it did not make him an enemy certainly underlined he was no ally. It was passed back to him by others that his refusal was attributed by Urban to arrogance and that was an impression the Pope would have passed on to his legate.

'I am obliged to ask, however, if the Emperor is marching to our aid.'

'I thought he was, Count Bohemund,' snapped Robert of Normandy. 'We delayed our own departure in anticipation, to no avail.'

Tempted to state how stupid that was, Bohemund held his tongue and smiled; he had to allow for the fact that these knights from the far reaches of Europe did not know the Byzantines as did he, so their mistake in reposing trust could be described as understandable.

'But when no evidence came of any movement from his camp at Pelekanum, I . . .' Adémar coughed rather loudly and Robert took the hint of the need to be inclusive. 'We could delay no longer.'

'Then it would give me pleasure to ride with you to Nicaea, Duke Robert, and you can tell me of the homeland from which my forbears came and a place I hope one day to visit.'

If it was an offer genuinely made, it was not taken so and that was plain on his face. The Duke of Normandy obviously held himself above the grandson of a mere petty baron, regardless of how the family had prospered since they left his domains.

* * *

Setting up a siege had about it a formula and part of the threat must be a demonstration of the strength of the besiegers, so the march that brought them into full view of the garrison was delayed until the host as assembled was in proper order and able to debouch onto the plain with pennants flying. Having done that, they proceeded to approach the walls, following the papal banner of the Crusade behind Bishop Adémar and his incense-swinging clerics, several archdeacons and a bevy of priests.

It was not merely religious; they sought to drive home their numerical advantage and would do so again when Raymond and his Provençal forces arrived to further drive home the point. If the hope was to instil fear in the Turkish defenders all they got for their trouble was jeers to assail their ears and many a bared arse from Turks standing on the battlements to assault their eyes.

When the leaders gathered once more to discuss their options, it was very obvious that the city was not going to fall to demonstrations; it would have to be overcome by force and Bohemund, the most experienced at siege warfare, made the point that such a thing would depend on time and numbers. These were not yet sufficient to entirely cut off Nicaea from succour by land and would not be so until Raymond arrived, so another attempt must be made to persuade the Turks their situation was hopeless, in order to avoid what would transpire, for it would come down to attrition.

'In which, my Lords, we might lose as much as those defending.'

'It cannot be done without great loss,' Normandy agreed.

'When we need our strength for what is to come,' added Godfrey de Bouillon, his mind ever fixed on the Holy Places.

That induced much consideration if not quite gloom as each leader contemplated what would be required. In an attritional siege the aim, starvation apart, was to inflict casualties on the defenders until they could no longer man the whole perimeters. The points of access were several high gates on the far side of that double ditch, which surrounded the city on three sides. Reached by narrow causeways that canalised any attack, the doors were so studded with iron bolts they would be near impossible to break down, the wood well seasoned and no doubt secured by great baulks of timber on the inside, while there would also be tubs of water on the parapet above to play upon the gates should the Crusaders manage to set the wood alight, as well as boiling oil to skin alive the attackers.

The towers could not be described as weak spots unless the besiegers could secure one and hold it, not easy when it required a force of knights to climb ladders or ropes under assault from rocks and burning oil, to then engage the defence at the top so successfully that one would fall into their hands. Siege towers seemed to offer the only way to get at the defenders at anything like equal strength, but were only possible if the ditch before the walls could be so filled in as to allow the passage across, something which the defence would not only challenge – they would sally out at night to clear any work done in daylight. Added to that, all the time they would look east to the horizon for sight of Kilij Arslan and his army returning to raise the siege.

'So,' Bohemund insisted, when all of these obstacles had been aired, 'do we agree it makes sense to try to talk?'

These men were not to be pushed into making a decision; each took his time before assenting, and when they had they also agreed that such a mission would be best undertaken by the man who had negotiated with them previously, with the Apulian leader tasked to instruct him in what was required.

'Offer them terms, *Curopalates*. They may march out with their weapons and move east to join their Sultan.'

'The city is home to Kilij Arslan's treasury and his family,' Boutoumites replied. 'They will not leave without those.'

'It is possession of the city your master wants and from what I have seen he has little need of gold.' When the Byzantine nodded, Bohemund added, in a firm voice, 'I have not been open with the others about the purpose of your previous efforts but they might suspect you will not act truthfully.'

'Then why task me with this?'

'You know them, you have met them, you speak enough of their language to sense their mood, we do not. Tell them that if we are many now we will be more soon and that the city will be cut off and assaulted. If it is, and it will be, all will die.'

Sensing doubt in the man's demeanour, Bohemund pressed home the point. 'Nicaea will fall, Boutoumites, for we will not go from here until it has and if you disbelieve that, think on this: we cannot pass on to the Holy Land without this city falls and so it will, if we have to take it apart stone by stone.'

'It may take time, days perhaps, the Turks will not be rushed.'

'Time spent is better than blood spilt, but I and my peers will want to know that progress is being made. Arrange to come to the walls and pass on a message of any developments, and if there is none, leave.'

CHAPTER NINE

U nder a truce flag for the second time, Manuel Boutoumites approached the main gate and was invited to enter, which prompted from Tancred the obvious question.

'Do you trust him?'

'I have no need. He has a clear set of instructions and this time the force outside the walls is large and about to grow.' A messenger arrived to tell that Raymond of Toulouse had broken camp and was now marching south. 'Once the Turks are convinced we will not, and cannot, let them hold Nicaea, and have enough strength to entirely surround the land walls as well as the means to stay here indefinitely, I think they will see the only hope of life is to agree to surrender the city.'

If it sounded simple it did not work out that way; negotiation proceeded at the pace of a sick snail, with petty demands being put forward to Boutoumites by the Turkish commander Acip Bey – these passed on to the princes to be agreed. Kilij Arslan's family, left behind, must be afforded special treatment, they and his treasury should depart ahead of the garrison, who would leave when they knew the Sultan had received his wives, sons and his gold, silver and precious jewellery. The Muslim non-combatants must be given free and unfettered passage too and an escort of Christian knights to protect them.

Adémar baulked at the demand that no mosque should be converted to Christian worship, agreeing only to respect those places that had not previously been cathedrals, churches, abbeys or monasteries. Nicaea had an abundance of such religious establishments – it was, after all, at the very core of the Christian religion, nearly as important as Jerusalem, being the city where, seven hundred years previously, the Emperor Constantine had forced the warring bishops of the faith, not one of whom agreed with the other, to agree a statement of belief to which all could adhere. The Nicene Creed had held since, albeit there was still the ongoing dispute between Greek Orthodoxy and Rome.

Each evening, as the sun sank in the west, Manuel Boutoumites would come to the northern parapet and report on his progress, if it could be called that, given he always postulated some fresh demand from Acip Bey. Yet he was far from discouraged; certain matters were progressing to a conclusion, and he hinted, since he could not say so openly, that the person with whom he spoke each day took more pleasure in the bargaining than they were ever likely to take in the finale.

'I grow tired of this,' Vermandois said, on the fourth day. 'Perhaps a few ladders on the walls and the need to fight might bring them to their senses.'

It was his brother's constable who checked him. 'We have an envoy inside, Count Hugh, who will suffer if we act.'

'What is the life of one man, Walo?'

'Perhaps,' asked Stephen of Blois softly, 'you would care to replace him.'

'How I wish my brother had come. Matters would soon be resolved if he was here.'

The implication of that remark was obvious and galling to those assembled, but no one was about to mention how badly the King of France stood with the papacy, caused by the difficulties of a bigamous marriage. Yet if Philip, a reigning monarch, had been present, it might have been hard to deny him outright leadership.

Technically, Robert of Normandy was a vassal of the French king regardless of how many times the duchy had fought whoever held the throne in Paris; by the same convention Bohemund, being a de Hauteville, still owed allegiance to whoever held the title of Normandy, as had his father and uncles before him. It would have been then, and was now, more of a myth than a reality, but certainly it was one to which lip service was paid, if for no other reason than to anchor the family in the Norman firmament.

'Could it be that this Acip Bey is just playing with us?' asked Bishop Adémar.

'Boutoumites would smoke that,' Bohemund suggested, 'and break off negotiations. If Alexius places so much faith in him he cannot be a fool.'

'And where,' Vermandois demanded, 'is our fabled emperor?'

'At his forge,' scoffed Robert of Normandy, 'fashioning rings.'

That reminder of his treatment was enough to send Vermandois out of the council tent, Walo obliged to follow, yet no sooner had he departed than a monk entered to say that Manual Boutoumites had been seen exiting the main gate of the city. Called upon to listen, the princes could just hear what sounded like jeers. This proved to be the case when, standing outside, they saw the walls of Nicaea packed with the garrison, all waving and shouting and in such a manner as to leave no doubt that it was derisory.

'I cannot comprehend it,' Boutoumites explained, once they had reconvened, the returned Vermandois looking particularly smug. 'Everything was proceeding well and I sensed Acip Bey and I were close to agreeing final terms, then suddenly there were armed men in my chamber, I was led to my already saddled horse and sent through the gate with clods of mud aimed at my back.'

'They were toying with you,' Vermandois snorted, looking to Adémar as if to say that if others had not seen it, he had.

'No, Count Hugh, I would have sensed that immediately.'

'What has changed, then?' Bohemund enquired, the Byzantine responding with a look of bemusement.

'Let us accept,' the Duke of Normandy said, 'that we are no further adrift of our goal than we were when our courageous friend undertook his mission.'

'Hardly courageous, My Lord.'

'Not so,' Robert insisted. 'I have had one occasion to send an envoy into a fortified place which my brother's forces have taken from me. The only thing that came back was a severed head.'

Adémar cut in. 'Perhaps they will see sense when Toulouse arrives.'

'Possible, but we have no choice but to continue with our own preparations.'

The news that a force of Byzantine soldiers was approaching raised the spirits on a day of gloom, until it was realised just how token it was, no more than two thousand men and with no sign, as Bohemund had surmised, of their Emperor leading them. The fact that such an absence upset his fellow princes, as well as the papal legate, underlined to him again just how little they understood their nominal ally, though Bohemund did not think it either tactful or wise to point up such a failure.

An imperial general called Tacitus, according to Boutoumites a highly regarded mixed-race mercenary, who held the imperial rank of *prōstratōr*, led the Byzantines. Half Arab, half Greek he had lost his nose when captured in some previous campaign and replaced it with one of precious metal. His greatest asset, aside from the amusement caused by his golden snout, was that he had been present at two previous sieges of Nicaea and he was thus able to give sound advice that would cut down on the possibility of errors of application by the Westerners, misjudgements he had observed before.

Less welcome was his assertion that he had come to take over the command on behalf of Alexius, which led many of Bohemund's fellow princes to express even more disappointment, which again showed they still had a very shallow grasp of the aims and pressures under which a Byzantine emperor laboured. He persuaded his peers to let Tacitus assume leadership, it being more formal than real; he could not, after all, with the few men at his disposal, do anything to which they did not agree.

More important than his troop numbers or his experience, Tacitus brought in trained carpenters and metal workers who set about the construction of a massive siege tower that would match the defence in height, while others were put to fashioning boulder-firing mangonels with which to bombard the defenders. Soon the ground before Nicaea resounded to the sawing of baulks of wood and the driving home of tight dowels, while metal was heated, shaped and bent to provide rims for the great wooden wheels.

The Christian soldiers, all other activities put aside, gathered stones of the right size for the mangonels and fashioned more by heating and splitting boulders. Others worked to provide the fascines that would act as protection for the various floors of the siege towers, while the supply ships were stripped to provide the cables by which they would be pulled up to the walls. For all their expertise and effort, such massive constructs took time to build, periods in which martial impatience wore upon the nerves of many of the leading knights, it being obvious that those with the least experience suffered from that most, a dangerous brew when they were intent on achieving the kind of glory about which men would talk for generations.

'Let us mount an assault with ladders first,' Tancred demanded, 'to test the quality of their defence.'

'Do not let your eagerness cloud your judgement.'

'It is not just I, Bohemund – you must have noticed how fretful some of our lances have become?'

'I have observed that the youngest ones are keen on activity, but I also see none of the men who have faced such walls many times, as have you, being easily tempted to test them. Remember you are a leader, not a follower, and a man who should know better than to allow those you command to press you.'

As he said that he looked over Tancred's shoulder, to where stood Robert of Salerno. He would be keen for glory and would happily see a blood sacrifice by others to achieve it, albeit he was no coward himself. Tancred, without turning round, guessed who was responsible for the frown on his uncle's face.

'You say that as a man who has much, Uncle. Try to see it from the view of those who have nothing.'

The response was quiet. 'So Robert is pushing to attack.'

'He is keen to win his spurs, but he is not alone.'

Still looking at the Lombard, who was studiously avoiding looking back, Bohemund understood what made Robert act so. He was the grandson of Prince Gisulf, who, if he had been a vainglorious windbag and a disaster both as a ruler and a soldier, had also been the reigning Prince of Salerno until he was deposed by the *Guiscard*. His profligacy left his heirs with little but their name and, since the recovery of the prosperous port city of Salerno was never going to be possible – both it and the title were held by Roger *Borsa* – then the need to make something of oneself became paramount. The trouble was it became so to the point of foolhardiness.

'I do not lack sympathy, Tancred.'

'I doubt that will assuage his pride.'

'I will speak with him.'

Bohemund was about to say he should be fetched over when his attention was taken, as was that of everyone in earshot, by a great commotion and his height allowed him to see what was happening, though not with any clarity. Men were abandoning their various tasks to make a sort of ragged avenue, through which a man was being dragged by some of the Byzantine levies of Tacitus, both victim and charges in black and yellow surcoats. They were heading for their *Prōstratōr*'s tent and the same noise that had alerted Bohemund had alerted him, Tacitus coming out, bareheaded, to stand, hands on hips, his golden nose glinting in the sun, soon followed by Manual Boutoumites.

'Robert must wait, let us see what this is about.'

Close to the Byzantine General's tent, the crowd following the fellow being dragged and pummelled had stopped, which showed that if there was one roped and staggering, there was another being hauled along as a dead weight, his surcoat more red dust than black and yellow. As Bohemund and Tancred strode towards the scene, Tacitus stepped forward and was obviously in receipt of some kind of explanation, that causing him to kick the inert body hard, before he turned to the other man, now on his knees and shaking his head at the question to which he had just been subjected, first as a whisper then as a shout.

'Turkish spies,' Boutoumites explained when the two Normans got close enough, 'caught counting our numbers.'

Tancred was bemused. 'That could be done from the walls by anyone with good eyes.'

Just then another Byzantine soldier elbowed his way to the front of the crowd and pushed on to hand something to Tacitus, which proved, when unrolled, to be a scroll. Following Boutoumites the two Normans edged closer, and when it was held out for them to see, it showed various lines and symbols as well as the outline of the lakeshore. It only took a second to work out the lines were of the defences of the southern edge of the siege lines, a shallow ditch deep enough only to slow a mounted assault, various drystone walls hastily thrown up to break up an attack, not comprehensive given they did not need to be; no threat was expected from that quarter.

'Not only have they ceased to talk,' Boutoumites opined, 'it seems they wish to sally out and attack us.'

Bohemund slowly shook his head. 'If they do they have chosen a stupid place to mount an assault.'

'One they could not get close to without crossing the front of half our host,' Tancred added, referring to the gate from which they would have to sally out, then the open flank. 'They would be slaughtered.'

Obviously reacting to a previously given order, the live prisoner had been lashed to the pole from which flew the black eagle standard of Byzantium. Even caked with dust it was plain the captive was young, clear-skinned and had a cast to his eye that spoke of some status. Added to that he would have to speak Greek to be of any success as a spy, as well as understand and make sense of any the besiegers dispositions, which probably put him among the more senior ranks of the garrison, if not the very highest.

Tacitus was now standing before him with a knife in his hand, the prisoner's eyes fixed on that even as he shook his head to refuse an answer to another question. The knife was used slowly to cut through his garments until his naked torso was exposed, what was visible, his scrunched genitals and black pubic hair, the subject of much ribald comment from the crowd.

Tacitus dropped the knife to the tip of the man's limp cock and used the blade to lift it, then looked directly at the fellow, who had shuddered, with those watching imagining a grim smile on their general's face. Not wishing to set in train anything not in the Byzantine's mind, Bohemund moved very slowly to get closer until he could hear the words being used. Understanding Greek only got him so far; Tacitus was a ruffian, a half-breed, and his accent demonstrated it, but through what he understood and what he guessed the gist had to be that the fellow should tell all or be rendered a eunuch.

'Ask him what time the attack will come,' said Bohemund softly.

Tacitus half turned, the sneer on his face that would have told another interloper to stay out of things disappearing instantly. Bohemund was pleased to observe, and he was sure of this, that it was not fear that made the Byzantine alter his expression but a degree of respect. Like most men who fought for Alexius, the mercenary had heard of Bohemund of Taranto and so knew of his stature as a fighter and a general. Maybe he and Tacitus had at one time shared opposite sides of a battlefield, though it would have been before the fellow lost his nose, that shining feature being too memorable to forget.

After a slow nod, the question was posed, the response an uncomprehending look that to the Norman mind utterly lacked authenticity and Bohemund concentrated on his eyes as he responded, talking directly to the prisoner in Greek.

'We have a way of questioning in Italy which you will not like. We light a fire and let it burn down to red, glowing coals, then we suspend the man who owes us answers on a spit above it and slowly roast him as we would a pig, with people on hand to keep him turning. First the skin becomes crisp, which is hard enough to bear, but then the juices of the body begin to drip onto the coals to make the heat even greater. The first part to roast to uselessness is that which hangs closest to the coals, so you will be unmanned quickly, though not as swiftly as with a knife.'

Delivered with deliberation, in a voice devoid of emotion, gave what was being said greater weight, that obvious by the growing fear in the Turk's eyes.

'Believe me, they will hear your screams in the city, and so loud will they be that they will seek to stop their ears. So at what time will the attack come?'

'Why does he say that?' Boutoumites whispered. 'If we can see them sally out, what difference does it make?'

'My uncle has discounted that because it does not make sense. Which means he is asking another question entirely.'

'Tancred,' Bohemund called over his shoulder in Greek, 'we have pits already alight?'

'We do.'

'You have no time to delay, then, my Turkish friend. Speak now and live, upon my honour, or be carried to a place where you will answer the question, but will it be too late for you to ever be a man again, perhaps too late to ever be anything other than a pariah? What time will the attack come?'

The voice was hoarse, either from fear or a sense of betraying his kind, and the Turk dropped his head to avoid the Norman gaze. 'At the third hour after dawn.'

'And where is your Sultan now?' That brought his head back up, the look in the eyes now one of quizzical surprise. 'To the east, I suspect, hiding in the hills. You merely have to nod if it is true, you do not have to speak.'

That was a jerk, which had Bohemund request the young fellow be cut loose and taken to his tent, an act which sent up a murmur of disappointment from a gathering that had been looking forward to at least a disembowelling.

'Let him bathe and find him some clothing,' he called, as he approached Tancred and Boutoumites. 'Now we know, *Curopalates*, why you were thrown out of the city with so little ceremony. Kilij Arslan has come back from fighting the Danishmends to try and save his city.'

'This he told you?' Boutoumites asked, not having heard the quiet exchange.

That got a smile. 'I think it was I who told him, but it matters not.'

'How did you know?'

'When the first thought makes no sense, then there must be other motives for the acts of man. We must prepare for an attack and soon; the Sultan cannot stay hidden in the eastern hills without we quickly get word of him, added to which he cannot be well supplied, so I suspect it will come either tomorrow or the day after. Tancred, ride to Raymond, who is on the road and cannot be far off. Urge him to move with speed. With the Provençal forces here we can plan to destroy Kilij Arslan rather than just drive him off.'

Tancred had just begun to move when he heard Boutoumites speak, not to object but merely to observe that Bohemund was making a lot of assumptions, which got him a very sharp rejoinder.

'I did not get my reputation by sleight of hand, *Curopalates*. If you doubt that, ask your Emperor. Now I must go and impress upon my peers that we must prepare.'

'Then you must include *Prōstratōr* Tacitus. The Emperor has given him command.'

It was tempting to tell this arrogant courtier just what that truly meant, but again there was a need for a level of tact, which, if it did not come naturally, was delivered with gravity. Bohemund spun round to address the Byzantine General with a request to accompany him to the council pavilion, and when Tacitus got there, and the others had assembled, the old Byzantine soldier made no attempt to take a leading position, which proved he knew his true standing if Boutoumites did not.

'Can we base all we know on the word of one captured fellow sent to scout our dispositions?'

The worry for Bishop Adémar was so great it produced a single crease of skin on his forehead, the question and the expression proving beyond doubt his lack of military expertise. It was explained to him by others, not Bohemund, that it would be madness to wait to find out if what the Turk had revealed was true, since if Kilij Arslan was going to attack, it had to be with a very necessary element of surprise.

The appearance of Tancred at the doorway was a sight to lift the spirits of his uncle, even more so when he informed the council that Raymond of Toulouse was less than half a day's march away and that he intended to bring his men on even if darkness fell before they made the crusading encampment.

'Time,' insisted Godfrey de Bouillon, 'to make our dispositions.'

Courtesy demanded he wait for a nod from each leader before he continued.

'Count Bohemund, since you hold the walls to the north I suggest it would be best if you move your men around to the south of the city so that the Provençal forces can deploy in the ground you vacate.'

'Agreed.'

'We, the rest, can take station to cut off access to the southern gate, for there will not be space for us to all man a common front.'

That too, being sound sense, got a nod as Vermandois raised his voice. 'I demand a place of honour.'

'But Count Hugh,' Adémar said, in his soft clerical tone. 'Wherever you are is a place of honour.'

It was testimony to his inanity that he took what was said at face value. Equally it showed a great level of tact that no one else present sniggered, especially the man sent to guide him.

CHAPTER TEN

It required a line of flaring twin torches to get Raymond of Toulouse and his men into place, a movement accomplished with much cursing, jostling and the odd exchanged blow. Not that he was with them; the Provençal leader was in the council tent discussing how the forthcoming battle might be fought, it being likely that the Turks would use the lake to protect one flank of their advance and seek to drive the Normans who were now in that position away from the city walls, so that they could get through to the gates and release the garrison, who would be waiting to sally out to join them.

Leaning over the map on the centre table, Bohemund made a sweeping gesture with his arm, outlining his view of how to counter that threat and not only beat off Kilij Arslan but inflict on him a crushing defeat, which put the majority of foot soldiers on the expected line of attack, with the majority of the lances out to the south in a position to engage once both forces were locked in combat.

'If you, Raymond and Duke Robert, backed by a good proportion of our *milities*, hold him on foot, then My Lord of Bouillon and I can use your mounted knights to wheel round and take him in flank.'

Vermandois, after Walo had whispered in his ear, made the point that such forces would be the most exposed.

'He may attack the position you take up and if you have your lances in the front line they will be at the mercy of the Turkish archers, which the Emperor told Walo and I we must at all costs avoid.'

Robert of Normandy spoke up next. 'Is it possible he would try to deny us a line of retreat by getting to our rear and cutting us off from the road to Constantinople.'

'Annihilation would follow,' Vermandois responded, clearly terrified at the notion. 'Like the People's Crusade.'

It was a potent and frightening allusion; every section of the host had marched through a landscape strewn with the bones of those slain under Walter Sansavoir, too many to even contemplate burying them. Even more, those visiting a market set up by Alexius at Civetot had walked on a carpet of the same that littered the landscape all along the shoreline. If there had been any doubt as to their fate should they fail, the proof scrunched under their feet; when facing the Turks it came down to victory or death.

'That carries too much risk,' insisted de Bouillon, speaking just before Bohemund had a chance to say the same. 'He cannot split from the garrison or he will be weak in both quarters. He must clear a gate to increase his numbers.'

'And his aim is to drive us from the walls,' Bohemund added, 'in short, to break the siege. The sight of our host retiring, as have the Byzantines before us, would be enough for him to claim victory.'

'Will he know that I have arrived?' asked Raymond.

'With the sun at his back he will see your banners and if he does not know your device he will be aware that our force has seen an increase.'

'He may know before that,' said Robert. 'Which could cause him to alter his plan of attack.'

'Impossible to tell if he has,' Bohemund replied. 'We have seen no sign of any signalling to warn him, but that does not mean there has not been any.'

'If I may,' Tancred cut in, carrying on when his uncle nodded. 'Any signal would have to be prominent enough to carry and be seen three *mille passum* or more away, so it would be seen and act as an alert to the presence of a receiver. It would tell us someone is out to the east and you, My Lords, would not miss such a sign as there is only one person that can be. He has come in secret and that he sees as his most potent weapon, so we should assume that the arrival of the Provençal host is unknown to Kilij Arslan.'

Raymond responded to Tancred with a nod, only for Baldwin of Boulogne to speak up, he doing so once more without seeking permission from his brother.

'It would be foolish to base what we do on a guess. I say we stand together on the defensive and let him batter himself on our shields.'

'That,' Bohemund growled, for once showing a degree of impatience, 'will leave him to fight another day. Which means, even if we drive him back, throughout the siege of the city we will be obliged to keep one eye over our shoulder and men deployed to prevent another assault.'

Baldwin and Bohemund exchanged a look that had within it none of the required delicacy for which this council had been formed, in fact it was openly defiant on the part of Baldwin. That was made worse when his elder brother agreed with the Norman and then sought to sweeten that rebuff with the instruction to command the foot soldiers alongside the Provençals. The Duke of Normandy and his lances would stay to the rear as a reserve, able to join the battle at any point where weakness showed and also to act against the possibility the Robert had outlined, an attempt by the Turks to cut the route of retreat.

Put to the vote, it was tied until Raymond agreed to the task he had been offered, not from amity but necessity. Last to arrive he was being given a pivotal role in the battle to come and that clearly tickled his pride, but he was scarce equipped for mounted warfare – having been marching for days his mounts were bound to require rest, which obligated him to a battle on foot. Finally Tacitus was invited, through his Frankish interpreter, to approve, which he did with a silent and enigmatic nod as if he thought it was all nonsense.

'Then all that remains,' intoned Bishop Adémar, 'is for each of you to be shriven and Mass arranged for the entire host.'

'That must wait,' Baldwin of Boulogne exclaimed, glaring at his brother, then Bohemund. 'First I want that ditch before the line My Lord of Toulouse and I are going to defend made deeper.'

Godfrey de Bouillon addressed Bohemund. 'And our men must take the spoil to fill and make smooth that part across which we are intending to advance.'

Bohemund nodded once he had considered the potential pitfall, namely that such a thing would be obvious. Yet with no high ground to observe the freshly dug earth, the only way Kilij Arslan would know of the changes would be by signal from the city, and he, like Tancred, had serious doubts that such a system existed. Even if it did, to send such a message was bound to be complicated.

Men toiled late into the night under the moon and starlight with spade and pail, digging and moving earth, spreading straw across the top of the filled-in part of the ditch to hide the obvious dampness of freshly dug spoil. Then they saw to their weapons, the grinding wheels spinning continuously to make deadly the heads of swords, axes and knives, as well as the points of the *milities'* pikes.

Sunrise found an army on its knees, facing the rising sun as the priests made their way through the ranks dispensing wine as the blood of Christ and a wafer of bread representing his body. Tacitus had brought his own Orthodox divines and they administered to his troops, even though they had been allotted a post of minimum danger, to the very rear of the crusading army. When suggested that he stay out of danger it was done with some trepidation – no one wanted to wound Byzantine pride yet it was accepted with good grace, bordering on alacrity.

Unknown to the Westerners, the *Prōstratōr* had instructions to keep his force intact, even to the point of abandoning the field if it looked as if these Crusaders would lose a battle. The empire could not bear any losses in men and arms; let these Franks and Normans bleed if that was required, then peace could be made with the victors.

All eyes were looking east to the hills that lined the far end of the Askanian Lake, the peaks plainly visible, before that a plain devoid of even a hint of an enemy, much of it hazily obscured by a wind that allowed the mist from the warming air playing on the cold lake water to drift across the landscape. By the side of each leader sat a glass of sand that had run twice and was now being anxiously watched as the grains slipped through the narrow bottleneck for the third time. To their rear were the sounds of snorting and farting horses, the clinking of metal weapons and a low murmur as the more pious continued to pray.

'Dust,' Bohemund said, which had Tancred peering forward at that hazy landscape.

Sure enough the colour of that mist had changed, the lower reaches dun-coloured, and in a few blinks of an eye the first shapes began to form in the cloud of their own making, eventually merging into a mass of horsemen coming on at a slow trot, the dust thickening to their rear as the men on foot jogged along to keep up. The sound of thousands of hooves took an age to materialise but by the time the sandglasses had run their course, the whole Turkish army was in sight, the sun high enough to show the glinting points of their weaponry.

Bohemund was thinking how much he had been required to restrain himself at the previous night's council. He knew absolutely in his own mind how the battle should be fought and he was now re-examining the points he had declined to add. First, these Turks were facing an army of a kind they had never met, most obviously his Normans; if they had heard of the tactics they might face that was no substitute for the actual experience of shock that was about to come their way.

Then there were the numbers; Kilij Arslan knew just as well as any Byzantine commander the level of force that could be maintained in the field so far from Constantinople, especially in the case of a siege, and he would have assumed his opponents to be of a strength encountered on previous attempts to invest Nicaea. But with a repaired Roman road added to comprehensive supply by sea, the Crusaders were much stronger. Added to that, all parts of the host were accustomed to winning battles – even the dolt Vermandois had enjoyed success alongside his brother the King of France. The Byzantines were more used to losing and that meant the mass of their men, in any battle with the Turks, would have been looking for a route to personal survival as much as they had looked for a way to achieve victory.

Looking to his left he picked up the glint of the Tacitus nose under his cone-shaped Byzantine helmet; if he was not about to be engaged with his men – they were well back – he nevertheless wanted his yellow and black banner to be seen at the centre of the defence, in the position which implied leadership. To the Norman right stood the line of lances under Godfrey of Bouillon, horses pawing the ground, and he reasoned that within a very short time he would know their worth, and that had nothing to do with courage, which he took as a given.

But did they have discipline, which was much more vital in battle, and could Godfrey and his captains control their men once combat was joined? That was the Norman secret – not just the shock of a disciplined charge but close battlefield control, and in years of fighting it had always amazed Bohemund how little his enemies had learnt about a way of making war that went back to the many decades before he was born.

'Time to take your place, Tancred, and remember, do not act on any other command than mine. Arslan will launch his mounted archers and once he has done so they will be committed and vulnerable, which de Bouillon will see.'

'He may be tempted to act prematurely?'

'Yes,' came the reply, with a wave towards Tacitus, who would do nothing in terms of control, and even if he did, no one would obey him, 'and with no man in command, who can stop him?'

'He will surely wait until the Turkish foot are also engaged.'

'Let us hope he does.'

They could hear the drumbeats now, a constant thud that grew until it was a near constant blow to the ears, intermingled with high-pitched cries and yells, no doubt exhortations to request Allah to smite the Christians who dared invade the lands of the Prophet. Most obvious was the fact that Kilij Arslan was doing exactly what had been predicted, attacking the host at a point where he could rive them from the Nicene walls. These were now lined with the defenders yelling to urge on their fellows, archers probably; those mounted would be waiting behind the south gate under their leader Acip Bey.

A horn blew and the mounted archers immediately broke from a trot into a canter, unhooking their bows of bone and horn to slot in an arrow, coming on in their thousands until the man leading them, distinctive in his decorated helmet, raised himself in his saddle and with a huge wave ordered the gallop, though he was soon obliged to order a wheel by the same method. Baldwin's deeper ditch was an obstacle that came as a surprise and impeded their progress, which drew from Bohemund a degree of admiration; if he did not much like the man who had proposed that it be done he had to acknowledge his wisdom and credit him with the ability to see ahead.

The inability to cross the ditch at the gallop took the vigour out of the charge and obliged the archers to loose their arrows at too long a range. That gave time to the Provençal and Lotharingian captains to order their men to their knees, shields up and joined to practically nullify the effect. Some bolts got through and the cries of those they struck could be heard, but most either embedded themselves in shields or ricocheted off harmlessly. For all they were quick to reload their weapons, the Turks had to negotiate the ditch before they could deliver a repeat, which broke up any cohesion.

All the Crusaders, Bohemund included, had been subjected to

lectures by Alexius on how to fight the Turks, too polite to point out that every time he fought them the Emperor had never achieved more than a stalemate and had too often been driven to surrender the field. Here, thanks to Baldwin and his spades, was a simple device that rendered those feared archers only half as effective as they were reputed to be, that made obvious by the fact that once they had got past the ditch, the salvoes of arrows ceased to as coordinated and instead became ragged.

Faced with an impenetrable wall it was impressive that they had the discipline to withdraw to the left on the sound of a horn command and allow the now yelling and charging foot soldiers to take up the assault. The shuffling of the shield wall looked ragged from a distance as adjustments were made but it was solid by the time the two forces came into contact, the noise deafening as their weapons and shields clashed.

Bohemund was aware of the way the lines of Godfrey of Bouillon were also becoming ragged as horsemen either failed to control their excited mounts or were in fact edging them forward to seek to persuade their leader to order the charge, which doubled the pleasure when he looked at his own lances, who showed no sign of becoming disordered.

Tancred was watching his uncle and he could guess for what he was waiting: those archers had not withdrawn and with Arslan's foot soldiers pressing their attack as near as they could to the city that left an area into which their commander could lead them to seek to take the foot defence in flank. They could not be unaware of the mounted lances to their left, but if the Turks could get in amongst the men under Toulouse and Baldwin that would render any disciplined attack impossible; to get to the archers the Crusader lances would have to plough through their own men.

The mounted archers had reformed and were returning to the battle. On they came and now they knew the ditch was there and its depth, so they crossed it before forming up to attack, and it was soon obvious as they rode forward, fired and wheeled away that they were doing more execution than in their previous attempt. Not that the defence faltered; if a man fell another moved quickly into his place. Looking at the mounted Lotharingians it was clear that Godfrey was losing cohesion and he being no fool ordered his men to move forward before that became too hard to control.

Tancred's eyes were on Bohemund, who studiously looked straight ahead as de Bouillon moved into a canter, riding across the Norman front kicking up great clods of earth and clouds of dust. Then with a yell and a drop of his yellow banner, crossed with a red bar, Godfrey ordered his men to charge, lance points dropping as they careered into the Turkish archers, who were busy loosing off arrows to impede their effort.

Yet they were adaptable in their fighting ability, these mounted Turks, for as soon as it became obvious that archery would not serve them they shouldered their bows and unsheathed their hooked swords, to ride forward and slash at the Lotharingian lance points. In no time the two forces were so intermingled that it was impossible to tell one from the other.

'Sound the horn to advance,' Bohemund shouted, signalling Tancred with a wave.

If it was an order to stir it was not an instruction to act alone. As Bohemund moved, his familia knights at his side, he and they set the pace of the horses that followed and with his sword held out at right angles, an act copied by Tancred, it was obvious that he had no intention of joining the embattled Godfrey of Bouillon. Egging his mount into a trot the Norman line rode right across the rear of the battle going on and only when past it did the order come to wheel north.

It was difficult to see what they were about to attack, so dense was the dust, but it soon became clear to those caught in the cloud what was coming their way, a line of dipped lances at a trot and in near perfect order. Another dig of the spurs had Bohemund's horse accelerate, a hard tug on the reins keeping that to a canter and it was only in the few paces before contact that he and his knights dropped back and the men behind him opened to admit them to form a single line.

Even if the enemy had been formed up to defend themselves they would have struggled to contain what hit them. In unison, they felt the effect of sharp metal points backed by the weight of men and beasts, the humans trained to a superior standard, the latter schooled to ignore the cries and waving weapons they faced. The enemy were not in good order, most of their fellow Turks were still fighting with Baldwin and Toulouse, so the Normans had taken them in flank, driving them back towards Lake Askanian so they would have no way to retreat.

Now in amongst the enemy, and with lances already embedded in the primary victims, it was time for swords and axes to be employed and in this Bohemund excelled. With his height and reach he did more execution than anyone, his great sword swinging to lop off heads or to strike an enemy body so hard as to progress right through to the vital organs, great founts of blood emerging from stricken bodies to fill the air with a red-mist spray.

With the pressure on their front diminishing, either Baldwin or Raymond ordered the horns blown to move from defence to attack, at which point Bohemund put up his sword and shouted to the knight who acted as the horn blower, a man who always rode close to his banner. The notes rose into the air, a signal for Tancred to pay heed to his uncle, followed by a blown order to disengage. With a discipline no other mounted force in Christendom could even begin to emulate the Normans fell back in good order to reform, once more able to assemble in an unbroken line.

'Tancred, take your conroys, wheel right and lead your men back into contact with Turkish foot. Be aware that our confrères are attacking and pushing them back.'

Given that was an instruction that needed to be passed on verbally it seemed an eternity before Tancred had detached the hundreds of lances under his command and led them further out onto the plain and mounted a second attack. Bohemund meanwhile had wheeled his conroys back to face west and the point from which they had set out, before them the still struggling mass of Turkish archers and Godfrey de Bouillon's knights.

The fellow who commanded the archers must have seen what was coming at his rear, for as soon as the Normans moved there was a ripple through the Turkish ranks that told Bohemund they were preparing to flee, which made him come to a canter quicker than he had intended. He wanted to catch them before they could break up and get round him and he had the horn blown to order that his lances open out to present a lengthier barrier. That was when he saw the man in command waving as he wheeled expertly on his mount, obvious by his decorated helmet, yelling for his archers to abandon the fight and flee.

There was no need for close discipline now and that he communicated to his men by the way he spurred his own destrier forward. The mount, if nowhere near blown, was not as fresh as at the first assault and anyway had never been bred for speed. Had it not been that the man Bohemund had set his mind on to engage spent too long about his business, they would never have met, but they did and close to. The Norman could see the pockmarked skin on a dark face, covered in dust, and the cold black eyes as he swung his sword.

The Turk's weapon came up to parry and as the blades connected he used the weight of Bohemund's blow to help him to wheel his lightweight mount in a way that no destrier could match. As he did so his blade swung low, seeking to cut into Bohemund's side, an act only stopped by the swift drop of the Norman pommel. The Turk felt that and the pressure on his blade took him down, he a fighter good enough to guess what was coming. He kept going forward so that the Norman weapon swished within a hair's breadth of his ducking head.

Again with outstanding horsemanship he spun his mount within less than its own length and if Bohemund had not spurred forward he would have been pierced instead of the flank of his horse, which, even well trained as it was, bucked as it felt the sword slice its flesh. The Turk had drawn back his sword to sweep it into the back of his giant adversary, but if he was a good horseman so was his opponent. With nothing but the pressure of his knees Bohemund forced his destrier round at the same time as the huge blade sliced down and across, taking the Turk at the joint of neck and shoulder and completely removing his head with such force that it flew several cubits away.

All around the mounted Turks were either fighting to get clear or in flight. Many of their foot-bound companions were being pushed back towards the lake by Tancred, while still having to seek to contain the advancing levies of Baldwin and Toulouse, this while the freed lances of Godfrey of Bouillon were streaming in to join the fight, and that combination broke all resistance, with many throwing away their weapons and pleading for succour.

What followed was great slaughter; soldiers who had walked on the bones of the People's Crusade were in no mood for mercy. Those who were not fleet of foot enough to get clear or who could not jump in the lake and swim were cut to pieces, while many drowned rather than face the blade. As for leadership, a glance to the east showed that Kilij Arslan and his personal body of defenders were fleeing under his streaming banner, with, it appeared, a very large portion of his army on his heels.

Bohemund rode back and leaning down used his sword point to lift the head he had severed, still with its decorated helmet strapped on, holding it up so all could see, at which point Tacitus rode forward, having taken no part in the battle judging by the lack of a mark on his armour. Looking up at the head, dripping blood down an already stained blade, the *Prōstratōr* smiled.

'That is the head of Elchanes, Count Bohemund, Arslan's best general and the man who led the massacre at Civetot.'

Looking up at the pockmarked skin, with the lips pulled back in a rictus of death, Bohemund replied, 'Then it will be fitting meat for the dogs.'

CHAPTER ELEVEN

Expecting in the aftermath of the victory to meet an ebullient Bohemund, Tancred was surprised by his gloomy demeanour. 'Baldwin and Toulouse behaved well, but de Bouillon's lances will not serve as they are if we meet a better enemy. He could not hold them back.'

'They did great slaughter.'

'And would have done more if they had stayed their attack. Our aim should have been not just to defeat Arslan but also to destroy him and perhaps even take him prisoner. That was possible if we Normans had been allowed to pin their horsemen and Godfrey had done what I had in mind he should, get behind the enemy and cut off any chance of retreat.'

'I do not recall you telling him that.'

'No, and you know why – I must be careful of the pride of others.'

'Just as they must have a care with you.'

'If they take their behaviour from you, then they will fail.' Seeing that his intended jest had been taken badly, Bohemund added something to mollify his nephew. 'In truth, Tancred, they could call me a goat if they fought as I would have them do.'

'Demand the command.'

'It would be futile, and even a mere hint would sow division where we need harmony.' Looking at the walls of Nicaea Bohemund produced a sigh. 'With Kilij Arslan in our hands, even dead, we might have no need to continue the siege. As it is . . .'

Both men fell into silence, watching the cadavers of the dead being stripped and mutilated, while those bodies floating on the lake were being used as target practice, men employing captured bows and the surfeit of spent arrows. It was testimony to the ability of the Turks who had owned them that so many were having trouble even drawing them properly, never mind loosing an arrow that found a target.

'Come, Tancred, there will be a feast and much rejoicing. Stay by me and if, in my cups, I look like telling the other princes of the opportunity we missed, I give you leave to buffet me round the ears.'

Tancred grinned. 'Lay a hand on you when you're drunk? Just what kind of fool do you think I am?'

The skins of wine were opened for all from high to low and soon severed Turkish heads were being displayed on lances, shown to the walls by the drunken revellers, some of the Lotharingians even taking to wearing them as trophies on their belts. Later, the newly constructed mangonels were employed to send a steady stream of bloody skulls over the battlements; bodies were tried but they generally splattered on the walls rather than carrying the parapet. All this was designed to depress the defenders who had, the next day, an even less cheering sight to trouble them, the rising shape of the great siege tower upon which work had recommenced.

Having restrained Tancred before, his uncle knew it was now time to assess the resolve of the garrison, to see what kind of resistance they could mount, that being the only true way to test their morale after the flight of their Sultan. Each contingent agreed to take turns with ladders and grappling hooks to launch an assault and try and get onto the parapet. This would require that they prepare in the dark, with good cloud cover to mask the moon, and get close before first light; at any other time of day the defenders would see them coming, allowing them to reinforce the point of attack.

Bishop Adémar was adamant that none of the commanders should risk themselves in such an enterprise, not, he stressed, through any lack of personal ability or courage – the nature of the task they were set upon precluded taking such a risk and the cleric was relieved when the sense of such a proposal was accepted. Vermandois apart, the princes were men with a firm grasp of what they faced in the future once Nicaea had fallen: twelve hundred *mille passum* of harsh territory, to be crossed in summer heat, over mountains and rivers, with enemies to fight on the way and very likely more great cities to besiege. If they were curious regarding the spirits of the defenders they faced, they were even more concerned about the morale of their own men, which would not be aided by them seeing their talismanic leaders slain.

The Normans drew first attempt, which meant Robert of Salerno got to execute the wish he had expressed before the battle; Tancred, much to his chagrin, was forbidden by his uncle to take part. Robert showed good judgement in choosing for his party twenty men who were not of great bulk, but slim and likely to be quick on their feet; speed might serve the assault more readily than muscle.

Once more a priest blessed the men, this time by torchlight, well out of view of the walls, and once confessed they lifted their equipment, four long ladders, and moved to get into position, not easy in the dark. Their leaders followed to observe and control the reserve, dozens of knights bearing, as well as swords and axes, a clutch of sharp, lightweight javelins. These men would follow in the wake of the lead party if they looked like achieving success. Behind them came *milities* carrying bolts of canvas. If Robert suffered a reverse the javelins would be used to seek to keep the defenders at bay until their confrères got clear, while the canvas would be spread and held taut to try and catch any falling fighter.

With the double ditch around the walls they needed to traverse one without being seen and use the land between to anchor the foot of their ladders. Robert had decided to use planks as well, the siege lines were littered with them, his intention to lay the ladders flat across the first ditch and use the planks to make a bridge by which to cross. Tiny strips of white cloth had been tied on the edges, visible to avoid them falling off.

Rough-hewn, made up of freshly cut wood full of sap, lashed with bark strapping and needing to be long enough to not only reach but also breast the battlements, the ladders were heavy. Robert's plan was to have them up and in position to drop on the walls as soon as the sun tinged the rim of the eastern hills, his fighters beginning to climb before it crested them. With men anchoring the foot, to get them up took real effort, to hold them steady so they did not fall against the stonework even harder, and it all had to be carried out without a sound.

Well back and looking at the same eastern skyline, both Bohemund and Tancred suffered from the anxiety common in such endeavours.

They were with their men in spirit, having undertaken many times what they were set to do, the last occasion at the siege of Amalfi. In the time of waiting their quiet conversation went back to that siege, to Roger *Borsa* and what a poor specimen of a ruler he was, Bohemund of the opinion that the duchy might well fall apart under his hand.

'He has a son now, remember.'

'Two years of age.'

'Still an heir.'

'Then the boy must be better than his sire,' Bohemund hissed, 'for I doubt he has the seed to produce more.'

Tancred could not avoid the thought: what will you do if he is not strong or your half-brother dies when he is an infant? It was almost as if Bohemund could read his mind.

'No doubt my Uncle Roger will take up cudgels for the son in the same way he has for the father.'

'Even if he is weak?'

'Roger too has sons now and I daresay he is as ambitious for them as you and I would be for our own.'

'For that we would both need a wife.'

'When I have what I feel I need is the time to consider a wife.'

That touched on a subject rarely raised; Tancred was young and if he was unmarried that was hardly surprising, but Bohemund would soon pass into his fourth decade. Many Norman and Lombard lords of Southern Italy had made suggestions to him regarding their daughters, all had been politely rebuffed and only intimates like Tancred were permitted to know why. When Bohemund came to wed, he was determined that the standing of his bride should reflect his own, and to his mind that was yet to reach its peak.

'I see a tinge of light,' Tancred hissed.

'Lord, I would rather be where our Lombard Robert is now than just being a spectator.'

Ahead of them and invisible, Robert's party were standing at the base of the raised ladders, hoping the tops, which had been tarred with pitch to blacken them, did not catch a sentry's eye. To keep them absolutely still was impossible; they were waving about, not much, but it was movement and thus dangerous. On a warm night and clad in chain mail they were sweating, no doubt like their leader thinking that an eternity had passed since they got to this point. That was when they heard his voice, for from behind him a slim line of grey had appeared in the eastern sky.

'Drop them slowly, try not to strike hard on the walls.'

One voice spoke in Norman French, but quietly and it was not identifiable. 'You need the Holy Ghost for that, Lombard, not us.'

There was no doubting when they did come to rest, aching arms were eased of the burden and no commands were required to get the first fighter to begin to ascend. Swords unsheathed and axes to hand they began to climb, Robert of Salerno in the lead, he like his men waiting for that shout which would mean their attempt had been exposed. Halfway up, Robert was beginning to believe they might get onto the parapet undiscovered, but that was dashed by the sound of a horn, which had men who had been climbing slowly and silently look instead for as much speed as they could muster.

In a part of the world where the sun rises fast, the outline of Robert, upright on the battlements, yelling and encouraging his followers, raised the spirits of all those watching. He had achieved enough of an advantage to not be immediately engaged and that held until half of his fighters could join him, which allowed them to fan out, though the first clash of metal on metal soon followed, this accompanied by the cries common in all combat: indistinct imprecations mixed with the odd shriek as a weapon struck home – frustrating for those watching, because while they could see their own, the defenders were hidden behind the crenellated walls.

'They are fighting hard,' said Tancred after a short while, time in which it was light enough to see clearly.

Bohemund knew he did not mean those attacking with Robert but the Turks of Nicaea; resistance seemed to be hardening, which could mean the original defenders were being reinforced.

'Move the javelins forward and get them ready, but caution them against being too eager or they will smite their own.'

All along the battlements the mail-clad Apulians were swinging weapons to both seek to maim their opponents and to parry the pikes thrust at them, but they seemed unable to achieve the prime objective, which was to get down off that higher elevation, onto the rear parapet and seek to secure a proper and defensible foothold. That would allow those waiting below to join them; get enough fighters up there and they could push back the Turks from their own walls and they could then seek to take one of the towers. That was not happening, and much as he was anxious, Bohemund declined to shout any instructions; another was in command up above and any decision was his.

It was not long in coming and Robert's signal was plain to everyone below, his shout to his fellow fighters, which implied they were outnumbered and in danger of defeat or death if they stayed. They were still in peril of such a fate in withdrawal, which was the hardest part of this type of action to execute. The line of battling knights began to collapse in upon itself, those at the rim now swinging weapons to hold back their assailants rather than wound them, while their confrères made for the ladders.

For those first to depart, the descent was achieved by first abandoning whatever weapon they were carrying – that was thrown into the ditch for later retrieval – then sliding down, feet clamped to the outer uprights, most of the weight of their bodies dependant on fast-changing hand holds, while below them and to the side the *milities* had spread their canvas, leaning back to stretch it in case they lost their grip.

The numbers were down to the last half-dozen, which compacted the area of fighting, so Bohemund ordered those carrying javelins to begin to loose them at the outer edge in the hope of creating a firewall by intimidation, for such weapons would not wound deeply, praying that what was a common problem would occur now: as defenders, assumed to be more numerous, pressed to get at the last of the attackers they achieved a diminishing return by being compacted into a crowded space, each getting in the others' way as they tried to achieve a kill.

Someone managed to get through the battlement defence; the fighter next to Robert of Salerno suddenly bent over and began to fall, his sword flying out of his hand, the weapon that had pierced him only becoming visible when his body spun full circle, the long pike detaching itself from his flesh by its own weight.

Shuffling, craning *milities* moved quickly to catch him and as soon as he thudded into their canvas they rolled the body out onto the ground, resuming their vigil, leaving him to be lifted and borne away by the men with whom he had fought. As he passed Bohemund, the Count looked down in what was now full daylight to see the wound, a great gash pumping blood, and that brought to his lips a prayer; the fellow looked set for the ministrations of the priest not the mendicant monk.

The point at which Robert of Salerno threw his axe at the defenders marked the end – he was the last to take flight – an act that got him just enough time to get a foot on the ladder. Now it was the Turks who were clambering onto the battlements, one of whom took a great swipe at Robert's head that only missed by a whisker. Unfortunately for the Turk, the effort, when he was off balance, worked against him and with a scream of panic he began to tumble, his scrabbling attempt to arrest his fall useless.

Tancred yelled to the *milities* to catch him – he could be a valuable prisoner – but either they failed to hear or ignored him and the falling body careered into the ground with an audible thud to lie there twitching. One of the just descended knights kicked him several times until he rolled into the ditch.

Robert, in company with the last quartet of his fighters, was several rungs down when Turkish pikes were employed to try and push the ladder tops away from the wall. This time their weight, added to that of the men still near the top, made such a thing difficult, too much for one man. It was a task requiring many hands and that was not achieved until the sliding knights were well past the fulcrum, but they could feel the way the ladders were going vertical and the point would soon be reached where they would pass that and fall.

What saved them was the length of the pikes, not long enough to get the ladders past the point of balance. Robert and his men got to the bottom and began to run as a hail of stones came down to try and crown them, the last act of the *milities* being to push the ladders so they fell backwards, saved for the next time they would be needed. Then they too bolted, dragging their canvas behind them, only one suffering from a rock that hit his head. Collapsed he was hauled out of danger.

* * *

'They fought like wolves,' Robert explained, making his report to the Council of Princes, the same he had made to Bohemund and Tancred. 'If they are to be judged by the fire in their bellies and the look in their eye then their spirit is high.'

'One attack,' was the response of Raymond of Toulouse, 'cannot be counted as a failure. We must keep up the pressure and see it we get a like result.'

'It is for you to choose,' Bohemund replied, slightly put out by the word failure; to his mind the Apulians had been as successful as was possible. 'It is your turn next, Count Raymond, and perhaps your knights can show we poor Apulians where we went wrong.'

Raymond knew he was being addressed ironically and that showed in his reddening face, which was enough of a high colour to begin with. Here was what Adémar feared: that men of such known ability would not stand to be diminished publicly, regardless of the high standing of their peers. He was about to intervene when Godfrey de Bouillon spoke, making his point for him.

'It can only be assessed when we have all tried. It may be, Count Bohemund, that your men met the very stiffest resistance, the best men in the garrison.'

'Perhaps,' Bohemund responded, forcing a smile.

He was well aware of Godfrey's deliberate attempt to ease matters; when it came to pride, that sin so quickly identified by Bishop Adémar, the Duke of Lower Lorraine seemed to suffer from it the least. It was rapidly being acknowledged that he was a good man, the very antithesis of his brother Baldwin, and one whom everyone present was coming to respect for both his sagacity and his genuine godliness and crusading zeal.

'Possible,' Raymond acknowledged, likewise obliged to react with grace by Godfrey's intervention.

Raymond made his attempt two nights later and for his men the cost was higher. On the south side of Nicaea, which he now occupied, the Turks had ballistae, huge catapult-like machines firing rocks from adjoining towers that created a killing ground between them that extended far beyond the ditches. His men got onto the walls, as had the Apulians, in the same manner and they suffered a few casualties there, but it was in seeking to withdraw that their losses were greatest as the catapults, able to swivel, bombarded those who had survived, one knight having his head removed completely by a boulder.

The other contingents had to make an attempt in their own section: Lotharingians, Normans and the French, and if they all managed to get up to the battlements, none could hold there, so stalwart was the defence. Matters were made more deadly with the Turks now alert to what might be coming, nullifying any advantage of surprise. If the results were the same, if the death rate compared to the Provençals was diminished, the conclusion was that advanced by Robert of Salerno: the Turks were in good heart, determined to defend their city and had to sustain them the previous failures of Byzantium.

There was another more telling reason for their confidence: the besiegers could not seal the side of the city which bordered on the lake, which supplied them with ample water, taking away thirst as a weapon, one of the staples of this form of warfare. Worse, even in daylight if they wished, the Turks could bring in more defenders as well as food and the Christian host had no means of stopping them, for they had no boats. This did not induce any sense of impossibility; well-supplied fortresses had fallen before and if it took numbers and courage, then that was outside the walls of Nicaea in abundance.

There was other activity over the following weeks, the mangonels firing stones that crested the battlements to drop on and catch the unwary sheltering behind them, the less cheering fact being they were too small to fire anything that would do damage to the walls and the means to construct bigger weapons was lacking. Two German knights were busy making what they called a 'testudo', consisting of baulks of timber bound together by lashed and tarred ropes in an attempt to emulate the Roman legionary tactic of advancing under linked shields like a tortoise.

That they did this without asking permission from the Council of Princes mattered not; that was a body quite willing to allow individual initiative, and when it was finished and ready to be employed the leaders all gathered to see how it performed as it inched towards one of the gates, there being a causeway across the double ditch. It was just as well the men who had set the idea in motion decided to let others test their plan, for the contraption turned out to be weighty for those who were under it and the bindings were too feeble to stay unbroken once the Turks began to rain down heavy stones.

It only took one rope to part and that put excess strain on the rest, not helped by flaring torches thrown onto the flat top surface where they set alight any strands of the tarred ropes. For a moment it looked as if the men bearing it would not only get to the gate but also be able to stay there and seek to set it on fire. But it was not to be; when another main rope parted it was only a matter of minutes before the whole thing began to come apart, individual baulks of timber falling to the ground to expose the men underneath.

What came down next was a potent mixture of burning oil mixed with grease and pitch that stuck to each and every body so that the fighters caught by it were turned into screaming, staggering torches that provided easy targets for the salvoes of arrows that followed. Few came back from that disaster and worse was to follow: those by the gate who had died or were wounded too badly to move were hooked by grappling irons and hauled up to the top of the towers, there to be stripped and mutilated before their cadavers were hung from the battlements, gut and entrails exposed, to tell the attackers what fate to expect if they too fell into Turkish hands.

Raymond of Toulouse spotted the flaw in the design the two German knights had used and he set his men to building a protective bombardment screen in the shape of a pitched roof, sloped at both sides so that anything striking would bounce off and away. Raised up it could be moved, static it could be dropped to the ground and provide total cover to those underneath. Following on from that which had preceded it there was no rush of volunteers and Raymond had to offer a money reward to see the execution of his experiment.

Again the leaders gathered and watched as the Provençal 'volunteers' inched forward. There was a small body of knights under the screen but the main party carried shovels, not swords, and had also a cart loaded with baulks of dry and turpentine-soaked timber, as well as planks to cross the ditches. It was obvious they were having more success because they got to the walls and remained there, seemingly impervious to all that was cast down upon them: the same combination of rocks, which bounced off, and flaming combustibles, which slid harmlessly to the ground while failing to set alight freshly cut timber lathes that made up the roof.

This allowed the diggers, and it took much time to achieve this, to attack the base of the stonework, their aim to create a deep hole and expose the underside of the foundations, into which they jammed their well-soaked baulks as supports. The rest of the dry timber was stuffed in and just before the bombardment screen withdrew it was set alight. Now the defenders had a dilemma: try as they might, no amount of water seemed to be able to reach and extinguish the blaze, which left the only option a sally out from the nearest gate to seek to put it out by hand, an eventuality covered by Raymond, who had mounted knights waiting to deal with such an attempt.

Every Christian eye was on that conflagration and so were those of the Byzantines, for here was a key that might unlock Nicaea. Smoke billowed up from the base of the wall, but inside that could be seen, very clearly, a red and orange inferno. Then a crack appeared above and it began to spread and fracture. With a mighty roar a section of the wall collapsed, stones tumbling as the mortar that held them gave way, the roaring sound of that overborne by the cheers of the besiegers. Half the stonework filled the ditch, the rest forming a pile that would have to be climbed to get at the defence.

Immediately preparations were put in place to launch an attack on that breech at dawn the next day but that only brought disappointment. Sunrise revealed that if the ditch was still full of stones, somehow, in darkness and without alerting their enemies, the Turks had managed to effect enough of a repair to close that breech to an assault that would have any chance of success.

CHAPTER TWELVE

Raymond's sloping bombardment screen was used more than once and each time it made the walls it seemed to achieve a result, if not one as successful as the first. Every time Acip Bey's Turks made good what the base fires had destroyed, and if there was frustration for that there was also a sneaking admiration for the man in command as well as those he led, who were showing a fortitude that was worthy of respect.

Baldwin of Boulogne tried a moonlight attack after another section of the wall had been damaged and that, always a risky venture, was repulsed. Climbing the steep fallen screed even in daylight gave advantage to the defence and the Turks, in lighter clothing that allowed easier movement, especially in poor light, fought off the mail-clad Lotharingians by flaying the slope with arrows fired blind, before closing in with daggers used to cut leg tendons rather than kill.

If casualties were slight there still emerged a steady stream of men heading back to Civetot to either convalesce or, if they were too badly wounded to recover, to seek passage home to whichever part of Europe from whence they had come. Also there were a mounting number of graves, each with a cross above it and a burnt-in inscription giving the name of the martyred victim and the legend that for his service to Christ his soul had ascended to heaven, where he now sat at the right hand of God.

Less to be regarded were those whose faith was too weak to keep going; they too left, to go home, no doubt to ridicule for their failure to maintain their vow. That did not mean a diminution of numbers; if some weakened in the face of the task there were more pilgrims, both knights and commoners, who were arriving in dribs and drabs to join the Crusade, the most welcome a company of Genoese crossbowmen who, with their deadly weapons, could outrange the arrows from any ordinary bow. Looking out from the walls of Nicaea, if they were counting, their enemies were getting stronger, not weaker. In addition, and less welcome, were the hordes of pilgrims, men, women and children, including Peter the Hermit, who had come to join the host on the route to the Holy Land, few of them the type to fight, so that here existed a large camp of useless mouths and it was growing by the day.

The time had come to employ the now completed siege tower – another was already under construction – and the bombardment screen was put to another use, this time to fill in the ditches with stones and earth so that it could be rolled close enough to the walls. Knowing what this portended part of the garrison, for the first time, sallied out to seek to destroy the screen, only to find themselves in fierce combat with the Provençals, set in place to contest such an eventuality. In this the advantage lay with the better-armed knights, and despite all attempts to hold open a corridor back to the gate from which they had essayed, the defenders were caught in the open and annihilated, none willing to surrender given they knew their fate was death, which they could face with equanimity; they too believed that to die for their cause was to be given entry to paradise.

Any siege tower had to be tall enough to overreach the battlements against which it was employed. It was faced at the top with a hinged platform, sharp-spiked at the base, that would be dropped to allow the first party of knights to cross and engage, hopefully killing some of the defenders who had taken up too forward a position, while above their heads was another level containing the newly arrived crossbowmen who would be tasked to force enough of a gap to get the knights over the top of the walls and onto the parapet that ran along the inner side.

In the tower, a series of internal ladders ran from the ground, up through the various floors, to the fighting platform, and once it had been rolled into place the reinforcements would rush to ascend and back up the leading knights. There was no lack of guesswork as to how the defenders would react; fire was a potent weapon, if one that would take time to get a hold on main timbers that were freshly cut and thick.

The problem was the tinder-like brushwork panels protecting the floors from arrows, both flamed and unlit, so there would follow in the wake of the mailed men *milities* bearing tubs of water with which to douse any blaze, this thrown onto the tight-bound reeds to prevent them flaring up, because that alone could ignite the main beams. Others, and this was a dangerous task, would have to move out to each side, where they would be exposed, to put in place the long outriggers that would anchor the tower and stop the Turks from toppling the finely balanced structure with ropes and grappling irons.

Raymond, given the tower had been constructed with his lines, claimed the right to man it with his men, for to partake in a fight from such a construct was seen as one of the highest points of honour for a knight, second only to single combat with a mounted foe. But carefully worded questioning established that the Count of Toulouse had never led an assault using such a weapon, whereas both the Apulian leaders had. For once, Bohemund, who usually kept a tight control of his counsel at the meetings of the princes, spoke with boldness and insisted it should be put, like the dawn assaults, to a ballot.

It was unfortunate, given the person who proposed it, that the Apulians once more drew the marked spill of paper. There was a moment when the florid-faced Provençal Count seemed set to vocally object against a policy mutually agreed – his high colour deepened remarkably – but a look from Adémar, who had been, after all, in his company all the way from his homeland and had his respect, stilled his protest.

'It would please me, Count Raymond,' Bohemund said, seeking to sweeten his disappointment, 'if my Normans occupied only the fighting platform. We would be more than content that any second wave should come from Toulouse.'

Godfrey de Bouillon cut in. 'As well as some from my Duchy of Lorraine.'

'France must have the honour also,' cried Vermandois.

That had all eyes on the Duke of Normandy; surely he too would protest that his knights must take part and they waited for his outburst, only to receive a dispassionate response, which had about it a reference to the fact that he held himself as titular suzerain to the Apulian Norman knights.

'Someone must plan for success. I suggest that with our cousins to the fore, that will serve well to represent my duchy. For my own knights, they will be mounted and ready to seize any opportunity that is presented.'

Was that the indolence for which Robert of Normandy had already been noted, or was it good sense? The object of the assault, made close to one of the gates, was to seize the nearest stone tower, each of which contained a stairwell, then fight a way down to the ground and drive off the defenders from the rear of the gate. If that could then be opened, a force of mounted knights charging through that could do great execution in the narrow streets of Nicaea, even more when backed by the crusading *milities* who would follow them on foot.

Not that it would be easy, as Bohemund was keen to point out; several siege towers might achieve such a result because they split a defence who had no idea where the main blow would fall, but experience indicated that with only one, and the Turks packed at the point of attack, all a single engine could hope to do was to deplete the numbers – a decisive victory could only come from a stroke of luck or a collapse of the defenders' morale. The best outcome to hope for was partial success, which might point a way to a solution to the taking of the city, for in truth no other avenue showed any promise.

With honour at stake, the others fell to bargaining for their place, which required much intervention from Bishop Adémar to prevent any of the point-making from descending into an open quarrel. Observing this, Bohemund was made even more conscious of what he had already surmised and imparted to Tancred: there could not yet be a single commander. Perhaps in the future a set of circumstances would change that, but that could only be, he thought, when failure of the entire Crusade was a risk.

Right of this moment there was a chance for glory, of the kind that every knight craved, an emotion to which neither of the men with de Hauteville blood in their veins were immune and, as the uncle pointed out, such a laurel could only enhance any later claims for leadership; if it was a distant prospect, it was one to keep in mind.

'Which,' Bohemund imparted to Tancred when they were alone, 'makes it worthwhile we try ourselves.'

'You and I both?'

'I cannot deny you what I will not refuse myself and, in truth, I have become heartily sick of watching others fight and not doing anything myself.'

'Our papal legate will not be pleased if he learns that we intend to carry out the assault in person.'

'Then, nephew, he must not find out.'

The Norman practice of training extended to the use of siege towers and if what they contrived was gimcrack it served to allow for mock preparation – a roughly hewn platform with a flat screen of canvas and wood that when dropped allowed the Apulian leader to set the pace of advance, for that could not just be a Gadarene rush, but had to be made in an unbroken line, while those following the first wave must be prepared for any number of eventualities. It also allowed Bohemund to think about innovation, a small addition to the normal tactics that might discomfit the defence, this carried on over several days until the morning dawned when the attack would take place.

First the siege tower had to be hauled by ropes to a point just out of arrow range, held to be two furrow-lengths, but that was not the only weapon they faced. The point of attack being obvious, the Turks had brought to bear their rock-firing ballistae and they had a surprise in store for the Crusaders, for these were used not to spew forth boulders but tightly bound balls of flaming straw wrapped around shavings, soaked with the same pitch and grease previously dropped on the attackers' heads, these fired at the near unmissable tower in the hope of setting it alight.

Too eager to see the effect, they began to employ them when the men dragging the ropes were in range, causing mayhem as the cables were abandoned and the lightly clad *milities* fled in all directions. That imposed only a temporary halt; over the last area of ground the tower had to be pushed anyway, Raymond's bombardment screen having been once more pressed into service to protect those both labouring and following, the bowmen and the mail-clad knights who would wait until the last possible moment to ascend so their weight would not make the task of moving it harder.

Bohemund and Tancred were under that, hidden from view, ostensibly along to provide encouragement, only wearing mail because it was wise to do so, their weapons carried by others. Hard as the Crusaders had toiled to make a smooth surface, the tower, because of its height related to its girth, was inherently unstable and top-heavy. It swayed alarmingly on what was far from even ground and that was more troubling when they came to crossing the filled-in ditches.

Finally, once it reached the point that would be covered by dropping the hinged platform a halt was called and the fighting men began to ascend, the Genoese crossbowmen leading the way to their upper platform, this fronted with a solid screen carved with slits through which they could fire in relative safety. They were the first of Bohemund's planned surprises, the second being his own presence and the Turks were not the only ones to experience that, given that a man of his height, once he emerged onto the fighting platform, towering over all around him, was startlingly obvious even amongst a race tall by nature.

The other leaders watching were split between a degree of envy and a less charitable emotion, Raymond of Toulouse being downright angry, Vermandois affronted and from de Bouillon a sense of admiration mixed with natural ire, while the Duke of Normandy pointed out that the family from which Bohemund sprung had ever been both rebellious and devious, which had obliged them to flee his father's wrath. Bishop Adémar was furious, yet obliged to hold in check any criticism lest it get to the ears of the Count of Taranto after the action was concluded.

On the fighting platform, two lines of a dozen knights each, Bohemund's doughtiest fighters were waiting, each with a javelin in their hand, while on the floor beside them were half a dozen more. It was a guess on behalf of their leader but he reasoned, from what he had seen of the garrison of Nicaea as well as their leader Acip Bey, they would not wait to be attacked, but would come onto the platform and seek to dominate the killing sector. The task of the crossbowmen above their heads was to create an area in which the Normans could fight on decent terms, initially outnumbered, obviously, but not so much as to render any advance impossible. Bohemund wanted to lower the odds even more.

The release of the platform was a case of simply slipping two knots, added to several kicks so that it moved at speed on its woven-rope hinges, crashing down on the battlements where it would crush anyone foolish enough to be standing upright. But instead of an immediate advance the Normans held their place, this as a group of Turks, presumably the best fighters, leapt onto the platform to stop their enemies prior to their being able to move. The javelins, thrown at short range by powerful arms, were lethal and three more groups followed the first salvo in what seemed no more than a blink.

With the area in front now full of the writhing, wounded and the odd dead Turk, Bohemund called for his men to pick up their fighting lances and step forward and that they did, one pace at a time and with no precipitate rush. Cohesion was the key to Norman warfare and that was the element they practised whether on foot or mounted. Stand shoulder to shoulder; present no gaps, always cover the flank of the man on your right as well as doing battle with what lay to your front, and trust the left-hand knight to do his task equally well.

The Turks had weapons suited to their general size and weight; the problem for the defence was that that applied equally to the Normans, who overreached massively what could be deployed against them. Their heavy fighting lances were longer, their swords the same and in a confined space, in essence a melee, manoeuvre was impossible; it was one man facing another, at best with a couple extra and that was not enough to overcome the inherent disadvantage faced by the defenders. Slowly, despite their best efforts and greater numbers they were pushed back, some of the men falling in the front doing so because their own people, eager to kill, were pressing them so hard on the back they could not fight properly.

Those bodies littering the platform became a problem for the attack as well, for to keep going they were required to step over recumbent bodies and not all of them were still, while the platform was now awash too with blood, making it slippery; a foot in the wrong place would bring a Norman fighter down and that, by creating a dog-leg, could jeopardise the whole if those in the second line failed to rapidly fill the vacated space. Also, some fires had taken hold below and the burning reeds were sending up clouds of acrid smoke, which hampered easy breathing for men who were exerting themselves to the maximum.

The greatest execution was being carried out by the pair of swordsmen with the longest reach, Bohemund and Tancred, with the former, his throat dry and hoarse, calling at intervals for the line to take a forward step, never more than that. As well as fighting to the front there were two other problems to deal with: the need to despatch or make still those Turks who had fallen but could still use their weapons achieved with a swift downward jab of a blade followed by a hefty foot being used to tip them, if they were close to the edge of the platform, over the edge. The fate of those they were obliged to step over was taken care of by their confrères, two of whom had been obliged to move up into the front line to replace wounded Normans.

The whole siege tower was rocking slightly as the support knights, the men of Provence, hurried up to await the point where they could get to the battlements and spread out, those rendered invisible because of what lay before them. In their eagerness they pressed upon Bohemund's second line, driving it forward until the space within which they could swing their weapons, should a thing be needed, was severely constrained, which had some of Bohemund's men turning to threaten to use those same instruments on their allies.

Bohemund shouted and that was the signal to push forward regardless; weight of numbers would get them off the platform and onto the stonework, for, in front, attack and defence were now so compressed as to have rendered the assault a pushing match, with a line of Norman shields now the most effective weapon. The

Turks were obliged to balance on the thickness of their own wall, a precarious place from which to fight an opponent of greater weight and reach. No doubt on a command they dropped back onto the wooden parapet and in another directive fell back a little to allow pikes to be used by those supporting them, one of which caught an unwary Norman; a hefty jab sent him spinning off the platform into thin air.

Bohemund and Tancred had split apart, creating space for the support to move up and broaden the fighting line, the men on the outer rim, supported by crossbows, required to keep extending it so that the Provençal knights could get into the fray. Conscious of the need for command, Bohemund called to Tancred to take control and eased himself back onto the platform, with some difficulty pushing through the crush of mailed knights. He hurried up to the very top level, from where he could see how the attack was faring and as of that moment it looked good.

It was the commander of the Genoese crossbowmen who pointed out where the hazard lay. Again Acip Bey had shown cunning in seeking to thwart the attack. No doubt assessing that a siege tower with outriggers set and jammed into the ground could not be toppled, he had set his grappling hooks to take away that support. In what must have been dozens of attempts he had been successful in removing one of the long steadying poles on the south side, then he had used massed archers and hot pitch and oil to stop it being replaced.

That left on that side of the siege tower only the one outrigger, with Bohemund able to clearly see the men recasting the grappling hook and trying to snare the remaining pole. That obliged him to withdraw the crossbowmen from supporting his knights to impeding those efforts; take away that pole and those same hooks, if they got a purchase on any of the main beams of the tower itself, in a place where they could not be dislodged or their ropes cut, could haul the whole thing over, which would cause havoc and much death to those on it and still inside. Certainly the men on the very top, bowmen and knights, would be lucky to survive, while the men who had made the walls would be stranded and no doubt die where they stood.

It was another testimony to the courage of the defenders that even under a hail of crossbow bolts they continued to try and sling their grappling irons and that brought admiration for the ability to offer oneself up regardless of the risk, the very quality that leaders like Bohemund looked for in his own ranks, and he judged it only a matter of time before they succeeded.

Below and in front the attack had stalled, not through any lack of courage or effort but because the fighting was more evenly matched, numerous pikes as well as swordsmen against knights who had a lesser reach than the former and were, as had the Turks been before them, vulnerable to being pitched off the battlements. It was also obvious the Provençal knights lacked the fighting discipline of the Normans – they let gaps appear in their ranks and were suffering because of it, which was diminishing the power of the attack.

The judgement of whether a battle is heading towards success or failure is a fine one and, if asked in repose, Bohemund would have replied it was instinctive, a feeling rather than a certain knowledge. At this moment it was very finely poised; the men for whom he was responsible were not falling back but neither were they advancing at a speed which presaged an imminent collapse, in truth they were inching forward into a situation in which the odds, man for man, would increase; the Turks could bring more men to bear than could he.

Even if he knew nothing of the Genoese tongue, he knew a curse when he heard one and he followed the pointing finger of the leading crossbowman to a see grappling hook round that second outrigging pole and hauling hard. Merely jammed against the siege tower it soon went, to be followed by a hail of small stones fired from Acip's ballistae, added to a hail of arrows, which precluded any attempt to set it back in place.

When he turned to look back at his fighters, he found himself staring into a very worried Genoese face. Fearing to be misunderstood he gestured that the crossbows should withdraw, which they did with alacrity, just as the first of those grappling hooks, now being thrown with impunity, thudded into the tower, though it failed to take a grip. But there was one other salient fact to take into consideration: get a grip on one side, then pull, and, even if it initially failed, it would dislodge the poles on the other side by the mere release of pressure, which would double the jeopardy.

The hope of an outright victory had always been slim to non-existent, wishful thinking, in fact, if you took into consideration Turkish tenacity. It aided Bohemund's thinking that he had the reputation he did, which precluded any judgement against his own bravery or experience. They had done enough for this day, learnt a great deal and were now faced with no possibility as he saw it of outright success. Indeed there was a chance of ignominious failure, with not only the men maimed or killed but also the weapon that they were employing destroyed as well.

It took threats to get those knights waiting to be engaged to withdraw with unblooded weapons and a man of less stature would have suffered, but you did not trade words with a giant sporting a ferocious glare. Luckily they were some of the Franks led by Walo of Chaumont, a good soldier who understood his commands. His men might also have noted that while the Norman leader had taken part in the fight their liege lord was well back observing. His other instruction to them was to get in place the hands needed to haul back the tower.

Then he had to get the Provençals to disengage, which was even harder given many had no common tongue, bar, in their case, a smattering of Latin, this after he had informed Tancred, in tactical control on the battlements and not actually now fighting, of his intention, using shouted words the Turks would not comprehend. Men were set on the ropes that would haul up the screen and told to be ready, while the people still fighting were Normans, so he was sure he would have no trouble with them and neither did he.

His next shouted instruction had them taking backwards steps, the execution controlled by inherent discipline rather than actual spoken commands, the whole attack collapsing in on itself until all his men were back on the slippery wooden surface. It was again his voice that had them break off and jog back, the platform hauled up as soon as they had passed the midpoint, though several Turks, who should have known better, sought by their weight to prevent it being raised. Another command had the Normans turn and swiftly despatch them before they again retreated to the main tower.

The screen was hauled up and that was the signal for the ropes to be employed to get the tower clear; slowly it began to move away from walls now lined with the jeering and triumphant enemy.

CHAPTER THIRTEEN

'We did well,' Bohemund insisted, to nods from his nephew, standing half to his rear. 'The Turks suffered more than us and if we had a trio of such towers I am sure, by splitting the defence, we could overcome and get inside the walls. Certainly we would inflict losses on the defenders they could not sustain and that, My Lords, may well bring about the fall of Nicaea.'

He had already outlined the minor modifications that would make the siege towers immune to the threat from those grappling irons, namely proper seating for the stabilising outriggers so they could not be so easily pulled away. Some of the 'princes' were nodding, but not all – Vermandois looked as if he was sucking a lemon and had already referred to the way his knights had been sent away without having had a chance to fight. De Bouillon then regretted that his men had never even got to ascend the tower.

Vermandois then changed tack in a bid to censure a Norman he clearly saw as some kind of rival, making it plain he still hankered after the leadership. 'You did not adhere to the agreement not to risk our persons, which we did.'

'No I did not, Count Hugh, but let me tell you this, there are occasions, and there will be more, when that cannot apply and is in fact unwise.'

That got a clerical frown from the Bishop; it had been the papal legate's suggestion, in fact his injunction, so Bohemund addressed him directly.

'I do not say, Your Grace, that if I had been absent that disaster would have followed, that the siege tower would have been tipped over, but I put forward the possibility it might.'

'Anyone could have seen the danger,' Vermandois insisted.

'But, Count Hugh, would everyone have acted on it?'

His nostrils flared then. 'Why would they not?'

'For fear that they might be thought of as overcautious.'

Try as he might, Bohemund, and he did by speaking softly, could not keep out of his response the implications of that: for all his vainglorious boasting, the brother of the French King lacked experience. He had never been engaged in a conflict where a siege tower was employed, while the man who disobeyed that injunction was close to being the most famous knight in Christendom.

'I judged that we had done as much as we could and were at risk. I have explained to you how this came about and if I have, in your eyes failed somehow, I am man enough to hear it from your lips.'

Adémar was quick, lest Vermandois say something stupid. 'No one of sense would express such a thing. If I admit to being irritated when I saw you on the tower, less so that your nephew was with you, I am now willing to say without equivocation that it was to our benefit that you were.'

'I am sure I would have done the same had it been I on the tower,' stated Godfrey emphatically.

'While I question your conclusions, Count Bohemund.' Raymond of Toulouse said and that had the two men lock eyes. 'To build two more towers will take much time and we have been about this business long enough, given our purpose. We must think of Palestine in all this and if we batter ourselves against Nicaea that must impact on our fortunes.'

'Lord Raymond, should you contrive a better method I am with you. All I have put forward is a personal view, which is the right of every one of us gathered.'

'More bombardment screens and mining would be quicker.'

'Even when the Turks merely rebuild what we destroy?' asked Robert of Normandy.

'Count Bohemund advances the notion that more siege towers will do the thing, but I say more mining will make it impossible for them to repair all the breeches we make and if one is left undone, that will be our opportunity.'

The Bishop spoke up, as usual his face showing the kind of concern meant to imply he took in all views and gave them equal credence, yet it was obvious to all he generally gave more weight to the man with whom he travelled and the magnate in which his bishopric lay than the others.

'I see merit in what the Count of Toulouse says.'

'I side with Count Bohemund,' said de Bouillon.

Vermandois spoke immediately. 'And I am with my cousin of Toulouse.'

'While I,' Normandy said, 'wonder what our titular commander thinks?'

All eyes turned to Tacitus, who had been silent throughout, not that anyone noticed; he was a man not of few words but going on none and when he did speak it was through an interpreter, even Greek speakers struggling to comprehend him, while with those who only knew Latin and the Frankish tongue it was essential. What followed seemed to consist of more words employed than he had ever uttered before and watching the face of the interpreter it was obvious that the opinion being advanced was not studded with optimism; the face was a positive picture of impending doom.

'The *Prōstratōr* wishes to remind you of how many times the forces of the empire have come to these walls in vain. He has watched your efforts with interest—'

That brought a growling interruption from Baldwin of Boulogne. 'He was supposed to stop us making the same errors as he had previously, not just watch.'

The interpreter stopped, and seeing the leaders react to yet another unwarranted interruption from a person not supposed to speak unless invited to, brought what amounted to an admonishment from Bishop Adémar, though it was voiced in a way that might have indicated the need of prayers for penance to a recalcitrant child.

'We must, My Lords, abide by the conventions we have set.'

'What he means, brother,' de Bouillon snapped, less the diplomat, 'is you speak through me!'

'If you spoke enough, I would not have to.'

'Leave the pavilion.'

'What?'

'You heard me, brother,' Godfrey hissed. 'Do as I say or by the faith I will send you home.'

That led to a silent stand-off lasting several seconds, but it could have only one outcome. When it came to arguing with his elder sibling Baldwin had no dice to throw. With as much huff as he could muster he strode out through the opening, leaving his brother to apologise for what had occurred.

'Be assured, My Lords, that Baldwin only acts as he does from an excess of zeal.'

'You see, Uncle,' Tancred whispered, 'being full-blooded brothers does not make for better bedfellows.'

'Quiet,' Bohemund insisted, as Adémar indicated the interpreter should continue, though his shaking shoulders showed evidence of amusement.

'My Lord *Prōstratōr* would point you towards the one wall, for all your strength, you cannot seal.'

'We are not blind,' Vermandois scoffed, 'and we have tried.'

That conveyed to Tacitus, he waved his hand dismissively. The Crusaders had set mangonels on the bank of the lake aimed at the entrance to the watergate. It was a poor weapon to employ because of its inaccuracy, every cast stone being of a different weight and the tension required to create the force to eject it a constant variable, which ensured that so far none had found a floating target.

'I do believe, My Lords,' the Bishop said, with a weary expression, 'that if we wish to hear the views of General Tacitus we should let this fellow convey them.'

'*Prōstratōr* means stable master does it not?'

Tancred once more hissed this softly, only to get an elbow in the ribs from his uncle, a sign that he should be as silent as Baldwin should have been, a correction following swiftly in a voice kept at the same whispered level as that of his nephew.

'Try Master of the Imperial Horse.'

The interpreter took up the translation once more. 'If you observe the lake, and examine the boats destined for the watergate, you will see that they arrive not only with food but also with men. Later they depart without them, which means, as we of Byzantium found out before you, that you cannot cut the number of the garrison by killing them, for the city will support a certain number of fighters and that will be maintained by the introduction of constant reinforcements.'

'We have greater numbers than they,' Raymond asserted. 'The problem we have is to employ those men in a way that has the desired effect.'

Vermandois was quickly on to that. 'Man for man, the Turks are no match for us.'

These responses were conveyed to Tacitus, who listened and nodded slowly, before speaking softly, the words following from his mouthpiece.

'Unless you can walk on water, the *Prōstratōr* says, and you would require the powers of Our Lord Jesus Christ to do so, you will not take Nicaea, for that opening sustains them.'

'Then we must have boats,' Tancred said in yet another whisper.

Bohemund spoke out loud, addressing the room. 'A valid point has just been advanced by my nephew. If we need to stop the flow of supplies to Nicaea and they are coming in on boats, then we have to employ the same means to prevent it.'

'Boats?' Vermandois asked, making a great point of looking all around him as though they might be hidden somewhere, which had Bohemund visibly stiffen; he was not to be the butt of any man's humour.

'We do not have any boats, Count Bohemund,' de Bouillon interjected, 'and even if we have timber we do not have the means, by which I mean the shipwrights, to construct them.'

'And how long would that take?' Raymond asked with a shake of his head.

'Heavenly chariots would be more likely,' said Normandy.

Feeling that he was being made to look like a fool – even de Bouillon, the man he considered closest to him in thinking, was looking at him askance – Bohemund searched for a solution and only one presented itself.

'Then the Emperor must provide them.'

The interpreter was conveying what he had said to Tacitus, and soon the *Prōstratōr*'s shoulders, even if he tried to contain it, were shaking so much he felt the need to drop his head to hide his mirth.

'Have we not put in repairs to his road, so that it is near as good as it was in ancient times?' Slow nods were the response to that – they were unsure where he was headed, and the road was somewhat less smooth than he was implying. 'We do not require galleys or even trading vessels, we need small boats of the kind that could be loaded onto a wagon drawn by oxen.'

Toulouse was quick with an observation. 'The lake boats the Turks employ are larger than that.'

'And we are, as the Count of Vermandois just said, more than a match for the Turks in one-to-one combat. We do not need to equal their numbers, we merely, as you said, Count Raymond, need to find a way to set our swords against theirs.'

That left the Vermandois in a bind; he was not sure whether to be glad that his words had been quoted or angry with the man who had used them.

'We would fight them on the water?' That was a question and one delivered with suitable doubt by Adémar.

'We would bar them from Nicaea,' Bohemund insisted, 'and if they chose to fight I will back my Normans to keep them from ever getting in that which they carry.'

That engendered a jaundiced look from everyone except the Duke Robert and de Bouillon; they were somewhat sick of being told of the fighting qualities of the Normans.

'No more is required,' Bohemund added, then he turned to Tacitus and spoke in Greek. 'A message must be sent to Alexius, your master, at once, demanding he provide boats, the largest he can get on an ox cart, by which we can cut off Nicaea.'

The interpreter replied after his principle had spoken. 'It cannot be done.'

Bohemund actually laughed out loud, which did not please the Byzantine General, aware that he was being paid back in kind for his earlier mirth. 'You never met my father, *Prōstratōr*. Those were words of which he did not know the meaning. I will go in person and demand from your master that he accede to our request.'

'Is it our request, Count Bohemund?' Robert of Normandy stated, his tone high-handed. 'I have yet to hear it even discussed, never mind agreed upon.'

The tone of the reply was cold. 'I await from the son of the Conqueror a better suggestion.'

'You dare to mention my father?'

'My Lords,' Adémar called, soothingly.

He was aware that a dispute was about to break out – the two were looking daggers at each other. The cleric also suspected that what he had heard was true: no Norman willingly bowed the knee to

184

another, whatever his bloodline. Looking at him Bohemund wondered what he would say if he knew the truth. The same blood ran through de Hauteville veins that ran through those of Robert of Normandy although not Bohemund's own, for he was descended from his grandfather's second wife. But the elder Tancred's first bride had been an illegitimate daughter of Robert's grandsire and it ill behove the son of William, known in the Duchy as the Bastard of Falaise, to come it high with his family.

'Forgive me,' Bohemund responded, suppressing the anger that threatened to break out into open dispute, which took a great deal of effort. 'I was thinking of my father when I used those words.'

'An admirable sentiment,' cried Adémar, with too high a dose of enthusiasm. 'Who could fault such a sentiment?'

If it did not serve to heal the breech, it was enough to throw a cloak over it.

'I do believe,' Vermandois said, 'that it falls to the man Alexius sent to aid us to ask for that which you propose.'

'Count Hugh, I have no interest in who asks, only in that the request is met.'

'The *Prōstratōr* can provide a messenger,' said Adémar. 'Perhaps, Count Bohemund, you may add a letter outlining your thinking.'

'Are they mad, these Westerners?' asked Manuel Boutoumites, when the Emperor imparted the request from Tacitus to him. 'Boats?'

'There is a communication from Bohemund as well.'

'Which I trust Your Highness will ignore.'

For once Alexius was sharp with a man he held in high esteem. 'Do not let your hatred blind you to his ability. He is a fine general and a mighty fighter and he is born from a stock that has beaten us at every turn.'

'Forgive me, Highness,' Boutoumites replied, his voice humble.

High in favour he might be but the *Curopalates* knew that could be withdrawn at the click of a finger. The monastic poorhouses were not full of those who had fallen from imperial favour, but there were enough inmates, many of them lacking eyes, to induce caution in even the highest-placed courtier.

'Which I do,' Alexius replied, well aware of the effect of his admonishment, this while pulling a paper from the pocket of his gown. 'In this Bohemund says, and I see it as a mark of the man, that the notion was advanced first by his nephew, not him.'

'He seeks to elevate Tancred?' Boutoumites asked, cloaking an opinion in a question.

Alexius was not fooled. 'He too is a de Hauteville, and if he is half the man his grandsire was I would fear him as much as I do his uncle. But, and this is the nub, Bohemund insists that what is required is not large vessels, but ones of a size enough to perhaps carry a dozen fighters, and that tends toward the most capacious fishing boats.'

'Heavily armed knights fighting on water in fishing boats?'

Boutoumites waved and extended an upright hand, indicating the obvious risk of capsize, not improbable given anyone fighting afloat would have to stand to do so.

'I think the Turks will fear to drown as much as a Christian and they may well do so, Manuel, and what is that to us in either case? But it might be a key to unlock Nicaea, so I say it must be attempted.'

'Am I to commandeer the boats?'

'Yes, but take a strong escort, the fishermen of Constantinople are feisty fellows and will not give them up easily.'

Other functionaries were despatched to get hold of the largest ox carts and the animals to pull them, which left Alexius musing on the possibilities. He sought to conjure up the scene on Lake Askanian, a body of water he knew well, having been a besieger of Nicaea himself and a failed one. This led him to wonder as to why he had not thought of the idea himself when he had been in command. It was the state of the old Roman-built road, of course, which had been in desperate repair every time he had marched an army to the Turkish stronghold.

The Crusaders had repaired it – was that too a de Hauteville suggestion? He did not know but it did alter matters. To transport the boats he had in mind would not be easy, but it was possible and there was a bonus if it did the trick. With Nicaea fallen the Western knights could be sent on their way to Palestine and that would remove them from any proximity to his capital, which he saw as being in danger as long as they were close by. Yet in his musings he thought he saw a way to improve the effect of these boats, one that would only be communicated to the likes of Bohemund when they arrived.

'For you see, you Norman devil, the Byzantine Emperor does not lack wits to match yours.'

The boats had to be loaded on the Galatea side of the Bosphorus and that meant breaking up the biggest crane from the capital's docks and shipping it across, a demand from Manuel Boutoumites that mightily upset the traders who used it to load their merchant vessels. Mollified with gold – the fishermen had needed to be bribed as well to prevent a riot – it was barely strong enough to bear a boat fresh out of the water and threatened to break, so days were wasted with them drawn up on the shore to dry out their timbers.

Once loaded and before they could be moved, the reverse had to occur: the innards had to be filled with water to reseal the planking and then that had to be bailed out so the oxen could move their specially strengthened carts, the cargo covered with canvas to hide them from the kind of prying eyes that would send a warning to Kilij Arslan, lurking somewhere to the east and licking his wounds, for he would certainly alert Acip Bey.

The road had been repaired but not for such wagons as these. Men had to work ahead, filling in depressions and clearing stones, and when it came to an incline double teams had to be harnessed together to get them up the slope, and to that was added sweating and straining human endeavour. This was made worse when they reached the passes through the mountains, where they could only ascend one at a time, with every beast and man employed and stakes used to secure the rear of the wheels at each small turn. The only one spared this was Manuel Boutoumites, sat on his magnificent horse, who earned much hatred and many whispered insults for his continual shouted exhortations to put in greater effort.

Descent was not without its hazards either, the need to keep the carts in line with the oxen paramount, for if they slipped to the side the whole would topple, which would certainly smash the boats and probably break the backs of the still harnessed animals. Up ahead were the impatient Crusader leaders, who knew the boats were coming and now were far from sceptical, quite the reverse – they were now seen as a salvation that would rid them of the need to assault the walls.

When they were close, the 'princes' rode out to meet the *Curopalates*, Bohemund in particular eager that such a weapon should not appear at a time when the garrison could observe their arrival. They stopped on the reverse side of the final hill and it was there that the Norman was apprised of the addition Alexius had made, four times as many banners as the vessels would have carried normally, all in the colours of the various lords who led the Crusade.

'His Highness believes that, at a distance, the Turks will see them and think the boats to be of a greater beam than in truth they are, thus carrying more men.'

'Clever,' Bohemund acknowledged, but he had a sting to administer as well. 'What a pity he did not see fit to take part in the siege and give us the benefit of his intelligence earlier.'

CHAPTER FOURTEEN

The boats were brought through the encampment at dusk, which fell to darkness so that again a twin line of torches had to be deployed, then taken along the lakeside, far enough to be launched well out of sight of the towers of Nicaea. Getting them into the water was accomplished at dawn by the simple expedient of using a slope and backing the carts into Lake Askanian until the boats floated free, the men set to man them sent aboard to become accustomed to rowing and manoeuvring them prior to them being employed.

Naturally every leader was keen for his men to take part, though that was not always welcome to the people they led, many of whom were confirmed landsmen. Again in this the Normans came to the fore; amongst their numbers were men who, like the de Hautevilles, had been raised in the Contentin, on the shores of the great ocean, and had fished for food and jumped the waves from a young age. Others resided along the banks of the River Seine and had kept alive the skills of their Viking predecessors when it came to boat handling.

Baldwin of Boulogne recruited men from those parts of his brother's Duchy of Lower Lorraine that came from the many lakes that dotted his domains. Vermandois too had men from towns that sat on rivers and so did Robert of Flanders, though it was he who had the most difficulty in manning his craft and the reason was prior experience. On departing Bari, one of the ships carrying his knights had literally split in half down its keel, sending to the bottom all who had sailed in her. That memory lingered, making his men, brave as they were, reluctant to risk anything that included water.

The other possibility, which had to be covered, was fighting; if none of the Crusaders had observed Manual Boutoumites refer to the possibility of capsizing to his Emperor, all knew it to be a risk. Exercises had to be carried out in water shallow enough for the Crusaders to survive their mistakes, like too many trying to stand up and making their craft unstable, albeit they had to endure, when they were drenched and struggling through the water, the jests and cries from those watching. In the end it was established that in a boat holding ten knights, only four could really engage in aggressive combat at any one time, while to go from standing to sitting or the reverse was a hard skill to master. The other matter was even more important: now that they had them, how were they to be employed?

'These are not vessels from which we can mount an assault.'

Such an opinion, advanced by de Bouillon, was so obvious as to not require any vocal agreement.

'Surely we must set up a blockade,' Vermandois suggested. 'A line of boats across the lake that cuts them off from their supplies and means that it is a true siege.'

Tancred asked for permission to speak and that was granted. 'I think the Emperor Alexius had something else in mind.'

'What?' the Frenchman demanded. 'Given he is not present.'

'The key to Nicaea is the spirit of Acip Bey and the men he leads.' That got a questioning look from Vermandois of the kind that implied, 'So?'

'They feel so secure because they have that one open side to their walls, it makes them certain the siege can never succeed and so it has proved in the past, as Tacitus pointed out.'

Robert of Normandy posed the next question. 'You think the loss of such will break their spirit?'

'I think it may persuade them that the time has come to seek terms.'

Raymond was scathing. 'You wish to offer them terms after what we have suffered these last weeks?'

That got raised eyebrows. Suspecting that his nephew would not wish to dispute with such a powerful figure, Bohemund came to his aid. 'How many more do we wish to spend here, for even if we invest the watergate and cut off future supplies the Turks are, of this moment, sitting on full storehouses?'

'And we have not come all this way,' de Bouillon added, obviously seeing the sense of what was being proposed, 'to spend a year or more taking Nicaea.'

'You have a suggestion, Count Bohemund?' asked Adémar.

'I think my nephew has, with your permission.'

With every eye upon him, Tancred nodded and explained his thinking, which had much to do with the many banners supplied by Alexius, and once that was outlined the sense of it was so obvious that his plan was put to the vote and given approval.

* * *

The primary task, given to those most able to quickly master the necessary waterman skills, was to mount patrols that would cut off Nicaea from its customary supply. In addition to that, the siege had to be pressed harder to prevent any news of the acquisition of the boats getting in through the gates, in short, the way the city was invested had to be pressed to the maximum, with nightly patrols set to catch anyone seeking to enter or leave by land.

Added to that, the main inlet in which the boats were berthed was rendered invisible from the water, which meant much cutting of reed beds to create a camouflage behind which they could sit unseen. The habits of the Turkish boatmen had to be studied, for it seemed to Tancred, if they left men in the city, it must be the same boat people who returned with their craft every time and he was soon proved to be both correct, which was encouraging.

Being unaware of what they might face, the Turkish siege-breakers were not given to taking precautions; one or two quite large boats came down the lake in daylight, rowing if the wind was against them, usually in the late afternoon, so they could make the watergate as dusk was falling, that obviously held to be the safest time. Also, being in the main concerned with the supply of food, they carried more cargo than fighting men, whatever number of those being left behind, it being easier to row an empty vessel than a fully loaded one.

Tancred sent two boats down the lake to prevent them reaching Nicaea and another pair were launched behind them as they sailed past the inlet, thus catching them between pincers, which proved absurdly easy. Never having seen a waterborne enemy they assumed everything they saw to be friendly until it was too late to avoid capture, and as soon as they saw the armed men on board they attempted flight, only to row into the arms of the vessels Tancred had sent out to close the trap.

That led to surrender, for if there were fighters aboard they were few and with unsuitable weapons to fight lances and Western swords, while the boatmen were not willing to bleed in a trade for which they were no doubt being well rewarded. Soon the creek was filling up on a daily basis with more captures, which meant more vessels the Crusaders could man.

'And as a bonus, Uncle, we can eat that which was destined for the city.'

'How long do you intend this should last?'

'As long as it needs to,' Tancred replied, slightly put out by the tone.

'The question was raised at a council today.'

'Let me guess – by Vermandois.'

'If he brought it up, he was not alone in wondering.'

'You?'

'I made your case, Tancred,' Bohemund growled. 'I reminded them that having given you the task they must bow to your judgement as to how long it should proceed.'

'Forgive me.'

'But I am telling you that is a position I will find increasingly hard to maintain.'

'Would I be allowed to show you something?'

'Of course, as long as it is of interest.'

Tancred called for their horses and once mounted he led his uncle to a point on the lakeside from which they could observe the watergate and the whole east wall of Nicaea. 'Look at the towers above.'

'Yes,' Bohemund said, 'they are manned, and poorly so, but what of it?'

'Acip Bey has no need to concern himself with this eastern wall because he knows it to be secure, but observe more closely and you may see the men up there are acting as lookouts, not defenders. Their eyes are fixed upon the lake and they are wondering what has happened to their supplies and reinforcements.'

The older man smiled. 'No doubt you are so far inside their minds that you know that too.'

'The plan agreed is working. They must suspect that something has prevented Kilij Arslan from keeping the flow coming, but they will be hoping it is a temporary break not a complete one. Yet the mere loss must affect the thinking of Acip Bey as well as his men, for such a lack cannot be kept hidden and it will be the cause of concern. Let that last for another week and then we will have them.'

'You're certain?'

'Do I have to tell you, Uncle,' Tancred hooted with a grin, 'nothing is certain in war.'

'A week?'

'If you can manage it and if the men of the council doubt we are succeeding, tell them to come down to the lake at dusk and eye that tower above the watergate, for that is when it gets ever more crowded as one day succeeds the next.'

Bohemund only passed that on to Bishop Adémar, knowing that if he stood against general opinion Tancred's wish for time would not be overturned and, in truth, he could understand the impatience of his peers. That evaporated when he saw what his nephew had hinted at, and it so impressed Adémar that all doubts were allayed. The tower went from having a few guards upon to being crowded as dusk fell, the shadows of those standing there eventually cast long across the lake as the sun set at their backs.

They paid no attention to those watching them or to any activity in the siege lines that were visible, all eyes were looking east, and it was almost palpable the hopes that they harboured: the sight of a boat or two carrying that regular supply of food and men that had allowed them to laugh at the infidels.

Tancred got his week and used it well, able to inform the council that he was about to put the next part of his plan in place on the following day. The launching of the boats was different this time; not only were they all to be employed but they were each and every one festooned with the banners of the Crusade leaders, several to each craft, and luckily there was wind enough blowing to cause them to show their devices plain: the red background to the blue and white chequer of the de Hautevilles, de Bouillon having the same in red and white on a yellow base; the blue shield of Vermandois dotted with yellow fleurs-de-lis; red shields for Normandy and Toulouse, only differing in the two lions for the former and an elaborate golden cross for the latter; while in the lead vessel and at the prow flew the blue device of the papal legate, Adémar de Monteil, Bishop of Puy, decorated with an image of the Virgin.

None of those who held those banners as a sign of their position were present, the whole enterprise being led by Tancred. They had taken up a position on the lakeside in clear sight of that wall they had so longed to invest, no part more than the tower that sat above the recessed watergate. There was no sight of the boats bearing their men – they were too distant to be seen even from the walls of Nicaea, but that soon changed.

First a sharp-eyed sentinel, unsure if what he was seeing was true, climbed from the parapet onto the battlements and peered into the distance, his call to his fellows unheard but the gesture with it plain. Within seconds the man had jumped down and disappeared, but it was not long before the top of the tower began to fill with bodies and that continued until it was crowded, and somehow they could guess that Acip Bey was amongst their number. It only took one to cheer for the rest to join in and soon their loud acclamation was echoing across the water.

'They think the boats are Turkish,' Vermandois said, obviously surprised, an indication that he had scant belief in Tancred's plan.

'Then,' Bishop Adémar replied, 'so much greater the shock.'

The cheering lasted for what seemed an age, evidence of just how much anxiety had been built up by the lack of their regular supply and it would not be just for what they carried. Those supply boats were a lifeline to their Sultan and their prophet, an assurance that whatever was thrown against their walls they could hold the city and deny it to the infidel. The cheering slowly weakened and finally died, for the devices on those billowing banners had begun to become visible and that told them that the impossible had occurred: the besiegers had a war fleet on the lake.

Part of Tancred's plan was that the boats should not come close, but should sail to and fro so far out of view as to disguise their size and numbers, far enough away to make the defenders think that every banner represented an individual vessel, and the success of that ploy came with the wailing that replaced the lost cheering, a ghoulish sound from hundreds of throats that brought forth from Bohemund words he had been hoping he would be able to employ.

'I think it might be time for the Emperor's *Curopalates* to offer Acip Bey terms once more.'

For a third time Manuel Boutoumites passed through the main gate of Nicaea, watched by a crusading host near to holding its breath, and it was an indication of how changed circumstances had become that he re-emerged within half a day. Abject surrender was not possible and in truth it had never been sought; Kilij Arslan's family would be safe, respected and returned to him, the garrison could also march out to rejoin their Sultan with their weapons, the only thing which must be left behind being Arslan's treasury, for without his chests of gold and silver he would be hard put to raise the kind of forces that would pose a threat to the Eastern Empire, whose troops would now occupy the city.

'When do we march in?' asked Tancred.

'We don't,' his uncle replied. 'This is going to be a triumph for Byzantium, not the Crusade.'

'It was by our efforts it fell.'

'And it is Tacitus and Boutoumites who will take possession for Alexius. Thus we have fulfilled one part of the vow we took on coming here, to aid Byzantium in throwing back the Turk.'

'I cannot believe you agreed to this.'

'But I did, for there was no point in standing against it. How many times have I said to you that our confrères do not understand Byzantium? The likes of Adémar accedes to this through his office as Pope Urban's legate, the others because they wish to be seen fulfilling the pledge they made to Alexius. Both the city and Arslan's treasury will come back under imperial control and we must wait to see what the Emperor thinks of our efforts and what rewards we will receive for them.'

'So Tacitus, the man who does least, gains most.'

'I should think he has spent the morning polishing his nose.'

It was late afternoon before Tacitus led his two thousand men into Nicaea to accept the surrender and not much longer after that Acip

Bey led his Turks out through silent ranks of the crusading host. It was a testimony to the grip that both the leaders and their purpose had on these men that they acquiesced in what was taking place, for there was not a fighter amongst them who did not serve for plunder and there before them, and they were barred from entry, was a rich city at their mercy.

'So we march on south?' Tancred asked.

'When we have arranged supplies, which I think will be readily provided. There are still Turks to contest with and they are yet a threat to Alexius. He will want us to render that void.'

If the treasury and plunder of Nicaea was barred to the host, reward was not. The leaders were called to Alexius's camp at Pelekanum and showered with gold, treasure sent back to Nicaea for their supporters and captains, rewarded as to their rank. When it came to the rank and file it was tubs of copper that they could spend in the fleshpots that had grown up around Civetot, now available to them given there was no enemy to fight and they could travel back and forth freely.

On the return to their encampment Adémar waited for Alexius to arrive in person and waited in vain, a message sent to the council that he had returned to the capital and he awaited them there to discuss future plans. Added to that was a telling postscript: they were welcome in Constantinople but it was felt their lances should stay south of the Bosphorus, with Raymond of Toulouse, the man who had refused to take the oath, in command.

Bohemund waited for his peers to be insulted and he waited in vain; even Vermandois seemed able to accept what the Count of Taranto saw as a calculated insult, though he understood well the reason the Emperor would never come near Nicaea while they were present. Alexius would see the Crusader encampment as a place of danger where he, surrounded by more men than he could muster to defend himself, would be at their mercy. He feared to step into their tents for fear of becoming their prisoner and the annoying fact was that he was the only 'prince' to see the truth that there was no real bond of trust between Byzantium and the Crusade.

The remaining members of the council, accompanied by their closest aides, rode into the city as a body, attended by their most powerful supporters and their familia knights, banners flying, to be cheered to the skies by the multitude. A Mass was said in Santa Sophia in which, much to the clear displeasure of the Patriarch of Constantinople, the head of the Greek Orthodox Church, Bishop Adémar was permitted to perform the liturgy in the Latin rite, giving communion to the kneeling lords of Europe and their closest followers.

A great feast naturally followed in the Blachernae Palace, during which even more gifts of gold and jewels were presented to the victorious Crusaders, and while the entertainment took everyone's attention, Bohemund kept an eye on Alexius, who if he was aware of it did not respond. The following day was spent in council with the Emperor, discussing the plans and needs of the next stage of their journey, plus the pitfalls they might face, which would take them to the vital city of Antioch.

There was a suggestion that they exploit the division amongst the various branches of the Mohammedan faith; the Fatamids in Egypt hated their co-religionists in his old domains, as well as the tribes who held Jerusalem, and might be persuaded to aid the Crusaders' cause. To this end he despatched an embassy to sound out their leader. After days of rejoicing, the time came to depart, but first Alexius sprung a small surprise.

It was a seemingly innocuous request that before the Franks and Apulians marched on they should restate the oaths previously taken regarding imperial property and that, because they were present, this included the likes of Baldwin and Tancred who had previously managed to avoid swearing. Baldwin acquiesced without a murmur, but Tancred was troubled to make a pledge he might not be able to keep. There was, however, no choice.

Golden-nosed Tacitus and his two thousand men would march with them to, as Alexius said, aid them in any task they undertook, protect them on their journey and to take possession, on his behalf and that of the empire, of any town and cities that fell to them on the way to Palestine. Vague promises were made about what would follow – some were sure that meant Alexius and the whole military might of Byzantium: Bohemund was not so sure and found in Godfrey de Bouillon a magnate willing to share such reservations. Yet there was nothing they could do to pressure the Emperor for a more binding commitment and they also had no choice but to march on when he gave the signal it was time to do so.

CHAPTER FIFTEEN

B ack in the camp outside Nicaea – the city and its churches was still barred to them except in small groups – the Council of Princes debated the next stage of their campaign, and some of the constraints which had applied to the previous endeavours existed now. In fact the problem was greater, for supply from Constantinople, either by sea or land, became increasingly difficult to maintain the further south they moved. Their numbers had previously dictated that they marched to Nicaea in separate units to avoid so stripping the land they passed through, for it would not support the whole.

Now at full strength and with a tail of camp-follower pilgrims that was made worse, even if the line of march, at least in its original phase, took them through very fertile country, but even the best of Anatolia could not feed a host which numbered in total seventy thousand mouths that arrived without warning. Foraging would be required, but more vital was to alert a wide area of the country that there was a passing market, and one with deep pockets for their excess produce, if they cared to make their way towards the line of march.

'We dare not be so broken up as we were coming here.' Godfrey de Bouillon stated this as though he expected it to be disputed, legs spread apart, his barrel chest thrust out and with it his jaw. 'We have driven Kilij Arslan off but that does not mean he will lie low like a dog and give us free passage.'

Bohemund permitted himself only a hint of a smile; de Bouillon was right, but would he ever acknowledge that he bore the responsibility for that situation, given his failure to control his lances in the first battle? Judging by his appearance the answer was no, and looking around the others there seemed no one, judging by their faces, who thought as he did.

'We cannot do as we did before,' insisted Raymond. 'In individual units we will be too small and vulnerable.'

'Added to which we have thousands of pilgrims.'

Adémar got a response that displeased him from Vermandois and standing behind him the Constable of France. 'I would leave them behind, let them make their own way to Jerusalem.'

'You would see them massacred, Count Hugh?'

'By whom?' Vermandois responded. 'We have given the Turks such a bloody nose I doubt we'll see sight of them between here and Syria.'

That, which flew in the face of everything that had just been said by the likes of Raymond and Godfrey, taxed the Bishop's seeming endless depths of patience and he sounded more irritated than he had ever allowed himself to be up till now, partly, Bohemund suspected, because when he spoke those words Vermandois had adopted a look of such arrogant indifference.

'They require our protection, and it is no less than our Christian duty to provide it to them. It seems you would throw them to the wolves, Count Hugh.'

'I would not see them harmed,' the Frenchman insisted, looking around as if he had somehow been traduced. 'But they complicate our passage. If they travel separately they will not want for protection even if Kilij Arslan can create another army to replace the one we have destroyed. Good sense tells me that he must deal with us first and that is another battle he will lose.'

'It has been my experience,' Bohemund cut in, with much emphasis on the last word, 'that when neighbours are threatened they tend to combine, in order to avoid being defeated piecemeal.'

'We should fear the Danishmends?' asked Robert of Normandy.

'Let us say we must be aware of them, for they are as numerous as the tribe led by Arslan and are his neighbours and fellow infidels.'

'As well as bitter enemies,' Vermandois said.

'Even bitter enemies sometimes come together. Let us remind ourselves that we did not destroy him, we merely put him to flight, and he will desperately want back what he had. This tells me he will pay a high price to get it, even by making peace with the Danishmends. But I would caution also that there are many other Seljuk tribes between us and the Euphrates, and if we are seen as instruments of Byzantium they will perceive that as a threat to them all and combine.'

'They would be wise to fight us before we got to Antioch,' de Bouillon suggested.

'Which is not yet threatened,' Raymond reminded him. 'It is many leagues distant.'

'They will have word from Byzantium of where we are headed, which in any case is not secret. As to our strengths and weaknesses, not all the mercenaries Alexius employs will be loyal to him, given too many are Turks or half-breeds.'

This Frankish conversation was being quietly translated for Tacitus; those words of Godfrey de Bouillon got the Duke of Lower Lorraine a filthy look that went right over his head, he being unaware of the insult.

'The decision we must make is this: can we march as a single body?' Adémar asked, nailing the important point. 'And if we cannot, how are we going to divide the host and into how many parts?'

'No is my answer to your first question,' Bohemund replied, a response that was backed up by the shaken heads of all the other magnates. 'Yet My Lord of Toulouse is right, we must be strong enough to battle if it is forced upon us.'

'Provided we do not have too much distance between us we can be as good as one.'

'Which obliges me to add that from Nicaea onwards we will not have the road we enjoyed previously, so rapid movement will not be possible. According to Alexius it is still a route, but one in which the old Roman Road only shows in very few places. Nor will we have the supplies in the quantity we require, which means we cannot just rely on forage and greedy peasant farmers. We must take with us food on the hoof and use the spare horses, oxen and donkeys as beasts of burden.'

After much discussion and several discarded suggestions it was decided that safety lay in numbers but the host could split in two and still be secure. Contact should be maintained and they should never be so far apart as to be unable to offer mutual support. The destination, where they would once more become complete, was an old Byzantine military camp at Dorylaeum, where there was ample water and pasture as well as a large farming quarter in the surrounding countryside.

The Normans, both contingents, would take the lead with half the pilgrims and camp followers, the rest coming on actually under Raymond, though pride was assuaged with the other princes by naming the titular leader as Adémar. Bohemund and Duke Robert exchanged a look then that might presage difficulties, for they had not, up till now, appeared to be natural bedfellows.

'I think he worries about acting in concert with me. Robert, with his title, sees himself as suzerain to anyone named de Hauteville and every Norman lance we lead, while he knows that it is not a condition I accept and that could lead to dispute.'

'And will it?' his nephew asked.

'I will try very hard to make it congenial. Nothing has changed, for in the end we will be as one again and all the complications of that will resurface. Little will be achieved by making enemies.' That was followed by a wry smile. 'And Normans are the worst to have.'

'And who does Tacitus march with?'

'Adémar, and it is my guess he will be bringing up the rear.'

'I long to see these Byzantines actually fight.'

'It would not be a thing to hold your breath upon.'

In that Bohemund was mistaken; if they had been supine at Nicaea they were the opposite now. In order that imperial rights should be respected and protected, especially any towns they passed or captured, Alexius had ordered his *Prōstratōr* Tacitus to advance with the very front elements of the Crusaders, in fact to take the lead and command, which also underlined their vow of service to him.

As soon as the forward element parted company with their confrères it was made plain to Tacitus that his position was one of advisor, not leader; neither of the Norman magnates had any intention of being led by a Byzantine, however highly he was regarded by his Emperor, and pressing home that agreement went some way to help them warm to each other.

The Norman host was in excess of fifteen thousand strong and half that number again would come on in the second wave, both a mass of mounted knights, who would lead their animals at least half of each day's progress, as well as the foot-bound *milities*, and, combined, the fighting elements made up two-thirds of the entire body. The rest – the pilgrims, and the camp followers attracted to any fighting force – straggled along in their wake led by a restored Peter the Hermit, either walking like him or, if they were of the wealthier kind, bestride an ass, creating a huge cloud of dust that rose to choke anyone not out to the front, which included Tancred, in command of the powerful rearguard.

With so many animals – each knight required three: one to ride, another to carry his equipment, clothing and personal stores and lastly his destrier – water was the paramount concern and that applied as much to an ox as an ass and to a pilgrim as much as a duke. Fortunately the lands of this part of Anatolia were well watered from the various mountain ranges that dotted the landscape, with peaks that in winter all held falls of snow, and these were melting to feed the rivers. They were traversing this fecund agricultural land at no great pace, passing alongside fields full of crops to purchase, so that the march, covering no more than ten leagues a day, dust notwithstanding, had a carnival air.

Out in front Robert of Normandy and Bohemund rode side by side with Tacitus, who was, as usual, not much given to communication. After an initial display of reserve it quickly became obvious that the two leaders had more in common than what might separate them. Away from the Council of Princes, Robert was a more congenial person by far, aware of the dangers of dissension and determined not to raise any hackles, so they soon fell to discussing the various things that troubled their life, both of which revolved around family.

'I would be at peace with William,' Robert said, referring to his brother, 'for I am content with what my father left me. He is not – even if I have given him my bounden oath not to attempt anything in England.'

'He wants everything?'

Robert smiled. 'Just as I am told do you.'

'I admit to wanting what should be mine by right.'

'I have been told of the nature of the man who prevents you.'

'Not *Borsa*,' Bohemund snarled.

'No, the Great Count.'

That was acknowledged but with a shaking head. 'If I knew the true reason why my Uncle Roger acts as he does I might be more content. Is it for an oath he swore to my father or a wily way to suit his own purpose?'

'Have you asked him?'

Bohemund shrugged and produced a grin. 'You will find, Duke Robert, that to ask a direct question of a de Hauteville does not get you a straight answer.'

Robert laughed. 'Then Italy has not sapped your Norman spirit.'

The easy talk continued at night, when the camp was set up, joined by Tancred, Robert of Salerno and many of the Duke's captains. Old campaigns were discussed, north and south – how Robert's father had subdued much of England by torching the country, especially the north, which was held by those listening to be a proper way to control a recalcitrant Anglo-Saxon populace and their rebellious carls.

Talk of family was again to the fore, for Normandy was troubled not only by William Rufus but also the Conqueror's youngest son Henry, even more implacably opposed to the Duke of Normandy than his sibling monarch. Then there were the Norman nobles who betrayed him one day to side with his brother, only to offer allegiance the next so he could never engage in combat and have any assurance of full support. He had already been captured once and imprisoned, forced to cede his inherited English domains to buy his release, and his tone left no one in any doubt he was sick of it.

The de Hauteville story was different. A lack of opportunity had brought them to Italy where William, the eldest, had shown great fighting and tactical quality to become the right-hand man to a powerful Norman magnate called Rainulf of Aversa, only to sense himself betrayed once he had aided Rainulf to recognition of the title of count. That had led to the near impregnable Castle of Melfi and a commitment to aid the Lombards against their Byzantine masters. William soon discerned that they were too untrustworthy to rule themselves, any one of a number of princes who rose to prominence seemingly ever ready to surrender leadership and the possibility of a kingly title for Byzantine gold.

So the de Hauteville brothers, now five in number, carved out a fief for themselves through their combat skills, first on the old Roman battlefield of Cannae, where William had done to the Eastern Empire what Hannibal had done to the Roman legions in antiquity. Much fighting followed across the whole of Apulia, Calabria and Sicily over four decades, de Hautevilles dying from age and the secret knife, to be succeeded by the next brother in line who could hold the Normans as one.

Byzantium suffered defeat at their hands everywhere until only Bari stood against them and that had fallen to the genius of the *Guiscard*. Not that he had enjoyed peace; plagued as he was by constant rebellion as well as a combination of all the princes of Northern Italy, arrayed against him under the banner of Pope Urban's predecessor. The fiery and intemperate prelate called Hildebrand, known to posterity as Gregory VII, hated the Normans and wished them gone. In defeating him and his combined forces Robert de Hauteville had been granted the full ducal rights, now held by *Borsa*, by papal decree.

It was easy to discuss with Robert the dispute Bohemund had with his half-brother, given his own sire had been born out of wedlock. Also there was much that did not require to be said, for these were men who lived in a world where much changed decade by decade and no lord was ever secure. If his sword could not hold them another would take his possessions. Robert's father William had come to the title aged just seven, the grandfather after who he was named having died on this very pilgrimage, and he had been required to fight hard to keep his inheritance, many times coming close to losing his life and his duchy.

Bohemund, having been born in Italy, knew from whence the family came and he saw it as a loss to have no actual knowledge of the Contentin, given he felt an umbilical connection to his heritage. To satisfy his curiosity Robert, who had been in those parts, was happy to describe the sea-battered shore and the rainwashed landscape of small fields and parlous demesnes of the region, perhaps the poorest part of his domains, yet fertile nevertheless. It had to be – Bohemund's grandfather on one such property had brought up a family of twelve sons and two daughters.

'They still talk of old Tancred in those parts,' Robert chuckled, with a nod to his young namesake, 'for he led those who saw themselves as his superiors a merry dance.'

'I was told he was minded to give them a drubbing from time to time.'

'That too.'

Over days they went from being guarded to find such commonality as to become, if not friends, at ease in each other's company. They had much in common being Normans and little to separate them that was not geographical, added to which they had both been sired by men not only potent but remarkable. Robert was as curious about the *Guiscard* as was Bohemund about the Conqueror and each of those had tales attached to their names that would keep talk going for a month.

'God forbid they should ever have met,' Robert said, with an accompanying laugh, his eyes raised to the clear, blue afternoon sky – it had been that way the whole day's march. 'Something tells me they would not have loved one another.'

'I cannot see my father bending the knee, even if he ever insisted that he was a true Norman.'

'And you, Bohemund, are you that too?'

'On both sides, Duke Robert, but I am as proud as my father when it comes to acknowledging a superior.'

'Never fear, Count Bohemund, I am not inclined to put such a thing to the test.'

A stirring to the rear of the host took their attention and both knew it came from the herd of spare mounts, these their shared property, part of their obligation as leaders. It was their responsibility, if one of their knights lost a horse in battle, to provide him with a replacement mount and right now the drovers in control of them were experiencing difficulties, which meant that over the horizon ahead and not very far there was another flowing river, something an equine could sense well before a human.

'A good place to camp,' Robert suggested, the sun being well past the meridian.

As a courtesy, Tacitus was consulted, Bohemund using Greek, and he grunted his agreement.

Almost as soon as they crossed the river next morning a horseman of the screening cavalry, sent out predawn, came back to report the presence of Turks, though not in any great numbers. There was no need to enquire what possibly lay behind that sighting. But these knights would carry out the task they were given and properly, so if the host was threatened they would be forewarned. This did not seem to qualify as that; it did, however, have to be thought on and, given the triple leadership, discussed.

'A raiding party,' Robert suggested, 'come to steal from our column.'

His interpreter dragged, 'Most likely,' out of Tacitus and Bohemund agreed.

Looking back to where they had crossed the river, less than half the host was on this side, the remainder patiently crowding the opposite bank, while ahead of them was open plain, a dangerous place to be, given there was no way to create a protected flank. Against that, stopping to fully assess any risk seemed an overreaction. Yet if there were raiders in the vicinity, this host and what they carried had to be the objective, which meant lightning raids, probably by archers, which would need to be rebuffed.

Another quick consultation with Tacitus followed and then orders went out for the knights, hitherto travelling in leather jerkins, some in only linen given that it was a hot day, to don their mail and Bohemund and Robert did likewise. If it would be uncomfortable it would render the lances near impervious to arrows, and they were also told to

212

spread out through the entire host in order to provide protection.

'Do we alert Adémar?' Robert asked, then answered his own question. 'We would need more of a threat, I think.'

'We should move on?' Bohemund said, looking at his co-leader and receiving a nod, then he gave orders to the scout, who was Apulian. 'Go back to your task.'

Nothing occurred that day or the next to disturb their progress and no alarms came from the cavalry screen so spirits remained high; they would reach the old Byzantine camp before the sun went down if the march went well, the only obstacles the endless small rivers, which imposed a check as everyone and every beast took in water. The animals did this downriver of the humans and strict instructions were relayed to the non-combatants – the soldiers knew better – not to use the river as a latrine. For that, on what they hoped was the last crossing, there was a marsh nearby.

Having just resumed progress, the trio of leaders saw the cavalry screen coming in at full gallop, which could only mean one thing: real danger threatened. Ahead of them, bounded by sloping hills, there was a junction to two valleys, seemingly empty when they first looked. They did not long stay that way; with what seemed no more than a blink the ground was filled with mounted men who could only be Turks and more began to cover the hillsides, which meant the leading elements were not alone in catching sight of this mass of warriors.

News rippled back through the host and when it came to the attention of the pilgrims it caused panic, understandable from people who feared another massacre like the one visited upon the People's Crusade, and if they needed reminding, there, at the head of their multitude, was Peter the Hermit. Men, women, children and their animals began to mill about in confusion, this while Bohemund and Robert watched as what

had been a substantial force before them became a multitude and one coming on without anyone seeming to be in control, seeking, by sheer speed and pressure to crush what lay before them.

No great genius was required to calculate they were outnumbered; Kilij Arslan had made peace with someone, probably the Danishmends, yet it mattered not who they were, more important was the sheer size of their combined force. Tacitus immediately swung his mount and made his way back to take command of his own men, who were somewhere in the midst of the host. Robert and Bohemund simultaneously grabbed their weapons, lances and swords from their packhorses, jammed on their helmets, then called for the knights nearest to them, who were doing the same, to form up.

This would have to be done at the canter and on the wrong kind of horse; there was too little time to do anything else, certainly not enough to saddle the destriers, nor was there any opportunity to issue orders regarding the rest of their forces. They would have to hope that those in authority behind them had the sense to do what was necessary, which was to stop the pilgrims panicking and fleeing, for that could only end in death, while simultaneously setting up some kind of defence.

To do that would take time and the only way to buy that was to impose a check on these Turks charging towards them. Lances couched they advanced, the line straightening with each spread of their horses hooves. Across the floor of the valley the line extended, perhaps a hundred men in number, who knew they might well be riding to their death, there being space to pass round on each flank. It swelled Bohemund's Norman heart to be amongst them and he looked to Robert Duke of Normandy, thinking how fine it was to be going into battle alongside such a man and such a title.

CHAPTER SIXTEEN

In battle the Normans never charged, for to do so was to lose cohesion, but this was not a contest of their choosing and the everyday riding horses they were on lacked the steadiness of destriers. Also they were up against another mounted force, not that which they more often faced, a line of shields in the hands of men fighting on foot. What gave their attack the power it unleashed were the opponents against whom they came up; lightly armed Turks, carrying bows, on fleet but small ponies untrained to withstand a galloping herd of bigger horses bearing down on them.

The enemy was thrown into confusion as much by the need to seek to control their mounts as by what hit them, a not quite perfect line of sharp pointed lances in the hands of men who knew how to wield them. Few missed their first target, none their second, the Turks lifted bodily into thin air off their saddles, where they would have remained if the knight that had pinioned them had held on to the shaft. The lances were quickly abandoned, replaced by swishing broadswords and eviscerating axes as each Norman took on every enemy within the arc of his range.

Trying to fight back, the Turks were once more up against a men of vastly superior body weight, with skills honed over years and the protection provided to the knights by chain mail. An arrow fired point-blank might have the strength to penetrate but it had to strike true; the slightest deviation and it would fly harmlessly off the tight metal ringlets, while those who had given up bows for swords had nothing like the reach of their Norman counterparts. What they did have was numbers.

In the midst of what was now a disordered melee were Robert and Bohemund, each with the standard bearer and in the company of their familia knights so that they fought as a compact body. One task for those body knights was to allow time for their liege lords to break off fighting for a short time and assess the state of the battle, which both men did, and it came as no surprise that without any communication they reached the same conclusion.

Too many Turks had got round their flanks and now filled the plain between them and the milling host. The time was coming when that number would be insurmountable and might cut them off. In truth, they had achieved what they set out to do, no more than check the initial Turkish storm. Swords waving in the air and without a horn to blow it came down to shouted commands to attend to their leader's banner and come together in two groups to fight their way out as a tightly bound unit and rejoin the main body.

That took time; the screaming mass of Turks, at least ten to their one, were determined they should not pass and they might have succeeded against lesser quality commanders. On this field they were up against two men who were not only doughty fighters, even within their own kind, but knights who shared a knowledge of battlefield tactics honed by their forbears over two centuries, both in their training manège and the field.

Little in the way of instruction was required to have their remaining knights adopt an arrow formation, their leaders, Bohemund and Duke Robert to the fore, their huge and heavy swords cutting a swathe through the Turks who got in their way, while on their flanks their companions sliced outwards to prise open a gap, leaving behind them a trail of broken and bleeding bodies as well as riderless ponies. It took time for this mass to thin, which revealed that a large number of the enemy had got in amongst the main pilgrim host and were engaged in fruitful slaughter.

Tancred had ridden forward as soon as the alarm was sounded; from his position at the rear he could see little or nothing, but was soon made well aware that panic was going to make what needed to be done a difficult task. It was not just the unarmed pilgrims who had lost all sense of order, some of the *milites* had allowed the surprise appearance of the Turks to crush their discipline, which was never of the highest order, a part of one body actually seeking to run for the hills, madness given they were full of the enemy, only to be cut down and butchered.

'Robert,' he called to his cousin, by his side. 'Take a conroy and ride hard for Adémar and Raymond. Tell them what we face and to come at once.'

That did not have to be spelt out; if they could not get some unity of purpose they risked being wiped out. As Robert rode off, aware he would have to fight his way clear, Tancred took command of every man he could muster and ordered most of them to form an outer rim on the edge of the host and drive everyone, fighters and pilgrims, towards the marshland that lined the nearby river.

'And do not be gentle. Kill anyone who disputes with you too hard.'

Now that Tancred could see ahead, one question was paramount: should he support his uncle and Duke Robert and gather a force to attack the Turks that ringed them, cutting a path for them to escape, for as of now, Duke Robert's senior captains having ridden into battle with him, he seemed to have the power of decision for the whole body? Momentarily, looking around him at what was a teeming half-fleeing rabble, he doubted if he had what was needed to exercise command, but that soon evaporated; he had men around him waiting to be told what to do.

'Form up on the edge of that marsh, seek to let through our people and stop the Turks and do not just let them charge you. Use your brains, get our *milities* into some form of defensive line and anyone of you that can take command of them and get them into fighting formation do so.'

The cry from dozens of throats had him spinning round, to see both Bohemund and Robert, in twin phalanxes, emerge from the dense mass of the Turkish forces, still fighting, still slaying but with more open and less crowded plain across which they could escape, intent on getting their mounts to the gallop. The cry 'to me' was hardly necessary as Tancred spurred his mount; there was not a mailed knight close to him who did not know what to do and as a body they rode into the rear of the Turks still trying to impede their confrères and scattered them like chaff. They then formed a body with the two Norman leaders to make good the escape of the whole, a breathless exchange following as he tried to impart to Bohemund what orders he had issued.

In their part of the field there was a temporary lull; a check had been placed on Kilij Arslan's initial attack and even a force as fluid as the Turks needed to regroup before they could recommence their assault. Yet it was clear that a large section of the enemy, those that had got round the flanks, were not only doing their killing in the open, they were busy penetrating the marsh and slaughtering the innocents there too.

'We must clear them out of there,' Robert shouted and without waiting led his men off to carry out that task.

All around him Bohemund could see knots of knights, it mattered not from which body, trying to herd pilgrims and foot soldiers in the right direction, while at the same time attempting to keep at bay the Turks seeking to break through to carry out a massacre. What aided their cause was stupidity brought on by sheer terror, men and women bringing on certain death because they knew they faced a possible one, breaking out into the open and seeking to flee, which drew off some of the Turkish strength who saw and pursued an easy kill.

All over the plain the ground was dotted with bodies and not just human, for the infidels were just as quick to cut down an ass as the pilgrim who had sought to get clear on its back. Even less cheering were the cadavers in the leather jerkins of the Apulian *milities* who seemed to have abandoned, in their flight, their swords and shields, leaving them utterly defenceless, as if being away from the collective was not dangerous enough.

Less heartening still were the hordes of the enemy now crowded on the nearby hills, a seething mass in numbers impossible to calculate, but certainly too numerous to take on in open battle within the area that they had chosen as the best place for them to fight. Looking behind them he could see Turks driving off the spare horses, yet more herding anything edible, oxen, sheep and goats, towards their camp.

Viewing such a depressing panorama of loss and death and problems to come took only seconds, and knowing Robert of Normandy was right Bohemund set off, not to aid him in clearing the marsh, Robert had enough men with him to achieve that, but to do what must come next, mount a form of defence that could withstand what was coming, and a clue was given as he felt his horse struggle to get its hooves out of the soft marsh ground.

Bohemund dismounted and ordered those that could hear him to do likewise, a command that rippled down the line as horses were gathered and tethered close by, the knights then forming a line on command. Behind him, yet at a distance, he could hear the screams of victims as the Turks still in the marsh cut down anyone who crossed their path, that mixed with the wailing of those wounded but not killed, added to the many who expected to be. Just in view also were Robert's avenging knights, taking on the enemy in a myriad of single combats that, if no more infidels got through, would secure the rear.

Had the Turks regrouped quickly it might have presaged disaster but that attack he and Robert had mounted did just enough to require them to assess their next move and organise their men to carry it out. Well out on the plain he could hear horns blowing and the odd trumpet as Arslan and his fellow leaders sought to get their milling masses of men into place for a concerted assault.

Fortunately, the captains who had control of the *milities* had got them into some form of order. They were on their way back to being a fighting force and despite the mayhem still going on in their rear Bohemund ordered them back, deeper into the marsh, until their feet began to sink in the soft earth above their ankles, his knights and those of Robert's who were not with him taking up station just in front, with a belt of marshy ground to their fore that would slow any charge by the Turkish cavalry, though nothing could be done to create enough of a buffer to render useless their arrows. There he had his standard driven into the ground; as long as that stood so did he.

Slowly, and it seemed an age, the killing diminished inside the depths of the marsh and soon Bohemund was joined by a dismounted Robert who never, even by a look, questioned the decisions he had made; in fact he made no comment on them at all, which told his confrère he would have come to the same conclusion. Robert took station close enough to stay in touch, where he too had his standard raised to flutter in a slight breeze, both banners an indication of just how personal was leadership.

There they would stay; they were up against a foe they would struggle too hard to beat in open mounted fighting and even if successful the bill would be disastrous in the number of casualties they would suffer; best to stand on the defensive and let the Turks break themselves in seeking to rupture their line, added to which they had another force, one greater in numbers, coming their way and quickly if they could be alerted to the danger.

Even standing still in the heat of what was now full day, clad in mail and wearing a metal helmet, could render a fighter near to useless and permission was passed along to remove the latter when not actually under attack. Someone had the sense to get the womenfolk coming round with water to assuage their thirst, the priests likewise, and they added their blessings to the skins they carried, while reminding the fighters of what awaited them should the Lord see fit to take them into his bosom.

'Where is Tacitus?' Bohemund demanded, searching the nearby marsh for any sign of him.

Robert nearly sighed. 'He has formed up his Byzantines right in the deepest part of the marsh in a ring defence.'

'We need him here.'

'You can try, Bohemund, but I think he is determined that we should take any wounds coming our way.'

'While he will offer to surrender if we fail and promise gold, and perhaps even the return of Nicaea, for his release.'

'You cannot think him that low?'

'When we have fought off these Turks, Robert, I will tell you of Byzantium and why it is never safe to repose trust in any of them.'

That got a shake of the head; what was being said clearly posited a notion too difficult for Robert to comprehend, even if he was no stranger to treachery.

The men who would control the sections of the now formed line were called together and quickly, given what was happening out on the plain did not appear to provide much time. The instructions, imparted by both leaders in combination, were plain. Hold your ground; do not advance whatever the prospects appear to promise. Let the Turks attack over the soggy ground before you that will dent the force of their assault. All, *milites* and knights, use your shields to provide protection from arrows. Knots of reserves were created; if a man fell they were to fill the gap.

'They are coming!' Tancred cried.

There was no need to say 'to your places'; each man crossed himself as, before them, with screams audible even at such a distance, the Turks were moving.

* * *

Robert of Salerno had halted briefly as soon as he was sure he and his conroy were clear of danger and were not being pursued, but the thinking of what to do next had been undertaken mounted. At a best guess the host under Adémar, Raymond and de Bouillon was a day's march to the north, but that was a distance for the mass, including pilgrims – they were moving as slowly as had Robert and Bohemund.

The distance for mounted and hard-riding knights was hours not a day, and it was a requirement that horses be pushed to the limit if need be and that had to begin now. Hard by a narrow defile he ordered half his men to seek shelter in there and stay out of sight if they valued their lives. For the rest they would ride and lead a spare horse till the point where the loaded mount became winded. That would then be switched for the fresher horse so that speed could be maintained.

Riding flat out, Robert and his half conroy had the advantage of the vast open spaces and cultivated ground, which they stuck to, that being flat, easy on the horses' hooves and free from impediments like rocks and sudden dips, or worse, holes in the ground made by burrowing vermin. As they passed those working in their fields they were cursed for the damage they caused but paid them no heed, not least because these were the same peasants who the previous day had charged them outrageously for what they sold to those who had no choice but to buy.

It took less time to make contact than even Robert anticipated, for they encountered the forward screen Raymond and his confrères had set out as protection, and he demanded their mounts to continue, while warning them to stay on the alert. Like Bohemund and Robert, the other leaders were out front, and seeing the riders coming on furiously they deduced the same message.

If Robert's new horse was breathing heavily so was he, and it took time for him to summon up the breath to explain what had happened, yet he was unable to answer the one question paramount in the council's mind: how were the Normans dealing with the Turkish attack and could they hold?

Alexius had given the Crusaders several old Roman maps of their route and no empire had ever been better served by its surveyors, so Robert was able to point out the field of battle in detail and every one of the Crusade leaders could see the salient features of the surrounding country and the possible avenues from which to attack. While orders rang out to get the majority of the mounted fighting men ready for an immediate move, the commanders of the foot-bound levies were instructed to set up a defensible camp into which they could herd the human and animal flotsam that was their tail, while more knights were instructed to throw out a screen to protect it.

Keen as they were to move, these were no tyro generals and that demanded a certain amount of deliberation. To just dash off and seek to engage the Turks might relieve the Normans, but the sight of such a mighty mounted force approaching would drive Kilij Arslan off, and if that would solve a problem it would not provide an ultimate solution, for it was the view of Raymond of Toulouse and Godfrey de Bouillon that the Turk had given them a chance to destroy him.

'I say we move out as a body but that a strong party of scouts be sent ahead to tell how our brothers are faring. If they are so pressed we must attack at once, so be it, but if they are holding them we can manoeuvre to get round Kilij's forces and annihilate them.'

'Which means we will no more be troubled by them,' Godfrey added unnecessarily.

'Robert of Salerno, you must lead that scouting force.' That got for Raymond a weary response from a tired man, but there was no doubt it was a mission he was keen to accept – he had blood relatives and friends in that field near Dorylaeum. 'We will be close on your heels, my title upon it.'

Hours had passed with repeated assaults on the Norman line, the Turks hurling themselves forward on horseback, releasing huge salvoes of arrows – and they did maim and kill – but too few to rupture the defence. Denied fortune by such tactics they tried a naked cavalry charge that got so bogged down they were hardly moving when they reached the Norman line. If they then expected a move out to cut them down they were frustrated; not a single defender took a step. An assault on foot followed and now it was men struggling in muddy and churned-up ground in what came down to single combat in which Norman discipline and steadfastness was set against Seljuk fury.

Constantly, eyes looked to the banners of Bohemund and Robert of Normandy, both red and both proudly flying in defiance of anything the infidel could throw at them, occasionally left behind by the men they identified as they rushed to a part of the line that seemed threatened to shore it up by personal endeavour. There they took place alongside their men to keep their line intact, doing the kind of slaughter that raised the spirits of everyone engaged. At other points of crisis the *milities* were led forward by their captains to impose a check on a dent in the line, but as soon as that was restored they were halted and ordered to withdraw, knights reforming to present to their enemies the extent of their failure.

Appraised that their confrères were holding, Raymond and Godfrey planned their attack – Vermandois was barely consulted, which irritated Walo of Chaumont. Adémar, surprisingly, put himself forward to lead a strong band of knights around the Turkish flank, ready to come on when the main attack was launched, for it was becoming plain that that would need to be a charge across the open country. No time was wasted in creating tight formations for as soon as they came into view the horns blew for the gallop.

The mere sight of these new foes checked the Turks and panic rippled down their ranks; the potency of the attack on the marsh line began to diminish and soon the defenders had sight of why, a horde of Frankish horsemen riding at speed in their own cloud of dust. Sensing that their enemies were seeking to go onto the defensive both Robert and Bohemund ordered the horses brought forward, their knights to mount, and, as Raymond and Godfrey at the head of thousands of lances crossed the river to their right, they broke out from the marsh to join in the attack.

Kilij Arslan could not stand against the combined might of the Crusader armies and he knew it, but he was determined to mount a defence that would allow him to withdraw in good order. At that point Bishop Adémar, in a breastplate and helmet he had surreptitiously purchased in Constantinople, appeared on his flanking hill leading five hundred more knights who, if they got across the Turkish rear, would spell doom.

The whole mass of Turks broke and ran, but not before the Crusaders got in amongst them and now it was their turn to engage in slaughter. No quarter was given, this was the People's Crusade in reverse, and nor was the pursuit ended when the Turks had quit the field. They were chased down the valleys and over the crest of the surrounding hills and far beyond that, the lead elements eventually seeing ahead of them the tented encampment from which they had sprung.

That put a check on the pursuit in the main, but not the flight. The Turks kept moving east and the leaders who had come to the aid of Kilij Arslan – Hasan of Cappadocia and Gabid ibn Danishmend it later transpired – abandoned their gold and silver, as well as some of their wives and all of their servants, horses, oxen, asses, camels and sheep. This provided, so rich were they, a proper set of feasts as well as sufficient treasure to make every fighting man feel as if, even without salvation, coming east had been worthwhile. Added to that, the Crusaders gathered back in what had been stolen from them.

Yet there was a bitter aftermath as they returned to the field of conflict, carpeted with the dead, too many of them Christians and too high a proportion of those fighting men. If panic had cost many of the pilgrims their lives, seeking to get them to safety had exposed knights to the need to fight alone against insuperable odds and it was a testimony to their prowess that not one lay alone; every Norman was surrounded by the corpses of those he had slain before succumbing himself.

Then there were the forces of Byzantium, who had taken no part. They had emerged from the swamp, and faced with men they had failed to aid they demonstrated no shame whatsoever, which had the Franks and Normans treating them as pariahs. Tacitus, insufferably, behaved as if nothing untoward had occurred and still expected to be consulted before any course of action was agreed.

It took three days to clear the battlefield and when they departed it was dotted with close to four thousand crosses, many without names for the Turks had so mutilated them as to render them unrecognisable even to their friends. A special Mass was said for their souls and a plea made to the Almighty to cosset the knights who had fallen, for they were truly soldiers of Christ.

The bodies of the slain Turks, which ran from the field of battle to and well beyond their one-time encampment, were left to the carrion, but even as they left them to rot, it was held that they had been a more than worthy foe.

CHAPTER SEVENTEEN

After regrouping at Dorylaeum they had to continue their march, only this time it was agreed as much of a composite body as the terrain imposed on them, without knowing what that meant in practice. Kilij Arslan was not done with the men who had invaded his lands; defeated he might be but the wily Sultan of Rüm adopted a policy of scorching the earth, denying them food and water in what was going to be, at the height of summer, an arid landscape in any case. Crops were destroyed by burning or being dug up and left to rot in the sun; peasants who might have food hidden were driven away or slaughtered to ensure their cache would not be tortured out of them by Westerners who would soon be reduced to starving.

In the heat of high summer the rivers were turning to trickles and eventually that would cease all together as they got further from the mountains which had already, in any case, given up what they had. For centuries the populace had lived with this and if they had not prospered they had learnt to survive. Cisterns had been dug below ground to store the precious liquid when it was plentiful so their fields could be watered and kept fertile and they could keep themselves alive. These the Turks destroyed, and if there was a proper artesian well an oxen killed and its carcass tipped down into the base was enough to poison that.

The temperature rose to a point that even those accustomed to the heat of Southern Italy could not bear. Metal was impossible to touch for humans, and the animals, who required huge quantities of water even in normal climes, had to have twice as much and even that was not enough in a country where there was little or no shade. This meant marching at night if no clouds obscured the moon and the stars, and continuing only in the short relatively cool period of the morning, which severely cut into the time it took to cover ground. In the midst of the day every piece of cloth was pressed into service as part awning, part windbreak, for that seemed to burn more than the air.

The army marched ahead and thus got what little sustenance could be found, though that was close to nothing; the pilgrims brought up the rear, eating the dust of those who had preceded them, suffering a degree of thirst that within days saw the weakest collapse. Since no one else had the strength to aid them – they had their own concerns about survival – that was a death sentence. Pope Urban's Crusade left in its wake a terrain dotted with desiccated corpses that a blazing sun would turn to bones within days and not all were human; many an animal lay down to die as well, while in amongst them were items looted from Turkish tents that, however valuable, had no more purpose.

The fighting men suffered too, if not to the same extent and Adémar sought to institute a system by which each contingent took the lead from one day to the next so that if anything edible or thirst-quenching was found it was equally shared, yet it could not and did not suffice and those whose spirit was weak, and most certainly those bearing wounds from the recent battle, began to die.

More worrying was the effect on the animals, most especially their horses for a force that fought mounted. With a landscape bereft of pasture it was a lack of food as well as water that began to decimate them; the host could not carry enough oats to feed them, and in any case dry oats were as useless as none. The flesh began to fall off them, their rib bones becoming so prominent that to image them as actual skeletons was easy. They were certainly in no condition to carry a knight on their back; they moved heads drooped, leg movements strained and their hides, which could not be shaved for fear of the sun, moulting in patches. The only saving grace was they would not be required to carry their burdens; if the Crusaders could not fight across a land like this neither could the Turks.

Occasionally the sky would darken on the horizon and hearts would lift; they soon learnt these did not bear rain but swirling clouds of stinging sand that choked even noses and mouths, well covered as everyone was, Tacitus especially, given his golden nose would get so hot in the sunshine as to burn his skin; not that he elicited much sympathy after his behaviour at what was now being called the Battle of Dorylaeum; he and his Byzantine levies were close to being despised, yet they had to be tolerated if the princes wanted any future aid from Constantinople.

After only days in what was a desert, how distant the glory of that victory seemed, and in the week that followed it became a hollow mockery, for if good Christians could beat the infidel in battle they could not conquer nature. Hundreds of pilgrims and soldiers died every day so it was a much diminished force upon which the relenting sun rose each morning, to be cursed as the immediate heat it produced hit red-raw flesh.

Now the horses were literally falling over where they stood and that included many who had struggled to their feet to move on in the first place. No packhorse could now bear a load, and the oxen, with a greater store of fat about their bodies, were pressed into service. The Normans took to excessive care of their destriers, for if other mounts might be replaced they could not, but the losses there too were enormous. Men, who had only prickly plants to sustain them – and they had to be beaten to a pulp to even consider consuming them – had little to spare, even sympathy, for the animals that had carried them into and kept them alive in battle.

'This is a battle no general can win.'

These words Bohemund croaked as the first grey daylight showed another flat and endless plain; they had marched half the night before exhaustion made a rest inevitable. That vista would soon lose all shape as the heat of the sun created what looked like a rippling pool of water between land and sky, a sight to drive some men so mad they rushed towards it, sapping what little energy and spirit they possessed.

'This is God's fight, not ours.'

'If we do not find water soon . . .' Tancred started to say, only to stop, not wishing to state the obvious conclusion.

'Then travellers will come this way and mark their route by our bones and they will say that in this desert our sins caught up with us. We were not men seeking purity but the bearers of our own curse.'

'We may be in hell already,' came the reply, as the orange rim of that massive blazing orb hit the horizon to rise in what seemed a blink to its full size.

'Rouse up our men, Tancred, we must make what progress we can before it gets too hot.'

That would amount to no more than an hour and before movement all the threads and strings which had been strung out to catch the dew had to be sucked dry, that being the only liquid these men would have until the next darkness. On this day the Apulian Normans had the lead, and as they moved, anything that looked as if it might be edible was scrabbled from the rock-hard earth, the spines of the only plants that could survive the daytime heat pulled off and the body broken up to be stuck on parched tongues in the hope of a modicum of fluid from that or the saliva it produced.

Leading his destrier, its head in constant need of being hauled up lest it expire from loss of spirit, Bohemund knew that his riding mount was not going to get through the day nor, perhaps, his fighting horse too. Then slowly the destrier's head came up and instead of dead eyes there was something in them, a sort of dull gleam. From plodding at his heels it sought to first come abreast of him and then get ahead in a sort of staggering gait. Looking round he saw the other equines to be less weary and that seemed to apply to all the lead mounts.

'Take firm grip on the horses,' he yelled and painfully, 'they sense water.'

If the command was the correct one – horses would drink themselves to death in their present state and men too if left alone – it hardly merited such precautions; neither man nor beast had a run or a gallop in them, whatever was over the horizon. All that could be managed was an increased stumble that did not even amount to a trot. It was testimony to the acute survival sense of the horses and how parched they were that it took what seemed an age before the ground began to green and the wide depression of a proper river became visible, although even in that the actual flow was right at the bottom and slow.

But it was water and the Apulians had got there first, both knights and *milities*; men and horses soon had their heads sunk below the level to drink deep after what seemed an eternity of want. How many did Bohemund and his fellow captains kick? He did not know. How many mounts did he drag back from the riverbank? That too was a mystery, but fight to maintain order they did. At least his men were sated enough to listen when he ordered them to move upstream and make way for those who would follow, in order that the sunken stone-filled bed of the river did not become a scene of men killing each other to get the vital sustenance.

From the position where he stopped his Apulians and looked back, Bohemund saw a scene biblical in its proportions, thousands of figures streaming across the desert towards that life-saving fluid and what he feared came to pass, the only one not moving, the easily recognisable figure of Peter the Hermit, arms open wide, crook in one hand, clearly thanking God for deliverance.

He would have been better to come on and impose some order. So crowded was the riverbank with both animals and men, and so far did those drinking from it extend, that those at the rear could not get to it. They began to fight out of desperation and if it started with fists it was not long before he espied the first flashing swords reflecting the harsh sun, while still yet to arrive were the poor, benighted and much-diminished pilgrims.

If there was a death toll for the crossing of that destroyed land there was another for the leaving of it. Desperate oxen had trodden many in their stampede to drink but the highest toll came from those who could not stop, people who drank so much and so quickly it killed them. They lay among the horses and beasts of burden that no one had bothered to seek to save from themselves. It took all day to restore some form of order, but at least there was water to drink and pasture for those animals that survived. Not that there were many, and all the leaders knew that if battle were joined now it would have to be fought on foot.

If that river did not bring an end to a land scarcely habitable it at least marked a boundary to what was, in summer, an Anatolian desert, part induced by Turkish malice, but one that would have tried the host even if Kilij Arslan had not made it worse. He and his allies had retired east and the Crusade was now moving south; there was pasture, sparse but able to keep the mounts from expiring, watercourses, which if they ran as a trickle in the high summer heat, at least provided vital fluid enough for the army and the pilgrims to make progress at a more normal speed.

That improved when they came across a series of fertile valleys surrounded by high and heavily wooded hills in the country called Pisidia, a point at which they could stop and seek to recover their strength, given what Turks had governed it fled at their approach. That required food, which existed in abundance, as did pasture and oats for their remaining mounts, half of which had expired. Better still, there were horses to buy and the treasure taken from the Sultans after Dorylaeum was put to good use.

'A hunt,' Godfrey de Bouillon insisted, 'is just what we need to finally restore ourselves.'

'I do not recall you needing much restoration, brother,' Baldwin retorted, to the amusement of all gathered, which included Bohemund and Tancred. 'You had more fat than most to live off.'

'I lived off my faith in Christ, Baldwin, which you so lack.'

'That I will find when I get to Jerusalem.'

'You should pray more often, as I do.'

'True, you have more leather on your knees than I wear on my back.'

'So what do you say, Bohemund? We have good horses now, so let us test them and us. It is near a month we have spent here and I long for activity.'

'We must look to move on soon.'

'Let the weather cool further,' de Bouillon pleaded. 'I have had enough of being baked.'

'You'd make a fine pie, though we'd be stretched to find a big enough pot.'

Godfrey frowned at the general laughter, but even he had to be amused by Baldwin's jest and soon his barrel chest was shaking with good humour. He got that which he desired and if it seemed frivolous to some it was the stuff of a nobleman's life to hunt game in the forest, and here in Pisidia they were surrounded by dense greenery in which there were deer, wolves, wild boar and brown bear. Word spread and it seemed a good notion, a way to finally restore morale, if the whole Prince's Council took part; even the Bishop was keen.

'You have never hunted,' Vermandois called, 'till you have sought prey in the forest around Paris.'

'My Lord speaks nothing but the truth,' added Walo.

'I have heard of French hunting,' Robert of Normandy said quietly to Bohemund, sat astride his horse beside him. 'Beaters chase the prey towards the King, who has beside him the best archer, and when some creature comes into view both he and his monarch fire together, the

King's arrow barely aimed. The beast is brought down and all praise their liege lord as a true champion of the chase.'

'I sense you have no love for your neighbours, My Lord.' Tancred opined, for he was close enough to overhear.

'East and west, my friend, east and west.'

The appellation cheered Tancred up immensely; to be called 'friend' by the Duke of Normandy was an honour he deeply appreciated and it had been one bestowed on him since Dorylaeum. Added to that, the Duke and Bohemund had become close, his nephew seeing that in many ways the titular suzerain was being seduced into an alliance and he knew why. If Bohemund ever claimed the right to lead the Crusade he could only do so with allies already in place, and it was generally held that Robert did not want it for himself.

When the horns blew everyone began to move out, heading for the edge of the deep forest. A hunt on this scale was massive, hundreds of beaters being sent out with the riders to start running what prey lay in the woods towards the hunt, which would otherwise just move out of the way. This particular quest had its own added difficulties for there were no verderers in this part of the world, as existed in the forests of Northern Europe, men who were tasked to keep the area in good order, to clear the dead wood – some of that was taken by the locals but not in a planned way – to keep clear paths through which hunting parties could move without becoming separated, to get to the depths where the game would run for security, and to advise hunters of both hazards and places of opportunity. Indeed, so ill maintained were these forests that swords were often needed just to cut a path.

As the man who had initiated the whole affair Godfrey was well to the fore, and to those observing him he looked a bit like an animal himself, nose twitching as though he had senses as acute as the prey he sought to smell out. To left and right the beaters were thudding everything in their path and soon their efforts bore fruit as a herd of deer broke cover and, with blaring horns, the mounted nobles set off in pursuit only to find that manoeuvring though uncut undergrowth seriously hampered their efforts.

De Bouillon cast the first javelin and so powerful was his throw, even from what was too great a distance, he managed to graze the buttock of the stag at which he aimed. Baldwin, right with him, had more success, aiming for a plump doe as it sought to jump a bush but which fell sideways as his spear struck home. His brother, in frustration, had grabbed another javelin off one of his accompanying knights and sped after his stag, soon to be lost to sight by greenery. Baldwin dismounted, putting his doe out of her misery and about to tell those knights he had brought with him to load it onto a spare horse when a series of roars and screams rent the air.

Still mounted, Bohemund and Tancred crashed into the undergrowth, following the path taken by Godfrey though that was far from clear, heading towards the noise, which now seemed to be more roars than cries of human pain. As in all forests there were clearings and the one they burst into presented the sight they feared: Godfrey, covered in blood, trying to fend off with a sword held by an arm that appeared to be broken, a huge brown bear, and with his mount nowhere to be seen.

Their arrival distracted the bear who turned, blood dripping from its teeth, to face them and that, if it did not give either man pause, made their hearts beat at a different rate. If such a creature was fighting there must be cubs somewhere close, for they were generally given to avoiding humans. That meant this she-bear would fight to the death and they were formidable creatures when roused to protect their young.

Godfrey, now collapsed, lay as a heap on the ground near its spread legs, and Bohemund for one certainly hoped that if he was alive he would stay that way; if he raised his head one swipe of a massive paw would break his neck. Without a word Tancred had edged right while Bohemund trended left, but for all they were in a clearing the low undergrowth was still heavy, too much so for a horse to charge through at any pace, which would be needed to avoid being unhorsed. Added to that, the mounts that he and Tancred were on were not fighting horses and they would likely baulk at getting too close to a bear anyway.

As Godfrey stirred – he was badly mauled but not dead – that obliged Tancred to cast his lightweight spear, which hit the bear on one shoulder and caused it to stagger back. The sound it emitted was a mixture of pain and fury, and even if it was stunned and did not comprehend what had happened, the creature had enough sense to pull the javelin out of its body before starting to lope towards the man who had thrown it, and that was when Bohemund came on, out of the animal's eyeline.

Yet he could not be silent with all the breaking branches he smashed through and he saw the bear stiffen to stop and turn. He dropped his own javelin – it might wound but such a weapon would have to strike something vital to kill – whipped out his sword and forced his mount to keep going as it bucked to refuse. Rising in his stirrups, he was tall enough to utterly overawe an animal that may well never have seen a human before, especially one that stood taller than itself, which forced it to seek to claw his terrified horse.

The blade of the sword swung down, to only catch the creature's eyes a second before it cut in and down to the massive furred neck. It was testimony to the depth of that and the muscles and tendons it contained that even Bohemund could not cut through, but he did enough to stop it cold, a great fount of blood spurting out of the sliced open main artery. There was a feeble attempt then to claw at his legs, but not for long; after several ineffectual waves of its paws, the bear toppled over in its death throes.

'Stay mounted, Tancred, there may be another close by.'

Bohemund clambered off his horse, his sword held out at the ready, his eyes sweeping the edges of the clearing, those kept moving as he knelt close to Godfrey who was so obviously badly hurt. De Bouillon tried to move, as if seeking to get to his feet, and it took a carefully placed hand to restrain him, for it was impossible to tell the location of all his wounds.

'Still, friend, help is coming.'

A horde of men broke through to the clearing, Baldwin with them, and if they looked down on the Duke of Lower Lorraine with pity, his brother did not; if anything he had the gleam of avarice in his eyes.

'Fashion a stretcher,' Bohemund ordered, 'and get him back to the monks, but gently. Tancred, down you come and aid me in looking for the cubs. I fancy they will make gifts for members of the council.'

'There must be more bears, Uncle.' His nephew replied with obvious trepidation, still in his saddle.

'Yes, males, who will eat the cubs if we don't find them.'

Godfrey was in a bad way, with many broken bones and open wounds from sharp claws and it was obvious his recovery would take time. When it came to the next council and to the planning of the move south, Baldwin of Boulogne took his elder brother's place and immediately ruined what had been, if not always outright harmony, any sense of shared purpose. He demanded primacy in all things for

239

the Lotharingians, openly stating that the Normans had been too often indulged and that Raymond of Toulouse had assumed airs to which he was not entitled.

He gave offence to all present, and watching him make these claims Bohemund exchanged a look with Robert of Normandy, and if it was a questioning one the Count of Taranto was not entirely displeased, for a little grit in the machinery of governance might in the end lead to a resolution of the entire question of command.

'It is to be hoped,' Bishop Adémar said, wearily, as he summed up the meeting in a rare display of feeling, 'that your good brother comes back to full health soon.'

Baldwin was content; for the sake of concord, he had been assured he would enjoy the lead position when the host moved out and that he would be consulted as an equal in all future operations.

CHAPTER EIGHTEEN

The next objective was the Seljuk stronghold of Iconium and the host was so arranged that on the approach they could move to an immediate siege, a precaution that proved unnecessary; the garrison, hearing of their approach, had fled and the gates were wide open. A rumble of discontent surfaced when Tacitus, as per his imperial instructions, took possession of the city in the name of Alexius and depleted his own meagre force to provide a garrison. His demand that it be respected and that the Crusaders be limited in their entry, as they had been at Constantinople and Nicaea, was ignored, though it was agreed that such a stricture should apply to the non-combatant pilgrims, over whom it was hard to exercise control.

There was no desire on behalf of the princes to delay; the weather was still hot but was nothing like as debilitating as barren Anatolia so it was possible to progress, while it was a reasonable assumption that their enemy was on the run, afraid to meet them in battle and not prepared to contest every step they took. With that in mind the march was immediately resumed, aiming for the ancient Greek settlement of Heraclea in the hope that there too they would find the place abandoned.

They came upon that city mid morning and the fact that the gates were shut and the walls were manned came as an unpleasant shock, less so when on examination they proved to be in poor repair, with parts of the battlements crumbling so badly they were meat for an attack with ladders, which could be put together and employed in no time, as soon as the ritual offer to surrender was delivered.

'An immediate assault,' Raymond of Toulouse advised, and getting the nod from his confrères, looked to the interpreter to let Tacitus know what he proposed; that the Byzantine *Prōstratōr* agreed was a mere formality and he knew it, so the response was no more than a sharp nod. 'Let us give them no time to settle.'

'Losses,' said Vermandois, 'could be heavy, without we make proper preparations.'

'We will incur more by delay, Count Hugh,' Bohemund replied. 'I admit we may be guessing but the garrison cannot be large and nor can their spirits be high. This is not Nicaea.'

'I will lead it,' cried Baldwin of Boulogne, his pigeon chest puffing out. 'I demand the right.'

Bohemund's reply was cold; he was in no position to demand anything. 'You are perhaps too eager for glory.'

That was received with a scowl. 'I am eager to show that my Lotharingians can fight as well as any Norman.'

It was Robert of Normandy who replied to that. 'I do not recall anyone in this council ever suggesting they cannot.'

'Many things are implied in this council that do not require words to be used or truths to be openly stated.'

'Your brother never thought so.'

'I am not my brother.'

'So very true,' growled Raymond of Toulouse.

Adémar, seeing Baldwin swell up to deliver an angry retort, spoke quickly. 'Your zeal is commendable, my Lord of Boulogne'

There was flattery in that; Baldwin had been born in Boulogne, as had his brother Eustace, now acting as his supporter, but it was not a fief of his and it was not a title to which he could lay claim; the man who could, the Count of Flanders, was present supporting the Duke of Normandy. Still Baldwin seemed willing to accept it, though it did nothing to soften his belligerence.

'When the Count of Taranto talks of an immediate assault he no doubt means by his own men or those of the Duke, his boon companion. You pressed a plan at Nicaea that favoured your men in battle, and who chased after the command of the forward section of the host before Dorylaeum if not the Normans?'

'Chased?' Robert demanded, very obviously affronted, only to be stopped by Bohemund.

'I care not who carries out any assualt, Baldwin, only that it is done and quickly in the hope that those Turks manning the walls will sense their situation to be hopeless.'

After Bishop Adémar's elevation to a lordship, the absence of any use of a title from the Apulian leader was significant and there was no doubt de Bouillon's younger brother resented it. He shared some features with Godfrey, the ability to go puce in the face one of them.

'It has to be acknowledged you have ever assumed a lead in these affairs, you Normans.'

That comment by Vermandois, which was as stupid an interruption as he had ever uttered, got a hearty nod from red-faced Baldwin, flashes of anger from the two Norman nobles and a look of horror from Adémar; the French fool was about to lift the lid on a tub of worms.

'My Lords, does it matter who does God's work?'

'Attack the walls, Baldwin,' Bohemund spat, 'but do let my Lord of Normandy and I know if you need help in making the ladders.'

'Damn you—'

'Baldwin!' No one had ever heard Adémar raise his voice to a shout; that he did so now shocked the man he had called into silence. 'Apologise to all for your blasphemy.'

It took several seconds and was mumbled, but Adémar got what he required. As soon as Baldwin had left, the Bishop took some time and much circumlocution in reminding those left behind of the need for harmony and to guard against the sin of pride; it was Raymond who underlined the only way that could be achieved.

'Then you have two choices, My Lord Bishop. Still Baldwin's tongue or pray that by some miracle his brother recovers before this council meets again, for I tell you if he insults me in the way he did our Norman brothers I will not let it pass without recourse to arms.'

'That you cannot demand of him,' Vermandois said.

'While,' Raymond growled, 'Count Hugh would be as well to adopt in this pavilion the same degree of assistance to our cause he employs elsewhere.'

Vermandois looked as if he had been slapped and he had been so, metaphorically; his nostrils flared and he looked set to issue a challenge, but if it was on his lips it stayed there, while everyone else present suffered a degree of awkwardness and Walo, at his side as usual, put a retaining hand on his arm. To say he was shy was an exaggeration, but he was not one to be to the fore when battle joined and had conspicuously never sought to act alone and in advance, much to the annoyance of the men he led.

The knights of France could stand comparison with anyone in the host, but they did not look to him as a leader of men and nothing showed that more than the looks he got from those he had brought to Asia Minor. To a man, it was assumed, they would have preferred to be led by his far more capable, if somewhat irreligious, brother.

'It would be churlish to leave Baldwin to assault Heraclea on his own,' he hissed, 'and I know he will welcome *my* aid.'

When he had gone, the look Adémar gave the three remaining senior members of his council was telling. Sad, for if concord had been hard to achieve, it seemed it was going to be impossible to maintain, especially with Baldwin representing Lorraine. It did not help that Tacitus, obviously apprised of what was going on, made no attempt to stifle his chuckling and that got him a clerical glare.

'I will go to Duke Godfrey and pray with him that his recovery is speedy.'

The assault was launched late in the afternoon and carried on until the light faded. That it was not completely successful did not dispirit those who had climbed and fought on the hastily thrown together ladders, for they had done great damage, claiming to have killed more than they lost. This indicated the defenders lacked confidence and another assault was planned for the next day in which they would open onslaughts at several points where the walls were in disrepair, all contingents participating, this insisted upon by Adémar to avoid another confrontation.

Baldwin was full of himself, boasting of his own exploits and never once pausing to praise his brother's knights, so it was no surprise that the only person listening was Vermandois – none of the others could stand it – and even he became bored, or was it annoyed that the participation of the French, who had attacked as a second wave and enjoyed equal success, was not acknowledged?

Preparations were made overnight, ladders strung together, weapons once more sharpened and everyone stood to for a dawn attack. When the sun rose it was to light up a delegation of leading citizens come to discuss how Heraclea should be occupied; overnight the garrison had decamped and fled east.

Tacitus was quick to step forward and claim Heraclea for Alexius and for once, when Baldwin objected, he got some sympathy from the rest of the Crusade leaders, though they suspected with Godfrey making a steady if slow recovery he hankered after the town himself as a personal fief. The Byzantines had done nothing here and would have done nothing at Iconium if it had shown resistance, while Tacitus had, since Dorylaeum, been ignored when it came to tactics or movement.

Yet nothing could be done to gainsay his actions; the next major goal was Antioch and to take that would require military help from Alexius – supplies shipped by sea and a force of fighting men put there by whatever method he chose. To offend him was to jeopardise that assistance; no one had to be reminded of such a need, nor that, just like Nicaea, a stronghold like Antioch could not be bypassed and left in Turkish hands, so many a tongue was stilled and irritation suppressed.

The next dilemma to surface was what route to take? This time it was not fear of starvation or thirst that preyed on the minds of the gathering, but the constraints of two high passes on the direct route, the Cilician Gates, through which Alexander the Great had passed, and beyond Tarsus, the Belen Pass. To thread such a host through these defiles would take no less than a week and would present the Turks, should they be able to regroup, with a target too tempting to ignore and one that would require minimal force – both passes could be blocked by the enemy while forcing a passage might be costly.

Mention of Alexander had Tacitus speak for once, to remind the Crusaders that history related that he had led a small, compact army and no tail of pilgrims. If food and water were plentiful on either side of the Cilician Gates the former was not in the pass itself; indeed, what little information he possessed indicated nothing but a track surrounded by rock, added to which they might again come upon an area that had been sown with salt by the Turks, so supplies enough to keep everyone fed would have to be taken through as well, which increased the risks.

The other possible route took the host east through a long, wide and lush basin between two mountain ranges that led to Caesarea where it was possible that Alexius, informed of their route, might join them. Regardless of easy forage, moving east would also drive back the Turks. From Caesarea the route to Antioch was through the lands of the Christian Armenians, who had no love for their Turkish overlords, and treaties could be made that would protect the rear of the Crusade and give ample warning of any approaching threat.

Raymond, while agreeing to the basic notion, had one point that needed to be made.

'It would be of benefit to send an expedition to secure the passes on the shortest road. We do not know, when Alexius comes, what route he will take – perhaps through Caesarea – but he, if he knows they are secure, might elect for the sake of speed to pass through the Cilician Gates.'

'To know what the Turks have planned would also aid us,' Robert of Normandy suggested. 'Do they intend to do battle with us before we get close to Antioch or is their strategy to hold that and deny us any progress?'

'Then we should split the host again,' opined Baldwin, his manner, as usual, making it sound like a demand not an option.

'No!' Adémar was emphatic; indeed he had shown more inclination to be so since the man he had just denied had so nearly caused outright dissension. 'As a host complete the Turks fear us.'

'You know that, Bishop Adémar?'

'If I lack your military knowledge I do not lack for common sense. If they do not fear us why have they kept their distance?'

'We must not separate again,' insisted Bohemund. 'If we won at Dorylaeum, it was a battle that could have been lost. Yet I take my Lord of Toulouse's point—'

Baldwin, interrupting, was loud in his scoffing condemnation, and the arch look of wonder that went with it was to imply he had just heard from a dolt. 'How in the name of the Lord Almighty are we to achieve it if we do not separate?'

'It is a courtesy we extend to each other to let every member of the council speak without interruption.'

If Adémar's check hit home, Baldwin did a good job of disguising it; his shrug was elaborate as Bohemund continued. 'A small force, pushed through the passes to ensure they are clear, which once south of them should ensure they stay that way, would be a sound move.'

The alteration in Baldwin's demeanour was so swift it was risible: his face lost its normal confrontational expression to be replaced by one that displayed wonder; he was also smiling, which was rare, almost as much as the words that followed.

'I agree and I put myself forward to lead it.'

Amongst men who were acquisitive by nature it did not take long to understand why Baldwin was so eager. Tacitus and his Byzantines would march with the main host, so any knight in an independent role might have a chance to grab a great deal of booty that in other circumstances would be sequestered for the empire, and no doubt it occurred to some of the magnates to put their name forward; only the loss of dignity by being so openly avaricious stopped them.

'It would be best to send men from more than one contingent,' Robert of Normandy said finally, in a gambit that precluded any loss of face.

'I agree,' Adémar responded, swiftly, 'but I would not stand in the way of my Lord of Boulogne.' He might as well have said it would be good riddance, and to make sure all present understood, he added, in what was probably an error of judgement brought on by frustration, 'And who knows, when he rejoins it might be to find his brother the Duke whole again.'

'Then,' Robert added, 'since none of we actual leaders can separate, let Tancred be given joint command.'

'Not joint,' Bohemund cut in, causing Baldwin to suck lemons again. 'Let them lead their own contingents, Tancred his own Apulian knights, and Baldwin whosoever he chooses, but in numbers agreed.'

That was tossed back and forth over some time, Baldwin's figure of a thousand beaten down to two hundred, with the same number allocated to Tancred. All would be mounted – the aim was to move fast and avoid battle against foes, superior or not. Times were discussed and, notwithstanding they might be wildly out, it was agreed a date they would meet up on the road to Antioch, Baldwin and Tancred tasked to reconnoitre the famous old city and report the state of the defences.

'You guessed why Baldwin was so eager?' Bohemund asked, when he and his nephew were alone.

'Only a fool would not; but I am bound to ask, if Duke Robert had not put forward my name, would you?'

'Yes, but it had more weight coming from him. How would it have looked if I had made the suggestion?'

'Like you were favouring your own.' The younger man took a deep breath before he posed his next question. 'Am I free to act for myself?'

'You would be a dolt not to. Baldwin is scarcely charging off to aid the Crusade but to line his own purse.'

'And perhaps take possession of any towns he can capture?'

'That too.' That got a hand on the shoulder. 'I had always intended one day to let you seek for yourself. If it has come sooner than anticipated the time has arrived. Ride out in the morning with your lances . . .'

'And some of your own.'

'They esteem you as much as do I, Tancred, and would chafe to stay with the main body. But I was about to say that you are free to do as you wish and to take for yourself anything that presents itself. If it disturbs you to grab land and plunder while on Crusade, do not let it trouble your mind, for there is not a noble knight on the council who does not harbour the same thought.'

'You?'

'Unlike them I have not pledged my lands to fund this adventure, but Godfrey de Bouillon sold most of his to the Church, and Robert of Normandy pledged his duchy to his brother for a huge sum of money. Why?'

'Robert I do not know, but Godfrey is pious.'

'De Bouillon is more so than I, that I will grant you, and I have enough of an opinion of him, for I think him an honest man, to believe he will ask for what he wants rather than take it. He is a true Crusader.'

'Not a trait shared by all the family.'

'Have I said enough?' Bohemund asked, to get a nod in response. 'I have a gift for you.'

That got a raised eyebrow from his nephew, which was not assuaged when Bohemund called out and a dark-skinned fellow entered and bowed.

'This is Anastas and I found him in Heraclea. He is an Armenian Christian as well as a trader and he knows the route to Antioch well. I questioned him closely and he has knowledge of the fastest and safest shortcuts. It may be that with his help you can get ahead of Baldwin and secure anything worthwhile before he arrives.'

They rode out the next day, after a Mass to bless their endeavour, on the best horses that the host could provide, animals that had been fattened on the ample pasture of the lands around Heraclea, able to cover the standard cavalry distance, including walking, resting and watering their mounts, of ten leagues a day. For Tancred it was sheer joy; much as he loved his uncle, to be in a position of independent command, to never have to ask if any act he desired to undertake was approved or not, was something he had craved for ever since he had been Bohemund's squire. For his cousin of Salerno it promised as much; Tancred trusted him more than did Bohemund, and for the knights they led, the prospect of plunder was enough.

It was dawn on the next day when it emerged that another two hundred Lotharingian knights had departed the host, no doubt to join Baldwin, which prompted Robert to suggest to his fellow Norman that Bohemund might consider reinforcing Tancred, given that those men, in such a number, would not have departed had it not been prearranged.

'It would not be wise, Bohemund, to place any faith in Baldwin's intentions.'

CHAPTER NINETEEN

Anastas proved his worth before they ever got to the Cilician Gates; he knew a route from Heraclea that cut out a great arc in what had been the old Roman road, with ample supplies of both water and pasture, not that Tancred availed himself of too much of either; he had to assume that Baldwin would not tarry so nor could he, but he was reassured when passing through the high and cool trail that traversed the Gates that he was ahead of his rival, for no one passing in the other direction had seen a mounted host.

Two days of hard riding brought the Normans into Armenia and the ancient city of Tarsus and, from a nearby hill, the sight was arresting for here was a city as solid in its historic glory as anything these Apulian Normans had seen in Italy, a major trading centre of antiquity with the classical architecture that such places could boast; temples erected to the Greek Pantheon of Gods, arches and columns raised during Roman times as well as the ubiquitous amiphitheatre and baths.

Less encouraging were the stout walls and several towering minarets that spoke of a strong Turkish presence, which posed a problem for such a small force as to how to capture it. Beside a small river where their horses were now grazing, they donned their chain mail to indicate they were planning an instant assault.

As if determined to drive home the message that he was not anxious, the Turkish commander led his mounted archers out to engage in immediate battle, which if it surprised the Normans did not send them running, it not being a large force, nor one with an excess of discipline. Tancred's men formed their line with the speed for which they were noted and the Turks found themselves counter-charged by a formidable wall of close-linked lances, which confounded them and broke up what little formation they had.

Arrows inflicted more wounds on animals than mailed men, so near impervious they went through the Turks and scattered them so comprehensively that their leader called an immediate retreat and fled back through the main gate, which they managed to shut behind them before their enemy could get through.

'Which does not serve us as well as it might, cousin,' Robert of Salerno gasped as he and Tancred trotted out of range of the well-positioned archers; the point was obvious – they were still on the outside.

'Let us set up camp and put our minds to some idea of how we might overcome that.'

Robert laughed. 'How long does it take to build a Trojan horse?'

'The garrison is small, a few hundred perhaps, and the population of the city is Armenian and Christian, so whoever commands cannot count on help from the populace. We will light double the fires we need after dark. Let them think we will be stronger on the morrow than they have seen today. If they think the whole host is coming to Tarsus, it may make them think of escape more than resistance. Meanwhile, let us throw a cordon around the walls while I seek, with our guide Anastas, to sow fear into their hearts.'

Throughout the rest of the day, Tancred rode round the walls in the company of his guide, who told the Turks in their own tongue of what was coming their way, a mighty host so large they would not see the tail from their highest minaret by the time thousands of knights were encamped around their walls, led by men who would not stand to be held up by so puny a city. There would be no mercy – it would be a painful death or Christianity for them all – and he gave good reason why, recounting in gruesome detail how their fellows had treated the pilgrims of the People's Crusade.

'They had sense at Heraclea,' Ansatas called, for the tenth time. 'They knew what fate held in store and took to their heels in darkness, which My Lord Tancred might, if he feels merciful, allow.'

Tancred's task was to glower and wave his sword, which he did well and frequently.

'Look upon him, look at the length of those legs, the build of the upper body and the reach of his sword arm. Think on this as you try to sleep: can you fight a man of such size? And yet he is but a dwarf to those who follow so close on our heels and whose banners you will soon see on the horizon.'

If the Turks tossed and turned there was little sleep for the Normans that night; over the hours of darkness the number of lit fires had to be increased, but not all at once – it had to appear as if reinforcements were arriving piecemeal and setting up camp, foreign devils who did not fear to march in the night. Others, including Tancred and Robert of Salerno, were out in the groves that surrounded the city, their task to keep silent watch and see how many people fled Tarsus, for if the fighting men did not, the non-combatant Turks would.

Happily, soldiers were leaving too, many on horseback, evidenced by their jingling accoutrements and in such a way, singly or in pairs, that hinted at individual endeavour, not an organised evacuation; the garrison would be smaller at dawn than it had been previously, yet Tancred sensed the same bold fellow might be in charge.

The messenger came with the rising sun, an invitation to the leader of the invaders to parley with the governor of Tarsus under a flag of truce. Gathering up that which he hoped he would need, Tancred, in the company of Anastas and his own body of personal followers, made for the main gate, to be greeted from one of the main towers by a fellow who went by the name of Gökham Bey, he issuing a guarantee that if the Lord Knight would enter in peace and leave his lances outside, all things were possible.

'They might string you up and hang you over the walls,' Robert said.

'Go back, cousin,' Tancred replied, as the gates creaked open, 'and do as you should. Take command till I return.'

With that Tancred rode through into the dark, shaded interior of Tarsus, carrying his own banner, and on through narrow, crowded streets full of the curious and fearful Armenians, eventually to enter the Governor's Palace. This stood inside a citadel of a different age and looked to the Apulian very like those of Roman vintage he had seen at home, an impression enhanced on entry to find fountain-filled courtyards, with cooling ponds and many shading trees and mosaic-tiled floors with designs of animals and birds.

The interior was Turkish in its decoration and there waiting for him was Gökham Bey, sitting on a pile of cushions nearly the height of a chair. The formalities of titles had to be exchanged, before Anastas took to the interpreting task he had been brought along to perform: what were the terms by which Gökham would surrender Tarsus? The demands were not unusual; for a Western mind it was the time taken which stood out.

'Tell him yes, all his men may depart with their weapons, but I must insist they take a route due east.'

The Bey understood that; the Crusade did not want them heading south towards Antioch. The delicate matter of his own family and possessions took longer and Tancred, by guesswork, tried to discern what was personal and what was gubernatorial – the latter he was determined to extract as booty and his bargaining position was wives. Gökham had dozens and many children; Tancred was only allowing him his one main spouse, and pressing home that no Christian could so condone polygamy as to agree to him taking a harem.

The Governor understood perfectly what this infidel was about but like his race he saw the bargaining as an essential to the ultimate trade. Slowly he surrendered goods of value to Tancred in return for things of value to him, giving up the Tarsus treasury, full of tax monies levied from the town and surrounding countryside, as well as the artefacts that he had inherited with his office.

For that he extracted a promise that he could keep his personal belongings, wives included. He would be able to take them with him when he left and time had to be granted to him for that departure, he being a man with much to carry. Also he wished for the Crusaders to stay out of the city till he was ready to leave, so that his dignity would not be offended and there would be no chance of conflict between his soldiers and those of the Christian Lord.

'Finally,' Tancred said to Anastas, 'I have one more demand to make and it is a painless one to the Bey. I wish for my banner, not the crescent, to fly above the citadel from this day forth, so that all should know that I am the suzerain.'

That took another glass of sand to negotiate, but it was agreed both banners should fly side by side on one of the outer towers until the crescent was lowered, that a signal that Gökham Bey was ready to take his leave.

The cheers rose from the Norman-Apulian throats as they saw the de Hauteville banner flutter up the flagstaff, and that was doubled when their leader rode out to tell them that within a short time they would be masters of Tarsus and their individual wealth enhanced with it, so it was time to prepare a celebratory feast, the means to make it memorable to be provided by the Armenian citizens of a city of which they would soon occupy.

That fluttering banner, as well as the fiery roasting pits, was the sight that greeted Baldwin of Boulogne, who arrived as the sun was setting. Tancred was not alone in counting their increased numbers and now it was plain why he was so far behind them: he had been obliged to wait to rendezvous with these additional knights. The attitude of their leader was not altered by being too late for the capitulation – he had the same blustering overconfidence that Tancred had observed in the council pavilion, his assumption that being present he was so very obviously in command, an idea the young Apulian scotched right away.

'You do not lead here, Baldwin, but I have sent to Tarsus to request more food so your men may eat as well as my own.'

'We must do more than just eat, Tancred.'

'Must we?'

'There are serious matters to discuss.'

There was no doubt what Baldwin was driving at, the look in his eyes being almost palpable, and when he spoke it was proved a correct assumption – greed masked as a desire for equity, that any spoils from Tarsus should be divided equally between the Lotharingians and the Normans, including him and Baldwin.

'We are, after all, joint leaders.'

'But we are not jointly successful. Perhaps if you had not taken steps to enhance your numbers you might have got to Tarsus before me, and I have no doubt that you are not behind me in the skills to get to where I am now. But share? Am I to say to my men, who did fight for this place, that they must not only divide it with the Lorraine knights but in a proportion never envisaged when we set out?'

'That I will forgo,' Baldwin replied, his manner suggesting he was being overly generous.

'You and your men will receive what I see fit to give.'

'If you are generous they will not be offended.'

He meant himself, which riled Tancred. 'Then stand by to deal with their displeasure, Baldwin.'

'What can I say? Your banner flies above Tarsus, so let us eat and I will seek, like Gökham Bey, this Turk you tell me of, to soften your position by long negotiation.'

Tancred ameliorated that by inviting his senior captains as well as those of Baldwin to eat with them and by seating himself as far away from the man as possible. Yet he was aware of the looks he was receiving, coming from a set of eyes naked in their calculation. Baldwin had not given up the contest and he was obviously busy thinking of ways to counter the arguments that would follow the next day.

He was sharper than that; when the sun rose Tancred was called out to look at Tarsus and there he saw flying from the tower not his de Hauteville standard but that of Baldwin, bright yellow with a triangle of red balls. The entire force of Lotharingians was up and fully clad in mail, clearly ready for a fight, and when he rode to the gate it was kept closed against him on the orders of the same man, who eventually came to the tower to tell him what he already knew.

'I command now, as it should have been ceded to me when I arrived. Had you deemed it wise to share we might have both our banners flying. As it is, by your miserliness you have forfeited everything.'

'It is your avarice that has brought this about. I invite you to exit with your weapons, Baldwin, and we will see this settled between us.'

That got a slow shake of the head; Baldwin was a doughty fighter, but he was not about to put his gains in jeopardy by engaging in single combat, especially with a fellow with the build and prowess of his de Hauteville blood.

'What did you offer Gökham Bey?'

'More than did you, and do not enquire as to what. Enough to say that as part of our bargain I will soon rule in the citadel, not you or he.'

'Without your soldiers.'

'Look behind you, Tancred.'

It was tempting to ignore that but not possible. A glance over his shoulder let him see what he suspected. Baldwin's men were mounted and heading for the gate, all four hundred of them, while his own Normans watched in silent fury.

The laugh was loud and very false. 'You may wish to offer them the same choice of combat you gave to me, Norman. If you do not I suggest you stand aside.'

There was no option but to do so; he could not fight that number and nor would he have done even if he had with him his men and them armed. They were outnumbered two to one and by Franks who, if they were generally in equal numbers no match for the Normans, were too numerous to favour the usual outcome. Back at his own camp he stood for an age watching the flag flying about the city, with his men waiting for instructions on what to do.

'Break camp and get ready your mounts,' he said finally.

'You are giving in to him?' Robert of Salerno asked, softly.

'I am doing so because we have no choice, Robert. If Tarsus was impossible to capture by force of arms before, it has not improved with a Lotharingian garrison. No, Baldwin is slimy enough to have outwitted me . . .'

'Which is to your credit, cousin.'

'Is it, Robert? Legend will tell all that I was made to look a fool.'

'No, legend will say that Baldwin of Boulogne was a deceiver and a cheat, who put his own need to gain against his service to God and our purpose.'

Tancred responded with a bitter smile; Robert was no stranger to his own motives. 'Then let us hope they do not examine my conscience as well.'

Mounted, Tancred rode under the walls at the head of his men, calling out to the watching Baldwin. 'You bested me in this, but one day you will pay for what you did here with your blood.'

'Boast away, Norman,' Baldwin replied with a sneer, dropping the de Hauteville banner over the walls, clearly with a stone inside to drive it into the dust. 'I piss on you.'

Heading north-east Tancred knew that another possible capture lay ahead of him, the town of Adana, not as ancient or as prosperous as

Tarsus but a place that might fall to the same threats issued there; go now while you can or face the whole host of Christendom. Baldwin was left not in control of Tarsus as he had implied – he and his men had taken possession only of the two towers that fronted the main gate – but still in negotiation with Gökham Bey about the final terms of surrender, talks which he was called away from in late evening because a force of around one hundred and fifty lances had been seen approaching from the north, eventually identified as Normans. Their leader, Roger de Liverot, he addressed from the walls and quietly refused them either entry or food.

'Make camp as did we on arrival and perhaps on the morrow we will grant you the means to ride on in pursuit of Lord Tancred.'

'Night is near upon us and we have ridden hard to catch him. We are in need of proper rest.'

'Hard ground never troubled a Norman, though grumbling is a trait.'

That made the Lotharingians on the walls with him laugh out loud, for what had occurred in taking Tarsus had opened up the kind of rivalry that had hitherto been kept under control in the host. The responses from the Normans, blasphemously crude, got like in reaction, the whole episode watched by the remains of the Turkish garrison.

Eventually Roger led his men away to occupy the same riverside ground as had Tancred, his men grumbling and weary from having ridden hard to catch him. Hungry, if not thirsty, they tended to their mounts and began to settle down for the night, Roger eschewing the need for sentinels to keep watch on the grounds that there was no threat nearby about which they need be concerned.

He could not be expected to know the effect on the Turks of

the exchange of insults that had taken place earlier; if they had not understood much of what had been said the sense was obvious: these Crusaders were not as united as they had first appeared, and added to that there was no sign of this fabled host. There was one man who reasoned that he might not, after all, have to surrender his governorship, but wisdom first dictated that he reduce the number of his enemies.

Half of Roger de Liverot's men, their leader included, died soundlessly, their throats cut by Turks who made not a sound as they approached the snoring Normans. A few awoke to see their fate just before it was visited upon them, the only sound to emerge the gurgling of blood spilling from a sliced open windpipe and main artery. Few, a very few, woke in time to get a weapon into play and fight off their assailants for a while before succumbing to superior numbers, and the very lucky, no more than a dozen in total, fought hard enough to get clear and head at a desperate run for the walls of Tarsus.

There they called to their Lotharingian confrères for succour, all insults forgotten, and had enough time to tell Baldwin's men what had happened before they were set upon and slain in sight of the ground lit by torchlight, the last men to die naming the person clearly responsible for their fate, none other than Baldwin of Boulogne in concert with Gökham Bey. The horrified Lotharingians were not stupid; they knew who would be next if they did not defend themselves, albeit some of their number were so incensed they set off to slay Baldwin for his crime, so that he was obliged to lock his door against them.

The rest set about seeing to the remains of the Turkish garrison, first closing the postern gate by which the murderous party had exited and hoped to re-enter, no doubt to continue the slaughter, they fleeing in the knowledge of what might exit from the gates any time soon, mounted warriors who would cut them down to a man. Emerging from the towers they occupied, the Lotharingians rampaged through the city cutting down every Turk they found, and quite a few Armenians mistaken for infidel, until they reached the gubernatorial palace where they found Gökham Bey, pleading through an interpreter that he had had no knowledge of what had occurred and offering gold to spare his life.

It did not serve him at all; two sturdy knights of Lower Lorraine took their swords and, with a series of blows, hacked him into half a dozen pieces, his blood running over an elaborately tiled mosaic floor, of a design that might have once been walked on by Roman feet. Others set about his wives and numerous children until there was none left alive. If many later claimed this was done to avenge their Norman confrères that was a lie; they did it for fear of their own lives.

It took Baldwin, from behind his locked, heavy, wooden door, an age to convince his followers that he had not conspired to commit the crime, and it was an indication of the man he was that they did not initially believe him. Some remained unconvinced even when he was allowed out, but without him they were leaderless in a strange land, and added to that, as a free man, he had the ability to offer them now that which he had intended they should receive once his talks with Gökham Bey were concluded.

Gifts of gold and silver, the right to loot the homes and places of worship of the Turks, a blind eye turned to those who extended that to Christian Armenians to fill their pouches and rape their women, this took any desire away to even chastise their leader. Added to that was the prospect to a senior captain of the position of governor of Tarsus, who could choose his own men to form the garrison, a duty of much comfort and little risk now the Turks were all slain or fled.

For the rest there were other cities ahead to plunder, and even leaving a garrison of an eighth of his strength, they still outnumbered the Normans Baldwin knew were ahead of them. Leaving the citizens of Tarsus to bury the Norman dead and cast the Turks into an open pit, Baldwin set off the next day to chase the man he now saw as the main rival to his ambitions.

CHAPTER TWENTY

It was impossible to ignore the discontent that began to surface in the ranks of Tancred's men; they felt cheated, and not having responsibility to the whole of the mission they also felt free to be angry with him for not either outwitting Baldwin or fighting him for possession of Tarsus. All he could do was to refuse to respond to their misery and talk confidently of what was to come – other rich places and the booty they would provide – with the added assurance that if he had been outwitted once it would not happen again.

The sight, after two days' riding, of a medium-sized walled town on the horizon raised all their spirits, only dented when, in coming close they saw a strange banner flying from the highest tower, deep blue and bearing heraldic symbols that were unrecognisable to Western eyes.

'Armenian,' Anastas said in Greek, aware that the identification did not bring a smile to Tancred's lips.

Naturally their approach had been spotted and as they came close to the town they saw the gates open. Soon a substantial force of mixed cavalry and foot soldiers exited to draw up on the plain in battle order and under that same blue banner, clearly intent on defending the town. A small party detached themselves and rode forward to a point well ahead of the battle line and stopped, clearly inviting a parley, and Tancred, ordering his men to prepare for a fight, rode to meet them. The leader, tall, handsome and dark-skinned, was out in front, mounted with his standard-bearer at his side and he disarmed Tancred immediately by bowing in greeting and welcoming him to Adana in fluent Greek, giving his name as Oshin and getting that of Tancred in return.

'As you will see, My Lord, the town is no longer in the hands of the infidel. We Christians have taken it from them.' There was no choice but to look pleased. 'But I must add that they were ready to depart for they had heard of the coming of this great host from Europe. If we rose up and drove them out it was with your aid, even if you were not present.'

'So Adana is now Armenian.'

'It is,' Oshin replied, his chest swelling. 'And soon all of our lands will throw off the yoke of the Seljuks, for we Christians combined will drive them away, back to the East. Now, My Lord Tancred, I invite you and your lances to enter our town as guests, to pray with us in our churches and to eat and drink all that we can provide.'

There was no choice but to accept, and also no alternative to sending back a messenger to tell his knights to take off the chain mail they had just donned, for there would be no fighting – they would be feted as liberators, yet Tancred knew that would not still the moaning. His men had not come all this way for wine and provender, and the fact that Adana was in Armenian hands, a race he knew the Crusade leaders saw as potential allies, meant the people and the property would have to be respected.

It raised the mood of all a little as, after entering the town, they rode through the streets to the cheers of a multitude of happy citizens, with flowers thrown at them to form a carpet under their hooves. When it came to providing sustenance Oshin was as good as his word, for the food was superb and the wine flowed, which gave some concern to Tancred who knew that, when drunk, some of his men were likely to go wild and start to look for women and booty, regardless of the fact that they were with future allies. He mentioned his worries to the Armenian leader, pointing out that would only increase the longer they stayed.

'So we must move on at the rise of tomorrow's sun for the Belen Pass.'

If Oshin was surprised that the cause for so many Crusaders was profit not absolution he hid it well. He was also wise enough, when told of what had occurred at Tarsus, to sense what Tancred was not saying: that his men were hungry for more than he could provide.

'My Lord Tancred, to get to the Belen you must pass Mamistra.'

'And pass it is all I will probably be able to do, for you will have seen that I lack the strength to take it if they resist, and if I camp outside to try to winkle out the defence, then the Baldwin I mentioned to you will only come and seek to dislodge me. I doubt I could stop that turning into a fight.'

'The garrison of Mamistra is weak.'

'And so am I.'

'If you were stronger?' Seeing Tancred's eyebrows lift Oshin added with a smile, 'It would aid Adana if Mamistra too was stripped of its Turks. People travel frequently between here and there to trade, for it is a far richer place than where you now sit. I know the Turks have heard of your arrival in Cilicia and I am informed they are in terror of seeing your banners from their walls. I wonder how they would act if they saw ours at the same time?'

'You think they might surrender?'

'If they fear you, they fear we Armenians just as much, for they have been oppressors and the fate of such people is not a mystery when power changes hands. The Turks of Adana did not die easily or swiftly and that will be known to them in Mamistra.'

'A joint attack?'

Oshin nodded and quickly added, 'We need nothing for ourselves, for with Tarsus and Mamistra in friendly hands our town of Adana is secure. It would serve both our causes well if a Frankish banner flew over both our nearest neighbours.'

Tancred could not keep the surprise out of his voice. 'You are offering me and my lances a gift?'

'One, I must remind you, that is not yet mine to give. But I will accompany you with part of the force that greeted you, enough I hope to terrify the Turks into surrender.'

'Do not denude your own town, for Baldwin will be hard on my heels.'

'Never fear, I will leave enough men to check him should he prove greedy.'

'Then we still must depart at the rising of the sun.'

'We shall, side by side,' Oshin replied, 'but may I suggest that you let your men know we do so as allies, so that before we go they do not misbehave.'

'Do you trust him?' Robert of Salerno asked, when he was told of the plan.

'Yes. He wants security for Adana.'

'But has he made a pledge?'

'Robert, I am in no position to demand one, but I do know we cannot stay here. We both know we must ride on, and not just for the sake of the task we have been given. The men are upset after Tarsus and I know they blame me.'

'A few malcontents.'

'That is all it takes to break the peace between the Armenians and us. If we rest here for any time those "malcontents", as you call them, will start eyeing what is available to steal, and once that commences every one of our lances will join in so as not to miss out. I think Oshin knows that too, which is his other reason for offering support. He wants us gone, and if we are going to plunder anywhere, let it be his neighbour.'

'Baldwin?'

'If he comes here the gates will stay closed against his men, but he will be allowed to enter himself and treated with courtesy.'

'Pearls before swine,' Robert spat.

Tancred grinned. 'I have a higher opinion of pigs than you.'

Oshin and Tancred rode out in company, leading a combined force that now numbered near five hundred men, all mounted, for the Armenian had left his foot behind to hold Adana. At his insistence they did not hurry, he sure that word of their coming should reach the Turks before they arrived.

'For their imagination of the fate that awaits them will do more to aid our cause than even your chain armour.'

That night, round the campfire, Tancred and some of his Greek-speaking lances were entertained by Oshin with tales of what Armenia had once been, a great and ancient nation that had dominated the whole of Asia Minor. He was proud that his race and its then ruler had adopted Christianity as the state religion before the mighty Romans; Armenian bishops had been prominent at the Council of Nicaea and they had held to their faith through invasion and occupation with an iron will that not even the sons of the Prophet could dislodge.

He was also curious, and enquired over two nights, about the lands from which these men he had adopted as allies came from, the ongoing dispute between Greek Orthodoxy and Latin Rome, the places they lived and the customs by which they led their lives. And he probed, if not too strongly, to seek their motives for coming this way, which exposed no more than their complexity; some had genuinely come for the sake of their souls, others in search of a better life or to drive back the infidel, a few with dreams of fabulous wealth which, under careful questioning, they could not disguise.

'On the morrow,' he said to Tancred before they retired, 'it may be that all the dreams you Normans hold can be met.'

Mamistra was three times the size of Adana and judging by the number of churches and mosques very much more prosperous as well, but its walls were in poor repair, worse than those of Tarsus. It sat on the River Pyramus, which Oshin informed them flowed strongly to the sea except in high summer. Thus every trader in Cilicia flocked towards it to exchange the goods they wished to trade for that which could be brought in from around the Mediterranean. In that exchange and the customs dues charged lay its wealth and, given such income, the Turks should have better protected it, and certainly the fortifications should have been better maintained.

'It is a mystery, Lord Tancred,' Oshin replied, when the very obvious point was made. 'Perhaps my fellow Armenians do not threaten, they are too busy trading and profiting to think of freedom. As for the walls, how long is it since the Turks had anything to fear, and the Governor would care more for the weight of his purse than the strength of his defences.'

The customary invitation to open the gates for the sake of their lives was offered and rejected, so the combined force made ready to attack, selecting a part of the walls away from the main gate in such a parlous state that they looked as though a hefty push would knock them down. The dismounted Normans carried ladders forward and if they were met with arrows the effect was hardly as frightening as they had previously experienced – the aim was terrible – and in any case their mail and shields protected them from most of the harm.

With real brio, led by Tancred and Robert, they got onto the battlements and began to fight to control them, which allowed Oshin's Armenians to approach in relative safety. As Tancred's men began to expand the area of combat, in execution of the standard tactics of seeking one of the towers, their allies got in the conflict and proved to be worthy supporters. It was a loud blowing horn that caused a slight let-up, with Oshin riding forward, leading Tancred's mount, to shout to him that there was a truce flag flying above the tallest minaret.

'Hold your positions, Lord Tancred, but push no more. I think our Turks are ready to seek to save their skins, so I beg you to join me in talking to them.'

Looking around him and the many dead who had already fallen to Norman weapons, not a few of them to his own, Tancred calculated that with a bit more effort they might achieve that rare event, the taking of a fortified place on the first assault; he was loath to depart from that.

'Talk to them, Oshin, speak for us all.'

'That would not be fitting. If Mamistra falls it does so to you. Come and bring with you your banner.'

'Take over, Robert, and hold the ground we have gained.'

Bloodstained and sweaty Tancred clambered down and mounted his horse, bringing in his own hand the de Hauteville flag. He and Oshin rode to the main gate to find a splendidly clad and swarthy individual on the barbican waiting to parley with them and he was seeking terms. Two notions were uppermost in Tancred's mind: the way Gökham Bey had betrayed him to Baldwin at Tarsus, and the fact that his and Oshin's men were still on the walls and in a position to press home the attack.

So pleas for time were denied; the Governor of Mamistra was given one glass of sand to get him and his Turks, military and civilian, out of the town on pain of death for all, including his wives and children. Nor was Tancred, egged on by Oshin, prepared to play the normal Turkish game of extended negotiations. He dismissed out of hand the man's attempts to bargain and swore he would personally make his death so painful that he would seek to convert to save himself.

'Take nothing,' Tancred added. 'Only what you wear and what you must ride. Your men must leave their weapons also, and if you abide by those terms I swear on the soul of Jesus Christ our Saviour that you will not be harmed.'

For a man that had no choice habit made him seek amelioration, until Oshin spoke up and began to describe what the people of Adana had done to their Turks. Argument ceased then, and for such a dark-skinned fellow it was strange how pale he had gone. Within the required time the Turks moved out, a long and slow caravan of horses, carts, women, each sat on an ass, children walking beside them, but no possessions of any size. When the last donkey left, Tancred called his men off the walls and with Oshin at his side rode into Mamistra to the cheers of the Armenian population.

The treasury of Mamistra was intact, as were all the furniture and artefacts held by the Governor of a wealthy trading city: chests of coins, gold, silver and bronze, beautifully crafted objects that would yield a fortune on their own. Now Tancred could still those moaning tongues and reward his lances with the kind of booty they had craved since leaving Apulia.

He too would gain much, wealth greater than he had ever possessed, for Oshin refused to take any share. Yet the pleasure in that was topped by the cheering sight of his banner flying over the city, its red background and blue and white chequer telling all who saw it that a de Hauteville was the Lord of Mamistra.

It was only two days before that was spotted by Baldwin of Boulogne, who stopped his men by the river and made camp. After that banner, the first thing he would have espied was much work being done on repairing the walls, tasks at which the Normans, endemic castle builders, were extremely adept. He would have wondered, while they toiled at the masonry, as to the identity of the men who were standing guard, for he would have no idea, even if he had been refused entry to Adana, that the man who commanded there was now here with half his forces. He took his time, but eventually Baldwin was obliged to ride towards the closed gates and ask to speak to Tancred.

'I come in peace.'

Getting no reply Baldwin asked that he and his men be allowed to enter.

'Denied, which is, you must admit, a fair response to Tarsus.'

'You were too arrogant, Tancred, unwilling to share as you should, for we are brothers in our endeavour. I acted as was necessary, and had you lingered you would have found me generous.'

'As generous as you wish me to be here?'

Try as he might to contain himself, Baldwin's natural bellicosity broke through and he positively snapped his response. 'As generous as you should be here!'

'And if I decline?'

'Then count my lances.'

'I suggest instead that you ride around the walls and observe that not all the men upon them are Normans. If you mean you outnumber me, you will learn that is no longer the case, and besides that, I sit behind these walls and if you wish to enter there is only one way you can do it. I will hazard that after you try, we Normans will outnumber you, for your lances will die on these battlements.'

'You would fight your fellow Crusaders?'

'Only if they seek to fight me.'

'I demand that you share with us that which you have taken here.'

'No, Baldwin, what I have here is mine. Ride on, I suggest, and do that for which we were sent. Make sure the Belen Pass is clear.'

'I will camp by the river overnight, Tancred, and in the morning I will come again and I expect a different answer.'

Baldwin did not wait to get a response; he spun his mount and rode away.

'We should ride out and teach him a lesson,' Robert hissed.

'He has his lesson already, cousin, we need deliver him no more.'

'A sound thrashing for him and his slime would be no more than he deserves and there is not a man you lead who does not share that feeling.'

'Then I look to you, Robert, as I should, to aid me in maintaining the peace. Baldwin will ride on, he has no choice.'

'To what, cousin? He is a member of the council if his brother is still not recovered, Tancred – you are not. If he makes a case to them to censure you . . .'

'Then I will rely on those who know me and know Baldwin to judge who has been honourable and who has not. Meanwhile, make sure none of our men meet his, for Baldwin has stirred up bad blood where there should be none.'

It was a forlorn hope; Baldwin's Lotharingian knights came to the walls to taunt the Normans, perhaps at his behest, and if it was plunder at the base of their jibes it was to their manhood and the chastity of their mothers that they alluded. The Apulians were not inclined to be insulted and do nothing, so as darkness began to fall a large party, weapons in hand, exited the postern gate to meet head-on their tormentors. Enquiries by Tancred never established who struck the first blow, only that when it was forthcoming the whole confrontation quickly descended into a brawl, and given these were warriors by trade it was not carried out with fist and feet, but with swords and axes.

Hearing the clash, Baldwin's remaining men rushed up from their camp, to find the Apulian Normans only too keen to pour out and meet them, with Robert of Salerno at their head. If it was a short affair it was a bloody one, with eight men dead at the count and many more carrying wounds. Each side had taken captives, Baldwin's men

276

dragged into Mamistra, Tancred's to the Lotharingian camp, and it required Oshin, the following morning, to arrange a truce. Matters were not improved when a trader from Adana arrived, to tell what had happened to Tancred's reinforcements at Tarsus and that made the meeting an even more bitter affair.

'My cousin of Salerno suggested you would seek to blacken me at a meeting of the Council of Princes, Baldwin. I look forward to hearing you explain how you allowed such a large number of Norman knights to be murdered in their sleep.'

'Accuse me and you will be required to prove it by combat.'

'Why wait till then, Baldwin? I am happy to face you now.'

Oshin did not understand what was being said in the Frankish tongue but he was sharp enough to know by the expressions on the faces of Tancred and Baldwin that a full-scale battle could break out at any moment, for the gates of Mamistra were open and all of Tancred's men were willing to come out and fight; if they did he would add his Armenians but it was far from what he sought and what should happen.

'Tancred, you have prisoners of your fellow Frank, he has prisoners of yours. Let us exchange those, then set a time for a proper parley in which your differences can be discussed without rancour. Translate that to the other side.'

Tancred nodded and seeking to moderate his tone he made the offer. Baldwin thought he saw a chink in the Apulian's intransigence and agreed, so men were led forward from both sides to rejoin their confrères.

'So when do we parley, Tancred?'

'I will not speak with you, Baldwin, until we face Adémar and the council.'

With that Tancred spun on his heels and led his party inside the gates, his order to shut them behind him loud enough to carry. Faced with a situation he could not solve and fearful of looking foolish, Baldwin rode off before the sun was at its zenith, heading due east, watched from the walls by a curious Tancred.

'What now?' Robert asked.

'We finish repairing the walls, garrison the city and then set about what we were tasked to do.'

'We might find Baldwin waiting for us at the Belen Pass.'

'Then we will take that as it comes.'

Days later Oshin and Tancred took their leave, with promises of friendship and mutual support, the garrison of Mamistra told to train an Armenian militia that could go to the aid of Adana if it was threatened, Oshin guaranteeing to come to Mamistra on the same purpose. The commander of the garrison was obliged to levy the necessary customs dues, to pay his men and put the excess into Tancred's treasury and guard it well.

'For when we have Jerusalem, I will send for it.'

There was no sign of Baldwin prior to passing through the Belen Pass, or indeed beyond at the port of Alexandretta to which the road led; if he was coming to Antioch then he had clearly chosen a different route, one that would, Tancred supposed, line his purse with plunder. If that laid to rest a concern, the news was better when it came to the Turks; local intelligence informed him the enemy, being small in number and afraid, had withdrawn to Antioch, and when he sighted the fortifications he could see why, for they were the most formidable he had ever laid eyes upon.

Unmolested, crossing busy roads full of traders, he rode round those parts of the perimeter easily accessible, marvelling at the ingenuity of what had been constructed on terrain which did not lend itself to straightforward building, battlements in one section that appeared to run up near sheer mountainside. He found, in a place called the Ruj Valley to the south of the city, a force of Provençal knights sent ahead by Raymond of Toulouse on the rumour that the Turks had abandoned Antioch, only to find it fully garrisoned and those inside prepared to come out and fight what was seen as a force posing some danger.

Driven off far enough to nullify any threat, even to communications, their commander Peter of Roaix had set up an outpost and intended to remain, if only as an irritant. Given there was nothing Tancred and his lances could do that would not amount to even a feeble spit on a stone wall, it was time to rejoin the main host and advise them of his progress.

CHAPTER TWENTY-ONE

The progress of the Christian army and their attendant pilgrims had been slow because of its size and the obstacles of terrain; crossing the anti-Taurus mountains over a single track in unseasonal mist and lashing rain had incurred heavy losses, especially of pack animals and their loads, which brought back hunger almost as acute as the Anatolian desert. Such a recurrence reduced some of the *milities* and even the odd knight to insist the Crusade was cursed and to offer to sell their weapons and shields to any local peasant for food, such misery only relieved when they got back down onto the plains and plenty at the Armenian city of Marash, albeit they were also once more at the mercy of the burning summer heat.

Expecting to have to fight they were relieved to find that the Turks, indeed the whole Muslim population, had decamped before they arrived. From high to low the Armenians of Marash were ecstatic, eager to provide them, albeit for payment, with all that they required to progress to their destination: food, horses, oxen and encouragement, their leaders also accepting the role of guarding the crusading flank from any incursions by their now joint enemy; if they could not stop the Turks from passing through – they lacked the military capacity to prevent them – they could ensure the Crusaders had ample warning of any looming threat.

From Marash onwards the Crusaders were able to form alliances with the numerous Armenian satraps; they ran large parts of Syria for Turkish overlords who would have been overstretched to do it for themselves. Such powerful local magnates had no love for the Seljuks and openly welcomed people they saw as their religious brothers, and many arrangements were made, not least for the transportation of supplies in the future.

Tancred met the forward elements of the Crusade on the road to Aleppo, able to assure Bishop Adémar, still acting as the titular leader and well ahead of the host, that the passes he had been sent to secure were open and the towns between Nicaea and Antioch garrisoned and safe should Alexius Comnenus wish to bring his forces that way; they had not joined at Caesarea as had been hoped. This also meant the Emperor would be supplied en route, which would speed his progress, while if he wished to send men by sea, Alexandretta was also in Christian hands.

'Where is Baldwin?'

'I have no idea, Your Grace,' was the abrupt reply.

Such a response to a gently posed question was strange, not least in the manner in which it was delivered. That this was so showed on the cleric's round face, and he was about to enquire further when the young Lord of Lecce added in an even less respectful tone that he was eager to meet up with his uncle. The last thing he wanted to do was explain Baldwin to anyone before he had spoken with Bohemund.

'Not ahead at Antioch, then?' Adémar pressed.

'No.'

'He will be happy to hear his brother is near full recovered.'

'I'm sure he will, Your Grace,' Tancred replied, with no conviction at all, before jerking his head in lieu of a bow and dragging his reins to take himself and his horse away, calling over his shoulder, 'The road ahead is clear, you have nothing to fear.'

'Do you think he contrived in the murder of our knights?' Bohemund asked, the shock of their death and the manner of it still evident on his demeanour. 'Of the Turks I can believe it, but for a Christian to slaughter his fellows . . .'

'I do not know, but some of his own Lotharingian lances think he might have contrived in the massacre.'

'They came to you and said so?'

'We fought them outside Mamistra and some of my men were taken captive.' Mistaking the reaction Tancred added, 'We killed and captured a few ourselves.'

'Fought!' Bohemund barked. 'You and Baldwin's men fought?'

'Perhaps it would be best if I told all.'

Which Tancred did, from the start to the very end and he left nothing out, even those parts that did not reflect well on himself, though he was keen to stress that if any bad blood had been created between Normans and Lotharingians, Baldwin and his naked greed lay at the root of it. He was sure that could not be gainsaid, given Duke Godfrey's brother had taken careful steps to ensure he had the greater number of lances under his command. When he finished, it was to look into an older face showing much concern, which was a relief – he was expecting to be chastised.

'These cannot be laid as accusations in council, Tancred.'

'For the sake of amity with the Duke?'

'Godfrey is not responsible for his brother, even although, in his soul, he will take upon himself that burden.'

'They are certainly very different people, and I would point out that even if they are not raised in the council these are rumours and claims that cannot be sat on. I can command the men I led to silence but I have no assurance I will be obeyed. Word will reach elevated ears by another route than that which is direct, while I, were I a member of the council, would also be obliged to ask where the disloyal swine has gone.'

'You got no indication?'

'Not a whiff, Uncle, if he is on a route it is not any one that will take him south. My guess is that he has gone off to look for conquests of his own and I would remind you he still holds Tarsus as his fief.'

'I will speak to Godfrey in private.'

'And the others.'

'If they hear by rumour of what you say happened at Tarsus, it is to be hoped they think as I do, that such matters are best not raised, lest we fall apart as a host before we even reach Antioch. I cannot bring back the men I have lost but there is too much at stake to make much of their fate, though I will have Mass said for their souls.'

'Then I hope no one whispers such rumours in the ear of Vermandois.' The grim response that got made words superfluous, so Tancred changed the subject. 'Let me tell you about the fortifications we are about to face.'

'You have no need for they are famous throughout the world. Every returning Jerusalem pilgrim speaks of them.'

'That does not tell you the tenth of it and, according to Raymond's man, Peter of Roaix, who has spoken to the ardent Christians the Governor of Antioch evicted, the city is strongly garrisoned to a number he thinks might go as high as five thousand fighting men.'

'It fell before, to Byzantium, and if they can take it so can we.'

Bohemund's conversation with Godfrey was elliptical in the extreme, more a case of the impossibility of Baldwin being involved in the massacre of his men than that he had contrived with the Turks to have it committed, yet the trace of an allegation could not be avoided.

'I wished you to hear of this from my lips rather than from any gossip that might circulate, Duke Godfrey, for that would likely come larded with malice.'

Godfrey, his broad face sad, sighed and crossed himself. 'My brother has ever been troublesome, but I have to think he would not stoop so low as you suggest.'

'I have suggested nothing.'

'You have laid out a case, Count Bohemund, and while you have not levelled any blame it is clear that some doubt exists as to how Baldwin acted. It is my experience that such a charge, even if false, levelled against a man's name is not washed away easily and, sad to say, his blood relatives suffer by association.'

'That is why I came to you and alone, for you do not deserve such a blemish. I have lost men I valued and I grieve for them, but I will not raise the matter in council, for to do so would embarrass you and would hardly serve our cause.'

That got a half smile. 'I have observed how often you have restrained yourself in council, Count Bohemund. You let others speak rather than take the floor in your own right, yet I think I observe you often disagree, much as you try to keep that hidden.'

'I must employ more effort to compose my features, and be assured, I would not let pass anything I thought endangered us or the Crusade.'

'That I do believe. It is to your credit and I thank you for coming to see me alone. Now I am doubly indebted to you.'

'If you mean the incident with the bear, you owe me nothing.'

'Allow me to decide where my indebtedness lies, Count Bohemund. Now, if you will forgive me I must say prayers for my wayward brother, who needs them whatever he has or has not done.'

If the tale of the massacre at Tarsus did circulate it was kept from public discourse and, in truth, Baldwin's absence was a relief to everyone including, Bohemund suspected, his own family, so that, if it was insincerely regretted as it had to be, it was far from troubling, for his natural bellicosity was being visited elsewhere. The future was of more import than what Baldwin was up to – before them was a Byzantine map of Antioch and the surrounding environs and plans had to be made as to how to subdue the city.

If the mass of the population of the city was Armenian and many of them adherents of their branch of the Christian faith that did not signify much; there would be those who through convenience or a genuine belief in Islam had converted, some of whom would fight for the Turks as well, either out of that same conviction or to hold on to what they had gained from being allies of the alien occupation. It was ever thus with conquest: some under a new master put personal advancement above principle, the powerless majority were swayed by their bellies, and those who stood out against the new dispensation were either killed or banished, and Yaghi Siyan, the Turkish Governor, had already expelled those who might stir up their race and religious brothers against him, careful, as an insurance, to hold the Armenian patriarch as a hostage.

Even discontented, which they might become when hunger struck, the mass of the Armenian indigenes would have no weapons with which to oppose the Turkish garrison and certainly no power to affect whether the siege would succeed or fail. None present thought it was going to be a simple affair, yet taken it must be – if Jerusalem was no more that a six-week march to the south, Antioch was the key to any chance of progress and much more beside.

It was no mystery, but here the Council of Princes came up against a stark reality that all knew but rarely mentioned: their host, though still powerful, was not as numerous as it had been outside Nicaea. Added to losses fighting there were the many more they had suffered in Anatolia due to thirst and starvation. There were the losses at Tarsus, and the march towards Antioch had taken its toll, several men lost from falls in the mountains. That did not include the number who had merely succumbed to accidents or the myriad number of diseases common to such a large body of men on campaign – foul humours, dropsy, sleeping sickness, seizures and the like added to the increasing number who had grown weary of seeking salvation and gone home.

Not everyone who left was abandoning the Crusade. A strong party of knights had been sent to secure the port of St Simeon, which gave the Crusade access to the Mediterranean and across that sea to Greek-held Cyprus and beyond, not least to Bohemund's possessions in Apulia, as well as fast communications with the Emperor Alexius, telling of the open route south.

Messages had been sent by Bohemund to his Uncle Roger, the Great Count of Sicily, who if he was not prepared to join the Crusade would do all he could to aid it – even *Borsa* would help. Requests were despatched asking for many things to be delivered as soon as humanly possible and to use the treasure given to him by Alexius to pay for it.

But that still left the here and now to be dealt with; Tacitus, for so long a time left out of deliberations, only coming to life when appointing Byzantine governors to towns and cities the Crusade had captured, now put forward a plan based on the successful capture of the city a hundred years previously. This had taken the form of a partial siege, operated at a distance and designed more to reduce Antioch by starvation than to take it by direct assault.

Strategic locations were identified and if these could be secured, he assured the council, the supply routes to the city would be severely interdicted. When winter approached, the host could live, well spread out, in relative ease and comfort while the garrison of Antioch consumed the contents of their burgeoning storerooms and perhaps become so reduced by the spring they would start to eat their horses. That was the time to invest the city more closely and demand surrender, when morale was already at rock bottom.

'Add to which, My Lords,' his interpreter said in conclusion, 'if your numbers are diminished now, they will, by then, surely be reinforced.'

'By the Emperor?' asked Robert of Normandy.

Tacitus, when that was translated, seemed to take that enquiry as some kind of affront and his reply when it came did not really answer the question. 'The *Prōstratōr* refers more to the fact that knights are still coming from your own lands to bolster your numbers, but that will cease with winter and only truly be at full flow in spring.'

'Ask him' said Bohemund, making no attempt to disguise his irony, 'if he has decided who is to be governor of Antioch yet?'

That brought from Raymond a frown as he took up the discussion, ignoring the whispered interpretation and Tacitus's subsequent growl. Likewise Bohemund paid no attention to the look of malevolence from a man he had come to mistrust, being more intent on what the Count of Toulouse was saying.

'Does the *Prōstratōr* wish to tell us how long he thinks such a way of proceeding would take?' He did not wait for any translation. 'Let me answer for him, so that we are not rendered impatient. He is talking of half a year before we even consider any form of assault, and I do not take to the notion of having my men idling for all that time and not fighting.'

He was not openly saying it, but all present understood: an idle army was one prone to illness, dissension and even disintegration, and besides that, they had already been about their business a long time, some of their number having left Europe and their lands two years since.

'This fellow we face . . .' Raymond stopped then, struggling to pronounce the Turkish governor's name.

Bishop Adémar came to his rescue. 'Yaghi Sayan.'

'. . . is by reputation a canny fighter,' the Count of Toulouse continued, 'but is he not at odds with anyone who might support him?'

'He plays games with the two sons of the Sultan of Baghdad, we are told,' the cleric replied, adding that the brothers were in competition for control of Syria, of which Antioch, once the third centre of Roman power in the ancient world, was the most important city. 'But our Armenian friends are sure he is really seeking Antioch for himself.'

'Then what are the risks of such people coming to his aid?'

Raymond's point was simple and again did not require to be

laboriously explained to men who were used to command: if they had nothing to fear from their rear, why waste time? What information they had implied that the Sultan had enough trouble in Baghdad to keep him from interference, while his sons hated each other and would never combine to pose a threat. Besides that there were the common sectarian disputes that had racked the Islamic faith almost since the time of the Prophet. The Turks were Sunni Moslems, while in the countryside to the east the Arab population was mostly Shi'ite. Therefore the notion of raising the whole region against the Christian host was negligible.

'We can do better outside the walls to starve out Antioch than from several leagues away.'

'You think starvation the only way?' asked Vermandois, making no secret of his own disdain for such an approach; no doubt he saw himself leading an assault over the walls and burnishing the legend he was sure would be his in posterity.

As kindly as was his way, Godfrey de Bouillon replied to that in order to kill off the reaction of the others, who were likely to scoff, stepping forward to the table on which the map was laid out, explaining why there was no other way, his tone patient.

'Look, Count Hugh, and tell me how we can assault the walls, half of which run up and down the side of mountains with only a small corner at the northern gate not protected by a river. The Orontes runs too close to the walls to allow for secure construction of siege engines. Even if we had the means to build such things, which we don't unless the Emperor brings them to us, how are they to be got into place? Even the bridge over the Orontes, the only place we could employ such a method, is too narrow, has its own barbican and is overlooked by the battlements.'

Count Hugh looked to Walo of Chaumont for assurance that what was being said was true, and the Constable responded with a silent nod.

'Is it possible to agree with both Count Raymond and General Tacitus?' asked Bohemund. 'We cannot lay siege to the city and leave the places he has mentioned, such as Bagras and Artah, unmanned – that is even more dangerous, and Artah must be secured so we have a route for supplies.'

That got nods of assent.

'Count Raymond has already secured the road south, so that leaves only the fortress of Harim, which has a small garrison and should be far enough distant to have no effect on a siege without we would know well in advance they are about to be a threat to us.'

If heads were still nodding that was not the end of the matter. A great deal of time and discussion followed before that was generally the course adopted, but it did not solve some problems that defied easy solutions. To completely surround Antioch and cut it off was impossible; only half of the six gates provided the host with the option to press on the defences while still being able to offer each other mutual support in case of an attack by the garrison, and it had to be accepted, even if it was unlikely, that might include outside reinforcements. The memory of Dorylaeum was still too fresh to allow for separation.

The gate that opened onto the western road, which led to the Antiochene port of St Simeon as well as its southernmost companion, lay right up against the east side of the wide Orontes River, with the only means to cross three leagues downriver. The southern gate was on the other side of the river as well, so any besiegers on the far bank would be isolated and exposed, while the remainder would not be able to offer quick support in case of any difficulties.

The most secure Turkish gate lay on the far side of the two mountains that dominated Antioch and was only approachable by a high and narrow pass between the twin peaks, while the Armenians who had been questioned indicated that to close that off was next to impossible. So half the entry and exit points could only be cut off by mobile troops and they had to be able in the event of danger to make a rapid withdrawal.

If these obstacles prompted sober reflection they did not deter, merely being taken into consideration, with each leader choosing one of the three sections of the defences where they could be effective, with the rest being a shared responsibility. Bohemund elected to take the northern gate that led to Bagras, the site of an old Byzantine fortress. Close to the hillside of Mount Staurin and therefore a place of danger, it presented the only part of the walls with an extent of flat ground on the approach, where it might be possible, should they ever have the means, to mount an assault with a man-made tower. This implied to the others present that while he accepted it was likely to be a siege of attrition, the Count of Taranto had not given up hope of a *coup de main*.

The northern Normans, as well as Vermandois, were next on his right between Bohemund and Raymond of Toulouse, the joint of their forces meeting at the next gate south. The last of the trio and potentially as dangerous as any, given the narrow amount of land at his back, went to Godfrey de Bouillon. Tacitus was asked where he wanted to be based and once he was clear as to the nature of the question he pointed to a place well to the rear of Bohemund and his Apulians. That it was safe was obvious; that it led back to Constantinople in the case of flight did not escape notice either.

With all agreed, Raymond of Toulouse had one more statement

he wished to make and it was clearly, to him, an important one. He pointed out that whatever happened, the siege of Antioch was likely to be of longer duration than that of Nicaea; he wished each leader to swear, as he was willing to do himself, not to abandon the effort, however difficult it became, on pain of eternal damnation, leaving Bohemund certainly, and probably the others, wondering what had prompted such a request.

'Every man present has sworn already,' Adémar insisted. 'What need have we of more pledges?'

'It concerns me that many have fallen by the wayside already and gone home. Then, when things are hard, there is the temptation to seek an easier route to satisfy . . .'

Raymond could not finish that, could not say the word 'ambitions' or refer to the absent Baldwin and the example he had set.

'We are jointly here and jointly we will stay,' Bohemund said, speaking before Godfrey could respond.

Robert of Normandy spoke up just as forcefully, knowing he was suspected of being a less-than-wholehearted Crusader and Raymond's request might be aimed at him and his brothers-in-law, Stephen of Blois and Robert of Flanders.

'If it aids our cause, let us make the pledge. If we are all acting in good faith it makes no difference, if we are not then God will be the judge.'

'I will swear and gladly,' Godfrey exclaimed.

This was close to comical – if anyone did not need to restate his commitment it was the pious Duke of Lower Lorraine; he was doing it because of the actions of Baldwin, who had quite obviously gone in search of personal profit, lest anyone ascribe the same motives to him. It did, however, because he was held in such high regard, oblige the others to agree and Adémar called for his priests and his missal to make it as formal as Raymond felt it should be.

Back in his section of the encampment Bohemund called his captains together and ordered an immediate move, his lances to travel fast and the *milites* to follow; he wanted the first thing that Yaghi Sayan spied from his citadel to be his banner.

Robert, Count of Flanders, was deputed to take a strong party of a thousand knights on a detour to capture the town of Artah, which controlled the road north-east and due east to Marash, Aleppo and Edessa. He arrived to find the town in Armenian hands, the locals having revolted and chased out a Turkish garrison that was reluctant to remain in any case, having heard that the Crusade was coming their way. The Armenians happily accepted a garrison of crusading knights and were equally pleased to have a banner of the County of Flanders fly from their citadel.

For the rest, with the Apulians in the lead, the only place to safely cross the Orontes was at a spot called the Iron Bridge, an odd appellation for an arched edifice made of stone that dated from Roman times or even earlier. No doubt there was some local legend of an ancient action to account for the name but it was not anything to trouble the host enough to enquire. They were pleased the bridge was unguarded and even more delighted, indeed surprised, when having crossed it they entered a flat plain in the full glory of its flowering, fed with water by a river in strong flow.

Yaghi Sayan, who should have sown the whole area with salt to deny them forage, had destroyed nothing. There was grain in plentiful supply, fruit on the trees and vegetables, the second harvest, growing in the fields while the fruits of the first harvest of the year were yet to be consumed. Livestock was plentiful and the population, being Armenian, was only too pleased to both greet and trade with these strange creatures from beyond their shores, while in the distance rising into a midday haze, they could see the massive twin hills that formed a backdrop to the city they were about to besiege.

Even to a warrior who had seen Palermo and had mighty Bari as a fief, it was sobering for Bohemund to examine Antioch when they got close enough to see the details of the fortifications, especially at the gate he had chosen to act against. Above them lay the top of Mount Silpius, while adjacent to that and only marginally smaller, Mount Staurin had set upon it Yaghi Sayan's citadel, itself a hard place to assault and capture should they ever get close, even more so given it was fronted by a steep escarpment.

From the flat ground on which the Apulians made camp the walls ran very quickly up a scrub-covered incline that would defy any man to walk upright – it was one for a scrabbling ascent at best made even more so by the loose screed of small stones underfoot – while all the way up there was a stout and near unassailable wall interspersed with dozens of towers. That crested the high summit of Mount Staurin and continued across a high valley lying just below the peaks of both mountains in which was set, as part of the main defensive walls, the formidable citadel; it was sobering to reflect that if it was like this on the northern approach, it was even steeper and more taxing to the south.

'As you can observe, Uncle,' Tancred said, pointing to the citadel, 'we can do nothing in preparation without that the Turk will see it.'

That was true; the whole plain would be laid out like a panorama from that high elevation. 'Let him first see we are determined.'

'Do you have a thought as to why he left all this food unspoilt?'

'I sense you are asking me a question, Tancred, to which you have your own answer.'

The two men exchanged grins, for it was no less than the truth, as the younger man replied, 'I think he hoped we would pass on and leave him in peace.'

'I think the same, but it was a foolish gambit. Only a madman would leave such a potent city untouched at his back.'

'Or is it that he does not fear us, and hopes to see our bones from his citadel when the food runs out?'

'One day, nephew, I hope you and I get to ask him the answer.'

CHAPTER TWENTY-TWO

In taking up their area of responsibility every crusading contingent took precautions to prepare for an immediate sortie by the garrison, indeed they did not expect to make their dispositions unmolested. Yet nothing happened for days; they were left to settle in, to eat well, drink wine, sleep soundly and celebrate their daily Mass with the numerous priests that accompanied the host. Camp wives, who were plentiful, settled in to look after their menfolk, which, much to the disgust of Peter the Hermit and Godfrey de Bouillon, included the more elevated divines, though not Bishop Adémar.

The whole turned into more of a settlement than a military camp and this lasted for one surprising week, then another. This left the princes with many questions but no answers, though it provided ample time to reconnoitre those areas not occupied as well as assess just how difficult it would be to shut off the city from resupply, very necessary if attrition was to work. Some wit, part of a party of horsemen reconnoitring the narrow track on the eastern flank of Antioch, having heard the inappropriate name of the Iron Bridge, decided that the equally stone-built point of entry and egress at the end of the valley should be called the Iron Gate as a measure of the kind of resolve that would be needed to invest and close it.

Not to be outdone, the Apulians named their gate after St Paul of Tarsus, where they had lost so many men murdered in their sleep. A dead dog cast over the walls where the Duke of Normandy and Raymond of Toulouse were camped gave the next one south its name while the third gate was more prosaically termed the Gate of the Duke after Godfrey de Bouillon's title.

The Bridge Gate was obvious but no one was quite sure how the last of these edifices got to be called the St George's Gate, probably more a patron saint of someone than for any other reason.

Mobile patrols were kept active, especially on the far side of the river, even if it was a long slog to the nearest crossing. Armenians and Syrians continued to be expelled or flee from the city, the suspicion that they were not all they seemed impossible not to consider after Nicaea, which, if true, meant that Yaghi Siyan knew much more about them than they did about him or his intentions; did he wish them gone or was he content to lull them into a false sense of security?

That period of peace broke on the garrison's first sortie, something they could do with impunity given half their gates were able to open and close at will, with nothing outside to impede them that could not be seen from the high citadel. It was to Bohemund's St Paul's Gate that they directed their first attack, using the western slope of Mount Staurin to assemble in plain view on a relatively flat ledge, then rain down arrows on the Apulian lines. Caught unawares and without mail or shields several knights were wounded, while one woman, the camp wife of a foot soldier, was killed outright.

To fight off such an attack was difficult; the men on duty and properly clad for battle sought, under Robert of Salerno, to advance up the steep slope of loose stones and scrub bushes under a hail of missiles that made the assent doubly hazardous since it was near impossible for them to both climb and protect themselves. They also faced the added danger of larger rocks deliberately set in motion to roll down the hillside and maim them, and they did not manage to even make contact. The Turks withdrew when their supply of arrows ran out, jeering as they retired, with Bohemund making a swift move to counter the threat.

'We will need to make up screens behind which we can shelter, for this will not be their last attempt using that tactic.'

Soon the whole Apulian host was hacking out and joining up frames while others cut and fashioned reeds in bundles thick enough to stop, or at the very least take the sting out of, a speeding arrow. Once erected the tents were moved into their shade, which had a double benefit of keeping out the sun for part of the day while a watch was kept on the hillside for a repeat, which was bound to come, it being so seemingly risk-free for the garrison. They had reckoned without the son of the *Guiscard*.

At night, in a thick heat haze that obscured both moon and stars, they could move without being observed and Bohemund led a party of his men in a wide arc and up the hill as silently as was possible, well away from the hearing of the sentinels on the walls. The aim was to find a bush behind which to conceal themselves, using their cloaks for added camouflage, the command to stay still and not move pressed home many times. The same band of Turks, at first light, no doubt using as an exit the Iron Gate, came over the brow of the mountain and began to slither down to that ledge from which they had launched their previous attack, making no attempt at subterfuge.

With the sun in the east and not yet fully risen, and the peak of Mount Staurin so high, the whole of the western slope was in deep shade, which helped to keep the knights hidden. Bohemund waited till he heard orders being issued, indicating they were getting ready to attack, before he stood up and called for his men to do likewise, immediately rushing forward and yelling like a banshee. At this elevation and given the incline it was not easy, running with one foot so much lower than the other, but it was possible and the Normans had surprise on their side.

The startled Turks, with their bows still on the shoulders, panicked instead of acting as they should and they were not aided by the fellow obviously in command shouting orders that seemed to be causing more confusion rather than less. Now it was the turn of the Turks to seek to scrabble to safety and quite a few, some dozen in number, did not get clear, falling to great swipes by flashing Norman swords as well as a pair of well-aimed axes; there was no jeering now, just screaming and much of that was coming from those fleeing.

Bohemund knew he dare not linger; the battlements were not far off and his party was in range of archery from there. It would not take long to muster the men needed to turn his attack into an untidy and potentially fatal retreat. His command to move came with an instruction to kick the dead Turks so they rolled down the slope ahead of them, and if the knights descending appeared inelegant, sometimes failing to keep their feet, they came back to ground level with the cheers of their confrères ringing in their ears.

'Now, we need a permanent piquet at the brow of the slope,'

Bohemund gasped. 'One that will stop them ever attempting that again.'

If such a tactic was easily advanced it was far from easily carried out and nor was it safe; it required the building of a drystone enclosure high enough to stop anyone just leaping over to slit the throats of those who were sent to man it. Every night it had to be resupplied with food, water and men, those left to hold it rotated from what was an isolated and extremely dangerous duty. But it worked; the Turks knew they would have to fight first to get into position and such attacks as had happened originally diminished, if they did not entirely cease.

Having begun to act the Turks expanded their efforts over the following weeks, employing mounted archers to inflict casualties on the Crusaders, small highly mobile squadrons who knew exactly the dispositions of their enemies and could see when certain groups were too remote from the main host to benefit from quick support, and such raids happened around the whole perimeter. Any companies caught outside the St George's Gate were obliged to flee for the distant river crossing, while those knights caught to the east of the mountains seeking to stop up the Iron Gate were being attacked by flying columns from a force based outside and to the east of the city.

But such actions happened right in front of the western walls too, for there was only a narrow strip of land between the Gate of the Duke and the Orontes in which to operate and too many times men were being trapped there and decimated, either killed by arrows and swords or else they drowned in the river trying to get clear. A frustrated Godfrey de Bouillon, whose knights were suffering the most, decided to build a pontoon bridge over the river using boats, so that the main body of men from his camp, of necessity on the far bank, could get across to aid their hard-pressed confrères.

This was only a partial solution given that aid came best from mounted and mailed knights; to ride a horse across an unstable platform was difficult and that imposed a strict limit on how many could use the pontoon at the same time – the greater the number who tried simultaneously, the greater the movement under the horses' hooves – which led to crowding on the west bank as frustrated warriors sought to get at their rampaging enemies.

Henry of Esch, he one of the pair who came up with the ridiculous bombardment screen which fell apart at Nicaea, became so frustrated he rode into the river, sinking ever more until his head was under the water and he was despaired of. God was with him, it was later claimed, as he emerged, still mounted and dripping water, to urge his mount up onto the far bank. Still soaked he went straight into action and did good service.

Of greater concern, as time went on, was the diminution of supplies; such a huge number of mouths – fighting men and pilgrims – required feeding on a scale that even the fertile plains to the west of the Orontes could not support, while bringing in food and fodder from the well-disposed Armenians was slow and difficult given it all had to be carried by oxen or donkeys and was subjected to raids by bands of Turkish warriors.

Those same bands made foraging difficult to near impossible, so from being a place of plenty the region in which they were encamped soon looked to be on the way to becoming a wasteland, and that was before the weather, hitherto benign, turned for the worse. Lashed by heavy rain and battered by strong winds the siege lines turned into an area of hard-to-negotiate mud and made everyone's life a misery, the Turks quick to take advantage of that by sending out short sharp raids to further lower the spirits of those they faced.

After days of such downpours the sky cleared, the wind dropped and news came from St Simeon that a fleet of Genoese ships had arrived in the harbour with supplies, and not just provender: there were new Crusaders too, if in no great number, but more importantly the Great Count Roger had responded to his nephew's request and sent from Sicily his most experienced artisans, men who had campaigned with him on the island and helped to take many a Saracen fortress.

Their first task was to turn Bohemund's temporary bastion on the slopes of Mount Staurin into a more robust fortress and if it could not match in strength the walls of Antioch it was well built enough to completely secure that flank and obviate the risk of what many feared, a mass attack being launched down that slope in an attempt to sweep the Crusaders into the river. Needing to be named, as did everything structured in the siege, the men who manned it called their temporary fort Malregard, a reference to the fact that it was still an exposed and dangerous position.

Yet if that arrival lifted the spirits it soon became clear just how short a period any food they had brought would last, and the ships were quick to depart once unloaded, with those who knew of the sea aware that they would not be seen again till spring, so dangerous was the Mediterranean for lengthy winter voyages. They still had Cyprus, much closer, but even there the crossing could be suspended for weeks due to storms, and in anticipation of dearth Bohemund sent half his horses away to the north where there was more pasture, an act which his fellow princes declined to emulate.

That still left him with enough mounts to be active in the ensuing sorties and the one most pressing was the need to counter the interdiction of supplies by roving raiders from the eastern hinterland. It was not just the loss of food to the Crusaders – every time a force sought to impede supplies getting in through the Iron Gate they faced not just the defenders of Antioch but a strong mounted force which threatened their rear and on more than one occasion had caught the Frankish lances unawares and inflicted heavy casualties.

As the contingent who would find it easiest to disengage and recross the Iron Bridge, the council deputed the Apulian Normans to seek to remove this threat, to find out where these raiders were camped and either destroy them or so harry them they would have to move further away to a point where their depredations would cease to be effective. From being static before the St Paul's Gate – only the other contingents had seen much work mounted – Bohemund's lances, one thousand strong, were delighted to move out on horseback. Tancred was left in charge of the rest of the host and Robert of Salerno taken along as second in command.

Across the bridge and riding east Bohemund was aware that the terrain to him was unknown. The plain he was on consisted of rolling hills, grassed after the recent rains, until far in the distance was an escarpment he knew was called Jalal Talat and the fortress of Harim. He suspected that somewhere in between there was a Turkish camp and a force of an unknown number, but one seemingly big enough to raid close to Antioch as well as far and wide to block the routes to the siege lines, so highly mobile and operating in country which they clearly knew well.

'Let us show them respect, Robert.'

That such a feeling did not come naturally to the Lombard showed on his face, but he kept any words to himself.

'We will split up. I want you to ride ahead at walking pace with half our lances and seek to flush out our enemy. As soon as they think you will discover their encampment they will be obliged to try and drive you off.'

'Happily.'

'You are not to offer them anything other than token battle. Make sure the fellow with the horn knows that you intend to retreat shortly after making contact.'

'I could tell the men.'

'Then you would have five hundred generals instead of one, best keep your own council. Understand this, Robert, I sense in you a desire to be popular and that is laudable in a leader, but my father taught me it is just as important to know your own mind and to be equally sure that no one who is not in your trust does not. Half the time in combat he was the only person who knew what he intended and that was total in his dealings with men off the field of battle.'

'Like my grandfather?'

'I only knew Prince Gisulf a little, Robert, but I can tell you he makes Count Hugh of Vermandois look like Alexander the Great, he was such a military dolt.' Seeing that it sounded like a slight on his bloodline, Bohemund softened his tone, which had been unsympathetic. 'You are not he and today, if we combine well, you will prove it. We may not see battle but if we do I want you to stand as well in my eyes as Tancred.'

'I thank you for that.'

'Robert, it is an aim I extend to all my captains, without exception. Now ride ahead and spread your men out to cover as much ground as the landscape allows without any loss of contact.'

'How will I let you know if we do find the enemy?' Bohemund just looked at him without answering, the obvious point that this was something he should be able to sort out himself and Robert acknowledged that. 'Men to the rear who will alert you?'

'I need numbers and how willing they are to fight. If, as I hope, they see you as meat for their table you are to take flight as if beaten, the rest will fall to me.'

Watching them depart there was a moment when Bohemund doubted the wisdom of giving Robert command; his lust for some kind of glory was high – he had a need to wipe out the stain of his inheritance being taken from him by the *Guiscard*, that made even more disagreeable by the fact that Duke Robert's wife, his Aunt Sichelgaita, had been a party to the removal of her own father – seeking fame, Robert might disobey his instructions. That thought had to be smothered; he had handed over responsibility and there was no point in fretting upon it. Instead he must look to how he was going to exploit what he expected to happen.

When the first half of his force was out of sight Bohemund ordered his men to dismount and walk; he wanted his mounts to be as fresh as possible for what he hoped was coming and it was a long time before that anticipation turned to frustration for there was no sign of Robert making contact, sending a hard-riding messenger to alert him to the approaching Turks. Throughout the morning they walked, exercising strict control over their horses when it came to cropping pasture or drinking, for a full belly was not an advantage in an equine when it came to rapid movement.

The sun was well past the zenith and he was getting closer to that escarpment called Jalal Talat when Bohemund realised he had made an error in thinking the fortress of Harim was too far off to trouble the siege of Antioch. So close had they come that a separate camp would have been unnecessary, indeed folly, much more vulnerable than even a small walled fort. Given cause to admire his enemies before, he was in that position again, there being no point in being upset that they failed to conform to his own tactical thinking.

'Mount up,' he called as he saw a rider, or rather the dust cloud in which he was near enveloped, his gaze ranging round for some way to keep his presence partly hidden. He wanted the Turks so fully committed they could not avoid contact and he spied to his side a low hill that, if it would not hide his men completely from anyone on an elevated slope, would serve to obscure their number. Riding slowly – he did not want dust in the air to alert the enemy – he led his men to where he had chosen to wait.

Robert was a long time coming, again raising the spectre of him acting for his own reputation, but eventually the ground began to vibrate with the effect of so many hooves and the one man Bohemund had put as lookout began to signal that the fleeing Normans were approaching and assured him that there were upwards of a thousand men in their wake. The lances went down as soon as the men had crossed themselves.

Now it was not vibrations but noise, a thundering and increasing cacophony of fast-riding horses, and then came the distant but faint whoops of excited and triumphant Turks, the same sound they had originally emitted at Dorylaeum. The forward element of Robert's section, the fastest riders, began to fly past the vision of the waiting Normans and yet Bohemund held still, for his presence remained unknown and that surprised him. Surely the Turks would have the sense to divert some of their pursuers to high ground to alert them to a possible trap, and if they did they could not fail to see what was waiting for them even if it was too late to avoid.

The sight of the bulk of his men riding by, neck over their withers, was soon followed by the first Turks, nearly everyone with a sword out and looking straight ahead, until those with wiser heads could not fail to see, by a flicking glance, what was on their flank. That they tried to pull up caused confusion throughout the Turkish ranks and that to Bohemund was the time to move. He led his men out at a fast canter, trusting the conroy leaders to exercise the requisite control, and they hit the first Turkish riders, spread out as they were, almost at once.

Robert must have been looking back, for as soon as Bohemund moved he had the horn blown and his men spun round to join in, with their young leader showing good judgement by leading them to the left flank of the Turks, the opposite side to which they were being assaulted by Bohemund. Riding flat out in pursuit it was near impossible for the Turks to either turn to meet the enemy in any disciplined manner or to easily realise how precarious their position was and retreat.

They sought to fight, but the odds were numerically against them as well as the tactical situation; they were disordered whereas the Normans were in close to full control, and that was not improved when they started to go down in droves to the couched lances. If there was a leader he had lost the battle before it started, for he could exercise no command that would save his men other than individual flight and, worse for his survival, those to the rear of his leading cavalry, unaware of what they faced, came on pell-mell into the battle, pushing forward their fellows into the rapidly closing jaws of the Norman maw.

The Turks died in droves; forced in upon themselves they fought as bravely as they could, but once more, when it came to even numbers the Normans, in their physical attributes and weapons, outmatched them in every way. For every one that died, another two were wounded to become a prisoner and when the battle was done the Turks had lost so many men to both that Bohemund knew the threat from Harim to be quashed.

The prisoners were brought back to Antioch to be paraded before the walls, a taunt to the defenders to tell them that their situation had gone from sound to questionable: without the support from Harim, the Crusaders' supplies would increase and theirs would diminish. The Turks jeered at that, so to still their mockery the men Bohemund had captured were brought into plain view and beheaded by a single blow of a Crusader sword, their heads then catapulted over the battlements.

The Turks, if they could not match the numbers, sent out a sneak sortie and caught a high divine, the Archdeacon of Metz, sharing an assignation with a comely young Armenian girl in one of the apple orchards. The cleric, clearly bent on seduction, lost his head immediately, the girl and his skull being taken back into Antioch, she to be, the besiegers were informed, a sound receptacle of the juices of Islam. They knew what that meant: she had been raped into stupefaction. Then she was beheaded like her potential lover, both their heads fired back along with contempt.

Day after day the Armenian patriarch of Antioch, an elderly man as befitted his office, was brought to the walls to be hung upside down while the soles of his feet were beaten with rods, an affliction he bore with more fortitude than those who observed his ill-treatment. Designed to drive good Christians to fury, it succeeded better than the Turks could have supposed and fired up the very people they sought to taunt to a level of barbarity that flew in the face of their stated beliefs.

CHAPTER TWENTY-THREE

For all the successes enjoyed by the besiegers, hunger soon became the abiding curse; all their plans for regular supplies foundered on the inability of those who had promised to deliver, and that continued even after the threat of Turkish interdiction had been removed. Then there came weather that was a surprise to the majority if not those who had a wider knowledge of the world; not just rain and cold, which they thought the region free from, but heavy falls of snow that completely cut off the routes to Antioch for even those trying to meet their commitments.

Supplies by sea, even after the Crusaders had captured and opened the southern port of Latakia, on a benign wind a day's sailing from Cyprus, were delayed by storms, and it had to be added that the island was a place of no abundance. The locals fed themselves first and no amount of payment would tempt them to risk hunger for the sake of a cause of which most of them had no notion. Foraging, from an area that had borne a heavy burden already, was producing less and less and the store of available sustenance was so depleted as to cause serious concern.

Naturally the fighting men were fed first, which meant that the pilgrims without the means to buy at inflated prices starved, and all the pleas of people like Peter the Hermit fell on deaf ears when it came to the Council of Princes.They worried about the health of their soldiers and it was far from good – disease always stalked siege lines and Antioch was no different, but if the men were weakened by hunger the death toll would escalate to dangerous proportions.

With no reinforcements coming in because of the season it was vital to maintain the numbers they could now muster and, with that in mind, it was decided that the act of foraging had to be extended beyond what would be considered safe or advisable in normal times. The decision was not unanimous that it should be so, especially given the lack of fit horses due to the need to put the feeding of men before equines, and it was this over which Raymond of Toulouse and the Normans came into open conflict.

'You are talking about sending away a high proportion of our cavalry strength and half our *milities*. What of Antioch?'

'The Count of Toulouse,' said Robert of Normandy in reply, 'does not seem to accept that without we can feed our men, there will be no siege to press home.'

'While the Duke of Normandy cannot grasp that Antioch must be in as dire straits as we. It is no time to relax our grip. If we must send men away let it be to a place where there is food.'

'Would not that equally deplete our strength?' Bohemund enquired.

Raymond had taken a position on the matter and over the

preceding weeks he had become fixed in his opinion that he knew how to press home a siege better than his peers, which gave Adémar a real dilemma, for he lacked the knowledge to know who was right and who was wrong. This made what he saw as diplomacy and some saw as fence sitting harder to maintain.

'At least, Count Bohemund, we might see those we favour back to good health.'

'Good! When they return they can bury the bones of those left behind.'

While Raymond sought to impose his views, Godfrey de Bouillon had moved to a position of much influence for his sound common sense as well as his complete lack of conceit and, while Adémar had seen his authority diminish, that of the Duke of Lower Lorraine had risen to the point that when he spoke all listened.

'The stocks of food are low and they are not being replenished in enough quantity. I would also remind you, My Lords, that we have another duty, which if it does not transcend what we are engaged in must have an effect on our thinking.'

'These pestilential pilgrims,' Vermandois spat. 'They eat food that should go to the men who fight. If you had listened to me after Nicaea it is a burden we would have shed.'

'Would it matter,' Godfrey responded, 'if they starved in Bythnia or here in Syria?'

'The Emperor would have fed and cared for them.'

'As he did previously, Count Hugh? Do you not recall we walked over their bones on the road to Nicaea? I would like to see you put that point to the sainted Peter who led them. He was in my pavilion today pleading that his pilgrims be treated equally and as Christians.'

'We lack the stores,' Robert of Normandy insisted. 'We have no more than a week of half rations and no idea of what will come in the days ahead.'

'I must have a formal proposal,' Adémar insisted, 'so I can put it to the vote.'

That got him a jaundiced look from Raymond, who expected support from the papal legate who had, to his mind, come here on the tail of his surcoat. But the Bishop was on the horns of a dilemma, still seeking to maintain harmony when he could see it fracturing before his eyes. It had come to the point that without Godfrey de Bouillon to aid him in keeping the peace there would have been constant dissent and disagreement.

'I propose,' said Normandy, 'that we send out every pack animal and ox cart we can muster, with men to both protect and lead them, to proceed to the plateau known as the Jabal as Summaq, in which we are told food is plentiful, and bring back enough to help sustain us until the spring.'

'Ten days to get there, ten to forage and ten back at least,' Raymond protested. 'Do you not think our Turks watching from their citadel will not notice?'

Bohemund spoke up then. 'Are you saying we cannot contain them even with half our strength?'

That flummoxed Raymond; if he believed he could not hold them he was admitting to the fact the siege was an error – the host outnumbered the defender six to one at even the most limited estimate.

'I would undertake to do that,' Bohemund added, which stung the Provençal magnate's pride. 'There is no need when my knights are present. They alone can seal the walls.'

'Then, Count Raymond,' interjected Robert of Normandy, 'you will not object to your foot soldiers driving the carts?'

'Do you intend to lead, Duke Robert?'

That gentle enquiry from Godfrey de Bouillon got a shake of the head. 'I will put forward my brother-in-law of Flanders.'

'An excellent choice,' Adémar exclaimed, with such faux enthusiasm he made it sound the very opposite.

Godfrey spoke next. 'Would you, Count Bohemund, agree to share the venture?'

'Surely it is the turn of others?'

'How can it be, my friend, when you so recently defeated our enemies in open conflict?'

'I am willing to serve as the council directs.'

The plateau referred to by the Duke of Normandy lay well to the south-east of Antioch and as had already been stated it was, for the kind of cavalcade led by his brother-in-law and Count Bohemund, a long and slow march to get there. Both commanded large bodies of knights, some three hundred each in number, enough to cow the locals into cooperation as well as to deal with any groups of Turks they might encounter.

Where Bohemund had come to enjoy common ground with Duke Robert on the way to Dorylaeum, he found the Count of Flanders less forthcoming in that regard, he being aloof and much concerned that he was as much a knight and commander as the Norman and that his authority over his own lances should not in any way be compromised. Added to that, those on foot were Raymond of Toulouse's men and they proved unruly, their captains just as unwilling to bow the knee to Norman or Frank.

The success of their mission made such a situation tolerable; while acting in concert they operated in a semi-independent fashion, ranging far and wide over what was a land full of milk and honey compared to Antioch, loading up their beast of burden and their carts until they were fully laden, eventually coming together to camp side by side with the intention of starting back for Antioch on the next morning, the troops of Flanders to the east and the Normans to their rear.

It was never established whose duty it was to send out scouts, each man blamed the other for the failure to do so and that continued all the way to the later chronicles of the Crusade; all that mattered was there were none, or too few to give warning of the threat that was approaching the foraging force. The sight of a large party of Turks at dawn, observing their positions, was in itself alarming and set the camp into a rush to get ready to move. Riding out to assess the level of danger Bohemund got a shock greater than any he had ever experienced, for, from an elevated observation point, he could see that the land to the east was covered in marching men; this was no roving squadron but a full-scale army, obviously headed for Antioch, and one that massively outnumbered the Crusaders.

Hastening back to the lines he harried the drovers and *milities* to get their carts and animals into motion in the hope of putting some distance between them and the Turks, quick to curse the Count of Flanders for the fact of such a force being a surprise. There were grounds for that, if they were slender – the mounted men of Flanders had operated close to the enemy line of march – but it was, in truth, the fault of both men to allow themselves to feel so secure that no duty for protection had been discussed.

To say it was a race to get clear was risible; the sole hope was that the approaching Turkish host would have in mind some other objective and that the sight of the foraging Franks would not divert them from that. It proved to be a false dream almost before they cleared the overnight encampment, as Turkish cavalry appeared on the far hillsides in numbers, clearly intent on forcing battle. With sinking hearts the two leaders knew the Muslim foot would be hot on their heels. Worse, the mounted warriors split into twin columns and set off with the clear intention of getting ahead of the Crusaders before coming together and blocking their route to the west and there was little either Count could do to prevent it.

Running for the whole foraging party was not an option; too many were foot bound, quite apart from their encumbrances, so they were ordered to make a corral with their wagons, into which they should lead their donkeys, mules and packhorses, and to then form a defence around that while the knights sought to drive off the enemy enough to create a corridor of escape. To the west the Turks were coming in from both the pincers to close the gap, leaving the lances no choice but to seek to force a way through.

Robert of Flanders declined to give first chance to the Normans – or was it their commander, for whose fame and reputation he now openly demonstrated his disdain? Gathering his knights he set off to stop the completion of that encircling movement, Bohemund electing not to join him but determined to hold his men together so that he could react to whatever came next. The knights of Flanders did good service, crushing the line of Turks before them, which allowed Bohemund to split his forces and attack the two wings which were now in confusion, thus opening the potential for flight by all.

With their weight superiority the Crusader knights were doing great slaughter and driving back the enemy so that the route west was clear. Hard as they fought to hold open that corridor, and despite an order to move, abandoning wagons and animals, including the stores they had worked so hard to collect, it soon became clear that the *milities* felt safer in their wagon-bound enclave than in the open and when they should have moved they stayed put. Never having the discipline of their mounted confrères, regardless of where they came from, no amount of browbeating would make them budge.

Both Bohemund and Robert of Flanders were in a bind: if they went to the rescue of their Provençal *milities* they would be riding back into the Turkish trap, and pouring towards that square of wagons were thousands of Turkish foot, too many for a force of five hundred knights to beat off unless they could be induced to panic. Why would they do that when on either flank they still had mounted men ready to fall upon their enemy?

It had to be attempted, there was no choice; mounts which had already been in action once were kicked into motion once more to filter round the wagons on both sides, one half of the field the ragged lances of Flanders, the other the near-to-neat line of Normans. The effect was immediate in that the Turks halted their onward progress, yet they were numerically so superior that the hoped for wave of dread and flight did not materialise; they formed a firm line ready to resist the charge of heavy cavalry under command of men who held them steady.

For their bravery the men at the front died in droves, speared, sliced, cut and trampled by the sheer weight of what hit them, and soon the knights were doing execution in staggering quantities, though not without losses of their own. Bohemund, in between slaying his foes, realised that the cavalry they had driven back were now re-formed and about to repeat their previous manoeuvre, only this time they would be close to and in support of their own foot, a potentially deadly combination.

Much as he hated the notion there was no choice but to withdraw or die in a situation where preservation of the mounted part of the crusading host was paramount. Added to that was the frustration that the Provençal *milities* had still not moved; this they could have done at a run and then at least he and Flanders could have acted to protect their back. Nor was he sure that his fellow leader would discern the same dilemma as he, leaving him no choice but to disengage independently, an act which left the Count of Flanders no option but to do likewise, a later cause of increased recrimination.

To get clear was not simple; the Turks did everything they could to hamper their efforts, but find space they did, riding hard towards the wagons, Bohemund yelling that there was still a slim chance to flee, a faint hope the Turks would not come on at speed. Now, as the knights rode by them without stopping – they could not without they sacrifice themselves – these Provençal foot soldiers finally realised the extent of their plight and some emerged to grab the stirrups of their knights so as to be dragged to safety.

Most remained, and when the mounts were blown and the knights stopped on the crest of a hill, it was to look back at a scene of slaughter as the *milities* fought and failed to hold off the Turks. For those who did not fall, slavery would be their lot, but nearly as depressing was the fact that all the supplies they had gathered were now in Turkish hands. Painful to watch, it had to be witnessed and it sat heavy on their souls as they rode back to Antioch, only to find there that the Turks had taken advantage of their absence to sortie out and attack the siege lines, inflicting a serious check using the tactic of the false retreat.

Emerging in numbers from the Bridge Gate they had enticed the Crusaders under Raymond and Adémar to cross the bridge of boats and seek to chase them off. It seemed to have been initially successful, but it was a trap and once the knights were on the wrong bank of the Orontes the Turks had turned upon them and engineered a rout, not a serious one in terms of dead and wounded, but a dent to their pride and also their faith: the Turks had taken the blue and gold Virgin banner of Bishop Adémar, which was held to be a thing no Christian God should have allowed.

Hope in any army is of paramount concern and the losses in men and food reported when the two Counts returned, added to the recent defeat before the Bridge Gate, sent that plummeting and it was not assuaged in the weeks that followed as food grew ever more scarce. First the non-combatant pilgrims began to die, and many of those who could not cling to life set off north in the hope of at least getting home. With soldiers reduced to eating berries and weeds death stalked the lines too and every morning produced more copses. The morale of the host led even powerful knights to seek succour: Stephen of Blois, claiming to be too ill to continue and his purse to be bare, removed himself to Alexandretta.

Every leader was emptying his purse to buy what could be purchased from those with food and they were selling at rapacious prices, this while the wind blew, the rain lashed down every few days and the occasional snow reduced the whole effort to stark misery, a state of which Yaghi Siyan took full advantage. No body of knights was safe, especially on starving, unfit horses, and even the trickle of supplies coming in from the ports of St Simeon and Latakia were subject to constant raids, all launched from the three Antioch gates the Crusade could not block.

Then Tacitus declared he must go north and seek reinforcements from the Emperor, a move that was greeted with much encouragement. That faded when it was realised he had taken his troops with him, abandoning his own possessions and much of their equipment to facilitate a fast march, the conclusion obvious: it was very doubtful if he intended to return.

Such gloom reached its nadir when it was discovered that even Peter the Hermit, that talismanic figure, in the company of a pious knight called William, Lord of Melun, had set off for Constantinople too and that could not be borne. Tancred was sent after him and he did bring both men back. Tempted to string them up, Bohemund, who was given the power of decision over their fate, felt he had to release them after no more than a stern lecture; to punish either severely would, in Peter's case, upset the pilgrims who saw him as their spiritual leader, and as for William of Melun, the knights in the host were restive enough without firing that up anymore, though he was treated as dirt and a carpet for the whole of the time he spent in Bohemund's tent.

Bleak as it was in want and dearth, there were occasional bright spots: the arrival of a fleet from England bearing supplies raised hope of assuaged hunger, until it was realised that most of the cargo was large quantities of oak and along with that came the woodworkers who could fashion it. Still, there was food too, and since oak was important, a large escort, hundreds of knights, went to bring it in safety to the siege lines, an indication of how difficult that was the fact that there were half a dozen small engagements on the way.

It was decided to use the oak to construct another fortress opposite the Bridge Gate, the site chosen that of a ruined mosque and a still used cemetery. If it was heartless of the Crusaders to disinter the bodies of the Muslim dead and throw them into an open pit, the fact that that caused great lamentation from the walls of Antioch was to the good – anything that lowered Turkish morale was to be welcomed. Soon the fortress stood four-square to block the exit. It was not intended to be so secure it did not need support, but it did mean that those who manned it could hold off the enemy in some safety until help arrived.

What was left went towards strengthening a derelict building opposite the St George's Gate, into which Tancred moved as an independent command. If he could not entirely blockade the entrance he could reduce the flow of goods going through it to a trickle, which left Yaghi Siyan only the Iron Gate for resupply, and mobile patrols made that risky. When the weather began to turn the Council of Princes found themselves in command of a much diminished force both in terms of man and horsepower.

If it was that, some comfort had to be taken from the hardiness of those who remained; these were the tough ones, the fellows whose faith or sheer tenacity had seen them through. If it was a lean force now, no more than thirty thousand strong and seriously short of horses, it was a resilient one and it had to be, for news came from their scouts of yet another Muslim army coming to the relief of Antioch under Ridwan, the son of the Sultan of Baghdad, which brought up a stark choice: to meet and defeat them or lift the siege of Antioch.

CHAPTER TWENTY-FOUR

If the number of reported Turks coming their way under Ridwan of Aleppo had to be an exaggeration, there was no doubt the Crusaders faced a massive force equal to their own and they could only detach so many from the siege to face it. Added to that their main weapon, the mounted knight with lance, was now so constrained by a lack of fit horses that doubts existed as to how effective it could be. When counted, it was realised that only some six hundred equines could bear a human load enough to do battle and they could not all be taken away from the defence of their siege lines.

At least they knew exactly where the Turks had camped, around the fortress of Harim, and they now had a greater grasp of the terrain than their enemy, which Bohemund pointed out allowed them to choose where any battle would be fought. This could provide a crucial advantage, for he still maintained, even after what had occurred so recently on the foraging expedition, that the Turks were not stalwart and the key to defeating them was the kind of surprise that threw their undisciplined levies into disarray.

'They are a mob, even the cavalry,' he insisted. 'Look how they acted at Nicaea. Let us commit them to battle and then shock them.'

'Mounts,' Vermandois said, and for once it was treated as a valid interjection.

'Most of our knights will have to fight on foot, Count Hugh,' Godfrey de Bouillon stated. 'That we have already established.'

'We must use our horses to good effect, and no one is more adept at that than we Normans.'

Even saintly Godfrey was put out by that comment from the Duke of Normandy, it being so crass, which was nothing as to the reaction of Raymond, who positively bristled; he had yet to forgive Bohemund and Robert of Flanders for the loss of his Provençal *milities*.

'It would be fitting if certain people were to accept that we are equals in combat.'

'Except in one regard, Count Raymond,' Bohemund interrupted, albeit softly. 'We Apulians have more fit horses than anyone else, the Duke of Normandy included.'

Two spectres were raised by that: the Count of Taranto had sent many of his horses away at the approach of winter where others had declined to do so and, if they had not all fared as well as he hoped, the number that came back battle-ready, some two hundred mounts, was significant. The second point did not have to be stated: there was no chance whatever that the Normans of South Italy would hand these horses over to anyone else. If there were to be a use of mounts in the coming encounter it would be led by Bohemund.

'My Lords,' he continued, 'even on foot, we knights mailed are

322

a match for the Turks, as you, Count Raymond proved at Nicaea, which I again take leave to mention.'

'And there,' Godfrey added, 'we chose where to fight.'

'That is our best hope,' Raymond agreed, his high mood assuaged slightly by Bohemund's reference to his previous success. 'So we now must spend time in the choosing.'

This time they were poring over maps that had been drawn by their own scribes; anything Roman after the desertion of Tacitus was seen as tainted. The obvious tactical need was a valley and one high sided enough to make it difficult for Ridwan to get over the slopes to outflank them, though given the numbers they could deploy it was hoped he would not even consider such a stratagem. The use of a false retreat was examined and discarded; the Turks employed that manoeuvre themselves and might not fall for it when used against them.

'Fighting on foot, cohesion is all,' declared Raymond. 'If we try to back away we will lose that and will struggle to re-form our line if they decline to follow. No, if we fall back, it must be pace by pace and decided by a single banner.'

'And once they are committed,' concluded Adémar, 'it is down to you, Count Bohemund.'

'Might I suggest the Count of Toulouse to command the knights on foot?'

Florid Toulouse was obviously taken with that notion and he glared at everyone present, Bohemund apart, daring them to decline him the honour.

'I am happy for you to lead,' Godfrey said, that backed by Hugh of Vermandois, who had lost some of his ambition since the start of this siege. Only the Duke of Normandy looked reluctant as he agreed.

In the event it was classic in its execution; Ridwan was so sure of his numerical superiority he came on as if he had already triumphed, to meet a line of mailed knights on foot, with shields and weapons at the ready, men who stood and suffered the attack by mounted archers and did not flinch. Then came the mass of Turkish foot, shoulder to shoulder and in deep and multiple lines that stretched across the valley floor, their kettledrums beating a loud tattoo and their cries to the Prophet rending the air.

At first the Crusaders were immovable, until Ridwan sent in several supporting waves so that the battle area became a crowded mass. The Crusaders took their first backward step, only one and in unison, each man eyeing the banner of Raymond so as to be sure that what order had been given was just that – one step and no more. Encouraged, Ridwan sent in more men and again, after a fierce fight the Crusader line went backwards, not much, but heartening to the Turkish general. Sure that one final push would break the Crusaders' spirit he committed all of his men and backed them up with his mounted archers. The whole milled about in the rear, ready for the pursuit, which was bound to follow.

Bohemund did not show restraint as he entered the fray; cresting the right-hand slope, he and his lances came over as a body and for once he let the slope dictate the pace of his attack, which was made at the full gallop over what was a short distance. To hold a line on such an incline was impossible, just as unlikely as that a force of a mere two hundred knights could put to flight an army numbered in the tens of thousands. Yet shock and astonishment are potent weapons and that was what fell upon the Turks now, and if the sight of these charging horsemen was not enough to dent their confidence, the sudden reversal of the actions of the mailed knights to their front was.

Raymond, Godfrey, Robert of Normandy and Hugh of Vermandois could not have acted in more unison and it was a miracle of coordination. Every one of their banners were dipped forward, following the command from Raymond, telling their knights to take back what ground they had surrendered, the aim not just to kill, but to pin their foes and make them stay and fight. Pressed into a confined space by the eagerness of Ridwan, what Bohemund and his knights careered into, the mounted archers, was such a solid mass there was no chance for anyone, man or beast, to escape and that they tried sent a ripple of panic through their entire host.

It was that, rather than slaughter, which determined the next phase, as men who felt themselves betrayed began to seek a way to save their skins and in doing so those archers ran down their own foot soldiers, trampling them under their horses' hooves and even swiping with their swords to clear a path. At the front killing zone, fighters who had thought they were winning were now dying in droves, for they had no notion of security to their rear, which took the passion that had so far sustained them out of their efforts.

A stronger general would have sought to rally his troops; Ridwan of Aleppo was far from that – he owed his position to his bloodline and was more concerned with his own life than that of the host he led. As soon as it appeared they might be checked, not defeated, the son of the Sultan called for his banner and fled the field, the effect on those who saw this disastrous. The non-engaged foot soldiers went after their mounted archers, leaving those at the front and the many others who stood their ground exposed to Bohemund's knights who were engaged in butchery at the rear. They began to die in even greater numbers or to fall to their knees and plead for mercy as they sensed they had been abandoned.

Now the shortage of mounts truly told; the Crusaders lacked the means to pursue their running foes – the horses were past their peak and too valuable to risk, while mailed men would struggle to walk at pace never mind run. They had won the day in this Syrian valley but did not yet know if they had prevailed in the contest, so they dare not let up, dare not let Ridwan regroup. It was a weary and dusty march towards the fortress of Harim, prayers being mouthed through cracked dry lips that they would not have to fight take it.

The joy when they saw the place in flames was unalloyed, that even deeper when they espied what Turks remained were hurrying east to safety. Raymond called a halt and Godfrey de Bouillon immediately beckoned forward Bishop Adémar, who had insisted he must share their fate if not their fight, and begged him to say Mass there and then for their deliverance. If any Turks of Ridwan's now crushed army did look back, it would have been to see the men who had driven them from the field of battle, both mounted and on foot, now on their knees in deep prayer.

In flight, the Turks had left abundant food, horses and valuables – silks, gold and silver, which were as rich a prize as victory – and also the Crusaders had prisoners in abundance, with Turkish banners to display to the defenders of Antioch, men who had known Ridwan was close and had fully expected to be relieved. Instead, they saw their religious brothers beheaded and knew that soon those skulls would be catapulted inside their walls.

The feeling that matters had tipped in their favour began to permeate the Crusaders' lines, yet any notion of a quick end to the siege was certainly not in sight – the Turks were still sending out sniping raids and their walls were intact, so it was a sentiment not a fact, the defeat of Ridwan of Aleppo being part of that. In addition, with improving weather the fields were producing food, and ships were bringing that in from Cyprus and more lances from Europe, which despite pleas to the papacy was a trickle not a flood. The problem, anyway, was not numbers but the sheer strength of the walls added to the tenacity of the resistance, and there was another matter that Bohemund was keen to raise in the Council of Princes: the status of Antioch after the siege was over, which was delicate.

'It will be handed back to the Emperor,' Raymond declared, 'as we promised we would do.'

'You would gift to a man who has done nothing to aid us since we gave him Nicaea?'

'We are bound by our oaths, Count Bohemund,' Adémar reminded him, which got support from Godfrey de Bouillon who referred to the ceremony at which he had sworn.

'I too kissed the relics as Alexius demanded of me, but I made him do so too, Godfrey, on the grounds that such loyalty extended in both directions.'

'Is an emperor bound by such things?' asked Vermandois; he meant a king, his brother.

'Alexius Comnenus is a man like you and I.'

That got a flare of the French nostrils and a nod from Walo, as ever by his side – Count Hugh thought himself superior to most men, an opinion not even shared by his own people.

'And I take the view that he has broken his oath to me.'

The Duke of Normandy laughed, his eyes twinkling with humour. 'Very convenient, Count Bohemund; that will allow a de Hauteville to take more Byzantine fiefs, which is a family trait, is it not?'

'Anglo-Saxon property is just as succulent, My Lord.'

That barb hit home and for once Bohemund thought that the man he had seen for months past as an ally might not be on his side in the discussion he was determined to force into the open. He also knew he had been too acerbic in his response to the mention of his family, and Robert replied in kind.

'While a legitimate claim to a kingdom trumps banditry, you will find.'

'None of those present can say that there is no other claim against that which we each own, My Lord.'

'I am curious to what you are driving at?' asked Adémar, seeing this conversation between two Normans as a distraction.

'When Antioch falls, as it will even if we are here for years, I say to hand it back to Alexius would be folly. He has done nothing to aid us, quite the opposite. If Tacitus withdrew on his own initiative, he did not return to us on imperial orders. Alexius has no intention of aiding us to take Antioch and the impression I get is he expects us to fail here.'

'I cannot agree that is so.'

'Where are his men, Count Raymond? We cleared the Cilician Gates and the Belen Pass to ease his journey south, and the towns on the way were free of Turks and would welcome him. He had a passage denied to us and no shortage of supplies, given he has ships at his disposal – vessels, I would remind you, we have not seen in the harbour of St Simeon.'

'All this may be true, Count Bohemund,' Adémar insisted, his face creasing, for it was not now as smooth and round as it had been before; many months of worry and the needs of his office had produced lines that now showed. 'But you have yet to answer the question I posed.'

'How, if there is no aid from Byzantium, is Antioch to be held?

How, when the Crusade marches on to Jerusalem, is it to be supplied? How, if the Turks are resurgent, is it going to be possible to ensure they do not get across our rear and cut us off?'

'It is rare to answer one question with three.'

'The answers are more important, Your Grace.'

Vermandois spoke up again. 'When we succeed, Alexius will send a fleet and army south to take possession.'

'Only if we agree he can and hold it for him until he does, which will not speed the journey to Palestine.'

'You would defy him?' Raymond asked.

'I would remind him that as far as I am concerned he has broken his oath to me, and therefore he has forfeited any right to my aid in giving him Antioch.'

'While,' Robert Duke of Normandy opined, 'any one of us here can claim that right if they share your view and are prepared to risk their soul by setting aside their oath.'

Vermandois was quick to butt in. 'Not least the Count of Taranto.'

'I still say that Alexius will send a garrison,' Raymond insisted.

'And if he does, My Lord, will you feel safe? Do you believe that if the Turks threaten his capital he will hold Antioch and risk that Constantinople might fall? Who amongst us has not felt let down by the actions of the Emperor up till now?'

That stopped any eye contact, for Bohemund had hit a very sore spot indeed – if they had not complained openly every one of them had railed at his lack of support in private.

'Alexius is clever, My Lords, he let us think he would take the field in person and aid us on our Crusade but he did not. Instead he has used us to free his borderlands and his men have stood aside when we have been in danger, as at Dorylaeum. We have crushed Turk

329

after Turk and who will benefit from their being diminished if not the Byzantine Empire?'

'We do.'

'And so, Your Grace, does he. I say we must hold Antioch ourselves and deny it to him, not for mere gain but for our own security and the sake of the Crusade.'

'And who,' Duke Robert enquired, 'will hold it?'

'We must hold it in common,' Adémar cried, before he realised he might be agreeing with Bohemund. 'Until Alexius makes his presence felt.'

'By the laws of conquest,' Bohemund said quietly, 'the man who holds it is the one whose banner flies above the walls when Antioch falls.'

There was a moment then when avarice came to the surface; Antioch was a rich fief, a great centre of trade and whoever was suzerain would not want for wealth. Then each mind, Bohemund was certain, turned to the notion that such a possession might fall to another and that, as a consideration, was less welcome.

'Pope Urban would not approve of even the thought.'

'Bishop Adémar, Pope Urban is not here, and I say if you wish to take and hold Jerusalem for our faith, you will not do so unless you hold Antioch as well. I have said my piece, but know this: my family has fought Byzantium for over sixty years and I will make a claim I do not think can be gainsaid. We de Hautevilles know them better than anyone in the council and to repose any faith in the notion that they, or Alexius Comnenus, will do anything other than that which protects their own interests, is folly.'

'Why do I think you have hankered after Antioch all along?' asked Tancred, when his uncle related to him the gist of the meeting.

'No, not Antioch, but it has been a long time since I felt that anything would come from going on to Jerusalem.' That raised a youthful eyebrow. 'Remember I told you by the River Vardar of all the things that were unknown. Then we had no notion of what to truly expect from Alexius or Byzantium, no idea of how or if this Crusade would progress. I tell you, if Alexius was here I would not even raise my voice regarding Antioch, it would be his by right, but he is not and we have not seen hide or hair of his main army, even at Nicaea.'

'He saw you as a threat.'

'Tancred, he saw us all as a threat. If he did not he would have come to Nicaea himself instead of Tacitus. No Roman emperor can afford to repose trust in any man and Alexius so mistrusted us our back was all he wanted to see.'

'Which angers you?'

'No, he acts as he sees in the interests of his empire. I am seeking to persuade the Council of Princes to act on behalf of the Crusade.'

Tancred grinned. 'But you would like that we Apulians should take possession of Antioch?'

'The man who held it for Byzantium was titled "Prince".' Bohemund laughed out loud, which had been rare these last months. 'Would that not be one in the eye for a Great Count and a mere Duke of Apulia?'

'Can we make that happen?'

Bohemund shook his head. 'Only God can make that happen.'

If Bohemund's views had struck obstacles with most of the leaders, Hugh of Vermandois was animated by the thought of his banner flying over Antioch, so when a message was sent to him offering to surrender the city, delivered by an Armenian smuggler, he eagerly pursued it and wanted to do so personally. This was a notion Walo of Chaumont, who had been sent to contain his follies, spent much time talking him out of and he only persuaded the Count to desist by offering to meet these Muslim rebels himself.

Every gate into the city had a postern and there were others at various places in the walls, small doors which only one man could pass through at a time and therefore very easy to defend or block up if threatened. In a time of peace these facilitated movement to and from the city, now they were used for smuggling and if the entry points were supposed to be guarded by men of the Crusade, inevitably *milities*, then a coin slipped into their hand, or food when they had been starving, was not to be sneezed at. If anyone had told Bohemund he would have just laughed; no place he had besieged had ever been sealed off completely and there were always folk within the walls willing to pay for luxuries or just good food, sometimes when the poor were eating weeds.

Walo took with him several knights and they were armed, slipping through the postern one by one on a dark and moonless night, with Vermandois straining to catch sight of them. He did see the door close behind them, but he heard the creak. The thick oak cut off the sounds that followed, that of his brother's Constable, the man the King of France entrusted to command his armies by his side, having his throat cut, the same fate visited upon those with him.

This was not a loss that could be hidden and Vermandois was obliged, when the heads of those men slaughtered behind the gate were thrown over the walls, to explain what had happened and without his main supporter to advise him he made a poor fist of it. It appeared a chance to gain the city by betrayal; it would have been foolish not to pursue such a possibility and he would do so again if chance offered it. The loss was heartbreaking but how many knights had given their lives in this endeavour? Walo had given his and would be esteemed for it and yes, the Armenian messenger, the smuggler, had not reappeared.

'Why do your think the message was sent to Vermandois?' Tancred asked.

'Yaghi Siyan wanted to warn us off dealing with traitors, on pain of our own death. What better way to despatch such a communication but through the hands of a fool?'

'He knows that Vermandois is a fool?'

'Why not? Everyone else does.'

CHAPTER TWENTY-FIVE

The makeshift fort opposite the St George's Gate, on the site of a long-abandoned shell of a monastery, was more a sieve than a true barrier; while it put a check on the Turks issuing in numbers to raid the lines of communication without warning it could not, and was not designed to blockade that entirely. Nothing demonstrated its vulnerability more than the need to keep it supplied and the efforts of the defenders of Antioch to impede that: every time food and water were brought to the bastion, it took a strong escort and a fight to deliver it.

It was effective at impeding anything of magnitude seeking to enter the city, as were the constant patrols out in the countryside seeking to cut off any supply being brought to the city by the Turks. Despite that, some got through, especially through the still-open Iron Gate, but the Apulians were the last line of obstruction at St George's and often an effective one. Not long after taking up the position Tancred and his knights captured a sizeable caravan carrying in large quantities things much desired by the Crusaders and even more so by those still inside: food, oil and wine.

When it came to small traders, exclusively Armenian, the gate was as open as it had ever been and once the screw was turned on the others points of access the amount of goods flowing past Tancred's position, while not a flood, was certainly significant to the ability of Yaghi Siyan to maintain the siege, if not in terms of fighting power, certainly as a means of stifling discontent within the Armenian majority.

Keen to have information about conditions inside Antioch and the state of mind of the besieged population, Tancred had taken to facilitating some of the smuggling, initially without side, but in time making things easy for those who passed him valuable information, while prohibiting those who refused to let him know what they had observed, so that he could advise his uncle in his dealings with the Council of Princes. What would happen to Antioch once it had fallen, now it was out in the open, had become a bone of some contention. That still, however, took second place to what lay before them, the actual act of capture, and for that the mood inside the walls was of obvious interest.

'My nephew reports a sense of increasing despair,' Bohemund informed them. 'Very little from Turkish caravans is now getting through and what the smugglers can supply will only serve to keep happy those who can pay the high prices they demand, and even they must guard against their purchases being stolen by the garrison. It is true, when we arrived they hoped we would pass on to Jerusalem—'

'Others have informed us of this,' Raymond interrupted; he

had become increasingly uncomfortable with the Count of Taranto holding the floor, which, given his greater knowledge of Antiochene morale he had been inclined to do. 'And that is history.'

'History with a point, My Lords,' Bohemund insisted, in essence ignoring the Count of Toulouse, which did not go unnoticed. 'For that first dented their optimism and we know that through the winter, when they saw us starving outside the walls, they expected each dawn to see us gone.'

'So now they know we are here to stay, which no one amongst us, I hope, doubted would be the case.'

In saying that, Godfrey de Bouillon meant it; if his faith had sustained him there was not another magnate in the pavilion, Bohemund included, who had not at some time contemplated that very outcome, either by individual action or a collective loss of will.

'The main food stocks on which the Turks rely, like the grain stores, are dwindling, what can be brought in without we appropriate it is reduced and so Yaghi and his Turks must impose ever more severe measures on distribution, which turns the populace against him, especially the poor who depend on Turkish largesse. They see the Turks feeding their horses while their dole is cut.'

'Not enough to overthrow him,' Duke Robert said.

'How could they?' Adémar responded. 'He still has as many as three thousand men under arms even after his losses. If anyone raises complaint I would suggest they are quickly executed.'

Bohemund then informed them of how many times that had occurred and told of the rumours of just how many Armenians had fallen to Yaghi Siyan's summary justice, for he was fierce when it came to sniffing out betrayal and swift to act. The aim of the Turkish leader was to hold out in the hope that an army would come to his relief and he would see the citizenry starve rather than surrender, so the Crusade, even if it frustrated them, had to be patient.

Raymond was not to be sidelined. 'I still maintain an assault on the walls will produce results.'

'It will.' Bohemund insisted, for he was aware, as were his peers, only he was in position to execute such a thing at the St Paul's Gate. 'It will result in many dead Apulians.'

'We must do something.'

For a man with such a reputation there was much irony in the reply. 'Yes, My Lord, we must wait.'

Which was a point he repeated to Tancred when he received a request that he visit his bastion.

'Raymond will not accept that there is no advantage in an assault if the Turks are still in good spirits and he is addressing men who are not known for their restraint.'

'Which would include you and I, Uncle.'

That got a smile and a nod. 'I nearly brought up my father, but that rankles even more than when I speak from my own experience. He knew never to throw men uselessly at a well-manned fortress. If we try and do not succeed that will affect our morale more than the Turks'.'

'And they are a long way from eating their horses.'

'True, so why have you asked me to come?'

'I may have a way to get inside the walls.'

About to mention the fate of Walo of Chaumont, Bohemund checked himself; his nephew was no fool, he would know better than to suggest anything that smacked of the same risk of a slit throat, and by a look alone he invited Tancred to continue.

'As you know, I have cosseted certain of the Armenian smugglers and if they have told me much I have hinted that they might achieve much more. I now know one of the towers on the walls is held by a force of Armenian converts, the others are manned by Turks.'

'Which one?'

'Halfway up Mount Silpius at a point were the incline is so steep we would never be able to try an assault.'

'Why give that post to an Armenian?'

The question Bohemund posed then was rhetorical, for it was not a vital part of the defence. Tancred agreed, but his uncle added that such a thing was not necessarily to the good.

'Converts are often the most stalwart when it comes to their faith.'

'True, but they have a limit when it comes to perceived slights and the fellow in command, who goes by the name of Firuz, I am told feels badly used by Yaghi Siyan. My informant tells me that the governor has stripped him of his property to ensure he stays loyal and it has had the opposite effect.'

'This your informant told you, which has to mean that such grievances have been spoken about, man to man.'

'The smuggler tries to supply Firuz and his men rather than the Turks, whom he loathes.'

'*Says* he loathes,' Bohemund cautioned. 'So can we be sure that the story is true?'

'No.'

Silent for a while, Bohemund sat deep in thought before speaking gain. 'Then let us discount this disaffection and work on the premise that this Firuz seeks to gain from our taking possession of Antioch.'

The response to that was jaundiced. 'Which without a Trojan horse is a long way off.'

'Meet with your smuggler, let him take to Firuz an offer of great power and wealth under a Christian prince, to gain which, he will have to convert back to his original faith.'

'Just that?'

'Yes, for if he baulks at reversion, Tancred, he is trying to lure us to our death.'

'Will you tell the council of what is possible?'

'It is too soon to say anything; let it lie and see what your smuggler brings us.'

Taking contraband into and out of Antioch was not a daily affair; those doing the supplying had to travel far to find the goods they wished to sell within the walls, for most of what was grown locally was consumed by the Crusaders. Added to that, Tancred's informant was no fool, certainly not stupid enough to be transparent with Firuz. Hints had to be dropped and less than entirely open responses needed to be carefully assessed, before inching to more intimacy. The Armenians would be fools to repose trust in each other too soon if they wished to keep their heads.

Slowly, over weeks, with Bohemund staying in the background – he had to be able to disown what he was doing in secret – the terms by which Firuz and his men would surrender their tower were fleshed out. That they would revert to Christianity was the first hurdle crossed and it was an important one, for the mass of the population would not, once freed from the Turkish yoke, take kindly to an Islamist in high office.

Now bribes could be offered – immediate riches in gold and silver and valuable offices promised, which no Christian prince yet held. Bohemund and Tancred alone, so as not to cause alarm, inspected the tower that Firuz held, an isolated one in terms of defensive numbers, commanding a stretch of wall as Tancred had said, almost impossible to assault due to the steepness of the slope. Finally a night had to be selected and the means planned as to how the Normans were going to get up that wall as well as get into position without being seen by the Turks in the adjacent towers, all this passed to and fro by that one single messenger on whom the whole enterprise depended.

With what he saw as a workable arrangement to proceed, it was time to ensure that if he did succeed, he should be the beneficiary – that the law of conquest he had sought to gain before was agreed, and in that he ran into a wall as stout as those of Antioch. His fellow Princes would not deviate from the notion of shared possession, while Tancred remained the only person he could be open with about his frustrations.

'There is a furtive tone when the subject is raised. Godfrey de Bouillon apart, I cannot help but think that others are on the same path as we and for the same purpose.'

'Then why not agree to what you propose?'

'Believe me, if they are scheming the time will come when, close to fruition and sure they will be the one that gains and that they have allies in place to support them, the right of conquest will be accepted.'

'Raymond?'

'Is, I grant you, the most likely, but Vermandois will be conniving, even if he has already had his fingers scorched. Our Robert of Normandy could buy back his duchy from his brother with half the revenues of Antioch, so he too will be conspiring.'

'Such a loss does not mean an end to opportunity, there is still Jerusalem, which is ten times a richer capture than Antioch and will be a fief to covet in Christian hands.'

That had to be acknowledged; Jerusalem produced massive revenues from pilgrims in bad times and Muslim hands; once back under the way of the true faith it would return wealth in untold quantities.

'If I have plunder to gain there I have little else, certainly not power.'

There for the first time, as far as his nephew was concerned, Bohemund had been open about his desire for domains, not just gold and silver.

'You cannot be sure of that.'

'Tancred, Jerusalem is no different to Antioch. Once captured how is it to be held?'

'By Crusaders.'

'In joint control, like Antioch?' There was no option for Tancred but to nod. 'It will not do. Where has such a thing as joint ownership of a fief led to anything but jealousies and dissension? All that kept my Uncle Roger and my father from conflict was the separation of the Straits of Messina. Whichever city you speak of it must be under the control of a single authority. Do not be fooled by the forced agreement we have enjoyed so far – that has been fed by necessity and some success. Once in Jerusalem, with the Crusade complete, that will not hold and the only solution is to hand the Holy City over to one of our number.'

'Which will not be you.'

Bohemund smiled. 'No, there is only one man who would justify selection, one of the council who would be content to stay and hold Palestine.'

'Godfrey de Bouillon?'

'I think that the case. Raymond is rich already and would not want to abandon his Provençal domains. Robert wants his Duchy of Normandy back, and the capture of Jerusalem will so raise him in wealth and standing, not even his brother William Rufus would be able to hold out against a successful Crusader with the Pope on his side and he would be bound by oath to leave Robert be.'

'Vermandois?' Tancred joked, which got a snort of derision.

'No, Godfrey sold nearly all he possessed to come on Crusade and he is a good man as well as true. If we do end up in the Holy City, I will expend every sinew to make sure that he is given whatever title is agreed upon and holds Jerusalem as his own fief.'

'If you can carry the principle, no one will dare vote for anyone but him.'

'I look forward to seeing Raymond of Toulouse's face when Adémar, a man he thinks his pet bishop, does just that.'

News had come from some of their eastern Armenian allies of another Muslim army being raised to come to the relief of Antioch and it was soon established that it was not being gathered – it was complete and ready to march in numbers that beggared the imagination; this had happened before and been proved to be much exaggerated, a point made by the Duke of Normandy, but it was decided to send out scouts to verify what the council were being told. The information that came back was worse than confirmation. Whatever threats they had faced up till now this was the greatest; the Turkish host was said to be beyond calculation and under the command of a formidable and experienced general called Kerbogha, and the conclusion drawn by Adémar was sobering.

'Up till now we have faced the forces of two brothers who hate each other and so they have only ever been able to bring to the field a part of the available Muslim strength. This host is different: it has been ordered to assemble by the Sultan of Baghdad and is led, I am told, by the Atabeg of Mosul.'

'This Kerbogha is a name that means nothing to me,' said Vermandois.

'It means a great deal to our Armenian allies, Count Hugh,' Adémar insisted, 'enough to strike terror into their souls and they begged us not to think the numbers are embellishment, but insisted it is three to four times the strength of anything we have yet faced, which our own scouts have confirmed.'

'Only if you choose to believe it,' Raymond said. 'Even our men can be blinded by sights they think they see.'

'My Lord of Toulouse, I admit I am still a tyro in matters military, but what would be the point of sending another army to dislodge us from Antioch if it were merely of the same size as those we have already beaten? My information from the Armenians tells me that the Seljuk Sultan has finally decided to brush us off the face of the earth and has ensured his commander has the numbers to do so.'

'Will Byzantium aid us?' asked Robert of Normandy.

This only proved to Bohemund he had yet to understand Alexius Comnenus, who would fear that such a host would turn on him if he took the field. 'Let us say it would be unlikely.'

'So,' Godfrey de Bouillon interjected, 'if we must fight this Kerbogha, and what we are told is proved to be the case, we must do so with every man we can muster.'

No more explanation was required; that meant lifting the siege and marching to do battle and with no guarantee that the Crusaders would win, which was an even more sobering prospect, for they still lacked enough horses of the kind that could stand in battle. It had always been a known fact that they had only successfully sustained their Crusade and got this far due to dissension between the Muslims, it being common knowledge that if they put aside those differences the numbers they might have to face would be staggering.

If the Sultan of Baghdad had hitherto see advantage to his own security in that family discord – men who fought each other could not combine to depose him – he obviously now saw the men around Antioch as the greater threat and he had the authority to force others to put aside their disputes and join in a counter-crusade.

'If we were within the walls of Antioch, this general the Sultan so esteems would have to besiege us.'

Every eye was upon Bohemund when he said that and all held the same expression. They were not inside.

'We have no prospect of that,' Adémar said, but there was a lack of conviction in his voice, a suspicion perhaps that a member of the devious family de Hauteville would not have said such a thing lightly.

'My Lords, I return to my previous plea that the common laws of conquest be applied, that whoever's banner flies over Antioch when we are within its gates has the right to claim it as their possession. I have not to this point alluded to what anyone of us must have sought, namely a way of entry by betrayal, but I would ask that we be open now and tell each other what contacts we have made for such a purpose.'

'You seem sure that the Lords assembled have done such a thing?' Adémar responded, clearly displeased.

'It is out of admiration for my peers that I think they are not so foolish as to have set aside the notion or that they have not sought to pursue it. And to prove my own sincerity in this I have very recently made contact with an Armenian commander willing to surrender to me a tower.'

'Where?' demanded Vermandois. 'At St Paul's Gate?'

'What stratagems have you employed, Count Hugh, since you so sadly lost your brother's Constable?'

'I have sought contacts, it is true, sent messages in by various means seeking to seduce the garrison to . . .'

He did not finish that, which was an indication of how far he had got.

'And tell me, Count Hugh, if you had succeeded, would you have willingly handed the city over to joint suzerainty by the council?'

'Of course,' the Frenchman contended, but he was a poor liar and Bohemund wondered if he was the only one present who did not believe him.

'Count Raymond?'

'As you say, Count Bohemund, a man would be a fool not to try, but do not think I would seek Antioch for myself.'

'Noble indeed,' Godfrey cried, as Normandy admitted he too had been active.

'What we have, if the Bishop's intelligence is correct, is a crisis, My Lords. I care not if you call it greed, but if I enter Antioch first and you are obliged to follow me I will claim it.'

'Very like a de Hauteville,' Duke Robert growled.

'Perhaps, but we did not get to eminence on the gifts of others, either in Normandy or Italy. Nor can I believe that men such as here present would act in any other way, despite their protestations, from which I exclude you, Godfrey, for you are the only saint among us.'

That remark produced more lines on Adémar's face than had ever been seen hitherto; he thought himself that.

'We must agree to what is in our hearts instead of our mouths and take steps to ensure that we have the means to defeat this great army coming our way, which I, for one, worry cannot be done in open battle when Antioch is still in Turkish hands.'

That did much to concentrate minds; with such a host approaching the siege would have to be lifted and worse than that, Yaghi Sigal could emerge from his walls to threaten their rear. The agreement was reluctant and had to be dragged out of each lord present, with the exception of Godfrey de Bouillon who spoke straight at Bohemund.

'I owe you my life and more besides, as you well know of. I also state here and openly that if others see in you avarice, I do not. If I disagree with what you contend it is not from antagonism to the notion. You may have the right of what you maintain and we here collected could have the wrong. What we are about is in the hands of God and if you are to be his instrument I am content.'

News that Kerbogha was besieging Edessa, which Geoffrey de Bouillon's brother Baldwin had taken as a fief, gave time for Bohemund to finalise his plans, but before he put them into practice he called upon Godfrey to advise him of what was about to happen and to seek his assistance.

'For if I can get into Antioch, I will not have the strength on my own to hold it. I want others standing by at certain gates armed and ready to rush in once they are opened. I need that to be set in train but in some secrecy.'

'Yet you still wish to claim it?'

'As I will be first over the walls, yes.'

Godfrey thought for what seemed an age, no doubt examining his conscience, to which he was a slave, until Bohemund could contain himself no longer; he was aware of what was closest to his fellow magnate's heart. 'Without support I will fail and so might the Crusade.'

'Then tell me what you need.'

EPILOGUE

The night was hot and cloudy, the moon and stars hidden, which made movement difficult, especially since it had to be silent. The men on the southern walls would have seen a large body of knights, over five hundred in number, both mounted and on foot, making their way at dusk around the base of Mount Silpius on one of their forays to close off access to the Iron Gate. If they had paid note earlier to Tancred's smuggler as he slipped out of the St George's Gate they would perhaps have wondered why he was accompanied by a youth instead of being alone, this being the son of Firuz, being taken to Tancred's bastion as a hostage, which required an extra bribe so both could pass.

Time was given for the garrison to bed down and get into a deep sleep, while the city behind them did likewise, so what they did not see, after the watch was set and in darkness, was the sixty knights that sneaked back to a point on the hillside opposite the tower commanded by Firuz, where they waited for several turns of the glass until the signal came, the short, bright flash from an unshaded lantern.

There was no way to approach the tower in silence, the slope was too steep and made up, as ever, of loose stones, so it was done at a rush, the hope that on a part of the defences poorly manned there would be no one between the adjoining towers able to hear, and those manning them would be inside. At the base of the wall, where the round fortification billowed out, Bohemund felt for and found the rope that Firuz had sent down, which eased somewhat, if not entirely, his fear that this was an elaborate trap; he had no idea if Firuz had sent a real son or some substitute he was willing to sacrifice, no idea if the smuggler had led him by the nose.

He was not alone in this dread and his intention to take the lead in what was about to happen had to be tempered by the needs of command. To ride into battle ahead of his men, to stand with them in line, both mounted and on foot, was expected of him. Not one of the men he led this night was willing that he should risk himself and they had drawn lots for who should go first, the honour, if it was that, falling to a knight called Fulcher. Quickly the cable-made ladder was tied on to the rope and hoisted up, it being in place when the tension was tested and it went taut.

'May God be with you, Fulcher,' Bohemund whispered, the swish of cloth that followed the man crossing himself.

Climbing a rope ladder was far from easy, made harder the more men got on it and began to climb, it reacting like a snake to every movement of foot or hand. Also the knights were keen and too many sought to ascend at once so, when they were halfway up, it parted in the middle, sending half a dozen men tumbling into the hard ground. If Bohemund could hear the sound of breaking bones, whatever wounds had been sustained brought no sound from the afflicted, some of whom might be dead for all their leader knew.

Caution had to be set aside and Bohemund called up for the ladder to be lowered, once the men still climbing were on the battlements, so it could be repaired. Time in the dark seems everlasting, this night being no different, and still Bohemund did not know if his men were safe. They had been ordered to remain quiet, the only indication of their wellbeing the lack of any screams as they found themselves betrayed. The rope was dropped, the reknotted ladder raised back up, but he could wait no longer and it was their Count who led the rest of his knights in the ascent.

When he got there Fulcher was waiting to hand him onto the battlements. 'Your Armenian is honest and has his men on the parapet guarding against anyone coming from the other towers. They have already taken care of the sentinels on both sides.'

Bohemund did not even know he had been holding his breath until the great gush of air escaped.

'You know your duty, Fulcher,' he said, passing him his banner.

'I do, My Lord.'

One by one his knights arrived, to be herded onto the parapet, then split up to move to the adjacent towers, past Firuz's Armenians who retired to their quarters. If all failed they would desert, if not it was the only place to be safe. Silent killing came as naturally to Normans as lance work and one party moved on and up to the small portal that led to the living quarters of the defenders in the adjoining tower. There they found them asleep, which should have made despatching them simple, yet it was not. Several of the detachment, twenty men strong and all Turks, managed to wake up and what followed was bloody indeed, only hushed because it was contained within thick stone walls.

Behind them the same execution was being carried out by their confrères and soon Bohemund had three towers under his control, all of which had stairways down to the city they were set to protect. The next target was the St George's Gate, two more towers down the sloping walls, outside which Tancred was waiting, but first Bohemund had to get the rest of his knights, those who had not ascended the rope ladder, inside through a nearby postern gate, while leaving a number on the parapet to deal with the remaining towers.

Thick planks of timber had been nailed into the mortar surrounding the gate, and for all the efforts at silence, ripping them away could not be done noiselessly, that made worse by those outside, in seeking to help, beginning to hammer with their pommels to knock it in. The noise was too much, Bohemund could hear cries of wonder or alarm from the dwelling nearby and he reasoned the time for subtlety was past. As soon as the planks were detached and the postern gate forced open he yelled at the top of his lungs, calling for the aid of God to their purpose, a cry taken up by all of his knights.

The move to the St George's Gate took only moments, this while above their heads the detachments in the gate towers woke and began to seek their weapons. When they rushed out of their sleeping quarters it was to be cut down by Norman swords, the same fate befalling the Turks guarding the huge wooden doors. Ten knights formed a ring of defence and held the torches that had been in scones while their confrères first raised the portcullis on its winch, the gates themselves rushed at as soon as men could get beneath the metal teeth, the great baulk of timber by which it was secured being removed and the doors swung open.

Tancred came through at a rush, leading hundreds of men, to find his fellow Apulians screaming like banshees and rushing down the various narrow streets, now becoming crowded with the alarmed populace who had come out to identify the commotion, many of whom died for their curiosity: the Crusaders had no time to do anything but cut down anyone who stood in their way; they needed to get to and open the Bridge Gate, which would allow entry to Godfrey de Bouillon and his Lotharingian knights, awake and ready to do battle as Bohemund had arranged.

The whole city was soon in uproar, the wiser citizens hiding in their houses, leaving the streets to become a killing zone for the Turks, many of whom fought desperately and well, but died anyway given their efforts were uncoordinated and they were unprepared. Added to that, on the outside the noise of battle had roused out all the other Crusader sections, Raymond and the Duke of Normandy, once they realised what was afoot, quick to get their men to a gate that would open before them once their confrères on the other side had secured it.

For many a glass of sand the fighting went on, still in darkness and torchlight. Blood illuminated by flaring flame was black and it flowed in the gutter like rainfall, only turning to red when the sun began to rise. Eventually that crested the mountains enough to light the great banner that Fulcher had raised on the highest tower of Mount Silpius, the red fluttering standard with the blue and white chequer of the house of de Hauteville.

Tancred and Bohemund stood in front of the Church of the Martyr, St Ignatius, chests heaving and covered in blood and gore, while all around them battle continued, for the Turks would not give up easily and if they had to die, they would not do so cheaply, their eyes fixed on their family ensign.

'What would your father say to this, Uncle?'

'Who knows? The *Guiscard* was never one for praise.'

'He might loosen his feelings in the face of this; he might say, "Hail, Bohemund, Prince of Antioch."'